Forever Grateful

Also By Aimee Martin

The Lake Shores Series
Forever Home

Forever Grateful

Aimee Martin

A Lake Shores Series Novel

Mercy Books,
A division of Mercy Pictures

ISBN: 978-0-9963063-2-4

FOREVER GRATEFUL

Published in the United States by Mercy Books,
a division of Mercy Pictures

To A. and M.
For your Inspiration

Acknowledgements

Once again this is the time for me to say thank you to everyone who took part in helping me with the creation of this book. And of course, the first thank you goes to God, without whom I wouldn't be the person I am today.

Thank you to my husband, the ultimate of all husbands who puts up with my weekend writing, mood swings as I work out a scene and always sticks by my side as we go through this crazy thing called life. Your love is worth more than words will ever express. Gu siorrádh, mo grádh.

To my three beautiful children, for loving me unconditionally and being part of my biggest support system. I promise to take that hike soon, babies.

To my editor, Dixie, who is the ninja of all editors. I'll always be thankful for the chance you took on me and still never be able to repay you. Thank you, always.

To Britney, Amanda, Lisa and Tanya for being my beta readers. Your words of advice and encouragement hold a special place in my heart. Thank you for believing in this book.

To my parents, mother in law, and all the rest of my ridiculously large family, thank you all for having faith in me.

And last, but in no way least, thanks to you, the readers. Thank you for taking this journey with me. I hope and pray that you'll continue to love these stories as much as I do.

Note from the Author

If you or someone you know has been the victim of abuse, please seek help through your local law enforcement, your clergy, or anyone else who can aid in bringing to justice those responsible. Or you can contact RAINN (Rape, Abuse and Incest National Network), the leading corporation in helping abuse victims.

RAINN Toll Free Number
1-800-656-HOPE (4673)

RAINN Website
http://www.rainn.org

If you don't feel comfortable talking to someone about abuse, seek out information in your bible, which is full of endless answers. All scriptures in this book were used from the King James Version.

http://www.kingjamesbibleonline.org

Forever Grateful

Prologue

"We lie down in our shame, and our confusion covereth us: for we have sinned against the Lord our God, we and our fathers, from our youth even unto this day, and have not obeyed the voice of the Lord our God." Jeremiah 3:25

November 15, 2009

Blue was supposed to be a comforting color. At least that's what she'd always heard.

But all Melanie Moore felt while she stared at the four walls surrounding her that were painted a sky blue was claustrophobia. Like the walls were closing in around her to secure her to the cold table she lie on, ready to centralize her shame even more than it already was.

Aimee Martin

She imagined it was similar to that kid–*or was it a man?*–that had been swallowed by a whale. She vaguely remembered a girl from her high school telling her the story. The man–Jonah, she thought his name was–had been swallowed up by the whale for not going where God had told him to go. Her friend, Ashley, had said it was why you should always obey the Lord for His punishments can be severe in ways you never imagined. But His blessings were even greater.

But given her reason for being in this room, on this cold table with the four walls closing in around her, she didn't give a damn what God, Mother Earth or anyone else had in store for her.

Melanie was a twenty-one year old young woman in a Planned Parenthood "procedure room" in the Costa Mesa office. She was ninety miles from her dorm room at San Diego State University. And she was getting ready to have an abortion.

Just the word sent a wave of uncontrollable shivers through her. This wasn't supposed to have happened. Her life wasn't supposed to be like this. She was a senior in college. She had two loving parents; even if they were a bit spacey at times. She guessed that's what hippie life did to people who embraced that lifestyle fully. She had great friends. She had been ready to graduate in the coming spring with a degree in Entertainment Business Management, and move to Los

Angeles to start her internship at Dalton Entertainment.

Instead she's lying here on this cold table waiting for a doctor to come in and remove a fetus from her body. Mel had never been a staunch supporter of abortion. But when this unexpected pregnancy had happened because of an unwanted sexual encounter, her views had changed.

Squeezing her eyes closed tightly, Mel tried to stop the images that wanted to weave their way into her mind from that night two months ago. The laughing men. Her blood curdling screams. The pain.

But it was all too much to block.

Jumping off the table, she ran to the trashcan in the corner of the blue room and threw up, not that there was much for her body to lose. All she'd had today were a few sips of water, per the "procedure" guidelines. When her heaving finally started to subside, she sat back on her sock-covered heels and wiped her mouth with a towel she'd found lying on the counter to her right. She didn't know if the sick feeling deep in the pit of her stomach was from the pregnancy, the nerves about what was getting ready to happen in the blue room, or the memories.

Memories... oh crap! Just as the thought passed through her mind, she leaned over that silver metal trashcan again. *Well, I guess that answers that question.*

She spotted a sink at the other end of the white Formica counter and slowly stood to make her way over to it. After rinsing her mouth out with cold water, she wet the towel and wiped it over her face and neck, trying to cool her overheated body and calm her nerves. Throwing the towel into a dirty linen basket next to the counter, she turned and crawled back onto that cold metal table.

Just as she was pulling the thin white sheet up over her lower body, the doctor knocked softly and walked in, a young nurse following close behind.

"Good morning, Miss Moore. How are we doing today?"

Doctor Finn was a seemingly sweet middle-aged woman with long brown hair the color of dirt pulled back into a low ponytail. The streaks of gray at her temples gave her a somewhat distinguished look, Mel guessed. But her ice blue eyes made her seem cold and aloof. Kind of like this table underneath her.

The nurse was only a little better. She had blonde hair and blue eyes with alabaster skin that made her look like a porcelain doll. Her nametag read Jennifer and she looked like she was only a year or two older than Mel. But her smile was kind and understanding.

Mel shrugged in answer to the doctor's question, not trusting her voice with the lump that was lodged there, unmoving. Doctor Finn smiled at her like she knew what Melanie was feeling.

You can't possibly understand unless you've been in this

FOREVER GRATEFUL

position yourself, Ms. Good Doctor.

"Is anyone here with you today, Melanie?" she asked.

"No. It's just me. Is that okay?"

"Absolutely. After the procedure is finished, we'll move you into an observation room so that we can monitor you for a couple of hours. Once we're sure that everything is alright medically, you should feel well enough to drive yourself home." Mel only nodded again so Doctor Finn went on.

"Okay. Let's get started. Move your bottom all the way to the edge of the table so that it almost feels like you're falling off. Great," she said as Mel scooted down the table. Then the doctor placed her heels into two stirrups at the bottom corners of the table that had been extended.

All of this felt fine, normal. Just like when a woman goes in for her annual exam.

But when she pulled over a tray on wheels and removed the green sterile sheet covering it, Mel's heartbeat started to speed up and her stomach started to cramp again. Every part of her body clenched tight with nervous tension as the doctor began showing her all the tools that would be used. She closed her eyes, not wanting to look at the offensive devices that would be used to kill a baby inside of her.

A baby born of rape.

"First off, Melanie, I'm going to give you an injection. It's just a local anesthetic, but it'll go into your cervix and help to alleviate some of the pain. After that, I'll____"

"Doctor Finn?" Mel interrupted, keeping her head turned to the side. "Would you mind if we just get on with it? I know you're just doing your job but if we don't get started soon then I'm afraid I'm going to lose my nerve."

Doctor Finn's frosty, ice blue eyes shot a knowing look right at her.

"Sure thing, Melanie. This is going to feel a little cold," was the last thing Mel heard before the speculum invaded her most private area and she felt a sharp stabbing pain.

And then suction machine was turned on.

To keep her mind off of what was going on below her waist, she concentrated on the bright white fluorescent lights above her. One was flickering like a strobe light, obviously getting ready to die. Funny that the word die is what came to mind other than something simpler, like 'burn out'.

Must be influenced by what's happening.

There was one set of lights in the corner that had a bluish tint to them. As the suction sound got louder, Melanie tried to think of all the different stores where someone could buy these light bulbs and wondered if that was the reason for the different color. Next she went over review questions in her mind for her Final Project course.

Anything that would help to drown out the slurp-slurp-slurp sound.

Tears pricked the backs of her eyelids and threatened to fall over her cheeks as she heard the doctor finally turn off the machine about twenty minutes after she had started the procedure.

"Alright, Melanie. We're all done," Doctor Finn said as she wiped a warm, wet rag over Melanie's now tender nether region. "Jennifer and I are going to help you up and we'll walk a few doors down to one of the observation rooms. It's a lot more comfortable in there. As I said, we'll monitor you for a couple of hours. Then you'll be free to go."

After removing her heels from the stirrups and gently placing her feet on the ground, Doctor Finn and the nurse helped Melanie slowly stand, each of them holding on to one of Mel's elbows. Keeping her gaze averted from the tray and suction machine to her left, Mel held tightly to their arms and let them lead the way down the hall.

Walking in the door, Mel decided it definitely appeared more comfortable. Dark green walls gave a calming effect. An en suite bathroom was in the far left corner. And directly across from that was a twin sized bed with a fluffy hunter green comforter.

Doctor Finn helped her lie down on the bed and pulled the comforter up to her chin, while the nurse filled up a pink pitcher with ice and water and set it down on the bedside table, next to a white Styrofoam cup. The plastic mat underneath Mel made an annoying swishing sound as she tried to move a little more to the center of the bed. Once the doctor was sure that Mel was comfortable and had the nurse call button within easy reach, she left the room, softly closing the door behind her with a faint click.

There was a low burning nightlight that was visible just inside the bathroom that drew Melanie's gaze like a moth to a flame. Holding a firm body pillow tight against her abdomen, she stared at that light and finally let the crying that she'd been holding onto take form.

As her vision blurred with the force of her tears, the last thought Melanie had before she fell asleep from emotional exhaustion was... *I'm going to Hell.*

Chapter 1

"And it came to pass, that, as soon as the days of his ministration were accomplished, he departed to his own house." Luke 1:23

June 6, 2014

Alex Lambert sat on the plane, staring out the window to his right at the dark clouds that were moving in from the tropical storm to the south of them and now surrounding the airport. He couldn't help but wonder if maybe it was some sort of omen that he'd been premature in his decision to leave the Navy. *No... it's been eight years. It's time.*

Still, the loneliness he felt while he sat waiting for the rest of the passengers to board the flight that was taking them from Jacksonville to Houston was overwhelming.

Maybe it was the crying kid sitting to his left that

couldn't be more than three or four. No doubt terrified of his first plane ride if the snot running down his nose was any indication. Or possibly it was the mother of the little boy who sat in the aisle seat of their row, gripping the bridge of her nose tightly with her eyes squeezed closed. Obviously she didn't know what to do about her son with tears streaming down his chubby cheeks like fat raindrops.

Those tears reminded Alex of his deployment to Brazil and the rainforest that poured down a never-ending supply of water from Heaven.

Leaning his head back on the headrest of his seat, he closed his own eyes and tried to block out all the sounds that were surrounding him. The crying toddler. The mother shushing him relentlessly. The flight attendant walking up and down the aisle, reminding everyone to buckle up their seatbelts.

I should have splurged for first class, he thought to himself.

Maybe then he could have caught up on some of the sleep he'd lost since he had begun his most recent internal debate. The one of whether or not to leave what had been his livelihood since he was eighteen.

But there hadn't been time.

His enlistment wasn't up for renewal until August but the aircraft carrier he was stationed on was going back out on deployment. He heard to Iraq for more airstrikes. Regardless,

his Chief had told Alex he had to make a decision ASAP.
Stay or go. He chose home.

Making the decision to go home to Lake Shores, Texas–
a small, country town with a population of about three
thousand people–was one of the easiest he'd ever made.
Once he got past his fear of hanging up his dress blues for
the last time anyways.

He was about to be twenty-seven years old. He was
single, with only a couple of steady girlfriends to claim in his
recent past. And neither of those had really brought his heart
to a place where it felt secure in another's hands. But being
gone for six months out of a year hadn't boded well for a
man's love life.

Now, though, he was ready to move into the next phase
of adulthood. Ready to find someone he could give his heart
to while accepting hers as a gift to him. So finding a little
woman to settle down with seemed like the most logical step.

Little woman. Oh man, I sound like my father.

Thinking about little women, however, brought Alex's
mind back to his sister Brinley's wedding a couple of months
ago. More specifically, the little woman he had met then
while at Jaxson's ranch for the reception. A friend of
Brinley's from her California days as an actress, before she
had moved back to Lake Shores herself to get married.

Melanie Moore.

Smiling to himself, Alex envisioned her long blonde

hair as it flowed around her shoulders that had been covered by thin black spaghetti straps that night. And the way it fell forward in a straight cascade as she laid her hand on his forearm and laughed at some of his horror stories from being overseas in Japan for nine months a few years ago.

But what made him fidget in his seat a little, and smile even more to himself, was picturing her eyes. That blue-green hue that seemed to change colors as she spoke or just listened. Like one of those mood rings his sister used to love as a kid; ever changing and yet holding you in a trance at the same time.

He wanted to see her again. Not just text and email with her a few times a week like they'd been doing as friends. Those virtual words just didn't hold the same weight as spoken ones. He couldn't hear her sweet, melodic laugh when she emailed "LOL" to him. Or see her beautiful smile when she sent one of those emoji face things to him in a text. The ones he had to ask his shipmate Tommy's wife about because he had no idea what they were.

He didn't want the acronyms and emojis. He wanted the real thing.

So caught up in her memory, he hadn't realized that the big seven-forty-seven was ready for take-off until he felt the speed pick up and the plane lifted off of the ground to be thrown into the dark sky.

Alex opened his eyes and watched out the window as

the clouds dissipated when the plane shot straight through them like a bullet from a gun. He watched the different shades of blue mold into one another as they moved higher and higher into the sky. And he couldn't help but wonder when–*not if*–he would be able to see the eyes that changed color as fast as those outside his window.

And if it would be anytime in the near future.

.   .   .   .   .

Melanie sat in her corner office on the seventh floor–Dalton Entertainment taking up the whole level–of one of the hundreds of sky-rises in Los Angeles, and tried like crazy to get her mind to focus. She had a ton of calls to make. Appearances and interviews to schedule for her two dozen clients, all ranging from actors to singers to athletes. Not to mention the contracts sitting on her L-shaped, glass top desk right in front of her that needed to be signed, initialed and delivered to various studios and companies.

But the people who were milling about on the sidewalk seventy feet below kept her in a daze, like watching ants crawl in and out of their hill to go to work, go home, go to work. That never-ending cycle of mundane life is what kept her high backed, black leather chair turned in the direction of the windows instead of the desk. It's what kept her from focusing on work, and instead had her daydreaming about things she knew better than to let have a place in her mind. Happiness. Love. Men.

Ugh... don't think about men!

Mel forced the chair back around and pulled up to the desk. She started signing her name on dotted lines and marking the spots that had to be signed and initialed by her clients, concentrating thoroughly on the way her cursive name should look page after page after page. *Melanie Moore. Melanie Moore. Melanie Moore.*

The only sounds coming from her office were the swoosh of papers and the tapping of her four inch, red stiletto heel on the black and gold speckled marble floor. When she realized that she'd signed her name on one of the of the client's lines, she threw her Mont Blanc pen down and turned back to the windows behind her.

She'd been like this–easily distracted–ever since she got back from Brinley's wedding. She had become Brin's manager about two years ago. And Mel had met Brin's best friend, Annie Cross a few times before a terrible accident took her life at too young of an age.

Since Annie's death, Mel had tried to step in to be there for Brin. Not to replace Annie. Those were shoes she could not, would not fill. But just to be around if Brinley ever needed her.

When Brin met her husband, Jaxson Mathews, the light that had gone out of her when Annie died came back full force. And the two women have been closer friends ever since. Close enough that Mel had gone to Brin's wedding and now, in the aftermath, sat daydreaming.

It could be that she hadn't had a vacation in so long that the brief reprieve to that no-name Texas town had given her a taste of freedom. She was only twenty-five. She shouldn't feel this weighed down from work yet. Shouldn't feel the need to be free from paperwork and galas and premieres and interviews.

But if she was honest with herself, Mel hadn't really been free since that night four and a half years ago. Not mentally free, anyways.

That is until she met Brin's gorgeous little brother, Alex.

There was really nothing little about the man that had kept her in la-la land instead of Corporate America like it should be.

It had to be the smile. The way his lips would turn up so far that his light brown eyes the color of honey would crinkle when he laughed. Or maybe it was those eyes themselves that seemed to look straight into her mind, past all the horrifying memories that rested there, tucked tightly under a rock the size of Alaska.

It could, possibly, be that body. Over six feet of pure, tanned muscle. The kind that is only developed by the constant exercise demanded of men and women who were in the military.

Aimee Martin

God, Mel, get over it already.

It was true that Alex probably fit into the mold of what her ideal man should be like. One with a strong hand. Mel remembered telling Brin about wanting that very characteristic in a significant other but realized that Brinley had probably misunderstood her meaning. If she had understood it at all.

After that nightmare four and a half years ago, Mel had decided that she needed someone who wouldn't be afraid to stand up for her. Someone to defend her honor and not sit in a corner, cowering like a little rat that hides from light and goodness and people. Someone with a strong hand toward others.

But not toward her. Never her.

Honestly, Mel didn't think that she would ever let a man who had even a hint of a heated look in his eyes anywhere near her again. The one time it had happened had brought more pain than any woman had a right to have to bear. Or person for that matter.

That's why she didn't understand people who stood up so proudly for their religion. Be it Christianity, agnosticism or anything else. What kind of God or higher being would let something as horrendous as rape happen to anyone?

No kind, that's who, she thought to herself.

Which is why more people needed to rely on their strengths to get them through life. And that brought her mind back to needing such a strong hand to protect her because no one and nothing else would.

All those thoughts mingled together and is probably why she felt like Alex would be a safe bet in that department. He came across as someone with the power of protection stamped on his soul so deeply that it would manifest itself like second nature to him. The way a mother bear instinctively protects her cubs, he, too, would instinctively protect those close to him. Almost how she imagined a big brother would act like.

Being an only child she wasn't sure, though.

Except you sure wouldn't be daydreaming about your big brother's smile. Or the way his corded forearm had tensed in pure strength when you'd touched him there at the wedding. And his light, honey-colored eyes wouldn't make your insides melt.

All this fantasizing was probably just a moot point anyway, Mel decided. She would more than likely never see Alex again. He was in Florida; doing whatever is was that Navy men did. And she was here, in California, with her senior level management job, a great condo that she owned and her sweet dog, Kassie. Who, Mel realized, she needed to get home to.

Pulling her gaze away from the ant-like people on the sidewalk below, she looked at the clock on the far wall and saw that it was half-past-five. Mel shut down her laptop and stuffed it into her brown leather briefcase on the floor next to her chair. She stacked up all the contracts into a neat pile and slid them to a corner of her desk, deciding that she would not take her work home with her today.

Straightening her black pencil skirt down her legs as she stood, Mel grabbed her purse and briefcase, shut off the office light and locked the door behind her. She said a quick goodbye to her assistant; a cheerful young woman named Becky Sanders who was fresh out of college at UCLA and looking to work her way up the company ladder.

Mel loved doing whatever she could to empower young women nowadays. Help them build their confidence. Then maybe others wouldn't be so ashamed to speak up and ask for help when they needed it.

Just like she'd been too scared to do when she had turned up pregnant after *that* night.

She shook off the memories as she rode the elevator down to the parking garage and pretended to be concentrating on her phone as men and women got on and off the elevator at different floors. Whatever it took to keep from having to talk to people when she was battling the painful emotions was always a welcome distraction.

When the final ding sounded, she walked to her little red Audi that was parked as close as possible to the elevators and right next to the security booth. She unlocked the doors with the remote in her hand when she was a few feet from the car and immediately locked the doors back once she was settled in the driver's seat. She set her case and purse in the passenger seat, started her car and reversed out of her spot. As much as Mel loved her job, when she pulled out of the garage and onto the busy boulevard with the sunlight beating its heat off the pavement, she felt free. Like she could quit hiding behind that front of "everything is perfect in my life" that those around her often saw.

In truth, she felt like the irregular-shaped white clouds that were visible through her front windshield and taking reign in the sky. Strong and confident on the outside but ready to shrink and dissipate into a ball of uncertainty on the inside.

I guess this would be when people would pray or meditate or whatever, looking for strength and guidance in their life. What a joke!

As Mel sat in bumper-to-bumper traffic, inching her way closer to her condo on Wilshire Boulevard, she thanked herself. Yes, herself, for finally seeing the truth of it all before it was too late. You want something in this life, go and get it yourself. Make your own dreams. And don't rely on anyone looking out for anything but themselves. Some people might think her kind of attitude was pessimistic, but Melanie thought of it as realistic.

Reality is something tangible that you can hold onto. Faith is nothing more than some mythical mist that evaporates right when you need it most.

By seven o'clock, Mel was finally pulling into the parking garage that took up the entire ground floor underneath fifty luxurious condos. Her assigned spot was only ten feet from the elevator, which was one of the reasons she'd bought this place two years ago. That, and the twenty-four/seven doorman as well as the high tech security system surrounding the premises.

She quickly gathered her briefcase and purse and jogged to the elevator, pushing the button for the third floor where her home was. She heard Kassie, her black Labrador-mixed baby, barking as soon as the key was in the lock. Walking inside and swiftly closing the door behind her, Mel bent down to give Kass some hugs.

"How are you, baby girl? Were you good for Momma while I was at work today? Huh?" Mel laughed as the dog barked again and licked her face. "Let me get changed and we'll go for a w-a-l-k." Mel refrained from saying the word walk so that her sweet, overly anxious dog, that absolutely loved going outside, didn't drive her nuts while she got ready.

She stood and placed her things on top of the eat-at bar of her kitchen with its cobalt blue granite countertops. The stainless steel appliances gleamed with the fading orange sunlight filtering in through the blinds in the living room. The light was blinking on her answering machine so she pressed play and listened while she grabbed a bottle of water from the refrigerator.

"Hello, my flower!" *Great. Just who I wanted to hear from today. My mother.* "I just wanted to let you know that your father and I have decided to leave Louisiana. There's just too much violence here with all that alligator killing. We tried to give the locals a taste of what it would be like if they gave peace a chance with those animals. But all they did was cuss us out! Anyways, we're heading north. Somewhere. We're not really sure where to but you know us? We just go with the flow and wherever the breeze blows us." *No kidding,* Mel thought. *Just like you breezed to Oklahoma right after I was raped.* "Well, I'll let you know how you can reach us once we get settled. Wherever we're going. Talk to you soon, my flower. Kisses."

Mel groaned at her mother's obvious flakiness and disregard to roots as she deleted the message and headed to her room. She'd been on her own for a long time. Since she was eighteen and went off to college. No need to care about her parents traipsing all over the country anymore.

She stripped out of her work clothes and heels quickly, changing them for a pair of yoga Capri pants, tank top with sports bra and tennis shoes. After hooking Kassie's leash to the bright red collar around her neck, she took her dog down the emergency exit stairs at the end of the hallway. They made it out of the revolving glass doors at the front of the building and onto the sidewalk, ready to chase the coming dusk to the west.

As the sky dimmed from that deep evening orange to a dark blue mixed with shades of purple and pink, she remembered the sunset from Jaxson and Brinley's ranch. Which made her remember Alex. Which made her wish she could see him again.

She could only imagine his deep voice to a certain extent when reading his emails and texts. She'd like to hear him say her name instead of just reading it.

Strong hand, she reminded herself. Look for someone to watch over her and nothing more.

If only her quickening pulse would get the message.

. . . . .

Fourteen hundred miles away from Los Angeles, Alex was walking out of Gate C at Houston Hobby Airport. With his black backpack that he'd used as a carry-on slung over his shoulder, he waited at the luggage turnstile for the rest of his bags.

He smiled to himself as he caught sight of the mother and little boy that had sat in his row on the airplane. They were weaving their way through the dozens of other people going to and from flights and they both appeared to be in a much happier mood.

FOREVER GRATEFUL

The kid was running circles around his mother's legs, laughing and saying "I wanna go on plane! I wanna go on plane!" But instead of seeming agitated like she had earlier, the mother just grinned down at him and picked up her little boy. She hugged him tight and gave him a big kiss on the cheek, whispering something in his ear that Alex couldn't hear. Whatever it was, though, had the boy smiling even bigger and throwing his arms around his mom's neck.

Alex had always loved kids and the scene before him made him wonder if and when he would ever get to be a Daddy. God willing, he'd have a house full of children.

But in the meantime, he thought as he finally spotted his bags coming around the big luggage belt, *I get to be one heck of a cool Uncle.*

Brin and Jax were expecting their first baby and he couldn't be happier for them. The upcoming new member of the family was one of the advantages that had cemented his decision to come back to Texas. To Lake Shores. Being close to family is one of the things he'd missed most while in the Navy and he was ready to be close again.

Picking up his big blue seabag and massive black suitcase from the turnstile, he gave a quick nod to the mother and son as he passed them and strode out to the pickup lanes. Scanning the crowd, he quickly spotted his father four cars back, leaning against his four-door Ford truck that was parked at the curb. His Dad, Mitch, noticed Alex as he started walking in that direction and met him halfway, wrapped him up in a big bear hug.

"Son. It's so good to have you home."

"Hey Dad," Alex replied, pulling out of the embrace. "Let's get out of here."

He threw his bags into the back and sat down in the front passenger seat while his Dad walked around the truck to get into the driver's side. As his Dad put the truck in drive and started to slowly pull away from the curb, a woman walking out of the airport caught Alex's eye.

Long blonde hair, beautiful delicate face, confident walk with her head held high.

Is that…?

But when she removed her sunglasses, no doubt figuring it was too late in the evening to need them, Alex saw her dark brown eyes and knew it wasn't Melanie.

I must be going crazy, he thought.

His Dad maneuvered the truck out of all the Houston traffic and finally headed south on Two-Eighty-Eight, the road to get to home. Alex leaned forward and turned on the radio. Willie Nelson started crooning about blue eyes that were crying in the rain.

Trying not to think about blue eyes, Alex looked out the window for a distraction. But then he noticed the way the evening sky was taking on a mix of colors. Pale blue and teal molded together to almost match the exact shade of Mel's eyes.

Alex continued to think about her even as he saw the cattle dotting the fields on either side of the highway, some nudging their newborn calves with their noses. Others hadn't given birth yet and were sitting in the shade of big oak trees.

As they passed one farm that was closer to the road, he saw a woman who looked to be in her thirties that was pregnant with a babe of her own.

And Alex wondered, for some unknown reason, what Melanie would look like with a belly that was swollen with a baby. What would he feel if she was pregnant with his baby? And would she be like some of the grouchy and exhausted mothers he'd seen on base in Jacksonville.

Or would she be as loving and forgiving as that mother from the airport?

Aimee Martin

Chapter 2

"Also I heard the voice of the Lord, saying,
Whom shall I send, and who will go for us?
Then said I, Here am I; send me." Isaiah 6:8

June 13, 2014

"Sometimes it's difficult to get used to civilian life
again. Best thing for you to remember son, is don't forget
your past. But find a way to look forward to your future."

Alex remembered his first Master Chief Petty Officer
telling him that little bit of wisdom about five years ago,
when the two of them had gone out for drinks to catch up
one night. His MCPO, Jordan White, had just retired after a
twenty-five year career in the Navy, and wanted to prepare
Alex for what he would eventually have to go through
someday.

At the time, Alex had played up the tears that had been evident in the man's eyes to too many beers and too much smoke in the bar.

But as he slung bale after bale of hay onto a trailer at Jaxson's ranch, The Burnt Aggie, he couldn't help but feel that maybe his Chief had been onto something.

Alex belted down the last of fifty bales of Bermuda hay with ratchet straps and went to sit under the shade of a large sycamore tree next to the barn. He stripped off his sweat-soaked white t-shirt as he went, tossed it on the ground next to the tree. He leaned back against the big tree trunk, stuck his jean clad legs straight out in front of him and crossed his booted ankles. Swallowing a big gulp of ice water from the gallon jug he'd brought with him this morning, Alex took stock of what he was feeling.

He was grateful, very much so, that Jax had given him this job. He was just a ranch hand but since he was staying with his parents for the time being–and they refused to take any rent money from him–he didn't need a lot of income. Despite eight years in the Navy, and what most civilian people believed, retired soldiers still had to work for a living. Jax was more than generous with Alex's paychecks. Which made him wonder if it was because he was the boss' brother-in-law, or if he paid all his employees that well.

Knowing the man and his giving nature, Alex suspected the latter.

FOREVER GRATEFUL

He felt a constant stream of love just being back in Lake Shores. His whole family was here. His good friend from high school, Bryant Moran, was still here along with his new wife Joanna and their twin, newborn daughters.

The town itself had given him a huge welcome home parade over the weekend. One of those 'Honor Our Local Hero' tributes that had made him feel a little self-conscious.

But loved nonetheless.

He felt strong in his faith being back here, too. Going to church yesterday at their childhood place of worship, St. Timothy's Episcopal Church, had given him a fulfillment that he hadn't felt in a long time. Even though he had attended the services on base—when he wasn't out on deployment—the traditional hymnals sung at St. Timothy's always made him feel closer to God.

And yet, despite all of those 'good' feelings, Alex couldn't seem to just feel settled. True, it had only been a week.

But he should feel some sort of normalcy by now, right?

He tilted his head back to listen to a blue jay that started singing in a soprano tune, almost like it was trying to answer his unspoken question.

When the bird flew off quickly at the sound of dead leaves being crunched into the ground, he turned his gaze forward to see his sister, Brinley, making her way toward him.

She smiled and waved ,which Alex returned in kind while he waited for her to walk over to him. When she reached the shade of the tree, Alex scooted over some and patted the ground beside him.

"Take a load off, sis. Or can you still get down here on the ground now that you're carrying my niece or nephew around in your belly?"

"Hardy-har-har," she mock laughed at him as she gracefully lowered herself onto the grass, crossing her legs Indian style and automatically bringing her hand to her still flat tummy.

"If you're going to be as over-protective as Jax, you can go right on back to Florida. I'm pregnant, not an invalid. And–" she shot a scowl at Alex, "–I'm only five weeks along. So cool it, little brother."

Despite her best efforts to appear scolding, her smile shined through and belied her attitude.

Alex studied his big sister for a moment. She looked good, healthy, in her white shorts and navy blue tank top with her strawberry blonde hair pulled up in a clip on the top of her head. No make-up marred her natural beauty.

"What?" she asked when she noticed him staring.

"Nothing. You just look good," he repeated what he'd thought to himself. "And happy."

"I am. Jaxson… he's the best thing that ever happened to me, you know? Brought me back from those last remnants of depression. Helped me see the beauty and grace of the Lord again." She sighed and smiled slightly off towards the distance at nothing in particular. "And he loved me. Even when I didn't think I deserved it. And he's kept on loving me. It's that love that's helped me see the reality of everything around us again. To find my place back in the world."

She gave a small laugh and shrugged as if that was all the explanation she could give.

Alex and Brinley had always been close when they were growing up. With only two years separating them, it was understandable to most people.

But with her sitting here, talking about the reality of the world and having to find her way back into it, Alex felt closer to his sister than ever before. Because facing that reality was what he was struggling with right now.

It didn't matter that their circumstances were different. The outcome was the same.

But he couldn't find a response that would come across as insightful or logical so he just nodded and turned his face back toward the open field.

His brow furrowed as he watched three of Jaxson's horses graze in the pasture. The sun was beating down on their strong backs, making their coats glisten with sweat.

He remembered the sun beating down on his own back as he stood on the deck of his ship when they shot the Suez Canal, headed to Egypt. Much of the training they had helped the Egyptian military with during that deployment had faded from his memory over the years.

But the heat from that big yellow-orange star in the sky was unforgettable.

Will I ever be able to view the wonders of life without comparing them to my naval past? he thought.

"Penny for your thoughts." Brin's soft voice made Alex jerk his head around in surprise.

He'd been so caught up in his own head that he'd forgotten she was with him.

"I was just remembering one of my deployments. Six years ago we went to Egypt. It was so hot that not fifteen minutes after we got dressed for the day, our shirts would be soaked through with sweat."

Alex shook his head and gave a short laugh at how much laundry he and the rest of the crew had had to do while they'd been on that five and a half month trip.

"And then I was thinking about how everything around me reminds me of my military days. And I'm wondering when that will ever stop." Alex looked to Brinley, hoping that maybe she had an answer to give him.

"Alex, you can't be so hard on yourself. I mean, really, it's only been a week since you've been home. Seven days. And you're trying to block out eight years' worth of your life."

"No, not block out," he interrupted. "I don't want to

forget my time in the Navy. I just don't want to flashback to different countries and deployments and missions every time I turn around. You know?" His sister nodded her head, chewing on her bottom lip with her teeth while she thought about what he was saying.

"When was the last time you had a vacation, Alex?"

He blew out a breath as he racked his brain for an answer to Brin's question.

"Man, it had to be when a group of four of us went down to the Keys."

"Uh-huh. But *when* was that?" Brin asked again.

Alex grinned sheepishly at her, knowing his response was probably not going to be what she wanted to hear.

"Almost five and a half years ago. Right after we got back from that deployment to Egypt and we'd all turned twenty-one."

"Well good grief, Alex! No wonder you're having such a hard time adjusting. You haven't had any time to just decompress. You need to go on a trip somewhere." She looked away but not soon enough for Alex to miss the hint of mischief in her eyes. "What about our place in California? You've never been there. It's in a great spot, right on the beach. You can have some solitude to reflect, pray… to deal. Or you can go enjoy the nightlife and let loose and have fun."

"I don't know Brin. I just started working here. Don't

you think I might come across as a little needy or a bit of a pansy if I'm already asking for a vacation?" Alex was skeptical about the intelligence behind Brinley's suggestion.

"Don't you worry about the boss. I have it on good authority that he has somewhat of a crush on me. I think I'll be able to talk him into it. Besides–" she leaned over and laid her head on Alex's now dry shoulder, seriousness taking over her playful banter about her husband, "–you need this, Alex."

Reaching up to rub his sister's hair, Alex sighed in acceptance. She wouldn't give up anyway so it was better to give in as early as possible.

"Ok, Brin. For you, I'll take some time away."

Her smile lit up the fields even more than the afternoon sun. She kissed his cheek and stood to go back inside, wiping the grass off of the backs of her legs and shorts. Turning to head to the house, she stopped and peeked down at him for one more word.

"I'll just give Melanie a call and make sure that she'll be around to be your personal tour guide."

She spun and strode toward the house so quickly that she missed the big grin taking over Alex's face.

·   ·   ·   ·   ·

Melanie had just gotten off of an hour-long conference call with one of her baseball clients and his publicist. They'd been hammering out all of the details for an upcoming commercial they were working on for a deodorant company, and had finally fixed the contractual glitches.

She was pinching the bridge of her nose, trying to hold off the headache that was trying to come on, when Becky's voice came through on her intercom.

"Miss Moore? You have a Brinley Mathews on the line. Can you accept the call or would you like for me to take a message?"

"No, it's fine Becky. You can put her on through."

Mel frowned at the time, debating on whether or not 'girl talk' was a good idea right now. It was only four o'clock and she still had a good two hours of work left.

But she hadn't heard from Brin in almost two weeks. Not since she had called to tell Melanie that she and Jax were expecting their first baby. Mel had congratulated her then gotten off the phone as quickly as possible. She hadn't wanted to chance having a freak out moment from disturbing memories. Late dinner meetings were always a plausible excuse because Brin knew how crazy celebrity schedules could be, which is what Mel had pleaded during their conversation.

By the time the third ring sounded on her phone, Mel was pulled out of *that* call and ready to take *this* one.

"Well hello, you beautiful married woman. To what do I owe the pleasure of this phone call?"

"Can't a girl just want to call and catch up?" Brin asked. But at Mel's silence, she must have known that Mel wasn't buying it. "Ok, don't be mad. Promise you won't be mad?"

"I can't promise anything until I know what it is that I'm not supposed to be mad about." Mel was definitely intrigued by the worry she heard in Brinley's voice.

"Well." Brin blew out a heavy breath. "It's about my brother, Alex. You remember him from the wedding?"

"Uh-huh. What about him?" Mel asked and tried to ignore the way her pulse picked up speed and her breathing became a little shallow at the thought of Alex.

"Well, he moved back to Lake Shores about a week ago and Jax offered him a job at the Burnt Aggie. So he's been working here and I went out to talk to him a little bit ago. You know, just to see how he was doing. If the guys were treating him alright. Stuff like that."

Brin was babbling. She never babbled. Something was definitely up.

"What is it, Brin?" Mel tried not to sound impatient but she was still at work and it sounded like her friend needed some help to get the conversation moving.

"Anyway, I could tell that something was off. He just didn't seem like his usual happy, carefree self. Basically, he's a little strung out trying to get used to being a normal person again instead of a military man. So I suggested a vacation. Somewhere he can relax, rejuvenate and re-order his life."

FOREVER GRATEFUL

Mel swore she could almost hear Brin chewing on her lip in indecision, even over the phone.

"What does all that have to do with me? And what's this promise that I need to make?"

"Well, I suggested he go to our house out in Malibu. I mean, it's just sitting there so why not? But, well, I..." Brin paused again. Mel ignored the umpteenth 'well' that was said and refrained from snapping at her to get to the point already. "I told him that I would make sure you would be around. You know, to act as a tour guide. Please don't be mad. I know I should have asked you first. But I also know that the two of you have been staying in touch since the wedding. And I really didn't think you'd mind. So will you? Show him around while he's there?"

Mel wanted to say no. She should say no. It didn't matter what her arguments to herself had been about Alex possibly being a strong-handed man to have around. She knew when there was danger in a situation.

And Melanie had a feeling that keeping Alex at a distance emotionally, and physically, would cross over into dangerous territory. Because it would be almost impossible to keep up.

But she needed to be honest with herself.

She did want to see him again. She did want to look into his light brown eyes and watch his smile transform his rugged jaw and sculpted lips. She wanted to hear his voice as he said her name.

So against her better judgment, she gave in to her pleading, pregnant friend.

"Alright. I'll be his tour guide. But make sure that he understands that I will not, cannot, be at his beck and call. I still have a job and clients."

Brin's squeal of delight on the other end of the line caused Melanie to have to set the phone away from her ear. When the happy screeching had finally stopped, Brin was a little out of breath.

"Thank you, Mel. Thank you, thank you. I know he'll be thrilled to see you. I mean… just because…" Brin stuttered on her words and it had Mel wondering if her friend knew something more about Alex and his attitude toward her than Brin was letting on.

"I know he'll be happy that he won't have to figure out California alone. So again, thanks."

"Uh-huh, sure. Listen Brin, I have to get back to work but tell Alex to text me or shoot me an email when he gets his flight information. If I can't be there to pick him up then I'll make sure there's a car service available."

"Will do. I'll talk to you soon, Mel. Bye," Brin said as she hung up.

"Bye."

Mel set the phone back into its cradle and, even though she knew she shouldn't, turned her big leather chair away from her desk and faced the window at her back.

Why was it that just the thought of Alex Lambert made her want to fantasize and forget her life, even for a minute? Dreams had no business in her world. The people she represented, yes. It was her job to manage those people and their dreams. But her own had died four and a half years ago along with her expectations for mankind.

Dreams were for people with misguided beliefs in faith and God and whatever other spirits they thought were out there. But Mel knew better than to believe in any of that foolishness.

She watched a couple, probably close to her own age of twenty-five, walk hand in hand down the sidewalk. Other patrons gave them a wide berth, almost like they were afraid of catching the all-too-well-known 'love-bug.' But as Mel watched the man lean down and kiss his woman tenderly on the forehead, she wished–for the first time in years–that she wasn't so cynical.

Three hours after her phone call with Brinley, Melanie was walking into the front door of her condo, kicking her heels off aimlessly and letting them stay where they landed. She set her purse and briefcase down at the kitchen counter and walked into her spacious, open living room. She plopped down on the cream-colored leather sofa and tucked her legs up underneath her.

It had been a long day at work with a dozen meetings

and at least twice as many phone calls. And she didn't want to even think about all the contracts she had waiting for her in her case ten feet away.

She stared out of the bank of windows to her left, watching the evening sun pour in from Wilshire Boulevard as it slowly sank lower in the sky. She could hear cars driving past her building, some honking their horns in an effort to get home themselves.

She was about to go get a glass of wine and head to her bathroom for a long soak in her claw foot tub when Kass came running up to her, having followed Mel from the door to the kitchen and now to the sofa. Melanie smiled at her sweet dog and reached down to scratch behind her floppy ears, jabbering nonsensical words like the dog was a baby instead of an animal. She decided, looking into Kass's big black eyes, that her pup needed some exercise and that her bath could wait.

But when she went to ask Kassie if she wanted to go for a walk, she heard her phone ding, signaling a text message.

Unfolding her tired body from her spot on the couch, Mel retrieved her iPhone from her purse and found a waiting message from Alex. She caught herself smiling even before she had touched the screen to bring up his text.

Crap, I gotta get over this infatuation.

When she pulled up the message, she was a little confused at the one, short question waiting for her.

Can you talk?

Mel gave a quick reply that yes she could, and went to get that glass of wine after all. Pulling out a chilled bottle of sauvignon blanc from her stainless steel fridge, she popped the cork with her automatic bottle opener and poured a half a glass.

Just as she was settling back into the corner of her cream sofa, the cell in her hand started playing the tune of Bon Jovi's *Always* and she answered a little too eagerly. Probably before the first ring had even finished on Alex's end. Mel took a deep breath before saying anything, trying not to sound too excited.

"Hello?" Her voice still sounded breathy.

Ugh. Smooth, Melanie. Real Smooth.

"Hello to you too." Alex's voice, deep and a little raspy tonight, came through on the other end. Hearing it, even for just that second, made Mel sigh to herself and sink even farther into the overstuffed couch cushion at her back. "How's my favorite California native doing?"

"I'm good, Alex. How are you? I heard you moved back to Lake Shores."

"Yeah, I did. It was time. Eight years in the Navy... well, that's another story for another day. I didn't catch you at a bad time did I?"

His voice sounded a little muffled and Mel distinctly heard the strains of an old Johnny Cash song, *Ring of Fire*, playing in the background.

"No you didn't. But it sounds like maybe you didn't plan this call too well according to your own timing. I can hardly hear you."

"Oh, I'm sorry. Hold on just a second." He paused and was gone for maybe half of a minute before Mel heard the music fade away and silence take its place. "Is that better? I wasn't really thinking about my surroundings. I guess I got a little anxious to call you. Brin said she talked to you earlier."

"Yes. She called and said something about you coming to L.A. for a vacation. I told her to have you text or email me your itinerary," Mel said, ignoring his comment about being anxious to call her. *Her.*

"Well, I wanted to talk to you. Blake, Jaxson's foreman, and I came over to The Bar with a couple of the other ranch hands. You know, shoot some pool, drink a beer. Unwind from the day. Anyway, I just got an email confirmation of my flight info a few minutes ago and decided to call you instead. Is that alright? I mean, if not I can always let you go. If you've got plans or something."

Mel giggled at Alex's sweet insecurity showing through. Of course it was okay but she felt the need for a little teasing.

"I don't know. You go out partying with a group of other single guys and then call me. How do I know you're not all taking over the dance floor with some of those country girls and then checking in with me while they make their way to the bathroom or something?"

"There aren't any gir…" he broke off, as he caught on to what Mel was doing. "Well, I guess you'll just have to take my word for it now won't you?" Now his voice sounded smug and more self-assured. Mel loved it.

"MmHmm. Take the word of a man I barely know. Are you serious?" Mel was having fun playfully sparring with Alex. She hadn't smiled this much with a man in, well, years.

"Now why would I go follow around a bunch of girls when I can talk to the most beautiful woman right here?" Alex replied.

Mel laughed out loud at his ridiculous statement. She barely kept from spitting the sip she had just taken across the room, and tried to hold her glass still to keep it from spilling.

She was still chuckling when she heard a door slam open in the background of wherever Alex was.

And then she heard the raucous and deep laughter of a group of men follow the door slam.

Her smile dropped and her glass fell out of her hand, shattering on the bamboo wood floor at her feet.

Aimee Martin

Chapter 3

"Howbeit, he would not hearken unto her voice; but, being stronger than she, forced her and lay with her." II Samuel 13:14

September 12, 2009

Melanie and her college sweetheart, Justin Ford, were just leaving a restaurant on the outskirts of the San Diego State University campus. Paddy's was a popular place for college kids because they offered a cheap menu with favorite foods like burgers, buffalo wings, cheese fries and the like.

Justin had asked Mel the night before if she would be his wife someday, pushing his black-framed glasses up his nose as he did. There was no ring. There was no bended knee. Just an honest question on a park bench at Mission Trails. She said yes and had been floating on cloud nine ever since.

Tonight had been a sort of celebratory dinner and they were on their way back to campus where they both lived in the dorms. They were seniors at the university this year. Mel was set to get her degree in Business Management, specializing in Entertainment, and Justin would be graduating from the Physics department.

They had the world at their fingertips and were ready to grasp it with both hands, together.

The moon, full and silver tonight, rose high and bright against a sky so black it seemed as if the stars' lights had all gone out. The only sound mixing with the silence around the two young people, walking hand in hand and in love, was the bass coming from different bars and other restaurants they passed on the street.

Mel and Justin had only made it four blocks from Paddy's when the door of a bar about fifteen feet in front of them swung wide open, slamming into the brick wall on the opposite side. Three men came barreling out, stumbling over each other in their obvious inebriated state, and laughing loudly at the struggle they had of walking. They all looked to be in their mid-twenties with physiques that suggested they worked out. A lot.

Justin pulled on Mel's hand, trying to move her to the outer edge of the sidewalk so that they could make their way around the group of men.

But right as they got even with them, the drunks took notice and all stood up straight, suddenly not as drunk as they were only a moment ago.

Justin and Mel stopped as the three men walked around them, caging them in. Mel began to worry about what they had planned as they came closer to her and Justin, slow step by slow step.

The first one to speak was tall and well built, blonde haired and had the aura of a preppy boy who always got what he wanted. His blue polo shirt and khaki pants only added to the effect.

"Well, well, well. Look wha we'f got here boys."

He stepped up closer to Mel and his breath smelled of stale beer and cigarettes. Mel tried to turn her face away to avoid the stench but he reached out quickly with his strong hand and grabbed onto her chin, holding her still.

"Wha's a pretty girl like you doing wiff a nerd like this guy, huh?" His slurring speech reiterated her concern about them and their intentions.

"Pp-please. Just let us go." Her voice came out shaky.

She jumped as one of the other two, this one dark skinned with long, shoulder-length hair to match and eyes that seemed soulless, made his presence known behind her. He looked like a thug in his black t-shirt, his jeans hanging halfway down his butt. He pushed Justin aside, ripping Mel's hand from his. The drunkard came up and began rubbing himself suggestively on Mel's backside.

"Awe hell, why'd we wanna go an do somefin like that? You're too sweet to leafe here a'lone."

This one reeked of whiskey and his burly arm came around Mel's middle, anchoring her to him.

"Come on, guys." Justin's arguments were falling on deaf ears. "We don't want any trouble. Here. Take my wallet. I've got about a hundred dollars in there and it's yours if you'll just let us leave."

The third man, who'd stayed in the background until now, came up and grabbed Justin's arms, pulled them taut behind Justin's back. The man's bulging biceps showed his brute strength as he held Justin's face forward, made him watch what was going on with Melanie.

"Nah, we're gonna stay right here wiff her. And you're gonna watch," the bully said in Justin's ear.

Mel's eyes bulged out of her head as she took in the meaning of those words. But before she had time to scream or run, the two with her began dragging her backwards into a dark alley.

Away from the lights of the street and any prying eyes.

Oh please, God, Spirits, whatever is out there… please help us. Don't let them take me back there.

But the heavens weren't listening to her today, Mel quickly realized.

Melanie yelped loudly as she was thrown against the

side of a dumpster and jammed her shoulder into the sharp corner. She desperately looked around, trying to find an escape, but found only brick walls and a burned out street lamp, shrouding the corner they were in with darkness. The blonde and dark haired men were on either side of her now, eyeing her like she was a piece of meat. The third man, who'd had a hold of Justin, threw him to the ground in the corner by the far wall and methodically walked to stand directly in front of her.

She saw now that he was bald with green eyes. And he was the most heavily muscled of the three. And intimidating in his leather pants and vest. He leaned in close to her face and licked her cheek with his raspy, beer soaked tongue. Mel gagged.

When he spoke in her ear, she realized he wasn't as intoxicated as his buddies because his words came out soft, precise and cold.

"Now it's time for a little fun," he whispered right before he tore her white sleeveless blouse from her body, exposing her upper body to waiting eyes.

Mel screamed and tried to break through but the bald man pushed her back, flipping her body around so that her front was crushed against the dumpster.

"N-no. Pp-please. I… I'm a v-virgin. Please don't do this."

She was sobbing and shaking, terror striking through her

at what these men were about to do. The blonde man on her left heard her whispered pleas and laughed.

"Well damn, this night juss got a whole lot better. A virgin, boys. Le's show her wha a real man can do," he boasted.

Then he reached down and lifted her blue-jean skirt to her waist and ripped her panties from her body.

Mel searched around frantically, desperate to find Justin. She found him curled in a ball, still in that corner where the bald man had thrown him.

When Justin looked up and saw her frightened face, she pleaded with her eyes for him to do something. Anything. But all he did was cover his head with his arms and tuck himself back into an even tighter ball.

Coward!

The blonde and dark haired men held her arms down on the dumpster and anchored her legs with their huge bodies, keeping her immobile. She tried to use her smaller frame to wiggle out of their hold but she was no match for their power, drunk or not.

When the bald man came up behind her, the sound of his zipper made her freeze with fear.

She couldn't fight anymore. It was like she had been shot with a tranquilizer gun and was now at their mercy.

"This'll only hurt for a minute," he said.

She looked back at Justin, hoping once more that he

would get up and help her. But he was still curled up in that corner. Sobs wracked her body and his form blurred before her when tears filled her eyes and streamed down her face in never-ending rivulets.

And as the bald man rammed himself into her, she let out a blood-curdling scream that would end up haunting her forever.

Aimee Martin

Chapter 4

*"And he said, My presence shall go with thee,
and I will give thee rest." Exodus 33:14*

June 13, 2014

Melanie heard her name being called but it sounded
hollow, like an echo that was far, far away from where her
mind had gone, stuck in that night. She knew she needed to
pull herself out of this flashback, away from the laughing
and screams.

But she felt her gaze stay steady, staring off into the
short distance straight ahead, at the television mounted on
the wall across from her. It was like she was watching the
scene play out on that screen rather than in her mind.

She felt her heart racing. The thump-thump-thump in her
chest made a heaviness settle there. Her breathing was

coming in pants, short bursts of air sucking in and blowing out of her lungs.

Again, she heard her name being yelled, louder now, but she couldn't find her voice to answer.

It wasn't until Kassie barked right next to Mel's face that she blinked and sucked in a breath sharply like she was starved for oxygen. And she realized that she wasn't in that dark alley.

She was home, in her living room, on her couch. And she was holding her phone? *What in the...* her thoughts were cut off when she heard Alex's frantic voice on the other end of the line, threatening to call the police.

"Alex?" she asked, finally breaking her silence. She listened as he blew out a heavy breath through the phone.

"Thank God. Mel, you scared the crap out of me. What the hell happened?" He didn't sound scared. He sounded angry.

"Nothing happened. I____"

"Don't you tell me nothing!" he cut her off. "I've been screaming your name for almost five minutes. I heard glass shatter. I heard you cry out. And a dog, I'm assuming is yours, has been barking almost the entire time. Now what is going on?"

Mel sighed in indecision. She knew that Alex deserved some sort of explanation. But what could she say?

I was just freaking out about the night I got raped by

*three drunken men. No big deal, it was like, over four years
ago.*

Yeah, right. All that would do is bring up more
questions. Or pity. And there was no way Mel wanted Alex's
pity.

"I just got a little scared at something I heard.
Sometimes that happens when I'm really tired and I zone out.
I'm sorry. But I'm fine now. Really."

"Melanie." His voice was softer now and the way he
said her whole name calmed her nerves even more. Everyone
called her by her shortened name and hearing it in full, from
Alex's lips, spread warmth through her belly. "That was
more than a little scared. What happened?"

"It was a long time ago Alex." She waited to see what he
would say but he stayed silent on the other end of the phone.
She sighed and gave him as much as she could right now.
"Sometimes I have these flashbacks from a bad experience.
But they're usually late at night. And never when someone
else is around. I don't know why it happened just now with
you on the phone. But it's over and I'm okay. I promise. Can
we just move on from it now?"

Again she waited. And again he was silent. Just when
Mel thought she was going to have to end the suddenly
awkward conversation, he cleared his throat.

"Alright, we can drop it. For now. But I promise you
this, Melanie. There will come a time when you're going to

have to tell me what this was all about. Not today. Not necessarily next week. But someday. Okay?"

"Okay. Now, you said something about getting an email for your flight information. When are you planning on coming?"

Mel was grateful that Alex was willing to let the matter drop. And glad the discussion had found its way back to safe territory.

"Right. I'll be flying into L.A. a week from next Thursday. On June twenty-sixth. Right now, I'm planning on staying through that Saturday night and coming home to Lake Shores on the twenty-ninth. But Jax and Brin encouraged me to take as much time as I needed to relax. So," he paused and Mel could hear his smile in his voice, "if you turn out to be an enjoyable tour guide, I might stay a little longer."

Mel ignored the flutter in her belly at Alex's threat to stay longer than just a few days.

"Well then if you'll forward me that email, I'll see what I can do to be there when you get in. For now, I really need to go. I've got a mess to clean up and a dog that needs to go out."

"Yeah, I probably need to get on home. I've got to be at the ranch for work at seven in the morning. I'll get you that email. And I'm looking forward to seeing you again. Bye, Melanie."

FOREVER GRATEFUL

She said goodbye to Alex but he had already hung up and didn't hear it. Mel leaned forward to set her phone down on the glass top coffee table and saw just how big of a mess her shattered wine glass had made.

Kass was sitting next to the side of the couch with her big head lying on the armrest. Her thick black tail thumped loudly against the wood floor when Mel reached over to run her hand across the dog's soft neck.

"I'm sorry girl. Let me get this cleaned up and then we'll go out."

Mel scooted to the other end of the couch and got up from there to avoid the glass shards. She grabbed the trashcan and a roll of paper towels from the kitchen, got down on her hands and knees next to the couch to pick up the larger chunks of glass. She mopped up as much of the wine as she could without worrying about cutting herself. Then she grabbed her vacuum cleaner from the linen closet in the hallway and made quick work sucking up the last bits and pieces of her mess.

When she grabbed Kass's leash from the dark brown entry table by the front door, the dog came bounding over to get hooked up. No longer in the mood for a lot of exercise, Mel took the dog down the elevator and out of the front doors to a patch of grass by the corner of her building.

She watched the sky morph from a dark orange into a deep blue. The stars started to twinkle lightly, just peeking out in the coming night.

Other pedestrians walked their dogs past her and Kass, oblivious to anything around them. So was the way of Los Angeles people. They tended to not pay attention to anything but themselves. Usually that's just how Mel liked it. To be left alone.

But tonight she felt the need for comfort and wished for once that those around her were friendlier, like the people in Lake Shores had been.

Once Kassie had finished her business and Mel had disposed of the waste in the bin on the sidewalk, the two made their way back inside and up to their home.

She filled Kass's bowls with food and water, grabbed a new glass of wine and walked down the hallway to the master bedroom. Her king sized bed with its sea green cotton comforter and mahogany sleigh-style headboard and footboard looked inviting. But Mel decided she needed that bath more than ever and walked past the temptation into her bathroom.

She set her glass down on the white marble countertop that gleamed under the low light put off from the three vanity bulbs above the sink. She turned on the water and set the temperature to hot, pouring in a heavy dollop of bubbles under the spray. While the tub filled, she retrieved her phone from the living room for some music and got undressed.

After she had put all of her clothes into the dirty hamper

behind the bathroom door, she lit a handful of candles that smelled like magnolia blooms and sank down into the white claw foot tub, letting the freesia scented bubbles cover her tired body.

The heat of the water and the sweet smelling suds made her skin tingle, like getting shocked by someone with static electricity. Mel sipped her wine and tried to put the last remnants of her flashback out of her mind.

Despite the warmth of the water, Mel still shivered at the memories wading around in her conscience. She hadn't had a flashback that severe in over a year. She didn't understand why it had happened again. Why now? And did it have anything to do with the fact that she was just starting to get to know a man again? At least in something outside of a work environment.

Frustrated at her own weakness from the past and her confusion over the present, Mel reached for her phone to turn on *Between* by Vienna Teng. But as she brought it in front of her to bring up the music application, the ding signaling a message sounded for the second time tonight.

Still thinking about you. Sleep sweet, Melanie.

Mel smiled when she read the text from Alex, relaxing more at his innocent words than from the wine and bath. She pressed play on her song and laid her head back against the rim of the bathtub. As the soft, haunting strains began with the music, she put all thought of green and blue and dark eyes that were full of contempt out of her mind.

And instead, focused on a pair of honey-colored eyes with nothing but light and goodness in them. A smile curled on her lips as she imagined seeing them looking at her in the future. She imagined the owner of those eyes seeing her like she was normal and not tainted by her past.

And she wished, more than anything, that her imaginings would come true.

.　　.　　.　　.　　.

June 26, 2014

Alex sat still while the other passengers moved to get off of the plane. He was content to wait because his flight had gotten in thirty minutes early and he knew she wouldn't be here yet.

For the last ten days he'd thought of nothing but Melanie. Sure he'd gone to work, visited with his parents. He'd even gone over to Bryant's house one day and met his babies.

But his focus had been elsewhere. It had been on this trip, on seeing her again. And now he was here.

When the last group of people—a father, mother and their two little boys—moved past his row, he stood and stretched, rolling his neck to get the kinks out from the three and a half hour flight. He retrieved his carry-on bag from the compartment above his seat and made his way to the door of the plane.

He gave a short "thanks" to the two flight attendants standing there and quickly walked down the gangway. When he was inside the terminal he stopped and looked around for that long blonde hair.

But as his eyes made a second sweep, all he saw was an older man holding a sign with **Mr. Alex Lambert** written in black marker on it. He sighed briefly in disappointment and made his way over to the chauffeur, forcing himself to smile.

"Mr. Lambert?" the gentleman asked.

He looked to be in his early fifties with a head of dark gray hair that was partially covered by the black hat he was wearing. His brown eyes were rimmed with wrinkles, his skin tanned from years spent in the sun. Despite the man's age, broad shoulders stood out like a set of footballer's shoulder pads in his black jacket and he maintained an aura of someone who obviously took care of himself physically.

Alex held his hand out to get past the icy image the man was showing.

"No, sir. That would be my father." Alex watched the man's lip twitch a little. "Or maybe my brother. He's getting on up there in age, too. Please, call me Alex." He gripped the driver's hand and was surprised at the strength in his shake.

"Yes, sir. Alex," he amended when Alex gave him a

reproaching look. "Is this the only luggage you have?" He pointed to the carry-on Alex was holding by the extended handle at his side.

"Yes, sir. I've got it," Alex said when the driver reached to take it from him. "So, which way to the car? And I didn't catch your name."

"It's Theodore Wilson. Ted."

"Nice to meet you, Ted."

Alex followed as Ted turned to walk through the large airport, heading in the direction of the pick-up lanes outside. It was coming up on three o'clock in the afternoon and the sun was high overhead, bright yellow against a pale blue sky filled with white clouds.

Alex pulled his sunglasses out of his shirt pocket and put them on right as Ted came to a stop next to a black Lincoln Towncar. Ted took Alex's bag and placed it in the trunk then opened the back door, waiting for Alex to get in.

He gently took the door from the older man's hands and closed it.

"I think I'll ride up front with you if you don't mind."

He got into the front passenger seat while Ted walked around to get into the driver's side. After checking to make sure there were no cars coming, Ted pulled out of the parking spot and headed into the busy L.A. traffic.

"Miss Moore suggested I take you to Mrs. Mathews' house in Malibu. She asked me to inform you that she would be stopping by this evening when she'd finished working for the day." Ted's manner of speaking was very refined and Alex wanted to loosen him up some.

"Do you have someplace else to go when you drop me off, Ted?" Alex asked.

"No. I've been hired to drive you wherever you need to go for the entirety of your stay. Was there someplace else you wish to go?"

"No, sir. I was just curious." Alex watched the man's mouth open and close a couple of times, obviously wanting to say something. "Ted, you don't need to be shy or reserved around me. If you've got something on your mind, just say it."

"Well," Ted began, "I'm not sure I understand why you refuse to let me call you sir and yet you have been saying it almost nonstop since we met at the terminal. Why is that?"

"I guess it started with my upbringing. Being raised in the south, you either have manners and respect your elders or you get your head slapped. I chose the former. And then my time in the military just cemented it. Now it's so ingrained that I don't think about it."

"Well, I can understand that," Ted responded and Alex thought he heard the man mumble. Something that sounded like 'We have a lot in common' before continuing. "And I'd like to thank you for your service."

Alex nodded his head and turned toward to window,

never having been comfortable with praise about his naval career.

He'd only been doing his job.

He watched the waves crash into the shore from the road they were on, high above the beach. He saw a road sign that said Pacific Coast Highway. The same highway that his sister had been on when she and her best friend, Annie, had gotten into a crash. He felt terrible that Annie had died in that accident but thanked God that Brin was alive and well.

How else would I have met Melanie? he thought, smiling. Alex wasn't sure what it was about her. But he knew, deep in his gut, that he was brought into her life for a reason. He couldn't wait to find out what that reason was.

An hour after his plane arrived, Alex was being dropped off at his sister's house by Ted. Alex refused help with his bag and Ted refused the offer to come in for a beer.

So much for loosening the man up.

Ted gave Alex his card with instructions to call if he had any desire to go somewhere, along with the house key that Melanie had asked he pass along. Then drove off in his Towncar.

Alex unlocked the front door and walked inside, feeling at home and in an alien place at the same time. He left the house key, along with his bag, by the white-washed entry hall table, tossing Ted's card on top, and walked into the kitchen. Cream colored granite counters flecked with gold shined and a note sat wedged by a basket of fruit on the island.

He picked up an apple and took a bite, carried it and the note into the living room. The note was from Melanie.

Alex- I've stocked the fridge and made sure any provisions are supplied. Please let me know if you need anything else. You have my number. I'll be in touch, soon. Mel

Alex laughed at the business tone coming off of the note in waves. He wanted to get her to let loose like she had at the wedding. To relax and enjoy herself and not be so detached. He couldn't wait to break down that tough outer shell and get to the soft woman underneath, like an egg.

But just like that egg, he'd have to be careful not to push too hard or else she might crack under the pressure.

To help pass the time, Alex unpacked his bag in the master bedroom where he'd be staying, per Brin's request. He took a hot shower to get the travel grime off, happy to find men's bathing stuff in the bathroom and not all women's fu-fu supplies. He dressed in a pair of jeans but left off his shirt and walked back into the kitchen.

Opening the stainless refrigerator, he saw beer, eggs, milk and the makings for cold cut sandwiches. He grabbed a beer, popped the top off and headed to the back deck, admiring the view from the wall of windows at the back of the house.

He sat in one of the wicker lounge chairs outside and listened to the ocean swoosh against the beach. He watched the sun sink lower into the sky as the evening came on, changing the light blue sky to teal.

He watched a group of high school kids play a game of volleyball off to his left, arguing over the position the ball had landed. He spotted some older girls off to his right, probably young college aged, sunbathing in their bikinis.

Not so long ago he would have made his way over to them, struck up a conversation and flirted. Maybe gotten a phone number.

Now, he just wanted to see Melanie.

He heard his phone ding through the open patio door and went inside to get it off of the kitchen counter. The object of his thoughts had sent him a message.

Want to meet for drinks?

The Taproom at seven?

He typed back a quick "sounds great" and waited for her response. It came almost instantly.

Brin's car keys are in the ignition.

It has GPS. The bar is on Melrose Ave.

See you there.

Alex looked at the clock on the oven and saw that it was almost six. He decided he'd rather be early than late and went to get dressed.

FOREVER GRATEFUL

He put on a dress shirt, rolled the sleeves up his forearms and kept the rest casual by staying in his jeans. He'd rather wear his flip-flops but decided that probably wouldn't go over well in a place called The Taproom. So he put on his black boots from his Navy days that he never left home without and walked out the door at six-fifteen.

He found Brin's powder blue Mercedes in the garage and sure enough, the keys were in it. He had to move the seat all the way back to fit behind the steering wheel and didn't understand how, if it was this tight for him, Jaxson was able to drive this thing. Not caring enough to dwell on the matter, he punched in the address on the GPS and left to go meet Melanie.

By six forty-five Alex was pulling up in front of the bar. He chose to valet since he didn't know his way around the streets of Los Angeles very well and was handed a ticket by a kid no more than nineteen.

When he walked into the bar, he felt a little out of place with all the wealth around him.

The black bar along the left wall was bordered with golden pipes and behind it more liquor bottles than he could count, their liquids reflected in the mirror behind them. Black iron stools covered in red leather lined the front of the bar as well as tables that were scattered around the room with black granite tops.

He chose one off in the corner where he could face the

door and watch for Melanie, away from the growing, after-work crowd, and waited for a waitress to come take his drink order.

When the petite brunette finally made her way over to him in black hot pants and a dark blue blouse, he ordered a light beer. She brought it back a few minutes later and he started a tab, still waiting for Melanie and looking around the growing bar population.

He spotted a tall, leggy redhead on the other side of the room staring at him. He gave a curt nod, not wanting the attention of the woman with more makeup than sense and a black dress so short she'd probably flash everyone if she bent over. But apparently she took that nod as an invitation because she started to make her way over to him.

"Hi there, handsome. Want some company?" she asked, her voice husky. But it wasn't natural. She was obviously trying to make it sound more passionate.

"Not really. I'm waiting for someone."

Alex looked back toward the door, praying Melanie would show up soon. He didn't want the audience of the woman but good manners kept him from saying anything more.

"Well, why don't I wait with you? My name's Denise."

She sat down in the chair right next to him and angled her body toward his. Her perfume was strong and musky, overwhelming. Alex leaned back in his chair, tried to look casual but really wanted to avoid the scent.

"Hi, Denise."

"Aren't you going to tell me your name?"

She batted her eyes in a flirtatious manner but it looked more like she had something stuck in them. *Maybe some of the two pounds of mascara,* Alex thought, a smirk appearing on his mouth at the image.

"Alex Lambert. Nice to meet you." Again he looked to the door and still saw no sign of Melanie.

He jerked his face back around when he felt a set of long, fake fingernails rake up and down his exposed forearm.

"Alex. What do you say you forget about whoever you were waiting for and we ditch this place? We can go somewhere more private. My apartment is just a couple blocks away."

He was just about to tell her thanks, but no thanks, when he felt a pair of eyes on him. He turned his head toward the door and there she was.

Melanie.

And she was staring daggers straight through him.

Dammit!

.   .   .   .   .

Mel had been anxious to meet with Alex all day. She really had wanted to be there to pick him up from the airport but in order for her to take off work tomorrow to show him around, she'd had to work double time today.

She hadn't thought to take a change of clothes with her to the office this morning so when Alex agreed to meet her for drinks and it was time to leave, she'd freshened up in the office's opulent restroom.

She had removed the jacket of her suit, making her white satin blouse, matched with the navy and white pin-striped pencil skirt, look more informal. She had touched up her makeup, what little of it there was. Just some bronzer for blush, a light brown eye shadow and a little mascara. When she got to The Taproom, she felt a renewed confidence.

Until she walked through the door and saw the redhead hanging all over Alex.

Jealousy clouded her vision until the two sharing a table across the room seemed to blend into one being.

Calm down, Mel. It's not like you're with him or anything.

Determined not to let her envy show, she held her head high, pasted a fake smile on her face and headed in Alex's direction. He stood when she got to him, effectively removing that redhead's hand from his arm.

She couldn't really blame the woman for being attracted to him. He stood tall with an authoritative bearing without being cocky. He looked gorgeous in his jeans and dress shirt with absolute control showing in his strong shoulders. And those corded forearms that she remembered feeling just two months ago stood out in stark contrast against the white of his shirt, his veins bulging in muscled strength.

His honey eyes gleamed under the low bar lights and gave off a look of determination and confidence.

But his mouth, which she remembered always smiling, was set in a straight line like he was mad. Until he walked around the table and bent to kiss her cheek, a playful half-grin on his mouth.

"Hey, beautiful. I've been waiting for you."

She heard his words but couldn't get past the feeling of his lips on her cheek. It was nothing more than a chaste peck but the feeling was unexpected. Electrifying in that it warmed her entire being. She had to swallow twice before she could make her voice work.

"Well I'm glad you didn't have to wait alone." She turned toward the redhead who was staring at her with a look of pure malice in her kohl covered eyes. "I'm Mel. Would you care to join us…?" she trailed off, waiting for the woman to give her name.

"Denise. And it looks as though *you* should be the one joining *us.*"

Denise looped her hand around Alex's elbow and Mel's gaze locked onto the connection. Her jaw clenched, she looked back up to find Alex staring at her with something akin to curiosity in his eyes. He confused her even more by winking and removing Denise's hand from his arm.

"Sorry, ma'am. But I told you I was waiting for someone. Since she's here now, I'll leave you to break the hearts of other men. Excuse us."

He took Mel's hand in his much larger one, led her to the bar and took two seats at the opposite end from that table. Mel looked back to find the redhead staring after them, retribution evident in her posture.

Alex got the attention of a short waitress and held up his beer with two fingers. She nodded back at him and then he finally turned toward Mel.

It wasn't until then that she realized he was still holding her hand and had them both resting on his jean covered knee. She marveled at the strength she felt in just his fingers and the way his hand engulfed her smaller one. The tan of his skin made her own seem even fairer than she already was.

That electrifying sensation from a moment before with his lips came back more powerfully. The feeling of being connected, on a deeper level than just the outside, was overwhelming. She looked up at him in time to see his mouth curve into a smile that was both puzzling and sexy.

But when their eyes met, she saw something scarier than the feeling at her hand.

She saw desire.

Chapter 5

*"Can two walk together, except they be
agreed?" Amos 3:3*

Alex couldn't decide what he was enjoying more at the
moment. The look of pure, feminine jealousy pouring off of
Melanie in waves. Or the feeling of her hand curled into his,
fingers laced together, palm to palm. Even though it seemed
tiny, almost fairy-like resting in his larger one, her hand felt
perfect there, like it belonged. And the coolness of her skin
made him want to bring her fingers to his mouth and blow
warmth into them.

Or maybe kiss her again just to see the pink flush that
had suffused her cheeks a minute ago.

He had been unprepared for his own reaction when he'd
touched his lips to her skin. Alex hadn't expected that
protective responsiveness to unfurl in his gut like a

Doberman ready to pounce on anything that seemed threatening. He hadn't anticipated the craving to kiss her again, only more forcefully and on the lips to show that man-eating, redheaded vulture–and anyone else watching–that she was his.

Except that she wasn't.

So after planting that quick kiss to her face, he'd dragged her off to this far corner of the bar in hopes of some privacy. And now, while they stared intently at one another, he saw that twinge of fear mixing with the jealousy in her blue-green eyes.

Fear of what? he thought to himself as she lowered her eyes back down to her lap.

He suspected he already knew the answer. Because no matter what Alex thought or did, he couldn't hide from his own eyes the desire to kiss her again and again.

When the waitress had placed the two beers he'd motioned for on the bar top in front of them and walked off, Alex rubbed his and Melanie's linked hands up and down his jeans to get her attention. She sucked in a deep breath, glanced at the movement of their hands on his leg and finally brought her gaze back up to his.

"It's not what you think, you know," he said just loud enough for her to hear. And couldn't help the grin that came when she tried to give him an innocent 'I don't know what you're talking about' look. "Oh, come on. You're gonna play like you weren't all upset when you walked in here a minute ago? I know what it looked like with that redhead hanging all over me."

"Well then it sounds as if it's exactly what I thought," Melanie said and tried to remove her hand from Alex's which just made him tighten his hold even more.

"You can't be mad at me for that. It's not my fault she was hitting on me." Melanie scrunched her nose up like a cute little bunny smelling something sour. Either she didn't like the truth or didn't like the words that described the truth. "I was trying to get rid of her when you walked in. Honest."

"Listen, Alex, you don't have to explain yourself to me. We're just friends. If that's what you're looking for while you're here in L.A., I'm sure you won't be needing my guidance."

"I don't want to take the redhead up on the offer to go home with her."

Melanie's eyes got wide and her mouth dropped open. Alex bit the inside of his cheek to keep from laughing at her expression. It's like she was surprised that a woman would offer something like that to a man. Or maybe, more specifically, to him.

"If I did, I wouldn't be sitting here with you."

"Now, look. I don't want you to feel like I'm holding you back from anything. Just because I made this date… meeting… whatever, doesn't mean you have to stick to it."

She glanced over her shoulder to see the redhead, Denise, still glaring at us. "If you'd rather go home with *Denise*–" she practically spit the name out, and the venom dripping off of those two syllables was enough to paralyze a lesser man. "–I won't stop you."

She managed to wiggle her fingers out of Alex's grasp and stood, slinging her big navy purse over her shoulder.

Right as she turned to leave, Alex stood up in front of her and laid a hand lightly on her shoulder.

"Melanie." She refused to look up at him, obviously more content to watch her toes. Alex placed a gentle finger under her chin to raise her head up. "Melanie. I'm sorry. I'm sorry for what you saw when you walked in. I'm sorry for teasing you about it. Honest to God, that's not what I'm here for. The only reason I agreed to this hair-brained idea of my sister's was because I was going to get to see you again. Please don't leave."

Alex could see the battle warring in Melanie's eyes. He could tell that she was debating whether or not there was any truth to what he was saying or if he was just blowing smoke. She chewed on her bottom lip and looked back over her shoulder again, toward where the man-eater sat.

He knew he was going to have to distract Mel, to get her mind off the redhead or else their whole evening would be shot.

He reached his left hand down and laced his fingers with

her right hand again. That brought her attention back to him, to where they touched. And when he brought their joined hands up to rest on his chest, her eyes followed and she stared at that connection, still chewing her lip. Finally she released her teeth and brought her gaze upwards until she was looking at him again.

The insecurity he saw there broke his heart.

Sweet, Melanie. What happened in your past to make you so timid?

"Would you feel better if we left and went someplace else?" he asked, willing to do whatever it took to see her confidence reign over her again. "Wherever you want to go. Just please don't walk out on me now."

Melanie searched his eyes, her own darting back and forth between his two. He was cracking her, he knew it. He just had to push a little more.

"Come on. Who's going to protect me from overly promiscuous women if you leave me here alone, huh?"

Try as she might, Melanie was unable to keep herself from chuckling. Soon her shoulders were shaking in laughter and her eyes crinkled with her smile. She doubled over, holding her side with her free hand when her laughs broke free from silent to noisy. A couple of minutes passed before she stood up straight and took a deep breath, regaining control of herself.

She shook her head at him with that smile in place on

her lips and sat back down.

·   ·   ·   ·   ·

I must be crazy thought Mel as she took her seat at the bar next to Alex again.

She knew what she had seen when she walked into The Taproom. Alex and that woman, Denise, sitting all cozy at a table in the dark corner. Why she had let herself be sweet-talked into staying was beyond her.

Possibly it was the tingling feeling radiating up her arm from where he held her hand against his chest. She wasn't naïve enough to deny the fact that the firm muscle bunching under her hand hadn't made an impact on her. Like it hadn't made her heart beat faster while wondering what his chest would look like bare, without the restriction of clothes.

Then again, it could have been the absolute pleading in his eyes mixing with the conviction of his words. His confidence shining through loud and clear in his tone.

And as she replayed the image of the two of them in her mind, some details stood out that she hadn't been able to focus on before, making her question her own certainty.

Like how Alex had been leaning as far back as he could from *Denise* without falling out of his chair. And how he had a look of annoyance, almost revulsion, on his face while watching the redhead drag her nails up his arm. And then there was the nervousness in his eyes when he'd caught sight of Mel at the door, like he was afraid she was going to bolt.

She was not too proud to admit when she was wrong but that didn't mean that it wasn't going to sting.

"I'm sorry, too." She sighed, desperately tried to ignore the pang of jealousy that still hung in her mind. "It was wrong of me to jump to conclusions. I had no right to make such a big deal out of that situation. Regardless of what was going on, it was your business. And for the record, no, I don't think it's what it looked like."

Alex just grinned at her, his eyes gleaming with something similar to admiration in the yellow glow of the lights behind the bar. He picked up his beer and took a quick swig, kept his eyes on her the whole time, before responding.

"No one said you had no right. In fact, if I had my way, you would have every right."

Mel couldn't have been more confused than if he would have said that he grew up on Mars. Who says something like that to someone they just met?

Me have a right to his business? Next he's going to want to be all in my business, too.

There was no way she would let that happen. With her business came her past and *that* needed to stay locked deep in the recesses of her mind. She managed to take her hand out of his grip and picked up her beer, just to give her fidgety fingers something to do.

"Ok, well… I've managed to take off of work tomorrow so I can show you around town. I was thinking of taking you to the normal places. You know, Rodeo Drive, the Walk of Fame, maybe the Hollywood sign in the hills. Unless there's something else you wanted to do."

She waited a beat to see if he had any suggestions but Alex remained quiet, watching her hand as she worked the label off the beer bottle with her nails. She forced herself to stop and brought her hands back to her lap. The movement broke into his concentration because he shook his head and looked back up at her then.

"Don't take this the wrong way. But do I look like the kind of guy who would want to see a bunch of letters on a hill? Or go shopping?" he asked with skepticism heavy on his last word.

And now that Mel thought about it, the only image she had of Alex on Rodeo Drive was of him running, trying to find a way off the couture store lined street. Mel giggled as she pictured him running in his boots and jeans, yelling for people to move as he made his way two streets over to Canon Drive safely. Which in all honesty could be just as bad as Rodeo except that there weren't quite as many tourists.

"Care to enlighten me as to what's so funny?"

"It's nothing. Just me realizing what a mistake it was to suggest those types of activities for fun. I'm used to hanging around women, not men, during after-hours. And let's face it; here in Los Angeles shopping is what women do."

"I can think of more entertaining things that women do."

The voice came from the side of Mel and her spine stiffened as she realized who it belonged to.

Can't that woman find someone else to harass?

She and Alex both looked in that direction to find Denise staring at them.

She had a smirk on her heavily painted mouth but there was something cold in her eyes. Malevolence. Mel had no intention of letting this woman ruin her night now that she understood what had happened earlier.

"I'm sorry, sweetie," Mel said as she tilted her head to the side, talking to the man-eater like she was a child. "We were talking about what respectable women do with their free time. Not a spoil like you who scours the bars for her next sugar daddy."

The screech that came from Denise's mouth–mixed with the loud, laughing snort that came from Alex–only fueled Mel's courage.

"Why don't you run along and find some other poor sap to kiss the ground you walk on? My friend here–" she pointed towards Alex, "–has already made it perfectly clear that he's not interested."

Not wanting to give the woman a chance to reply, she withdrew a fifty dollar bill from her purse, which was more than enough to cover the tab. After getting the attention of the little waitress that had served them, she waved the bill in the air to show her they were ready to leave and laid it down on the bar.

"Come on, Alex. The atmosphere in this place is making me feel dirty. Let's go someplace where they keep the trash outdoors."

Mel stood, slung her purse over her shoulder and grabbed Alex's hand. As they walked out of the bar, she ignored the snide comment of 'you'll pay for that' that came from the man-eater, knowing that the odds of ever seeing that poor excuse for a woman again were slim to none.

Once outside in the warm summer evening, Mel handed her valet ticket to the boy standing behind the podium and Alex did the same. As the kid ran off to get their cars, she turned toward Alex to find him smiling at her, his shoulders shaking as he tried to hold in his laughter.

She wasn't so controlled and burst out laughing so hard that she bent over at the waist, her purse sliding down her arm as she did. Tears filled her eyes as she thought about the offended expression on that woman's face. She felt no remorse, though. Nothing was said that wasn't absolutely true.

Still, that outraged look along with her own shock at saying such things made her laugh so hard that she lost her breath and started coughing, struggling to pull air into her lungs to breathe. Alex patted her on the back a few times and reached down, grabbed her elbows and slowly pulled her back to a standing position.

"You'll catch your breath easier if your diaphragm isn't constricted," he said in between his own deep breaths.

Mel was too caught off guard to speak.

The way his hands gently held her arms made her feel fragile. His callused palms rasped against the tender skin on the inside of her elbows, making her skin tickle. The happy expression on his face transformed his normally commanding look to something more playful, approachable. His smile was wide and his full lower lip stuck out a little as he laughed.

Her gaze was drawn to his mouth. She wanted nothing more in that moment than to lean forward and press her lips against his. To see if he tasted of the beer he had sipped earlier. Or if his lips were soft, hard or somewhere comfortably in between.

"What's going on here, Alex?"

He didn't even pretend to act like he had no clue what she was talking about. They had been dancing around this connection all evening and she wanted, needed, to know what it meant.

"I'm not sure. But I'd like to find out." He moved his right hand from her elbow and brought it to her face. He softly placed his fingers against her cheek and ran his thumb along her jaw line. Very tenderly. "I want to know you. The real you."

"I don't know if I can," she whispered, closing her eyes as her feelings of insecurity bubbled up to the surface.

Right then she hoped those men who had raped her were burning in hell. Not only for what they did, but for what they took from her aside from her virginity. Her confidence. Her beliefs in something greater.

Her ability to trust.

Mel felt Alex's thumbs both run along her cheeks, wiping away tears that had slipped from beneath her lashes. The gesture was so caring that she cried even more, trying to figure out how to get past the fork in this road they were traveling on.

"Don't cry, sweet Melanie." Alex pulled her into his chest and wrapped his arms around her back. "Just let me in. Let me be your strength."

Her breath caught and she hiccupped past her tears as she processed what he said.

My strength. My strong hand. How could he…?

She didn't understand why those would be the words he'd chosen.

"Has your sister been saying anything to you about me?" Mel asked, afraid that maybe Brin had broken her confidence. She pulled her head away from the hard planes of his chest and looked up into his eyes.

"No. Why?"

"Because of what you said about being my strength. Why would you say that?"

He sighed and a peaceful look came across his features. He brought one hand up from her back and held onto the back of her head, keeping her eyes focused on his.

"Sometimes you just have to accept that God is in control of your life. Not only with what ultimately happens but what we are led to do and feel and say." Mel snorted and covered her nose quickly, embarrassed that she had let that out. "What is it?" Alex asked.

Well, I guess if he really wants to be with me then he'd better know the truth. Now or never.

"Alex… I'm an atheist."

Aimee Martin

Chapter 6

"Judge not, that ye be not judged." Matthew 7:1

June 27, 2014

Alex sat in one of the lounge chairs on his sister's deck and stared at the sun peeking over the horizon to the east, its deep amber rays casting shadows over the sand. The gray light over the ocean, still untouched by the sun, felt like it matched his feelings, worried and doubting.

It was early. Not even seven in the morning. But he hadn't gotten much sleep, tossing and turning all night before he finally gave up and dragged himself out of bed thirty minutes ago.

Alex had come out here hoping the peaceful serenity of the morning would help him get his thoughts together.

An atheist. I had no idea.

Melanie's confession to him last night had caught him off guard. But what was more was that while that might have scared some people away, he didn't feel the need to tuck tail and run. He truly believed God had brought them together for a reason. And he believed that this was probably just Satan's way of trying to keep him from showing Melanie the way to Christ.

Lord, I need your help here, he prayed. *Guide me in the way to bring her to You.*

Last night, after hearing those three words, he and Melanie had left separately and both gone home. The kicker was that it was her idea. He had wanted to go somewhere and talk about it. Find out more on why she felt like she couldn't believe in anything. In God.

Alex guessed that admitting her atheism wasn't something Melanie did on a regular basis. Her running seemed more like a defense mechanism. So he'd let her go, watched her drive off in her little red Audi before climbing into Brin's car and heading home to the beach.

When he'd gotten back here last night he had stripped down to his boxer briefs and climbed into bed. Even though it was only ten-thirty, the flight out here mixed with the crazy few hours at The Taproom had caught up with him and he'd fallen asleep right after his head hit the pillow.

But visions of Melanie–hurt, alone, crying and desperate

for help–filled his subconscious into the wee hours of morning. When the clock on the nightstand said six-fifteen, he finally just tossed the covers aside and sat up. He'd thrown on a pair of jeans and white t-shirt, brushed his teeth in the bathroom and headed to the kitchen for a cup of strong coffee.

And now, with the morning emerging more fully in front of him and his coffee slowly waking his brain up, Alex couldn't help thinking of that old saying 'It's the dawn of a new day.'

He watched two women jog by on the beach in running gear, chatting and laughing as they went as if all was right with the world. And he thought of Melanie again. He pictured her running just like those two women.

Only instead of laughing she was crying and frightened and running from whatever had pushed her into her beliefs. Or lack thereof, rather. He got the feeling that she'd been running alone for a long time now with no one to help her or be there for her. No one willing to let Melanie just be herself.

That's probably why she's so standoffish and scared to interact with people.

His brow furrowed in concentration, an idea taking hold and not letting go. Plans formed in his mind of how he could get her to open up and be young and carefree like she'd been at Brin and Jax's wedding.

He watched a handful of fish jump out of the water

about ten yards off the shore and the thought hit him. He smiled when he decided on what he was going to do.

Just like the new day, Alex wanted to give Melanie a new dawn, too. For herself and her life. And hopefully, God willing, in time he'd be able to show her the wonders of the Lord.

But first, he had to show her the wonders of life.

. . . . .

Mel sat on one of the barstools at her kitchen counter, nursing a hot cup of tea. Normally she went straight for coffee. But this morning, she had a headache brought on by lack of sleep and regrets.

Seeing the look on Alex's face when she'd told him she was an atheist last night had felt like a punch in the stomach. The surprise followed by disbelief and ending with something she could have sworn was disappointment.

She was used to people being surprised by her because of how well she did her job. After *that* night and her trip to the clinic two months later, Mel had promised herself that she would never be a doormat again, forced determination to be the front skill in her repertoire.

Because of that promise, she was now a career oriented woman who never took no for an answer when she was bargaining for her clients. She was sharp in every aspect of the business, knowing when to sign a new client or back off of a deal that seemed too good to be true.

Her boss, Timothy Evans, had told her once that even he was surprised at how focused and determined she was. And that promoting Mel to a senior level management position, even though she was only twenty-five, was one of the easiest decisions he'd ever made.

The disbelief in Alex's eyes had been a little harder to handle. That he could be so doubtful of something she had shared about herself had hurt. He had just said that he wanted to get to know her. *The real her.* And with her first big contribution he had acted completely put out. It made Mel feel like maybe Alex just wanted to know the good parts of her life.

Unfortunately for him, aside from her job and her dog, there just wasn't a lot of good.

But what had cut the deepest was the disappointment. The way it had been written all over his face like a clown wearing makeup.

She could handle a lot of things from a lot of people. She handled the absence and indifference of her parents. She handled the jealousy from coworkers who felt she had been promoted too quickly. She could even handle the scorn from that woman last night because none of those things mattered to her.

They just were.

But Alex did matter. What he thought and felt and saw in her made her want to be better for him. Why, she wasn't sure. But he made her wish that she wasn't the troubled soul who held onto a fear of men like a second skin. He made her want to open up her heart and let go.

And wasn't that just entirely ludicrous? The last man she'd done that with had sat idly by and watched while three monsters tore her apart. It was Justin who had set the premise for what she felt toward the population with the 'Y' chromosome.

But Alex isn't Justin, Mel, she thought to herself.

No, Alex wasn't one to cower in a corner. He would fight with everything he had for anyone that he felt was important to him. And maybe that's why that disappointment had hurt so badly.

She wanted to be important to Alex. But if he was unhappy with her now, then how long would it be before he decided she wasn't worth the risk?

She set her mug down on the counter and raked her hands through her unbound hair. Frustration made her tug lightly on the ends, hoping she could tug the confusion right out of her head.

God, this is so stupid. You don't know what he felt. You're jumping to conclusions. Just call him.

Her little pep talk did little to alleviate the insecurities running through her brain. She halfway wished she could just call and plead an emergency with a client, maybe cancel the whole day.

But, while she might be a loner and at times a little phobic, a liar she was not.

So she stood, rinsed her mug out at the kitchen sink and placed it in the dishwasher, then made her way to her bedroom.

The bed was still unmade, the sheets thrown all over from her thrashing about last night. Mel picked up her cell from the nightstand, unplugged the power cord and walked back into the living room. She curled up on the couch facing the windows to her left.

While the noise from this busy L.A. street corner rose in volume down below, she dialed Alex's number and waited for him to answer. He didn't make her wait long, answering before the second ring had finished.

"Good morning!"

He didn't sound nearly as exhausted or lost as she was. Maybe Mel really had been reading too much into his expressions last night.

"Hi," she said. Her voice sounded meek so she cleared her throat. "I hope you were able to get some sleep last night. I know how hard that is to do sometimes when you're not in your own bed."

"I got enough. How 'bout you? Did you rest any?"

"I got enough."

She smiled when he broke into laughter on the other end of the line. Hearing that sound come from deep in his throat made her feel warm all over. She imagined his Adam's apple bobbing up and down and his lips curved into a big smile. And his gorgeous eyes bright with a happiness that she had made him feel.

"Well, I hope it'll be plenty. We've got a busy day ahead of us," he told her when he'd finally gotten a hold of himself.

"Did you decide what you wanted to do?"

"I did."

That was it. That's all he said. They were both quiet for a minute before her curiosity finally got the best of her.

"Are you going to tell me what it is? I need to know so I can figure out what to wear. And what time do you want me to pick you up?"

"First, no, I'm not going to tell you. Second, just wear something casual and you should be fine. And third, you can meet me here at Brin's house if it's not too much trouble. Say, in about an hour, hour and a half?"

Mel glanced at the clock and saw that it was almost nine.

"Alright. By the time I get ready and drive over there it should be right at ten-thirty."

"Sounds perfect. And Melanie…" he trailed off.

"Yes? What is it?" She didn't know what he wanted to say but the fact that he was hesitant made her nervous.

"It's nothing, really. I just wanted to tell you that there is no judgment on my part about what you said last night. Who am I to judge anyone, you know? I didn't want things to be awkward when you got here so I thought it'd be best to just get it over with."

"Like ripping off a Band-Aid."

She blew out a small breath, relieved that he seemed to be okay with her admission. She could hear him smile when he replied.

"Yeah," he said softly. "Just like that. I'll see you in little while, Melanie."

He hung up before she had a chance to say anything.

Mel stood up from the couch and went back into her bedroom. She took out her clothes for the day and laid them all on the messy bed then went to take a shower.

Once the water was warm, she walked under the spray inside the white ceramic tiled space. She shampooed her hair and washed her body, taking the time to shave her legs since she'd be wearing shorts. Then she applied a healthy dollop of her jasmine scented conditioner and ran it through her long hair.

By the time she had finished bathing and gotten out of the shower, the bathroom was filled with a floral scented steam.

She took a little more time than usual on her makeup, choosing some taupe eye shadow that had a shimmer to it to help bring out the blue in her eyes. She decided to stick with her bronzer blush but added a pale bronze lipstick rather than the clear lip gloss she normally wore.

After thoroughly blow drying her hair, she opted to pull it up into a low ponytail since the day was already warm at eighty-five degrees, and only expected to get hotter.

Back in her bedroom, she put on her white linen shorts. She had chosen a dark cream, cotton, sleeveless blouse, knowing that it would go well with her makeup.

She slipped her feet into a pair of brown leather Stuart Weitzman, Grecian style sandals. She walked to the corner of her bedroom where there was a standing oval mirror in a cherry wood frame and surveyed her handiwork.

Fun, a little flirty.

Perfect, she decided and headed back to the kitchen.

Mel had already taken Kass out for the morning so she gave her pup a pat and kiss on the head then made sure she had enough food and water to last for the day.

She grabbed her purse, checked for her keys and cell, then walked out the front door after one last 'bye sweetie' to Kassie.

Five minutes later she was in her car, heading south toward the highway. The clock on her dash said nine-fifty-five and she guessed that she'd be at Alex's right on time.

She smiled when she hit the PCH, thinking this day may turn out to be just what the doctor ordered.

FOREVER GRATEFUL

. . . . .

Alex had been searching Google all morning trying to find the information he needed to set his plans in motion for the day. After making a couple of calls and giving his credit card number over the phone, twice, he finally had the first half of the day organized and ready to go.

Now he just needed Melanie to get here.

Once he got off of the phone with the caterer, he went to the master bathroom and cleaned up quickly in the square, all-glass shower, choosing to forego the shaving today. He dried off and dressed in a pair of khaki cargo shorts and a red polo shirt, made sure he had his wallet and cell phone in the side pockets. He slipped his feet into his favorite pair of brown Reef flip-flops, hung the towel on the rack in the bathroom and headed to the kitchen for one more cup of coffee while he waited for Melanie.

No sooner had he poured the brew into his mug did the doorbell ring. Glancing at the clock on the stove he saw that it was ten-twenty-six.

Right on time, he smiled to himself as he went to open the front door.

The sight of her took his breath away. There was nothing fancy about the way she was dressed. White shorts, some sort of tank top and sandals all fit her body to perfection.

The shorts made her legs look like they went on forever. The top fit her loosely and flowed around her upper body like a blanket blowing in the breeze. And the light colors of the fabric made her look innocent.

But it was the sight of her hair pulled up in that ponytail, out of the way of her angelic face, that did him in. Her features were so utterly feminine. Soft cheeks with high cheekbones, lips that were just a little pouty and begging to be kissed and long eyelashes that framed his favorite feature on her. Those beautiful blue-green eyes that looked more like the ocean this morning. All combined it made her look young and relaxed.

And that's exactly how he wanted her today.

"Is something wrong?" Her soft, hesitant voice broke through his mind and he realized he'd been staring.

"Not at all. You look beautiful."

Melanie ducked her head down toward her chest. But Alex was having no part of that. He wanted her to embrace life, not hide from it. He placed his index finger under her chin and slowly brought her face up so she was looking into his eyes.

"Don't do that. Don't hide from me. You're beautiful," he said again and this time a small smile curved around her lips.

And just because he couldn't help himself, he leaned down and lightly placed his lips against her cheek. He wanted to taste her lips but had to remind himself that this was a marathon, not a sprint.

He caught a whiff of her perfume as he pulled back. A faint floral scent that had him breathing in deeply, hoping it would stay with him throughout the day.

When he stood straight before her again, Melanie's eyes had opened a little wider and her mouth was open slightly. Her reaction pleased him. It showed Alex that she was just as affected by his lips being on her as he was.

"Are you ready to go?" he questioned.

"Y-yeah," she stuttered a little then cleared her throat and came back with a stronger voice. "Are you going to tell me where we're headed to now that I'm here?"

Instead of answering, he reached down and laced his fingers through her left hand, pulled her into the house and smiled at her cautious enthusiasm.

"I thought we were going somewhere," she muttered under her breath as they made their way through the living room.

"We are. But we're getting there by way of the beach," Alex reassured her as they made it to the back doors and out onto the deck.

The morning was warm, the air tinged with salt from the sea. The sun was rising brightly in front of them and the blue of the sky was unmarred by any clouds.

Beach goers were starting to make their way to the sand, carrying blankets, ice chests and chairs. A few teenage boys came running out from a house on the left carrying surfboards under their arms.

Alex and Melanie walked down the steps of the deck and headed right. He knew there would be a large dock about a half of a mile down from Brin's house, if the directions he was given were accurate.

Melanie pulled her sunglasses off the top of her head and placed them over her eyes. She hitched the straps of her brown suede purse higher up on her right shoulder and looked over at Alex.

He was staring at her again and he knew it, but couldn't help it. He was mesmerized by the smallest actions she performed. Everything about her screamed grace and poise.

"You know Alex, if you don't quit looking at me like that it's going to get very uncomfortable."

"Looking at you like what?"

"Like you're trying to figure out some puzzle. Or see into my mind." Her voice was soft, like either of those options scared her and she didn't know how to handle it.

Alex didn't want to start the day off on a bad note so he forced himself to look forward and watch out for the dock.

They walked in silence a while, their sandaled feet getting covered with sand and neither of them caring. The waves crashed into the shore on their left and laughter rang out around them from people enjoying the warm sun and surf.

FOREVER GRATEFUL

When they were about halfway to the dock, Alex jiggled his hand a little in Melanie's to get her attention.

"You grew up here right? In California?"

"Yes," she said. "Why?"

"What did you used to do for fun with your parents when you were younger?"

"Well, my parents were gone a lot when I was growing up. Usually off to concerts or sit-ins, things like that. So I stayed with my Gramma most of the time. She used to drive me down to Venice Beach to see all the street vendors."

Melanie laughed and Alex found himself smiling, waiting to see what memory was going on in her head.

"There was one guy. I think he was supposed to be a fire breather or something. I don't know. I was, like, ten. Anyway, when he blew out the fire he turned his head in a circle for more 'wow factor' but he didn't look at what was around. He ended up catching his entire booth on fire. No one was hurt but everything in his station became an inferno."

She paused and looked thoughtful for a minute before turning to face him.

"You know, now that I look back at it, it's really not all that funny. How sad for that man. He goes to put on a show for dozens of people and all he did was make a fool of himself."

Alex heard her empathy for the fire breathing man but

her lips were clenched tightly, trying not to laugh. He wasn't so keen on holding back and let out a loud roar when he pictured a booth up in flames at the hands of its owner. Melanie giggled with him but not loudly.

"Your parents didn't ever go there with you and your Gramma?" he asked when he caught his breath.

Melanie immediately closed up emotionally. He could see it. *Crap,* he thought and made a mental note that discussions on her parents were off limits. For now.

Before she could snap at him or try to cancel their day together, he asked a different question to distract her.

"Did y'all ever go out on boats or do anything like whale watching?"

His change of subject had the desired effect. Melanie turned to look at him again as they walked on down the beach. Her tinted glasses were still light enough that he could see the interest in her eyes.

"No."

Alex nodded his head a couple of times and looked forward, happy that he had chosen something that would be new for her. When he didn't say anything more, Melanie stopped, tugged on his hand to get him to stop, too.

"What did you plan for today? You can't just ask me something like that and not tell me why."

She was cute when she was irritated. Her chin was hitched up and her right foot was tapping away in the sand.

FOREVER GRATEFUL

"Let's just say that I hope you don't get seasick."

Alex pulled on her hand and they both started walking again. In the distance in front of them, about a hundred yards away, he saw the outline of the dock. He looked at his watch and saw that it was eleven, figured it would take them about another fifteen minutes to get there.

"So we're going on a boat. I'm surprised that's something you'd want to do so soon after you got out of the Navy. I mean, didn't you have enough of the water while you were enlisted? There are millions of places to go in L.A. and you chose the ocean. It doesn't make very much sense to me."

Melanie was rambling, one of those people who talked a lot when they got nervous. Alex got the feeling that she hadn't spent much time on boats. She was edgy.

But instead of trying to calm her fears, he let her talk about nonsense until they finally reached the dock.

He marched up the steps and she followed closely behind, the grip she had on his hand getting stronger by the second. When they reached the cleat that the boat was tied to, he turned to face her and placed his free hand on her lips.

She stopped talking. But he was momentarily speechless, too. Her lips were soft under his fingers. A little moist, a little full and a lot perfect.

Not now, man! he scolded himself and quickly removed his hand. When he was satisfied that she wasn't going to say anything else, he finally told her their plans.

"We're going to get on this boat here–" he pointed to the forty foot, flybridge trawler boat he had chartered for the afternoon that was to her right, his left, "–and drive about four miles offshore. We're going to eat some lunch and, hopefully, see some dolphins and whales."

Alex watched as a light came over her face. Her nerves about the boat seemed to vanish with the thought of seeing some of the mammals of the sea.

"Really?" Melanie asked, her voice full of childlike wonder.

Alex smiled at her before turning to greet the man stepping off the deck of the boat. He was older, in his sixties, with a head full of silvery gray hair. His skin was darkly tanned from years on the water and appeared even more bronzed with his white button-up shirt and light khaki shorts. His eyes were hidden behind a pair of polarized wrap-around sunglasses but he had an easy smile with teeth that were a little too white.

He reached out to shake Alex's hand as he stepped onto the dock.

"Morning! My name's Sal, Sal Jones. I'll be your captain today. You must be Alex and Melanie." His handshake was firm.

"Yes, sir. Alex Lambert. Nice to meet you." He turned toward Mel and held up her hand that was held in his. "And this is Melanie Moore."

FOREVER GRATEFUL

She gave a small smile to Captain Jones but didn't say anything. She was too preoccupied looking at the boat like it was a death trap. Alex thought of Peter when he was told to walk on water by Jesus. He imagined Melanie having the same lack of faith right now that Peter had had then. Only hers was in a machine rather than the Lord.

Of course there's a lack of faith, Alex. That's what you're trying to help her see.

"You'll have to excuse Melanie, Captain. I think she's a little afraid of the water."

His assertion made Melanie's head snap up to the two men. She stood up straighter in an effort to save face.

"I'm not afraid of the water. I've spent my life on the beach." She looked back at the boat again and some of her bravado left her. "I'm just a little nervous about the boat. It's safe, right?"

The captain gave a little chuckle before he reached down and took Melanie's free hand, pulled her towards the port side of the bow.

"One hundred percent safe. I assure you."

Alex took his cue from the man and they both stepped over the rail. Once on the deck, they turned and helped Melanie step over and onto the deck as well. She let go of the captain's hand but held tightly onto Alex's. Alex rubbed his thumb over the backs of her knuckles, trying to soothe her nerves.

But he knew that she wouldn't be able to calm down and enjoy herself until they were out in the open water.

"You two feel free to look around for a few minutes. Pete's my first mate. He and I are going to run through our checklist one more time then we'll be ready to head out." He excused himself and left Alex and Melanie to their own devices.

They watched Sal walk up the three step ladder to the flybridge–where the controls were–and start talking to a younger man who looked to be in his thirties. Alex pulled Melanie along the rail and into the door on their left.

They walked into a salon that was bright and airy, the windows on three sides allowing the sunlight to stream through like fingers reaching out to hold them. There was a u-shaped white leather couch that surrounded a dark russet table centered in the space along the bow wall. Midnight blue accent pillows were placed neatly in a row along the back section.

A small galley took up the space on the stern side of the boat. On the starboard side were a stainless steel refrigerator and microwave, a six-foot-long black corian counter with chestnut cabinets above and below, as well as a glass wine cabinet nestled in the corner of the counter space.

On the port side was another counter, this one with double stainless steel sinks, a four burner electric stovetop and a stainless oven. Flooring over the entire boat was teak and polished to a high shine.

"It's like an apartment."

Melanie's sweet observation brought Alex's attention to her. She was looking around the room with something similar to awe on her face, taking in all the décor like a kid in a candy store.

"Kind of, yeah. You've never been on a boat before, huh?" he asked, wanting confirmation for his earlier assumption.

She vehemently shook her head no. Again, he rubbed her knuckles softly, hoping to keep her attention on him rather than her fear.

"There are a couple of state rooms below this area." Melanie looked over at him, confused. "A state room is a place where there's a bed, maybe some sort of drawers or closet and the head. The bathroom. I'll show it to you if you want or we can go back out on deck. Maybe Captain Sal and Pete will be about ready to ship out."

"Let's go back out."

Melanie was already headed back toward the door that led back outside. Alex followed her out but directed her to the left by placing his hand on her elbow. She walked along the deck to the stern but stopped suddenly and he heard her gasp.

He smiled, knowing that the rest of the surprise he had planned was setup.

Not waiting for her to say anything, he slid around her and walked over to the mahogany table in the center of an eight foot by ten foot open space. There were two matching chairs placed on either side of the round table. A white linen table cloth lay across the hard surface, and on top of that were two place settings of food.

Roasted chicken with a white wine, rosemary sauce took precedence on the dishes. Sautéed zucchini and squash lay off to the sides of the plates. Caesar salads sat in small bowls at the top left of the settings and empty wine glasses sat at the top right. A stainless ice bucket rested in a wrought iron holder in between the two chairs with a bottle of chardonnay chilling inside.

Alex walked over to the closest chair and pulled it out. He stood, waited for Melanie to come sit.

She hesitated for a minute then slowly walked over and sat down. He took a seat in the other chair and watched her. She was looking down at her hands that were twisting together nervously in her lap.

He reached out his left hand and placed it over hers to stop the fidgeting. He watched her throat work up and down, twice, before she finally looked up at him.

"Did I do something wrong?" he asked, praying that he hadn't made a mistake. Or maybe gone too far too soon. She gave a small smile and shook her head no but her eyes looked sad.

FOREVER GRATEFUL

"Then what is it?"

"It's just..." she paused, swallowing thickly again. "It's just that no one has ever done something like this. Gone to this much trouble. For me."

"I'd go through more, Melanie. If only you'd let me."

"Why me? I mean, you could have your pick of women. Last night is evidence of that. So why do this for me?"

Her insecurity brought out his protective instincts because he knew somehow she had been hurt and that's why she was so uncertain of herself. And of him.

"Why not you?" he countered instead of answering.

Her brow furrowed a little in thought. Just when he was sure she was going to give some lengthy retort she smiled again. Only this time is was fuller and more real. She gave her shoulders a shrug as if to say 'I have no answer.'

"There's something you need to understand about me, Melanie. I'm not like other men you've dated or been around. The way I was raised, and my training in the Navy, taught me what it is to be a man. Respect the Lord. Respect your elders. Respect women and children. That's what matters most. I respect you and want to show it."

"You do that by renting a small yacht and having some fancy lunch provided?"

She was smirking at him and he took a deep breath, happy that she seemed to be accepting what he was saying. She was so stunning, especially when she smiled and her youth came out of hiding.

She took his breath away.

"No, that's just a little extra to get some brownie points on my side. The way I show respect for you is by listening to you and not judging you. Letting you be yourself. By being myself and taking care of you. That's how a real man does it."

The grin instantly fell from Melanie's face and her skin went sheet white, the way it would when someone is about to be sick. Her mouth fell open and he could imagine the silent scream that wanted to come forth. Her eyes got wide, glazed over and stared straight through Alex.

He didn't need her to talk to know what had happened.

He'd just lost her to one of her flashbacks.

Chapter 7

"For he found her in the field, and the betrothed damsel cried, and there was none to save her." Deuteronomy 22:27

September 13, 2009

Mel had zoned out.

She experienced that first stab of pain and it felt like something–or more specifically, someone–had just torn her in two. Like a knife had been shoved into her most feminine area and twisted three hundred and sixty degrees. And then twisted again.

She gave up screaming. She gave up fighting. She just laid there like a broken rag doll, unable to hold herself upright any longer. What was the point? All her screaming and fighting did was excite the three monsters even more.

She lost track of time.

When the bald man had finished with her, the blonde man took his turn. And after that, the dark haired man. She thought they were finished and she'd finally be free to run, to hide.

But no.

They started the entire disgusting, agonizing rotation all over again. That's when she quit trying to figure out how long she had been stuck in this dark corner of a dark alley with nothing but dark hearts surrounding her.

Mel closed her eyes and imagined she was a kid again. She imagined walking down the boardwalk with her Gramma, eating hot dogs and cotton candy, watching street performers put on a show for any dime they could get. In those memories there was nothing painful, only peaceful.

Gramma would hold her hand while they walked. Stroke her hair as they watched the waves crash into seawall. Laugh with her at the mimes pretending to run into brick walls.

But… why is her laugh so deep? Why is she pulling… OW!

She wasn't with her Gramma. The dark haired man with soulless eyes was pulling her hair, trying to see her tear streaked face while the bald man roughly shifted into her yet again.

"Lemme see tha pretty face. Y'know you like dis don'cha?" His whiskey-soured breath two inches from her face kept her from going back to her peaceful place. Back to her Gramma.

Mel tried to wrench her head away but all that did was make him rip out a hunk of her hair. Just more pain.

Please, please just let this end.

She quit looking for Justin, too. The weak excuse for a man was still cowering in the corner the last time she had chanced a glance in his direction.

He'd heard her pleas for help and had done nothing. Nothing.

Between him and these three drunkards, all her hope for humanity was quickly flying out the window, lost on a breeze of alcohol and smoke and hatred.

"C'mon man. Iss my turn." Mel thought it was the dark haired man again but she didn't know for sure.

The more they rammed into her, the higher her pain climbed, the less she heard and saw around her. It was like the throbbing torture on her womanhood took all of her other senses and beat them into the ground.

All she felt was the sting, the ache. The humiliation.

Sometime later–could have been minutes or it could have been hours–the bald and blonde men threw her roughly against the dumpster again. Her ravaged body slid down to the cold pavement, landing in a weak, bloody heap.

Mel glanced up in time to see the all three of the men zipping up their pants, almost in unison. They were glaring down at her like she was some sort of rotten trash left outside to draw the rats from the corners of the alleys.

You all are the rats, she thought to herself.

She flinched back and covered her face with her hands when the bald man leaned down and spoke softly in her ear. Again she recognized that he was not as inebriated as his cronies and his menacing voice came out in a threatening whisper.

"You'll keep your mouth shut about what happened here." He grabbed her chin roughly with his burly hands, keeping his green eyes locked on Mel's. "Or we might have to make our way to your fancy University and pay you another visit."

Too late, Mel realized he had taken her student identification card from her purse. He was holding it in front of her, showing Mel that they now knew how to find her.

"I w-won't. I-I swear." Her voice was hoarse from all the screaming and felt as wrecked as the rest of her.

Satisfied that she would not breathe a word of this to anyone, the bald man stood straight and walked off with his two companions. She felt revolted when they all patted each other on the back like they had just won a championship football game or maybe were headed to a bachelor party for a night out.

When they turned right at the corner of the alley and finally were out of site, she took a deep breath that caused sharp pains to spread throughout her body. She gingerly ran her hands over herself to try to assess the damage.

Starting at her head, she felt the tender bald spot on the left side of her scalp where the dark haired man had ripped out her hair. She felt her lower lip, swollen and trickling blood from being slammed against the dumpster. There was a tightness on her chest bone where she had been held down so roughly, no doubt already turning into a black and purple bruise.

When she finally allowed her gaze to travel farther south she saw her torn panties lying on the ground. There were blood spatters all over them but not nearly as much as the small puddle directly underneath where she had been standing.

Her body fell forward in a nauseated lurch and everything that was in her stomach came out in a violent rush.

Her right palm landed in the pool but she was took sick, too devastated to care. Minutes passed with her bent over until her gagging finally subsided into dry heaves.

When there was nothing left, she carefully sat back against the dumpster.

Tears, unheeded and unchecked, ran in streams down her face. The salt mixed with the blood in the open cut on her lip but she felt no more pain.

She felt robbed. She felt dirtied.

Aimee Martin

She felt broken.

Chapter 8

"Confess your faults one to another, and pray one for another, that ye may be healed. The effectual fervent prayer of a righteous man availeth much." James 5:16

June 27, 2014

Alex stared at the frightened woman in front of him and felt helpless. She was pale, like someone who hadn't seen the sun in years. She was shaking all over like she had been left out in freezing temperatures all night. And her breathing was so fast that it looked like she had just run a marathon.

Melanie was stuck in some memory, some horrible event from her past that had literally rendered her speechless and immobile. He needed to find a way to bring her back to the present. Fast.

Aimee Martin

What the hell am I supposed to do? How do I help her now?

Gently, he leaned forward and laid his hand on her left knee. When she didn't flinch he gave her leg a little shake. Nothing. He wanted to grab her by the shoulders and shake her but he held himself back.

Alex remembered a buddy of his from the Air Force, Jim Stanton, who had come back from the war with Post Traumatic Stress Disorder. All the bombing he'd had to do in Afghanistan had taken a toll on Jim's peace of mind and he suffered for it. Tremendously.

Jim had told him once that when he was in the throes of a flashback, the worst thing someone could do was grab at him. That sometimes it would make the person suffering lash out.

Regardless of what had happened in Melanie's past, Alex was sure that this was the same thing. And it was killing him to sit by and watch her go through it.

Not caring what would happen to himself, Alex placed his hands on either side of Melanie's face and held her, softly but with purpose. He angled her face up so that her eyes–still seeming to be staring off somewhere else, somewhere in the past–were aimed directly at his own.

"Melanie."

He waited, hoping his voice would bring her back. Still nothing. He tried again, gave a gentle shake to her head.

"Melanie, look at me. Look at me now!"

She let out a loud yelp and flung her arms up, trying to wrench free from Alex's hands but he held fast, refusing to let her leave.

"It's me, Melanie. It's Alex. Look at me."

He kept repeating it over and over, ignoring the hits his arms were taking from her hands. Finally, like a thick morning fog clearing with the rising sun, her eyes slowly started to refocus. Her arms settled slowly back down in her lap. She blinked, twice, and then looked directly into Alex's eyes.

"That's it honey. It's me. You're okay," he spoke quietly. "You're going to be alright."

He knew the moment she realized what had happened. Her eyes got wide with realization and there was no hiding the glossy moisture filling them. She took a deep breath, tried to regain her composure.

But when her lower lip started to tremble, Alex pulled her into his arms to give her comfort.

"Shh. I'm here, Melanie. I've got you," he murmured when her shoulders started shaking, soft moans breaking free from her normally poised self. "Let it out. Just let it go."

Alex pulled her from her chair and set her down on his lap, rocking her back and forth. He gave no thought to propriety or his vow to take things slowly with her. She needed reassurance that she was safe. So he held her head tight against his chest, rubbed her back soothingly, and just let her cry.

Melanie latched on to the front of his shirt, grabbed tightly to the red material like it was a lifeline. She buried her face even deeper into him, like she was afraid he would disappear if she let go.

I'm not leaving you, sweet Melanie. Not now. Not ever.

The declaration that only he had heard made his head come up in surprise. They barely knew each other. He shouldn't be thinking about forever. But he had, subconsciously at least. And he recognized the truth behind it.

Alex wasn't going anywhere.

.　　　.　　　.　　　.　　　.

Mel couldn't seem to relax her fingers. She couldn't put an end to the tears that were falling. She just couldn't stop.

She had come completely out of the flashback. She knew where she was and who she was with. She kept telling herself that again and again in her mind, hoping it would ease the terror and shame filling her.

I'm on a boat with Alex. I'm on a boat with Alex. Not in that alley. Not with those men or Justin. I'm on a boat and I'm with Alex.

Finally Mel started to relax; her heartbeat slowed and

her breathing became less erratic. She forced herself to quit crying but little sniffles snuck out of her nose like a child fighting off a cold. She tried to loosen her white-knuckled fingers that were holding on to Alex's shirt.

But they were so stiff that she couldn't manage it alone.

Alex must have felt her struggling because he removed his right hand from her back and brought it around, gently uncurling her fingers one at a time. When he had all ten of them open, he laid her hands flat against his chest and returned his hand to her back, his strokes absorbing her tremors and reassuring her anxious self.

Even through her blouse she could feel the strength in his hands, the control. She could also feel the defined muscles under her cheek, hard and unyielding but smooth under her palms. Things that had always terrified her.

But for once that power didn't scare her. It made her feel safe. Whole. Which didn't make a lick of sense but she was finished trying to figure things out where Alex was concerned.

She hadn't spoken of the attack to anyone since her last therapy session a couple of years ago. She hadn't needed to because the flashbacks had stopped. It'd taken two years of intense therapy but she'd finally made it past that dark time in her life and moved on.

Or so she thought.

Mel knew that after this episode Alex wasn't going to let

her explain the flashback away like she had last time. He wasn't going to let her escape to the safe confines of her mind.

But really, her mind wasn't exactly safe anymore so she might as well tell him. And resolving herself to that decision, she felt relieved. Like a weight was being lifted off of her chest.

She took a deep breath, tasted the salt from the ocean they were floating on and hints of rosemary from the chicken on the table to her left. She ran her palms along the planes of Alex's chest and flinched a little when she felt the muscles jump under her hands.

She licked her dry lips and brought her gaze up, past his Adam's apple and his chin, up further to meet his eyes. Those honeyed depths stared back at her with concern and empathy. Mel felt her lip start to quiver again and sealed her lips tightly together to stop it.

"I'm sorry."

"You don't have anything to apologize for."

"Yes, I do. You planned this amazing surprise and I ruined it by having a… an episode. So I'm sorry."

Mel watched as his eyes took in every detail of her face. They roamed over her pale skin–chin, mouth, cheeks, even her forehead–before coming back to rest on her eyes. She knew what was coming even before he had opened his mouth.

FOREVER GRATEFUL

"What happened, Melanie?"

That's it. That's all he said. He didn't need to expand his question anymore because Mel knew what he wanted to know. And she wanted to tell him.

She realized she was sitting on his lap, though she didn't remember how she got there. Mel knew she needed a little distance to get the story out, physically and figuratively.

So she pushed back from his chest and stood on shaky legs. Alex placed his hands on either side of her hips to steady her. They were so large that they covered her from hip bone to hip bone. She stared at the contact for a minute before she took a few steps back and sat down in her own chair, ignoring the heat that lingered like a branding iron where his hands had just been.

Mel looked out to her right, past Alex, at the water stretching for miles. The bright sun shone down on the surface and it looked like obsidian. The disturbances in the water from the ripples caused by low tide made the normally calm sea look jagged, just like that volcanic glass. White clouds began to form in the bright blue sky above the horizon like pillows ready to soften the blackness below.

Mel couldn't help but wonder if her comparisons to the elements before her–jagged and soft–had anything to do with her emotions. They were shifting through her like a rollercoaster; up, down, up, around, down. Panic, doubt, pride and resolve fought their way to the surface of her soul.

She pushed down everything but her determination and turned back to face Alex.

He was watching her closely but patiently. His hair was blowing in the breeze, falling across his forehead but not quite covering his eyes. There were blonde streaks that she had never noticed before scattered around his head making his tanned skin seem even darker. His strong jaw, angular with a light scruff already showing, was set in a straight line. His lips were neither smiling nor pouting, but tempting with their fullness.

And his eyes. His beautiful, honey-colored eyes stared at her in such a way that she felt exposed. Like her heart was laid open for him to pick apart and possibly put back together again.

Please don't let this be a mistake, she thought to herself.

Swallowing thickly to get past the frog in her throat, she finally opened up to someone other than the therapist for the first time ever.

"It happened almost five years ago," she said and then stopped, the words stuck against her lips like water backing up in a bathtub from a drain stopper. A few minutes passed before Alex broke the silence, willing her to go on.

"What? What happened, Melanie?" he repeated his earlier question.

His voice was deep and sure. Encouraging. And the words began to flow from her like a geyser, the pressure from being kept inside for so long causing her to reveal everything.

"I guess I should start at the beginning. My parents are hippies. Not in the 'this is a fad and will pass' kind of way but real, true-life hippies. Because of their lifestyle, they were never around very much when I was growing up which is why I spent so much time with my Gramma. She was a Christian. She always took me to church on Sunday mornings when I stayed with her."

Mel smiled sadly thinking about the woman she had admired most in the world but decided to keep those memories tucked up inside. At least for a little while longer.

"But I never really latched on to the while religion thing. I guess it's because I wanted to be a part of my parents' lives so badly that I took on their beliefs as a way to get closer to them. They were agnostic, believed in a higher power. Not necessarily God, per se, but… something. Whenever they were home they would take me to the park and go on and on about the elements of the earth surrounding us. How we needed to protect those elements and that they, in return, would protect us.

"My parents tried to teach me to rely on the universe to help me. They certainly never did," she muttered and then, "So as I grew up, that's the way I thought. That the universe and the elements and karma would watch out for me as long as I was a good person and treated them with respect. I'd done a really good job of it, too. I never got into trouble. I was respectful of others. I did well in school; even got a partial scholarship to San Diego State.

"I was a sophomore in college when I met Justin. Justin Ford. He was what some people would call nerdy but I loved him. At least I thought I did. He was a very studious, non-violent, dry-sense-of-humor type of guy. Safe. He asked me to marry him at the start of our senior year. I said yes. It was one of those no muss-no fuss situations.

"There was this avenue about a mile from campus that everyone used to call College Row. It was nothing but restaurants, bars, a few coffee houses. It was always full of students. The day after his impromptu proposal Justin and I went out to dinner; no place fancy, just one of the Irish pubs on the row. It was late when we left to head back to the dorms, around midnight I'd guess.

"Neither one of us were paying as close of attention to our surroundings as we should have been. So when a door flew open in front of us we both just kind of stopped." Mel paused and closed her eyes, memories starting to flood her mind as she saw in vivid detail everything that came next.

You can do it, Mel. Just say it and get it over with.

She opened her eyes and stared straight at Alex, hoping that what she was about to expose to him wasn't going to be a deal-breaker. He gazed back at her with compassion and strength and Mel fed off of it.

FOREVER GRATEFUL

"There were these three men. They were ridiculously drunk, stumbling all over each other. Justin and I tried to give them a wide berth and walk around. But they took notice of us first and cornered us right there on the avenue. Two of them came up to me, one in front and one in back, kept me pinned between them. They were teasing me for being with someone like Justin and taunting me... sexually. When Justin stepped up and tried to get them to back off and let us go, the third man came up behind him and grabbed him. He's the one I remember most. The third guy. He wrenched Justin's arms behind his back and held him tight, said something about having some fun. That's when they all pulled us both into the nearest alley."

Mel was having a hard time keeping her voice steady. She felt the trembling vibrations come through in her words but there was nothing she could think of to stop it. She spotted her wine glass on the table, half full of the chardonnay that had been poured but untouched since they sat down. She reached for it and drank it down quickly, hoping that courage would slide into her system just as the cool liquid had.

She clutched her hands together in her lap, watched as her knuckles turned white from the pressure she was putting on her fingers. She didn't want to see Alex's face when she told him of the disgusting act that had taken place so she kept her gaze down, traced the veins in her left hand with the tip of her right index finger. That blue line marking life inside of her seemed even more pronounced now that her skin was pale with the memories running through her mind.

"The two that had a hold of me threw me against a dumpster and held me there. I remember a sharp pain in my side from where I hit the metal but I was so scared at the time that it didn't really register until later. That other guy threw Justin into the corner of the alley and came up to me. He whispered something in my ear and that's when I realized he wasn't as drunk as his buddies. He was so… calculating. And callous. After he ripped my shirt off, he turned me around and slammed my chest into the side of the dumpster. I tried to run. I did. But the first two just held me even tighter, bruising my skin where their fingers gripped into my arms.

"Then I tried pleading with them. Even told them I was a virgin, which I was. They just laughed even more. I think it excited them to know that I was untouched in... that way. I looked around for Justin and found him still sitting in that corner. I begged with my eyes for him to help me." Mel paused and gave a short, humorless laugh that sounded hollow even in her ears.

"Little jerk just laid his head back down and ignored what was going on in right front of him. That was when reality settled in. I knew what was getting ready to happen and there wasn't a damn thing I could do to stop it."

FOREVER GRATEFUL

Mel's breathing came out in little pants now, her chest heaving shallowly and rapidly with every slight release of air. Her eyes welled up with tears, desperate to fall over and land on her hands but she refused to let them fall. Not yet. Her nose started to run and she sniffed but not before a drop trickled out and landed on her wrist.

Great. I'm gonna have one of those ugly cries with swollen eyes and a runny nose and choked voice. Not exactly the strong persona to give Alex, Mel.

Her thoughts did little to alleviate her wayward emotions and reactions. So instead of trying to reason it all away, Mel swiped harshly at the wet spot on her arm, anger at her past and its ability to still torment her making her movements rough. She sniffed again and took a shaky breath, determination rising up inside and forcing her to resume her story.

"The pain was unlike anything I had ever felt before. It still haunts me. I actually thought I was being torn in two, like someone had stuck a knife in me and was ripping it upwards to cut me in half. I cried and screamed and tried to kick out at them. But when I realized how much they liked that I was fighting, I stopped. I thought that maybe if my body was limp it wouldn't hurt so badly so I tried to sag down. It made me feel like a withering flower that's left out in the heat, its petals wilting from over-exposure. Only it was my body and I was wasting away under their onslaught of cruelty.

"When my voice became hoarse from all the screaming I just kinda zoned out, tried to put my mind in a different time. A happier time. It was working too until one of them grabbed my hair, wanting to see my face. He ended up ripping some of it out when I tried to wrench free." Mel instinctively reached up to run her fingers over the small spot on her head where even now, five years later, hair refused to grow.

She flinched when a warm, solid hand wrapped around her wrist. Alex brought their hands down to rest on his knee, linking his fingers with hers, and laid his left hand over the top. She watched as he rubbed softly against her skin and noticed that her hand was trembling. Slowly Mel brought her gaze up to meet his stare. Something in his eyes–reassurance, definitely and maybe a little compassion–seemed to break the hold she'd had on her tears.

Like a dam bursting forth under the pressure of a thousand storms, Mel cried. Thick rivulets of salty tears ran down her cheeks and chin, resting in a small puddle in her lap. Her lips trembled so hard that they felt like a miniature earthquake was taking place right on her face. Her upper body shook with her weeping, shoulders rising and falling with the sobs wracking through her. She hiccupped when she tried to suck in a breath to speak.

Alex released her hand and got down on his knees in

front of her. He grabbed her face gently in his large hands and held her steady, his eyes searching hers for strength that she didn't feel was inside her anymore. She felt nothing but weak and hollow as she finished her tale.

"When they were finally done with me the bald man and one of the others threw me into the side of the dumpster again. My body was so exhausted, so ravaged, that I just kind of slithered down to the ground like a snake going down a tree trunk. And even then, when they were… zipping their pants back up… I was scared that they weren't finished. I didn't feel even remotely safe again until they left the alley with me still huddled next to the dumpster and Justin still cowering in the corner.

"As soon as they were out of sight I tried to pinpoint what was hurting the most. But as soon as I saw the blood on the ground, I…" she stopped, memories of what was left of her virginity making the words impossible to come out.

Mel could still see the red in her mind, bright and pooling like a puddle of Kool-Aid, only thicker. She could still feel the cramping in her stomach that gave way to violent retching. She could still feel the shame and disgust that surrounded her heart that day and held on for years to come.

Mel looked into Alex's eyes as she cried, searched for any sign of regret from getting involved with her. Or maybe his own disgust at being with such a tainted woman. But then his thumbs wiped at the tears soaking her skin and it all became too much. He wasn't showing any indication that he wanted to tuck tail and run in the other direction. It was just the opposite, in fact. His tenderness and concern and actions made the question that had plagued Mel for years bubble to the surface like lava flowing from a volcano.

"Why, Alex? Why would someone do something like that? Why me?" she choked out, sobbing harder with each syllable that came from her mouth.

"I don't know honey," he said quietly as he sat on the deck of the boat and pulled Mel down into his lap. "I just don't know."

Mel wrapped her hands tightly around his neck and held on like her life depended on it. She buried her face into the side of his throat and wept.

For her lost innocence, both physically and emotionally. For her lost faith, what she used to have of it anyway. For everything that she thought she had repressed long ago and was now front and center in her mind, heart and soul.

.   .   .   .   .

Dear God, Alex thought to himself in horror, *I never would have guessed something like this was going to be her big secret.*

He could only imagine the all-encompassing pain she

must have gone through. No, that's not true at all. Despite the vivid details Melanie had given him, he still couldn't imagine what she had felt. What she had thought. What she'd had to experience every day since then.

And by herself, no less.

He knew that she was anticipating him to be disgusted by her revelation. Maybe even push her aside and get as far away from her as possible. He had seen the expectancy of it in her eyes, in the way her shoulders sagged with resolution as she relayed her dramatic history.

But running away was the furthest thing from his mind right now. What he felt, what he recognized in his own heart, was the utmost need to protect her. From both her heartbreaking past as well as the evil of the world around her today.

He wanted to comfort her, and not just in the physical sense. His arms were still holding her close but the small measure seemed so inadequate when compared with what she had been through. She needed someone to take her torturous memories away and replace them with something good. Something loving and pure.

He wanted to be the one to give that to her.

And as much as he wanted to be her strength, he needed her to see just how strong *she* was. How strong she *is*. That Melanie could endure what she had and not only survive it, but work through it to become the independent and successful woman she was today was nothing short of a miracle.

He knew of other sailors that had crumpled under the strains of being out at sea for six or even nine months at a time, having to be flown home at their next port because they were unable to handle the mental struggles. Some might not believe that the two scenarios are even relatable. But in his mind, a woman being raped–viciously and repeatedly–held the worst kind of psychological strains in the aftermath, leaving her broken and fighting for a reason to go on.

But she had fought, was still fighting.

It's no wonder Melanie felt like she couldn't believe in God. For one, it didn't sound like her parents had a very firm grasp on what it meant to have faith. In something other than the dirt, anyway. And since she was a girl who yearned for the acceptance of her parents, she had now become a woman with that same misguided principle.

Second, she, like too many other people, believed that being a Christian meant nothing bad would ever happen to them. And that if they are just religious enough then the dangers of the world will be kept away, their life protected inside a spiritual bubble.

But that's not what faith is about. It's about knowing that even when something cruel happens God has His reasons. His will. And it's realizing that the trials and tribulations He puts us through are meant to make us stronger and bring us to the point in life where we can choose… our road or God's road.

Alex firmly believed, now more than ever, that he was brought to Melanie for a reason. Or maybe she was brought to him. It didn't matter either way.

What mattered was that they were together now and he had no intention of letting her slip through his fingers.

He would help her see how strong she is. And that being strong doesn't mean she can't rely on him or God or her faith. Just the opposite, in fact. He wanted to show her that her strength will grow *because* she hands some of her self-assuredness over to them.

And he had a feeling she would teach him a thing or two about humility. That it's okay to let his own worries and meekness shine through every now and then. Maybe he doesn't have to keep his guard up at all times and come across as the big, tough sailor.

But that would have to come later.

Hopefully the rest of the plans he'd made for their day would help to open her eyes and her heart, even just a little, to God's grace and what it does for a person's emotional well-being. That's something that he would have to ease her into, though. Because right now, she needed what strength he could lend her.

Her tiny hands were still clutching onto the back of his neck and he felt how cold they were. Reaching back, Alex unwrapped them from his nape and brought them around and up to his mouth. Melanie gave a teary sniff and leaned away from his throat, curiosity evident in her sea green eyes as she watched him.

Keeping his own eyes focused on hers, he slowly brought her hands up to his lips. One by one, he lightly kissed each of her trembling fingers. When all ten had been touched by his mouth and the trembling had stopped, he wrapped her hands in his large, warm ones and held them with his left hand against his chest. Melanie had watched as his mouth made contact with her hands and now stared out their joining, right next to his heart.

He brought his right hand up to her face, gently wiping away the last of the tears that had slipped free from her lashes, and lifted her face to his. He tried to show her that he was here, that he was going to be here. But the doubt and worry still lingered.

"I know how hard it must have been for you to open up to me like that." When Alex saw her flinch he mentally kicked himself for not just going straight to what he really wanted to say. He quickly went on. "You listen to me, Melanie. You are beautiful. And intelligent. And so damn strong. You have stirred something inside of me that I was beginning to think didn't exist. Not just a desire to protect but a desire to love."

Melanie started to pull away but Alex held her tight,

making sure she felt the beating of his heart and the truth that lay hidden there with the flow of life.

"I'm not saying it's a complete feeling, a whole feeling. But it's there, just waiting for the chance to grow. And I know you feel it too, honey. All I'm asking is that you give it a chance. Give me a chance. And let's see where this grows together."

Melanie's eyes searched his, looking, he suspected, for any manipulative statements. She looked down again where he held their hands against his chest, rubbing smoothly over hers to try to bring warmth back into them. Her lower lip started to quiver. Alex hadn't realized he was holding his breath from watching that tremor until she looked back up at him with a small smile playing around her perfect lips. He breathed out and back in heavily, drawing in deeply to replenish the lack of oxygen.

Melanie pulled her left hand free from his grip and brought it up to rub against his stubbly cheek. Her delicate hand made its way down to his jaw and around to the hair on the nape of his neck. The trail of fire left by the whispering, soft touch of her fingers had him swallowing thickly past a lump in his throat. A lump brought on by the need to kiss her.

When her fingers found their mark, she gripped him tighter and leaned her forehead against his, quietly breathing words that gave him hope.

"Okay." Her gentle voice broke through the silence. "But I need you to promise me something."

"Anything."

"Baby steps, Alex. I need you to promise me that we'll take this—us—in baby steps. Because I'm scared."

The vulnerability in her voice brought out every protective instinct Alex had. But if this was what Melanie needed, then he would do whatever was in his power to give it to her.

"I promise. We'll take baby steps. Together," Alex assured her and for the first time in as long as he could remember, he looked forward to the mission ahead.

Chapter 9

"Out of Zion, the perfection of beauty, God hath shined." Psalms 50:2

Hearing Alex give his word made Mel sigh in relief. She wasn't sure why it was so important that she get that reassurance from him. The promise that he stick with her at the pace she needed. She just knew, deep down, that it was. And the fact that he gave it to her so willingly made her appreciation for the man in front of her that much stronger.

Replaying all of the sordid parts of that night had caused her a lot more emotional stress than she would have guessed. Each detail spoken brought forth more anxiety, more shame, drained her mind and body in every way. She thought she had put those degrading responses behind her, buried them in the dark recesses of her psyche.

So the fact that those feelings had come out into the

open today, in front of Alex, brought embarrassment along with them.

But Alex stayed right there with her through every word, never wavering in his obvious empathy and support.

Usually that empathy would make her pride rear its ugly head, ready to fight off anyone who tried to feel sorry for her. Like the pity she used to see from the therapist she went to right after the attack. That woman's expressions had portrayed, *"You poor, little thing"* and *"How horrible for you,"* with no real remorse for what Mel had gone through.

But with Alex it felt genuine.

And he was still here, supporting her in more ways than one, despite her history.

Maybe good things happen to good people after all.

Looking into his eyes right now, with their faces mere inches from each other, Mel felt her appreciation grow. She felt it morph into something else, something that exceeded the emotional connection of just two friends. It scared the crap out of her.

But she was tired of being some timid little slip of a woman when it came to men. She wanted more.

And she wanted it with Alex.

She was acutely aware of the way his large hand still cupped her face, his thumb slowly rubbing along her cheekbone. She could feel his calluses–brought on, she suspected, by years of working with steel on a naval ship–

against her tender flesh.

But instead of feeling abrasive and hard she only felt warmth seeping from his skin to hers. That warmth grew and spread, flowing out from her cheek, down past her throat and settled in her belly.

Her entire body heated with the realization that Alex literally held her in the palm of his hand. As the temperature of her skin rose, so did her heart rate. She parted her lips slightly to take in more air and try to calm the racing. Alex's gaze latched onto the movement and he watched her mouth, stared at it with a look of longing radiating from him.

Mel's lips felt dry under his scrutiny and she licked them quickly. Whatever control Alex had been showing seemed to go out the window with that one small action.

His beautiful eyes lifted and focused on hers again. She saw so many emotions reflecting in those honey-colored orbs; want, need, anticipation. But most of all, she saw hope.

In her.

It was enough to send a crack striking through the fearfulness that had encompassed her heart for almost five years.

They both moved at the same time, slowly closing the small gap between them. Alex's hand remained gentle on her cheek but she felt her own hand tighten around his neck, determination and fear waging a war with each other for the front position in her mind.

When she felt his breath barely graze her top lip, her eyes fluttered closed and she waited. One heartbeat. Two. Her heart beat a third time and still nothing happened.

Mel reopened her eyes and found Alex staring at her.

"I want to see you," he said and then, "I want to know that you're going into this with both eyes open. I need to know that you know it's *me* kissing you. Not Justin. Not some maniac. Me." He grabbed the other side of Mel's face so that she was caged by his hands.

"It will always be me."

His declaration barely registered as he brought his mouth to Mel's, sealing their lips together tightly. She desperately tried to keep her eyes open. But the electrifying touch of Alex's mouth on hers had her lids falling, blocking out everything around them except this. Except him.

His lips–his kiss–made Mel feel like she was holding her breath, waiting for the first firework to burst open in a night sky. And then releasing in a rush with the boom that followed that light. Pure exhilaration and awe.

Mel brought her hand to rest on his chest and she felt the difference between the parts of Alex's body. The hard planes under her palm were a complete contradiction to the fullness and softness of his lips. Having his mouth connected to hers, unyielding but tenderly, had her clenching the front of his shirt firmly, trying to grab hold of something real to keep her in this moment.

FOREVER GRATEFUL

It had been so long since Mel had been kissed with anything more than friendly regard. She savored the feeling of rightness settling over her, the heated anticipation of what more could–and hopefully would–come between them. Never had a chaste kiss held so much power over her.

Alex didn't push to move the caress of his lips against hers to something else, something more passionate. It's like he knew that this was all Mel could handle right now.

Instead he kept his mouth closed as he pulled away, leaned in for another sweet peck and sat back again. The absence of the heat from Alex's lips forced Mel to open her eyes, searching for the source of the warmth that was spreading through her and wanting to bring it back.

As her vision cleared from the enflamed daze, she found Alex staring at her, his gaze moving from her eyes to her mouth and back up again. Indecision of whether to kiss her again or not rolled off of him for a few seconds. Mel saw when restraint won the battle he was facing. His chest rose and fell underneath her hand in a deep breath. Resignation made him close his eyes and drop his head a little, almost in defeat.

To her surprise, she was a little disappointed herself. But that response didn't leave her feeling like she was being rejected. Because she knew, with absolute certainty, that Alex had just opened the door to that something more she wanted with him.

When he raised his head back up and opened his eyes to look at her, she was sure the expression on his face matched the one on her own. Surprise, wonder, confidence. None of which she had felt with a man since Justin. And she was beginning to question whether she had ever felt it with him or if maybe it was just something along the lines of convenience.

She wasn't sure and she didn't care.

Right here, right now, with Alex still holding her like she was something precious and the taste of him still lingering on her lips, there was only one thing going through her mind.

"Wow," she whispered, that single word drifting between them on the breeze from the sea.

"Yeah."

Alex continued to look at her, the urge to lean in again evident, his eyes probing for a sense of what she wanted. But she didn't shy away, not this time. Instead of waiting for him, she took initiative and leaned in herself, desperate for the taste of him once more.

Right as she felt his breath on her mouth again, and the eagerness of feeling him grew to almost unbearable, there was a throat clearing beside them, causing her to jerk back.

Captain Jones stood off to her left, trying to hide his amused and slightly embarrassed expression by looking up at the bright blue sky. She'd completely forgotten that they were on a boat, getting ready to go out and look for whales and dolphins.

Embarrassed herself, she realized she was still sitting on Alex's lap in a telling embrace.

Quickly, she scrambled to scoot back and get off of Alex but his big hands wrapped around her hips, holding her still and making her skin burn through the thin material of her shorts. He directed his attention to the Captain.

"Yes, Sal?" he said to the man who was still looking at the sky like it held some sort of deep secret.

"I just wanted to let you two know that we're ready to push off." Sal hesitated before looking back down at Alex and continuing. "Unless you've changed your minds about going out."

Alex looked back at Mel with a question in his eyes, his eyebrows–the same color as his hair–rose slightly, waiting for her to make the decision. And as much as she wanted to go right on kissing him, she realized she was actually looking forward to hopefully seeing the animals in the ocean. And that she was no longer afraid of the ship and its (according to Sal) unlikely demise.

Because Alex was with her.

Keeping her eyes on Alex, she answered, "We haven't changed our minds. We're ready." And then quietly, so that Alex was the only one to hear, added, "I'm ready."

And as Mel watched the relieved and proud look come

over Alex's face, she knew without a doubt that she was ready to move forward not just in this boat, but with him, too. More than ready.

.   .   .   .   .

Never had Alex's world been rocked as hard as it had in the last half hour

Not his time off the coast of Ukraine, when the aircraft carrier he was on was a sitting target for any missiles to be launched at them.

Not when they were housing the jets being sent to Iraq for strategic bomb drops on terrorist strong holds.

Not even when he'd been a nineteen year old kid being told about his first overseas deployment to Columbia.

While all of those instances had scared him, made him pray to God for safety and peace as he never had before, none of them had made him feel anxious, like he'd lost all control.

This one did, but in a freeing way, like that first downhill drop of a rollercoaster. Melanie, with her innocent abandon and surprising reception, had set loose in him the desire to be exactly what she needed.

Until he'd kissed her.

Her lips–sweet, soft, lush and perfect–had sent every rational thought out the window until all he could feel, all he could sense, was Melanie. Her taste lingered on his lips and he resisted the urge to run his tongue along them. Her scent clung inside his nose, something lightly floral and utterly feminine and completely Melanie.

But it was her eyes that kept him on the edge of pushing this moment too far. Those blue-green depths were still dazed, her pupils not quite focusing again. She looked like a woman on the verge of letting herself go.

Not now, Alex... he scolded himself. *Wait. For her and for you.*

With that decision persistent in his mind, he leaned forward for a quick kiss to her forehead. He removed his hands from her enticing hips and set her on the deck of the boat. After standing he reached down with both hands, pleased when she willingly placed her own in them, and slowly lifted her up.

He pulled her chair back out at the table and waited for her to seat herself, then took his seat to her right again, holding her hand on his leg.

"I hope you can eat with one hand. Because I don't plan on letting you go."

His declaration brought forth a blush on her cheeks, hopefully because she recognized the double meaning behind it. But she ducked her head, picked up her fork with her left hand, and took a bite of salad.

He followed her lead and began to eat his salad as well,

finishing well before her and moving on to his chicken. It was good, the rosemary wafting into his nose and making the flavors even stronger, but in no way diminishing the scent of his Melanie.

He watched her out of the corner of his eye as she ate, noticed the dainty way her tongue slipped out to lick a small drop of sauce from the edge of her mouth. She didn't use her teeth to get her bites off of the fork, instead using only her lips. And each morsel she brought up was never too big, but the perfect size for her delicate mouth.

Everything about her–from her straight posture to her calm demeanor to the way she ate–screamed poised and refined. Even after the horrible flashback she had endured moments before, which just showed how resilient she was.

And she was beautiful in that way.

But now that he knew a little of what lay under the surface, he was more determined than ever to break open her moderate manner and release that fireball he caught a small glimpse of.

Tonight. You'll open her up tonight.

"How's your dinner?" he asked, trying to focus on the now.

"It's wonderful! I'll have to remember this preparation for the vegetables."

Personally, Alex thought the zucchini and squash were a little too feminine of a food for him but if Melanie ever wanted to fix it for him, he'd be more than willing to eat them.

"You like to cook?"

"Oh, yes," Melanie answered. "And I love to try new recipes. Although, sometimes they turn out a little... off."

"You mean like over-seasoned?" Alex asked.

"With too much garlic or under-seasoned or too raw or maybe, sometimes, too burnt. I said I love to cook. Not that I was very good at it. My Gramma tried to teach me but I just wasn't with her enough as I got older to really learn. It's still enjoyable, though. Especially since it's just me."

This last she said quietly, almost sadly. Alex wanted to tell her that it wasn't going to be 'just her' anymore. He wanted to tell her that it would be both of them. Together.

It was on the tip of his tongue, too, but something held him back. Something that said it was too soon. He knew it was too, but found it difficult to remember his personal pep talks about taking things slow with Melanie.

Rejoice in hope, be patient in tribulation, be constant in prayer.

Reciting one of his favorite verses from *Romans* gave his mind peace and he promised to himself that he would remain hopeful, patient and constant.

"Do you like to..." Melanie started to ask him something but abruptly stopped when the boat began to sway right and left. Her eyes got wide and her breathing got a little faster.

When the engine started, a dull roaring that echoed in the emptiness surrounding the dock, she jumped in her seat and turned to look behind her. Alex watched her head move from side to side, searching, before finally turning back to him with something like panic in her eyes.

"Where's the motor? I thought the Captain said this was safe! How can it be safe if there are no motors back there? Maybe we should get off."

"Melanie," he interrupted her. "Calm down. Take a breath." Alex waited for her to do as he asked and then went on. "This boat is safe. I promise. On a vessel this size, they don't have those little outboard motors you're used to seeing on the stern of a boat. The back. The engine is in the space underneath us, in the hull. That's why it sounds a little louder where we're at because we're basically sitting on it."

"Are you sure?"

"Positive. Try to relax."

To hide the smile playing on his lips at her unwarranted fear, he reached over and grabbed the bottle of wine still sitting in the ice bucket. Alex filled her glass halfway and did the same to his own. After replacing it back in the bucket, he lifted his glass in her direction.

"A toast. To showing *you* the beauty of the deep ocean." He waited for her to lift her glass and softly clink it with his before going on. "And to gracing *me* with the beauty that it is you."

And there it was. That beautiful smile that was both shy and flattered and transformed her panicked expression from a moment ago into one of excitement.

Melanie took a small sip from her glass and set it back on the table right as the boat started to move forward. She closed her eyes for a few seconds, took a deep breath and opened them to look directly into his.

"Will you show me?"

Alex didn't need to ask her what she wanted to see. Pride at her determination swelled in his chest as he stood and pulled her with him.

But instead of walking to the rail like she probably assumed he'd do, he walked her to the ladder leading up to the flybridge. When they were right next to it, her hand tightened around his fingers slightly before releasing them to walk up the few steps. He was right behind her and tried to focus on the steps at his feet rather than her perfect backside that was directly at eye level with him.

Easier said than done. I am only a man, after all, and she's a beautiful woman.

Standing in the area on the top of the boat, with a dark blue canopy shielding them from the sun, they were essentially open to everything around them. Melanie looked at him in confusion.

"Isn't this where Sal and his mate were a few minutes

ago? How are they supposed to… drive… without being at the… you know?" she asked, eying the unmanned controls in front of them.

"There's another place to drive. Under this area, in front of the section where the galley was, is a room called the bridge. It's basically the same as this except it's surrounded by windows and this is out in the open. I thought you might like it better up here so Sal and Pete went down below."

As they made their way slowly out into open water, Melanie turned to watch the ocean, visibly trying to overcome her worries.

The salty breeze blew her ponytail out behind her and reminded him of golden wheat bending with a summer wind. Her shirt ruffled around her body, catching on her curves and showing Alex just enough to entice him even more. The sun peeked through underneath the canopy and highlighted her toes with its rays, making the pale pink polish there glisten.

He could see the moment she began to relax and enjoy their surroundings.

A small smile crept onto her face and her eyes crinkled at the corners. Turning to face him, Melanie grabbed Alex's hand with both of hers and brought it to her chest, right over her heart.

"Thank you."

He grinned at her and pulled her a little closer, wrapped his left arm around her and settled his hand in the center of her back.

"You're welcome. Would you like to see how some of this stuff works?" he asked, tilting his head to the controls in front of them.

She nodded her head quickly, enthusiasm finally overtaking her apprehension. Alex sat down in the captain's chair and pulled Melanie over so that she was standing directly in front of him, between his legs.

Reaching his arms around either side of her, he began to explain what some of the different electronics were, like the GPS, radar and sonar. He pointed to the gauges, telling her which showed their speed–and what knots versus miles per hour meant–and the RPMs, or Revolutions Per Minute, of the propeller. She paid attention and asked questions, her fears shifting to curiosity.

Alex was glad for the distraction of answering her questions because it kept him from thinking of how perfectly she fit with his body. And then, because apparently self-torture was his new forte, he wrapped his arms around Melanie's middle, crossed them together and held her against his chest.

She just felt right.

She brought her hands down and rested them on top of his, linked their fingers together, silently giving him confirmation that she was okay with this. With him. He kept his head next to her right arm, watching the waves break to the sides of the boat and the sun glitter down on the surface of the water like diamonds.

Thirty minutes after they had set off from the dock, the engine slowed and shut off causing Melanie to jump again in surprise, breaking the tranquility of the moment. She twisted around and looked down into his eyes.

"What's going on? Why did we stop?"

Just as he was about to answer, Sal came up the steps behind them.

"You guys ready to see some whales?" he asked.

All of Melanie's hesitation from earlier was gone now. In its place was enthusiastic curiosity as she happily said yes.

"Let's go then," Sal said, turning to walk back down the steps. "You two come with me back down to the cockpit. Pete's already cleared away the table and chairs so there's plenty of room to watch."

Alex stood from the chair and walked in front of Melanie, holding her hand while they walked down the three steps back to the area they had vacated a half hour before.

They reached the rail on the port side just as Pete came walking toward them from the bridge.

Up close, Alex could tell that he was definitely in his thirties. He was darkly tanned, like Sal, with light brown hair streaked through with blonde by the sun. Alex also noticed that the two men's faces held strong similarities, from their thin noses to their squared chins. Wearing the same polo shirt and shorts as Sal, he guessed the two to be father and son but refrained from asking since it wasn't of any concern to him.

"Anchor's down, Pop," Pete said when he reached the three of them.

Alex chuckled to himself as he got confirmation for his personal thoughts. Pete came to stand at the rail with him, Melanie and Sal.

They were all looking down into the ocean below, a blue so deep and dark it was like looking down into an abyss. Down here, out of the shade from the canopy on the flybridge, the sun shone down brightly, making its way to the middle of the sky overhead as the time approached twelve-thirty.

Several minutes passed with the four of them not saying a word before Melanie began to fidget and finally broke the silence.

"What do we do now?" she asked, turning to Sal.

"Now," he began, returned her gaze and smiled, "we wait for the show."

"Do you really think we'll see the whales? I mean, I don't know a lot about the fish—"

"Mammals," Sal corrected.

"Right. Mammals. Anyway, I don't know a lot about their living conditions or habits or whatever. So, you think they'll make an appearance today?"

Alex loved watching how she'd gone from timid and scared of being on a boat to now embracing what was to come. The excitement in her voice and the optimistic expression on her face said she was finally starting to enjoy herself.

He knew that she'd never looked at the wonders of the world as anything more than things that were "just there." She'd never given any thought to how and why and by whom.

It made being here with her, where she was getting her first honest glimpse at what God had made, all the more pleasing. Alex prayed those animals would show up while they were out, too, so he could show her more of His beauty. He couldn't push her with words of who created these wonders.

He just needed to introduce her to a world that every human had a chance to see. And pray that she would come to accept it.

．　　　．　　　．　　　．　　　．

Mel stood at the rail next to Alex, with Sal and Pete on either side of them, and stared into the water. She'd never cared much about what lay beneath the surface of the ocean, or about seeing any of it with her own eyes.

But something had changed inside her in the last thirty-six hours with Alex.

That's so ridiculous. You can't change what you've always felt and thought in a day and a half just by being around a certain person.

And yet, even as she thought that, she knew it to be a lie. The question was *when* exactly had those things changed and how.

Was it last night when she had told him of her atheism and he had easily looked beyond it? Or today when she told him about her... past?

No. You know exactly when things changed.

It was the kiss. It was his lips. And his hands and arms and entire body. The way Alex had wrapped himself around her like a koala clinging to a bamboo tree had made her feel protected. Safe.

The sensations he'd set loose inside her when he'd kissed her were confusing and exhilarating at the same time. She had sworn off men and anything resembling a romantic relationship after the debacle with Justin that night.

But Alex made her feel special, and beautiful, and desired for who and what she was. Not in spite of it.

Her lips still tingled from his kiss. Her face still flamed from where he'd held her still for his mouth. Her whole body felt alive and primed, ready for something she wasn't sure she would ever be able to go through with. But if there was ever a man to try it for, it was Alex.

And that's why she desperately wanted to see these whales.

Mel felt that if the elusive animals would come to see her then it would be a sign. An omen that proved that sometimes the things you never expect to happen, do.

Still warmed from Alex's embrace, Mel wanted this–them–to happen, also. But she needed some indication that it was possible.

Come on, whales. Let me see you. Show me hope.

A splash out in front of them brought four pairs of eyes up, looking into the distance for the source of the noise. Instinctively, Mel reached down and grabbed Alex's hand that was resting on the rail. If he was surprised that she'd done so, he didn't show it. He simply laced their fingers together, kept them connected while they waited with bated breath.

And then out of nowhere, fifteen yards in front of them, a big brownish-gray whale leaped out of the water about a dozen feet and landed on its side, its pale belly shining from the sun bouncing off the water.

No, not just big. The thing was huge! Mel gasped at the sight of the monstrous mammal splashing in the water like a baby would in a bathtub. How she could think that whale was comparable to a small child, she wasn't sure. It just looked so playful.

She yelped in shock when two more jumped out on

either side of the first whale. One about the same size and the other much smaller. A baby. A smile crept on to her face at the image. The three leaped and splashed together, like they were playing a game. It was one of the most beautiful things she had ever seen.

When the whales' images blurred before her eyes, she realized she was crying. Alex noticed, too and pulled her to him, directly in front of his chest. He wrapped his arms around her and rested his chin on her shoulder while she stood, mesmerized, by the display of pure animalistic joy.

"Those are Fin whales," Sal told them. "They're also called Razorbacks. See that long dorsal fin along its back?" He pointed to the fins on each of the whales and at Mel's and Alex's confirmation, went on. "That's where they get the name from. Because the fin looks like a razor along their backs.

"Winter and Summer are the best times to see them migrate through here. They usually travel in groups of six to ten. So if you watch... There," he said, nodding his head toward the left of the three they had been spying.

Four more whales, all different sizes, were taking turns launching out of the water, too. Mel thought it looked like they were playing a game of stationary leapfrog. Laughing, Mel pointed to the baby who was again leaping and almost landed on the head of the biggest whale.

"Look, Alex! Isn't it the most beautiful and amazing

thing you've ever seen?"

"Yes. It is."

Mel turned her face to look back at him only to find that he wasn't looking at the whales at all. He was staring at her, a slight grin on his lips and a twinkle in his eyes. He leaned towards her and Mel, with Herculean effort, kept her eyes open.

When his lips softly touched hers, she cupped his cheek, loving the feel of the stubble against her palm. She kissed him back, their mouths moving slowly against one another.

But then Alex turned her around so that she was facing him and Mel's lashes fluttered closed at the feel of his hard body against hers. She thought she heard the click of a camera going off but was too absorbed in the moment to care. Her arms twined together around his back and Alex's cradled her face, anchoring them together.

Mel's head was spinning and she felt like she was running out of oxygen so she pulled back slightly, opening her mouth to drag in a lungful of air. Alex looked no less affected. His heavy breathing caused his chest to expand against her own and made her realize how closely they held each other.

"Is it always like this?" she whispered, hating at that moment her lack of experience in this area of life.

"No. This is special. You are special." When Mel started to shake her head to deny his words he spoke again. "Yes,

Melanie. You can't convince me differently from what I already know. And I'll prove it to you, but you have to let me. Will you? Will you take that leap of faith and let me show you why we deserve this chance?"

His gaze bore into Mel, pleading and sincere and utterly intense. How could she deny him this when he'd already done so much for her? But really, it wasn't about denying him. She wanted to see what it all meant, too.

His words and actions. Her responses and openness. Alex was right.

This was special.

"I trust you, Alex."

And maybe someday he would understand just how hard it was for her to give that trust. For now, the look of satisfaction on his face, highlighted by the golden streams wrapping around his head from the sun, was enough.

"All right, you two," Sal said, breaking into their quiet moment. "What do you say we head on back to the dock?"

Still looking at Alex, Mel nodded and he turned to look at the Captain.

"Sounds good, Sal."

The father and son nodded in return and headed back into the bridge. This time, when the motors started underneath them, Mel didn't jump. With Alex holding her tightly against him, keeping her pressed to his hard chest, she felt protected.

He turned her back around to face the rail but kept his hands at her waist, the constant contact making her appreciate his attentiveness. Together they watched the waves spurt up from the sides of the boat as it was maneuvered around to head back the way they had come.

As the boat picked up speed, the wind blew her ponytail around her face. She brushed it back and tried to tuck it behind her ear, not wanting to miss the white caps cresting the waves or the way the water sparkled under the watchful eye of the sun.

Never had she imagined the ocean held this much beauty. It could be that her imaginings never allowed her to move past the ugliness in the world outside of her office and home. Or maybe because she didn't open herself up long enough to anything–or anyone–to see what more the world had to offer.

Of course, it could be that the man behind her was allowing her to see things in a different light. An optimistic and unguarded light.

Whatever the reason was, she was glad to be able to see the brilliance of it all with her own eyes now and not settle for trying to take someone's word for it anymore.

Fifteen minutes into their return trip, Alex pointed to the wake of the boat, drawing her attention to the water down in front of them rather than up at the horizon. At first Mel didn't see what he was pointing to.

She started to turn her head to look at him and ask what he was pointing to. But he stopped her.

"Just wait," he said. "There!"

A laugh escaped Mel's mouth as she saw about a dozen dolphins jumping out of the water, racing alongside the boat's wake. Like the whales, they looked to be playing leapfrog. Only instead of with each other, they were leaping over the wake with a speed that was both unexpected and exciting to watch.

She had heard that dolphins were fast. But other than a trip to Sea World San Diego when she was eight, she had never seen them in person. And that trip was so long ago that she only vaguely remembered them. She did know that what she'd seen then, with the dolphins in captivity, was nothing compared to the free-spirited way these mammals swam.

There was something so playful and majestic in the way they arched up and out of the water only to plummet back into the waves with their pointed noses slicing through the surface first. They were magnificent.

How can anything be that magical to watch?

Mel had never paid attention to how amazing her surroundings were. For years, she believed that people and animals–everything on the earth, for that matter–were just here, in existence by some unknown entity and blurring together in everyday life.

Kind of like the Big Bang Theory and everything

coming from a speck.

But now, seeing these small marvels of the ocean, she had to wonder if maybe she had been wrong. Because how could something as grand as the Fin whales and these dolphins come from a speck?

And even more, how could this man behind her–this strong, caring, patient man–come from a speck? He wasn't made from a dot. He had to have been created by something more.

Or someone, she thought to herself.

Which really confused her. All these years she had believed in nothing; no God, no higher power, no spirits or karma.

But now, well, she wasn't sure what or who it was she believed in. Just that it was more than the nothingness of atheism.

She wasn't sure how to handle it but she knew that she needed to find out. For herself and for any future she might hope to have with the man who was making her see life in a different way, a happier way.

"Alex?" she asked, nervous about the bridge she was getting ready to cross.

"Hmm?" he said and placed his chin back on her shoulder. He swayed them side to side slowly, rocking them as a whole while they watched the dolphins jump over the wake once more and swim off, looking for some other boat to chase.

"What can you tell me about your God?"

Aimee Martin

Chapter 10

*"For I know the thoughts that I think toward
you, saith the Lord, thoughts of peace, and
not of evil, to give you an expected end."*
Jeremiah 29:11

June 28, 2014

Mel kicked off her tennis shoes right after she walked in
the front door of her condo, wiggling her toes in an effort to
stretch them out a little after her run with Kass. Her dog went
straight to the water bowl on the kitchen floor, lapping
deeply, before lying down on the tile to cool off. She
grabbed a bottle of water from her fridge and sprawled out
on the couch, directly underneath the ceiling fan to try to
cool off, herself.

It was still fairly early, not even ten in the morning. But

the summer sun had been brutal and the sweat dripping down her face and neck only proved it. Normally, she wouldn't run outside in the summer, preferring instead to use the building's gym equipment located on the second floor.

In the air conditioning.

But thoughts of Alex and what all had happened yesterday crowded her mind like a too small room stuffed with oversized furniture And the only way she felt like she could clear it was to get out in the open.

It was funny, really. Thinking of him talking about the beauty that God made had been what plagued her, made her doubt everything she believed.

And yet being out there, *in* that beauty, was all she'd wanted to do.

She felt like a newborn baby opening its eyes for the first time, looking at everything around her in absolute wonder. She had watched the decorative crepe myrtle trees–the ones that were planted on every corner for eight blocks–blow in the gentle breeze. And she'd thought of the way Alex had swayed with her on the boat. She had seen the sun beaming down through the small, white clouds in the sky and thought of the whales falling down through the surface of the ocean.

Even watching the people hustle about, quickly moving along the congested sidewalk to get to their destination, made her remember the dolphins and how fast they were in the water as they maneuvered around each other.

All of it seemed different today. Hopeful, when only twenty-four hours ago it was just normal. Mel knew it was because of the things Alex had told her regarding his faith.

Not that she was totally convinced of there actually being a God. But something he had said yesterday after she asked him about his God had stuck with her and she replayed his words in her mind.

"There's a verse in First Corinthians, one of the books of the bible. It says that God is not the author of confusion. He's the author of peace. That's what He wants for us... peace. That and our faith. In Him. He doesn't want us to be confused about what He has laid out before us. He wants us to embrace it with faith in our hearts."

It had been so long since Mel had felt anything resembling true peace that she wasn't sure she knew how to find it anymore. And she'd voiced that concern to Alex, who had a ready response for that, too.

"I do," Alex had said quietly to her. *"I'll show you. But you have to trust me."*

Is that what I want? she thought to herself, taking a gulp of water.

She watched the fins of the fan spin around and around, a quiet click sounding every time the pull cord gently slapped the light fixture in the center of the piece. Seeing the motion of the blades in their never-ending, never-changing circle made her realize that she already knew the answer to that one.

Of course that's what you want, Mel. Otherwise you're just like that fan... leading a never-changing, monotonous life.

And she did want it. To be able to go to sleep at night and feel at peace with herself and her life–with her past– would be a welcome change to the torment that still sometimes tracked her in her dreams. There was a place in her chest, very near to her heart, that yearned to have tranquility.

But put my life in someone's hands just to have it happen?

That wasn't something Mel thought she'd ever be able to do. She was intrigued, sure. Curious about how Alex could, did, trust in someone so much without ever seeing the person. He had said that's why it was called *faith*.

Mel liked having control over her life. To give that up to someone, or something, else meant losing the only part of herself that she had worked so hard to get back after the rape. She couldn't get back her virginity. She couldn't take back the trust she had put in certain people.

But regaining control of her life? That she had worked for and she wasn't ready to just let it go to some God that she wasn't even sure was real.

Alex was real, though.

And for some reason she felt like she could put her trust in him. Mel wasn't sure what it was that made her feel that way so certainly. What drew her to him like bees to honey.

It wasn't just that he was incredibly good-looking, although that fact didn't hurt. And it wasn't just that he was the brother of a good friend of hers, whom she trusted, thereby making him trustworthy as well.

There was some deeper, emotional pull that enticed her. No, it was more demanding than that. This pull was insistent that she follow him, lean on him, believe in him.

She had never been one to argue with her gut feelings before. Her instincts are what have gotten her this far in life and Mel wasn't about to start ignoring them now. Not when something that was bigger than she could've ever imagined lay on the horizon, waiting for her to grab it with both hands.

What's that saying? "In for a penny, in for a pound."

With that thought in mind, she picked up her cell where she'd laid it on the coffee table before her run and went to her previous calls list. Taking a deep breath for determination, she hit send on the most recent number.

"Hello?" Alex answered on the fourth ring sounding out of breath.

"Hi. Alex?"

"Melanie," he said her name on an exhale, something like relief coming through in that one word. "Good morning."

"Is this a bad time?"

"No! No, not at all. I was out for a run on the beach when I heard the phone ringing as I was coming up the back deck steps. I might have pushed a little harder to make it to my cell before voicemail picked up."

"Oh. Okay, good." She pushed the image of his lean body running on the sand–and her crazy wish that she'd been with him–out of her mind. "I went for a run this morning, too. Just got back about a half hour ago, actually."

"Really? Next time maybe we can go together."

Mel smiled at the coincidence that they were apparently thinking the same way. She heard the fridge door close on the other end of the line, followed by deep gulps coming from Alex.

"If you need to call me back after you've had a chance to catch your breath I don't mind. I know it takes longer for some than others to slow their breathing down," she teased, biting back a giggle.

"Woman, you go run twelve miles and sprint the last two and tell me you're not winded for at least five minutes after."

Twelve? Good grief! I'm lucky to get in three before I'm huffing and puffing.

"Okay, okay. I'm sorry. I have no room to talk since I only made it a fourth of what you did."

"Uh-huh." She heard the smile in his voice. "I guess I

forgive you."

They were both quiet. Mel pictured Alex leaning on the kitchen counter at Brin's house, the water bottle he'd just drank from resting against an open palm while he held the phone in his other. She could see him with a smile on his full lips while he looked out the bank of windows at the ocean.

She guessed that he was sweaty from his run. Was he in track pants and a shirt? Or maybe just a pair of shorts in an effort to stay cooler in the heat, with beaded, salty droplets running down his chest and back. Mel glanced down at her left hand as she unconsciously made a fist, imagining how slick his skin would feel under her touch.

Her breath caught in her throat at how real the little fantasy seemed. Alex heard it.

"Melanie? You alright?" he asked softly, evenly.

"Yeah." Clearing her throat, she continued. "I was actually calling to see what you wanted to do today. Or if you'd like for me to make the plans."

"So does this mean I get to see you again?"

"Of course. Why would you think otherwise?"

"I'm not sure. Yesterday was… well, eye-opening, thought provoking. For both of us. And a little intense, too. I wasn't sure if you'd want to take a day to yourself or something."

"You're right. It was all those things. But you leave tomorrow and I don't want to miss any opportunities."

"Opportunities for what, honey?" he asked.

The endearment caught Mel off guard. She remembered him saying it yesterday, more than once. But she'd played it off as him being sweet and comforting after all her confessions. Now, him saying it in the light of a new day, made her warm and fuzzy all over, like a preteen's first crush taking notice of them.

"To see you, be with you," she answered simply and heard his heavy sigh.

"I like that answer."

His deep voice spoken quietly made something deep in her belly clench. Something that felt both foreign and familiar at the same time and made her want to clutch that feeling inside.

To hold onto it forever.

"Good."

"Six o'clock tonight. I'll have that handy driver you hired for me pick us both up and be our transportation for the evening."

"I guess this means you're making the plans, then," she responded with a touch of fake annoyance.

That he obviously saw completely through when he laughed loudly in her ear.

"They were already made. I was just waiting on the go-ahead from you," he told her, confidence oozing from his little declaration. "Six o'clock. Be ready."

She answered with an "okay" but he'd already hung up. Holding the phone in her hand, she smiled at the now blank screen, excitedly anticipating what he had in store this time.

And went to take a shower.

.   .   .   .   .

Alex laid his phone down on the kitchen counter and took a deep breath. He felt like a weight of uncertainty had been lifted off of his shoulders.

When the sun came up this morning he had been a mixed up ball of feelings.

On the one hand, he had felt good, encouraged, by the day he and Melanie had had yesterday. A sense of rightness had settled over him when she had asked about God. And explaining scripture–a small part of it, anyway–had given him hope for what might lie ahead in terms of their future.

He was excited to move forward with it.

On the other hand, he had been nervous, maybe even a little panicked. The things he'd told her and shown her would be enough to scare a nonbeliever off. What if she took what he'd said about God wanting our faith and Him having our lives planned for us and decided it was too much control to give up?

All the opposing thoughts plagued him until he felt like his head was going to explode.

So he'd run, hoping the sea air and physical exertion would help to clear his mind. Somewhere around mile six he realized it wasn't working and turned to make the return run to Brin's.

He was preparing himself to make a call to Melanie, to say whatever he had to say to make her see him again. To not turn and run away but to stay. With him. So when he'd heard her voice on the other end of the line, sweet relief washed over him and all he could do was sigh with it.

And she wants to see me again. Dear God, please don't let me mess things up with this woman.

With his small prayer hanging in the back of his mind, he pushed off the counter to get to work on the plans he'd thought of yesterday but decided to postpone after their emotional day. But when he heard the squeak of his sweat-soaked tennis shoes on the tile floor, he decided a shower was at the top of the list and headed to the master bathroom.

Fifteen minutes later, clean, barefoot and in a fresh pair of jeans, Alex sat down on the living room couch and opened his laptop.

Google was his friend as he searched for the type of place he wanted to take Melanie to tonight and promptly found three within a thirty minute drive from her condo (according to Google Maps). He decided on the one that was the most out of the way so that there would be less traffic, hopefully enticing Melanie to open up more.

After choosing the entertainment, he looked for restaurants that were in the same vicinity. Nothing too fancy, just casual with good food. There was a place called The Seafood Café about two miles away from where they'd end up that had good reviews. The menu looked like it had a nice selection and it wasn't overpriced.

Perfect.

He wrote down all the information on a notepad sitting on the glass top of the coffee table and went to the entry hall where he had left the business card two days ago. He dialed the number as he walked to the back deck.

"Wilson," the voice said on the other end, curt since he probably didn't recognize the number.

"Ted? Hey. It's Alex, Alex Lambert."

"Hi, Alex! How are you? Is Los Angeles treating you alright?" The curtness was gone, replaced by a kind familiarity.

"I can't complain, Ted. It's definitely faster paced than I'm used to but I've spent most of my time here at the beach, so it hasn't been too bad. How about you? Any other out-of-place tourists to drive around?"

"No, sir, Alex. Miss Moore paid me to be at your beck-and-call so I've just been catching up on some… personal stuff. I'm assuming that you need me to drive you somewhere if you're calling." Ted let the statement hang in the air like a question.

Alex noticed the way the man had paused when he'd said 'personal stuff,' like he was hiding something more. He still remembered that mumbled comment from the drive to the airport and wondered what exactly they might have in common. But he chose not to dwell on it. It wasn't his business what the man did in his spare time.

"Actually, I do. I was hoping you might be up for driving Melanie and I on a, well, a date of sorts this evening."

"Of course," Ted replied. "Just tell me when and where you'd like to go and I'll be there to pick you up."

"I'd like you to get me first. Say, around five tonight? From here we'll go get Melanie and head to the restaurant."

"That's no problem. I'll pick you up at Mrs. Mathew's home at five sharp. Do you know where you'll be going tonight?"

"Yes, sir. I have the names and addresses of the places here. Would you like them now or later?" Alex asked.

"Later would be fine. I'll see you at five, Alex."

"Five o'clock. Thank you, Ted."

"It's my pleasure, sir," he said to Alex and hung up.

Alex looked at the time on the clock that hung on the wall across the room from him, noted that it was just past twelve, and decided to fix himself a sandwich. He closed down his laptop, left it on the coffee table along with his cell, and headed into the kitchen.

FOREVER GRATEFUL

Right as he got out the mayo and sliced cheddar cheese, his phone dinged with an incoming text. He went back to the living room and retrieved it, smiling when he saw Melanie's face appear on the screen. He opened the message.

I need to know what to wear.

Alex couldn't hold back the laugh. Out of all the things he imagined her questioning him about, clothing was at the bottom of the list. He quickly typed back a reply.

Are you asking me for fashion advice?

You do know I'm a man, right?

He waited patiently for the ribbing response he was sure was coming. He didn't have to wait long.

I'm asking you because you're so secretive about plans and now I need to know how to dress.

I can always stay home.

Crap, he thought. *This could turn downhill fast if I don't give her a good answer.*

Before he could come up with a witty response, his phone went off again.

And yes, I definitely know you're a man.

And that right there was enough to take the wind out of his sails. How was he supposed to respond to that? He did feel a sense of pride knowing that he was apparently affecting her as much as she was affecting him.

And affect him she did.

He could still smell the fragrance of her long hair as it

blew past his face. He could see her flawless lips, remember the feel and taste of them under his. And her petite little body, how it fit perfectly nestled against him.

Alex cleared his throat and shook his head a little, tried to focus on the task at hand.

Casual top and jeans. Boots if you've got them.

As beautiful as Melanie was when she was all dolled up for weddings and work, he couldn't wait to see her dressed down again. He could already imagine how great her backside would look in a snug pair of jeans, long and lean legs...

Thank You. That wasn't so hard was it?

I'll be ready at six. See you soon.

Alex read her last text and knew that the next five and a half hours would go by at a snail's pace. He couldn't wait to see her tonight.

Man, I have got it bad.

·　　·　　·　　·　　·

At five-fifty that evening, Mel was pacing her bedroom, debating for the twentieth time on whether she had chosen the right pair of shoes. Boots. That was all Alex had told her.

Did he not realize how many different types of boots were in most women's closets? There were stilettos, low-heeled, over-the-knee, booties. Not to mention the choice between leather, suede, several different types of reptile skins.

But he had told her jeans and a casual top. So she'd opted for a pair of black, matte leather boots that came up to just above her ankle with a short heel. Well, two inch heels but that was quite a bit shorter than the normal four and five inch pumps she wore to work.

Her pale blue jeans were cut in the skinny style, fitting her legs all the way down to the tapered ankle. Her black sleeveless top was sheer-satin and she wore a black camisole underneath. She had decided to wear her hair down tonight, the long blonde waves curled at the ends that rested halfway down her back. She kept her makeup light with some pale pink blush and lip gloss, a little mascara.

She stopped in front of her mirror and looked over her ensemble again, turning from left to right to get a view of every angle.

Casual. Yes, definitely.

When her doorbell rang five minutes later, she took a deep breath and told herself to stop fretting. Alex wouldn't care one bit about her shoes. She stuck her chin in the air, even though no one was around to see her prideful maneuver, and went to answer the door.

Alex stood in the hallway leaning casually against the doorjamb with one ankle crossed over the other. He looked relaxed, and gorgeous, in a pair of dark blue jeans that were worn in all the right places. Mel tried not to look too closely at those places. His beige button up shirt made his honey-colored eyes shine bright, like streams of gold spun from Rumplestiltskin.

His hair had been finger-combed back and for some reason, seeing those waves in ordered disarray made Mel want to run her own fingers through it just to see if she could make it look the same.

And on his feet were a pair of faded brown cowboy boots.

"Do I pass inspection?"

Mel jerked her head up, realized she *had* been staring and felt her cheeks flush in embarrassment.

"I'm sorry. Staring at you like that was rude of me and I____"

"You can stare at me any time you want to, for as long as you want," he interrupted and Mel rolled her lips together inward to bite back a grin.

"Alright. Now, I should be asking you the same question. Do I?" she asked and did another spin like the one she'd done in her bedroom, for Alex this time.

"Always," he told her, even though he never took his eyes off her face. "because you always look beautiful."

Now he looked her body up and down, from the top of her head to the tips of her toes, taking note of her clothes. His eyes lingered on her legs and Mel forced herself not to fidget under his gaze.

"And you look perfect."

She smiled at him, a coy smile full of timid hope. But when he only continued to look at her, seriousness etched across his brow and making the skin there break out into three vertical wrinkles, her smile started to slip.

Just as she was opening her mouth to ask if something was wrong, he stepped across the threshold and abruptly took her face in his hands.

Mel barely had time to register the feel of his rough palms against her cheeks before he brought his lips down to hers. She expected urgency, maybe a little roughness because of the way he'd moved to her so suddenly.

She had not planned on the softest of touches. A faint caress of his full lips over her own. The tenderness made her dizzy and she brought her hands up to rest on his chest, as much to feel the muscle there as for the need to find something to steady her.

Alex's breath rushed out quickly at the contact and Mel jerked her hands back. But he quickly removed his right hand from her face and caught her fingers, kept them pressed against him.

More pecks of his lips across hers, from one corner of her mouth to the other, had Mel closing her eyes in sweet surrender. At the light touch from the tip of his tongue to her lower lip, Mel opened her mouth in surprise. Alex took the opportunity to stroke his tongue against hers, softly. He'd barely made contact before he retreated, placed another kiss on her upper lip.

She felt the chill when he lifted his head, allowing the air to come between their heated faces. Her eyes opened slowly, her brain sluggish in its attempt to understand what had just happened.

Why he had done that? Why she had responded so easily?

When her focus came back, she looked up and saw Alex grinning, looking like he had just snuck the last slice of pie after Thanksgiving and gotten away with it.

"I'm sorry." His muttered apology said he was anything but that. "But I've been thinking about doing that all day. I couldn't wait any longer. I promise to be a perfect gentleman the rest of the evening." He laced the fingers of his left hand with those on her right, pulling her toward the hall. "Come on. Let's go eat. I'm starving."

Mel grabbed her purse from the entry table to her right and shut the door behind them, locked it quickly and rushed to keep up with Alex's long stride to the elevators.

And she couldn't help but hope that maybe he wouldn't be the gentleman *all* night, if it meant he'd kiss her like that again.

Twenty-five minutes after they had left her building, Alex and Mel were pulling up–via Ted and his Towncar–in front of a plain looking building about three blocks to the east off of the Four-Oh-Five.

Faded white clapboard shutters were open on the eight windows lining the front. A worn, wooden porch wrapped across the front and curved around each side, with white, wrought iron tables and chairs placed every ten or so feet.

Several couples sat at a few of the tables on the porch while more could be seen through the double-wide screen door leading to the interior.

Alex held Mel's hand as they walked up the three porch steps and inside the restaurant. A dark stained oak podium stood just inside to the left, with a girl of about seventeen manning the station.

"Good evening! Welcome to The Seafood Café. Table for two?"

"Yes ma'am," Alex told her and the girl blushed a little. Whether from him addressing her as a "ma'am" or just him in general, Mel wasn't sure. Not that she would blame the girl for blushing by looking at Alex. One look at him and Mel did the same.

"Great." The girl cleared her throat. "Inside or would you rather sit on the patio?"

Alex looked at Mel for an answer and she shrugged her shoulders, leaving the decision in his hands. He turned toward the hostess and said, "I think we'll stay inside tonight."

"No problem. Right this way."

She picked up two menus from a cubbyhole on the wall behind her and led the way to the back of the building, nimbly weaving in between tables until she reached the one she wanted. She placed the menus on the table in the back right corner, smiled sweetly and walked away quickly.

Mel sat and smiled up at Alex as he helped to push in her chair before taking his own seat to her left. The table was worn, like the front porch, with shallow ruts and grooves from years of use. Mel wondered what the stories were behind some of the marks; if they came from a couple like her and Alex who put their symbol there to remember a first date. Or maybe a family with kids that were too ambitious with their silverware.

In the center of the table was a single white tapered candle, its soft glow casting shadows on the two of them.

Alex picked up a wine menu that was leaning against the salt and pepper shakers, held it out to Mel and asked, "Would you like to order a bottle of wine? You probably know more about that than I do. I'm not much of a wine connoisseur."

Mel smiled at his boyish admission and took the menu from him, opened it and scanned through the two dozen wines they had listed.

Before she had a chance to give him an answer, their server appeared, a young man of about twenty with dark brown hair and eyes and the ruddy complexion of someone still maturing.

"Hi guys! My name is Greg and I'll be taking care of you tonight. Our special this evening is the roasted salmon on top of an arugula salad with tomatoes, avocados and mushrooms and a side of rice pilaf. Now, can I start you two off with something to drink?"

Again Alex looked to Mel. After hearing the special, she knew exactly what she wanted.

"We'll take a bottle of the Terlato Pinot Noir," she looked up and told him, then laid the menu back against the condiments.

"Excellent. I'll go get that for you and be back to take your orders."

When she looked back at Alex, he was staring at her, a half grin on his lips and a playful expression making his face look younger than he was.

"What?" she asked.

"Nothing. You. How did you know what wine to order?"

"When he said the special, I knew we would want a pinot noir. It's a red wine, a little dry with some berry undertones. It goes really well with salmon." A thought hit her. "I'm sorry, I didn't even think to ask if you wanted the special. It sounded so good I decided that's what I was going to order but if you want something different…" she trailed off, feeling self-conscious about her assumption.

"No, it's okay. The salmon sounds great to me."

Greg came back, bottle and two glasses in tow. He set the glasses down and popped the cork, pouring a small amount of the deep red liquid into a glass before offering it to Alex. He shook his head and pointed to Mel, who took the offered glass from Greg. After a quick swirl and sniff, she tasted the wine and gave an approving nod. Greg poured them each a glass of wine then set the bottle in the corner of the table.

"Have you decided what you'll be having this evening?"

Alex ordered for them both, saying, "Yes, we'd both like the salmon tonight."

"Another excellent choice. I'll just go put that in. If you need something, let me know. Otherwise, I'll be back to check on you shortly." The server walked off toward the kitchen, leaving Mel and Alex alone.

"What made you decide on this place?" Mel asked Alex as she took a small sip of her wine.

"Well, it was supposed to be a casual place, nothing high-end or fancy, which is what I wanted for tonight. Someplace laid back, you know? But I got to tell you, I think it's a little classier than the website portrayed."

"Oh no, you had it right. This is casual. By L.A.'s standards anyway. I think it's great. The rustic porch, the worn tables give it an older feel. But the food and service steps it up from a dive to a more elegant setting. I love it."

"Well then if you're happy, I'm happy."

Alex reached across the table and took Mel's hand in his. It felt so natural to curl her fingers with his, to feel the brush of his thumb across her knuckles. She could have stayed just like that all night, gazing at the gorgeous man across from her and not saying a word.

But she was anxious to find out more about him.

"So, tell me about adolescent Alex."

"'Adolescent Alex'?"

"Yes!" She laughed at his expression, one that said he thought she was crazy.

"What do you want to know?"

"I don't know. What sports did you play? Did you have any serious girlfriends? What was your favorite subject in school? You know... the normal stuff."

"Okay." He leaned forward and took a drink of his own wine. *For courage, maybe?* "This is good." He nodded to the bottle and set his glass back down on the table.

"And you're stalling." She smirked at him.

"Okay, okay. Where to start... I never really was one to like school," he began and told Mel about how he scraped by in class, passing usually with B's and C's. How Brinley helped him a lot when they were both still in high school.

But what made Mel laugh into her glass of water was his story about skipping school in second grade.

"Wait! Wait just a minute. You skipped school in second grade?" she asked, dumbfounded that a kid that young would even consider something like that.

"Yeah." He laughed at her shock. "I really hated school. Used to get anxiety about going, although we didn't know that's what it was back then. There's this ditch that Brin and I used to pass by every day on our bikes when we rode to school. So one morning, I stayed at the ditch and told Brin to 'pick me up' when school got out for the day.

"We did that a few times. I think it was either day two or three in a row when the teachers called my Mom, wanted to know if I was sick. When we got home that afternoon, Mom was waiting for an explanation. Scowl on her face, toe tapping away, the whole nine yards. I didn't want to tell her but Brin never was good at keeping secrets from our parents. She ratted me out."

"Oh, come on, Alex. What did you expect her to do? You kind of put her in an awkward situation."

"I know that. Now. But at the time I was just an eight year old kid who was pissed that his big sister told on him. Looking back, I see the humor in it. But man… I wouldn't share anything with her for the longest time." He shook his head with a smile at the memory and Mel could see the love for his sister shine through.

I wouldn't mind him having that kind of look with me.

Mel froze at the new thought, wondered where in the world it had come from. Before Alex had a chance to see her alarm–or worse, to question her about it–she put a happy mask back on her face and pretended like it never came to mind.

Alex went on to tell her that even though he despised school, he really loved art when he was in junior high and high school. He said that he didn't have the talent to take him anywhere with it; but, that it gave him a kind of peace.

He played all types of sports. From football to baseball to soccer and even some cross country.

"I don't know. I loved playing sports, loved being active. But I never felt like it was where I belonged. It was more just something to help pass the teenage years. I didn't get that sense of rightness until I was in the Navy."

And now he was out of it. Mel could imagine just how hard it would be for him to adjust to civilian life. She gave his hand a squeeze, showed him she was there. He smiled graciously at her but was kept from saying anything when their food arrived.

Greg set her plate down and then Alex's, asked them if they needed anything else, then left when Alex told him no. They ate in a comfortable silence for a few minutes.

The salmon was delicious; moist, tender and seasoned to perfection with hints of thyme and lemon coming through. The salad was crisp and refreshing and the rice had just enough spice in it to give some heat to the dish.

"What about you?" Alex asked, finishing off his salmon and moving to his own salad.

Mel thought about it a minute. What could she tell him that wouldn't reveal just how scared she used to be? She decided to stick with earlier years, leaving the college stuff for another day like he did, subtly, with his naval past.

"There's really not a lot to tell. I didn't play any sports. I did really well in school, studied all the time. I did my best work in writing and English. I used to love to write short stories and poems in high school."

"Did you want to be a writer?"

"Me? No, no I just loved the freedom that putting words on paper gave me. Professional writers scare me. I think they're all a little crazy to be able to come up with stories out of nowhere. I didn't want any part of that when I grew up.

"So when I applied for college, I actually had plans to go to the school of arts at SDSU. But I changed my major before the end of the first semester."

"Why is that?" Alex pushed his now empty plate aside and leaned forward, more interested Mel's history.

"I found out during my first audition for the college's rendition of *The Glass Menagerie* that I apparently have a terrible case of stage fright. I was petrified, couldn't even get my name out before I started to hyperventilate. I started sweating so bad that I swore everyone could see the wet stains under my arms."

Mel scowled at Alex when he started laughing. Not just a little chuckle; a deep throated laugh complete with him holding his stomach while his head was thrown back. She would have been embarrassed about the scene he was making if it weren't for the fact that he looked so magnificent with his joy shining through.

Even if it is at my expense.

But, if she were honest with herself, the memory was pretty funny. It would have made a great newspaper headline. *Drama Student Fails Class With Worst Case of Stage Fright Ever Recorded.*

At that thought she laughed with him, ignoring the curious glances from the other patrons, some looking on in annoyance. But most had knowing smiles that said they appreciated the enjoyment at their table.

When Mel and Alex had both calmed down and were able to talk again, he reached across the table with both hands and grabbed Mel's fingers. He pulled them toward his mouth, lifted her left hand and kissed her knuckles. Mel's breath caught in her throat at the sweet, barely there touch that sent a fleet of butterflies loose in her belly.

His lips on her caused all conscious thought to go out the window. Even on her hands, apparently.

He placed his strong hands on the outside of hers, keeping them locked in his warm embrace. Mel focused on the different shades of their skin, the feel of his callused palms against the backs of her hands, and slowly brought her gaze back up to his.

Alex's eyes, more like the color of dark caramel under the glow of the candle, looked back at Mel with something like adoration evident. She swallowed thickly at what she saw there before he finally spoke.

"I'd say it sounds like God had a bigger plan for you, after all. And I'm very thankful that I get to be a part of it."

Chapter 11

"And the Lord God said, it is not good that the man should be alone; I will make him an help meet for him." Genesis 2:18

Melanie was quiet when they left the restaurant. She was quiet now, too, in the car. Alex looked across the seat at her, her face in shadows with only the faintest of glimpses visible when the car passed underneath the florescent glow from a streetlight.

He didn't see any signs of nervousness or reluctance; but, he didn't notice any further openness, either.

He worried that he had pushed the envelope too far with his statement back at the café. About God having a bigger plan for her.

But at the time, the words had just slipped out and he hadn't even given it a second thought. Especially when she smiled at him, accepted his words with ease. At least compared to the way she had reacted on previous, similar situations these past few days.

But now her retreat into the corner of the seat had him on edge.

He reached over and took her right hand in his, softly running his thumb across the backs of her knuckles. She seemed to like it whenever he did that. When Melanie slowly brought her face around to look at him, Alex kissed those knuckles and rested their joined hands on his leg.

"You okay?"

"MmHmm. Just thinking."

"Anything you want to share?" he asked, hoping to untangle some of the tension that hung in the air between them.

"Not yet." She took a deep breath, releasing it steadily. "But soon."

Melanie didn't say anything else but she did scoot across the seat to be closer to Alex and rested her head on his shoulder. He reached his free hand up and ran his fingers through her hair. The movement made the scent from her shampoo wash over him–something sweet like gardenia or jasmine–and Alex breathed it in deeply, filled his lungs with her.

The softness of the strands that moved through his fingers had him envisioning what that hair would look like, feel like, lying across his bare chest. Or curtaining their faces, blocking out the rest of the world with a silken, blonde barrier as she leaned over and kissed him.

Come on, Alex. Get a hold of those wayward thoughts. The last thing Melanie needs is evidence that you are, indeed, a man.

Alex fidgeted in the seat, trying to readjust himself a little. Melanie sat up quickly, probably mistaking his movements for being uncomfortable. He unlinked their hands and brought his arm around her shoulders, urged her head down into the crook of his shoulder, taking advantage of the situation.

"You're fine. I just didn't want to hurt you with my shoulder. Thought this might be more comfortable."

Melanie murmured an agreement and nestled in closer. Alex turned his face and placed a lingering kiss on the crown of her head, tightening his hold on her. He felt like if he didn't hold on tight enough, this moment might run from him. And he would do anything to keep her right where she was.

But too soon, Ted pulled up in front of their second stop for the night and he had to let her go.

Alex exited the car on one side while Ted held the door for Melanie on the other. When she stood and turned to look across the top of the car, her eyes lit up at the neon twinkling behind Alex with a mixture of surprise, excitement and apprehension.

"You brought me to a Honky Tonk?" she asked incredulously, walking around the back of the car to stand next to Alex. She looked up the flashing cowboy boot lit up in bright brown, blue and red that moved from one position to another at every blink. It looked like it was dancing. "I don't know whether to hate you or love you right now."

Alex's heart leapt in his throat at her words. He didn't think she realized what she'd said; she was still looking up at the boot with a smile creeping up on her lips. He swallowed so hard he felt like his Adam's apple was going to push through the skin on his throat.

Hearing that four letter word–love, not hate–come out of her mouth and directed at him, even unconsciously, made all sorts of hopes burst through his mind.

It's too soon. Isn't it?

Before he had a chance to answer his own question, Melanie pulled on his hand and headed to the oak door of the building.

"I'll be right here when you're ready to leave," Ted called out to their backs.

Melanie gave a little wave behind her head with her right hand to say that she'd heard him (even though Ted was probably talking to Alex) and pulled the door open with enthusiasm.

They stepped into a dimly lit room; though "room" was

probably too tame a word for it. The square building was at least fifteen thousand square feet. Lights hung from thick silver cables every ten feet with deep red globes keeping the bulbs covered, giving the space a cozy feel.

A bar took up the entire back wall with a black, rubber bar-top. Stools with dark brown, leather upholstery and deer antlers for legs stood in a line for people to sit at. Five bartenders ran up and down the length of the bar while they took orders, made drinks and chatted up their patrons.

In the center of the room, taking up at least half of the space, was a light brown, parquet dance floor, crowded with at least fifty people currently doing a line dance to Blake Shelton's remake of *Footloose*.

Surrounding the dance floor were tall tables with the same black rubber tops and deer stools as the bar. People huddled together around the tables, all laughing animatedly and having a good time, while ten or so waitresses walked around and delivered orders, some flirting with the customers.

On the right wall were six dart boards, men and women all throwing their darts and trying to get a bulls-eye. On the left side of the room were a handful of pool tables. Men hunched over the tables to line up a shot with their pool cues while their women sat at even more tables to cheer them on.

To their immediate left, on the same wall as the entrance, stood a DJ balcony with a lone man. He had on a set of headphones and was speaking into a microphone in front of him, counting out the steps of the song to the dancers. Alex saw a large computer screen in front of the man with a long list of various artists and songs.

A young woman around Melanie's age walked up the booth and stood on the steps in front. The DJ leaned over, took the headphone off of one ear and listened to whatever the woman said, nodded his head at her request.

Framed pictures showed scenes from ranches and farms as well as popular country singers from over the years

It was loud and relaxing and fun. It was perfect.

Alex spotted a free table off to their left, right to the side of the dance floor. He pulled Melanie's hand, gave her no choice but to follow as he made his way over. They both took their seats and within minutes a waitress came up to them in a tight pair of jeans with cowgirl boots and a white tank top tied at the waist. She laid out two napkins on the table, smiled and said, "Hiya guys! What'll it be tonight?"

Alex ordered a light beer and looked over to Melanie. She nodded her head at the waitress, returning the woman's smile as she said, "Make that two!"

By the time the waitress returned with their beers, the music had changed to a slow song. Alex watched Melanie sway from side to side in her seat with a small grin playing on her lips as she watched the people dance in front of them. He took a quick sip of his beer, stood and held his hand out to her.

"Dance with me."

Melanie placed a trembling hand in his and he closed his fingers around hers. He admitted to himself that even though her hand was cold he could feel the heat from her touch radiate up his arm. Alex walked backwards, kept his eyes focused on her soft blue-green ones as they made it onto the floor.

He was not prepared for what he'd feel when his arms went around her waist and hers circled up and around his neck.

He'd held her before, when they kissed as well as on the boat.

But something about this–the atmosphere or the new information bouncing between them or maybe just the intimate way they held each other–had his heartbeat drumming wildly in his chest. His pulse picked up speed when Melanie licked her lips. He felt his stomach do a flip when she played with the tips of his hair at the nape of his neck. And when she looked into his eyes with that one emotion so openly evident, he knew he stopped breathing, if only for a second.

He saw trust.

At the question in his eyes–the one that said "are you really trusting me?"–Melanie gave and almost imperceptible affirmative nod of her head and laid her cheek against his chest, taking a deep breath. Alex laid his cheek down on the top of her head and held her closer, his arms like a band around her waist.

They swayed like that, back and forth but never moving positions, for the entire length of the song, relishing the warmth of each other. No words were spoken. No words were necessary.

The gift of that trust was enough to make the silence that stretched before them fill with hope instead of fear.

One song turned into another and Alex found himself humming to the tune from George Strait. He felt Melanie smile against his chest and took a chance. He leaned back, took her right hand in his left and placed his other hand on the small of her back. He guided her in the way to dance the Texas Two-Step and moved them in a slow circle around the perimeter of the dance floor.

When Melanie looked down at their feet he tipped her chin up, made sure she focused on his face as he sang the words to her.

"I cross my heart, and promise to, give all I've got to give to make all your dreams come true. In all the world, you'll never find, a love as true, as mine."

"Do you always serenade the woman you're dancing with?" she asked with a sheen of tears in her eyes.

When one rolled down her cheek, like a drop of dew rolling down a window, he brushed it away with his thumb and cradled her jaw in his hand. He brought his forehead down to rest against hers, lightly laid his lips across hers before answering.

"No, only you."

Melanie brought her head back to look into his gaze; her own bounced back and forth between his eyes as she searched for some kind of explanation. He gave her the simple one he knew she wouldn't misunderstand.

"It will only ever be you."

.   .   .   .   .

It will only ever be you. What does that mean? It's too soon to say something like that. Something so permanent. Right?

Mel's thoughts bounced around in her head while Alex led her back to their table by the dance floor. They had danced to two songs in a row.

But that second one by George Strait–she might be a Cali girl but everyone knew who George Strait was–had loosened something inside of her.

No, it wasn't the song. It was Alex. The way he sang the words, not like he was just singing them because he knew the lyrics but as if he really meant them. For her.

Was it a little corny? Maybe.

But she loved it nonetheless because it was so real and

honest.

There was a barrier around her heart that had been on guard, kept it closed off like Fort Knox, for five years. But when he'd gazed at her and whispered those sweet lines, the barrier cracked open. Exposed her heart to feelings both unknown and confusing. But not altogether unwelcome. Which is what was strange, but again, Mel knew she was through trying to figure out the "whys" when it came to Alex. Those didn't matter anymore.

She just wanted to figure out where they went from here.

And even though they had both opened up a lot to each other this weekend, she knew it started by getting to know one another even better.

Since it was loud, Mel leaned across the table and grilled Alex for more information about his past, about what made him who he is today. They talked about favorite foods and she told him she loved German food, especially schnitzel. Alex apparently had a weakness for Mexican food. They both loved golf but admitted to not getting to play as often as either of them would like.

And Mel told him that even though she was new to the 'Honky Tonk scene,' she loved to dance and was looking forward to getting back out on the floor.

"You know, we don't really call these places a Honky Tonk," he told her.

"Well then what *do* you call it?"

"It's just a bar. Or a country bar if you really need to be more technical."

He laughed at her when she rolled her eyes at his answer and she stuck her tongue out at him. But sobered quickly when his expression changed from playfulness to one of yearning when he honed in on her action.

Seeing that desire for her in his eyes didn't bother Mel, now. Not like it did the other day at the Taproom.

That look, that emotion, made the bottom drop out of her stomach and she felt a yearning of her own. Deciding it was time for her to make the first move, she leaned closer toward him and smiled when he followed her lead with an appreciating grin.

But when his eyes quickly glanced to the side, and he straightened as the smile fell from his mouth, she did the same and fought down a feeling of rejection. Until she looked closely at his face.

Gone was the happy-go-lucky man that had been with her tonight.

In his place was a man with annoyance, and maybe even a little anger, shining through. He stared behind her, to the left, at something that had him fuming. Mel turned in her chair to see what he was looking at and immediately froze in her seat.

Across the dance floor, just walking into the bar through the big front door, was Denise.

What the hell?

She turned back quickly to see if that woman was what had Alex getting so upset. He glanced at Mel and gave her a small smile that was obviously forced. He tried to shake off the frustration with a roll of his neck. But Mel could still see evidence of it in his rigid shoulders and the clenching of his jaw. Any other time and those actions would look sexy, masculine.

But not now, not with that man-eater just steps away.

"Well, well, well. Who do we have here?"

That woman's voice grated on Mel's nerves worse than nails on a chalkboard and she fought off the urge to shudder. Alex reached under the table and grabbed Mel's hand. She didn't know if he did it for her or himself but she drew strength from those callused fingers and turned to look at the overly promiscuous woman who stood directly behind her chair.

Denise was in another tiny dress tonight, this one a teal color with black high heels. The neckline was square cut and low, which left nothing to the imagination, and barely covered her private areas. Her red hair was pulled up into a messy bun on the top of her head and again, the woman wore pounds of makeup. From the black eyeliner to the pink blush to the bright red lipstick, she looked like a classy clown.

No, I'm pretty sure clowns have more class than her.

Mel giggled at her immediate thoughts and earned a

scowl from the newcomer.

"Something funny?" she asked Mel with a leer on her face.

"What a coincidence seeing you here, Denise." Alex saved Mel from having to respond. "I didn't peg you for the type of woman who liked country music. Do you come here often?"

Denise's eyes widened a little at Alex's words and she stammered a bit when she answered.

"Yes! Well, no. I mean... sometimes. What kind of a woman did you peg me for?"

Mel rolled her eyes at the way the woman tried to get seductive with Alex. Denise leaned an elbow on the table to show off more cleavage and almost purred her words.

"Honestly? I haven't given you any thought. I've had other... pressing matters to stay focused on." Alex smiled at Mel and she returned it, felt that openness in her heart as he put Denise in her place.

Denise didn't like the lack of attention. She pulled up a chair and sat, as gracefully as she could in her too-short-for-public dress, right next to Alex. He didn't take too kindly to her nearness and made it known when he scooted his chair two feet to his right, closer to Mel.

Mel heard a small huff come from across the table and turned to watch Denise. She scowled at them through narrowed eyes that roamed down and noticed the way she and Alex naturally leaned into one another. His hand might have been hidden under the table but there was no question as to where it lay by the angle of his arm, which was across the front of Mel's body like a shield protecting her from the woman with the death stare.

Something about her set Mel on edge. Los Angeles had a population of almost four million people with close to a thousand bars. Out of all those she just *happened* to show up at the one that Mel and Alex were?

No, something was definitely off and she intended to find out exactly what it was. But first she needed a little information.

"Do you work around here, Denise? It seems like this is a great place people come to after they clock out. I mean, that would definitely account for the coincidence, right?"

Please don't let her see through my game here.

Denise looked back up at Mel, shock evident with her wide eyes and open mouth. She quickly recovered and answered, "No, actually I just graduated from college at UCLA recently and haven't had a chance to get a job yet."

Mel didn't miss the way she cast her eyes down when she spoke, like she was trying to hide a lie that would have been visible in her kohl-covered gaze. Instead of commenting, Mel just nodded her head.

If a look of doubt crossed her face then it was purely accidental and not meant to get Denise to keep talking at all.

At least that's what Mel hoped her look portrayed.

"I did just rent a new apartment over on South Grand Avenue. It's only a studio but it *is* just me."

Now that had alarm bells going off in quick succession in Mel's head. Number one, she saw Denise look straight at Alex and emphasize the words *just me*, like that would make him want to go home with her. Never mind the fact that she came across as desperate since Alex was clearly here with Mel.

Number two, and more disturbing, was that Grand Avenue was not far from Mel's own condo on Wilshire Boulevard. A chill ran up her spine knowing that this spiteful and vicious woman had a place that was only four and a half blocks from her.

"And how long have you lived there?"

"About twenty-four hours," Denise told her with a sinister smirk that crossed over her heavily painted mouth.

Mel's throat felt parched as suspicions danced around in her thoughts. She took a quick sip of the beer in front of her, let the cool liquid soothe the dryness before she asked the man-eater one last question.

"I'm so sorry. I don't think we ever got your name the other night. Denise…?" Mel squeezed Alex's hand under the table and hoped he caught on to what she was doing.

Of course he won't catch on, Mel. He doesn't know who you've planned on talking to after this. Or what for.

But he squeezed back so she took that as a sign that he knew she was up to something.

"It's because I never offered it to you," Denise finally said. Her words dripped sarcasm like a sundae melting in the hot sun.

"You didn't give it to me either," Alex broke in and played it up when he leaned a little in Denise's direction and fed her haughty attitude. It worked.

Denise batted her thick lashes at Alex and again almost purred as she replied to him.

"Sanders, handsome. My name is Denise Sanders."

Gotcha! Mel thought as she stood from the table.

"Excuse me a minute. I need to use the ladies' room." She leaned down and gave Alex a kiss to the cheek. She kept her mouth turned in the opposite direction of Denise and whispered just loud enough for him to hear, "Don't worry, I have something I need to do real quick. Keep her talking. I'll be back in five."

Their faces were so close that Denise couldn't see the slight nod Alex gave Mel before she turned from the table and walked away. When she was even with the big oak door, she looked back to see Denise focused on Alex.

And turned to slip out the front.

The small, gray stones crunched under Mel's boots as she hurried across the gravel parking lot. Ted was right where they had left him an hour ago, sitting in the front seat with a laptop out and a manila file folder in his lap. Mel knocked on the driver side window.

Ted looked up quickly and a hand moved to his left side before he visibly relaxed when he saw it was Mel who stood there.

He got out of the car, placed a hand on Mel's upper arm and asked, "Is everything okay, Mel?"

Alex didn't know that she and Ted were friends, had known each other for four years since she was a twenty-one year old intern during her senior year of college. He used to work security at Dalton and had been the head of the department until two years ago when he quit it all. He'd told the bosses that he needed a change. Mel had overheard some of the other agents who'd talked about him having a midlife crisis, but Mel knew better.

Staring at a bunch of computer screens and strolling the halls to deal with menial inter-office quandaries was too slow paced for Ted. He was an ex-marine who had served in the Gulf War when he'd been twenty-six. He needed something more exciting. So now, at fifty, Ted owned a private investigating firm with three other veterans.

He took this "chauffeur" job as a favor to Mel because she'd wanted someone to watch over Alex since he was in a new place. She knew he was catching up on paperwork from other cases while he waited for her and Alex so Mel cut to the chase.

"I'm not sure, Ted. I need you to run a name for me. Don't think of this one as a favor though. I want to pay you for the information."

"C'mon Mel. You're like the daughter I never had. I'm not charging you a dime. And besides, it's just a name. So what's going on?"

Mel smiled graciously at the man who was like a father to her just as she was a daughter to him.

"There's a woman. She was at the Taproom the other day and I didn't think anything about it. It was probably just bad luck that we, Alex and I, ended up at the same place. But tonight she showed up here. She's inside now. I don't know, Ted. Something about that woman has rubbed me the wrong way."

"Are you sure it's not just because she's hitting on your man?"

"Alex isn't my…" Mel stopped. Because saying Alex wasn't her man would be a lie and she couldn't lie to herself, or anyone else for that matter. Not anymore. "No, that's not what's going on. I'm telling you, something's not right."

"Okay girl. I'll look into it. What's her name?" Ted asked and grabbed a small white notepad and pen from the dashboard of the car.

"Denise Sanders. She said she just graduated from UCLA, no job. Oh, and she told us that she just rented an apartment over on Grand Avenue South."

FOREVER GRATEFUL

Ted paused for a moment when he heard the woman's address–he knew how close that was to Mel–but quickly finished scribbling all the information down and laid the notepad back in the car.

"Alright. I'll see what I can dig up and let you know."

"Thanks, Ted. You're the best."

Mel smiled and gave him a quick peck on the cheek.

She turned on her heel and headed back inside, anxious to stake her claim on her man.

·　　　·　　　·　　　·　　　·

Alex sat as still as he could at the table. He hoped that if he didn't move then Denise wouldn't feel the need to move, either. Specifically any closer to him. The strong musky scent of her perfume choked him worse than it did the other night.

Probably because all he wanted to smell now was the soft and sweet fragrance of Melanie's shampoo.

He glanced around the room, looked for Melanie again but didn't see her anywhere. He knew she had been gathering personal information on Denise, could tell an amateur interrogation when he saw one. So he'd sat back and let her do her thing and only stepped in when Denise started to clam up. But he couldn't help much when he had no idea where Melanie had been going with her line of questioning.

I'll definitely get the answers from her when we leave.

When he felt a hand slide up his back and land on his shoulder, he sagged a little with relief that she was back. He didn't need to turn around to know that it was Melanie with her hand on him. He knew her scent and feel anywhere.

He turned his head to look at Melanie when she didn't sit, just stood to his right with her hand on him and looked at Denise with a gleam in her eyes. He knew that look. He'd seen it at the Taproom, at the boat, tonight before they walked in here.

It was the one of determination, with a little possession thrown in, and clearly told Denise "*This one's mine.*"

Alex smiled at Melanie and laid his hand on top of hers, kept her hand where it was on him as he thought to himself, *I'll be her possession any day, every day.* When he saw that greedy look on her face that said she wasn't about to let him go, it made pride swell in his chest at her obvious claim on him. He'd thought of Melanie as *his* for weeks and could only thank God that she now shared his feelings.

He slid his right arm around her waist where his big hand rested on Melanie's hip and he pulled her into his side. She looked down at him and winked which made him laugh before they both turned their faces back to the woman across the table.

Denise was obviously jealous and frustrated at being rejected but Melanie didn't seem to care. Not that he blamed her for her lack of sympathy. This man-eating woman just didn't know when to take no for an answer. As her heavily painted mouth opened to say something, Melanie cut in before her words could come out.

"Well, it's been interesting seeing you again, Denise. But if you'll excuse us, my boyfriend and I are on a date and we'd like to get back to it. Alone."

"Boyfriend?" Denise spat out. "Isn't that a little childish?"

Alex had had enough and stood from his chair. He kept his arm around Melanie tightly as he looked down at the other woman.

"It's only childish if you're not into monogamy. Good thing for us that we both are." He threw a twenty dollar bill on the table and turned with Melanie stuck close to his side. "Have a good night, Denise."

Alex walked them to the front door and out into the dark night. Melanie pulled on his hand several feet from the door, stopped his forward progress and made him come back to where she stood. He held his left hand out to Ted to let the man know that they'd be there in a second and faced Melanie.

She looked at him with hope and doubt in her eyes and she chewed on her bottom lip with the most adorable embarrassed expression. Alex bit his tongue to keep from chuckling. He wrapped his arms around her waist and pulled her into his chest. He kept a hand firmly planted on her lower back and brought his right up to cup her cheek, stroked her high bone softly.

"Does this mean I get to call you my girlfriend, now?"

"I'm sorry for that. I know it was presumptuous but I really wanted to–" Alex cut her off with his lips.

Slowly he moved his mouth over hers, gave her time to catch up to his sudden advance. When Melanie relaxed into him and kissed him back, he moved his hand from her cheek to the back of her head. He kept her steady while he kissed her thoroughly. He traced the seam of her lips with his tongue and when she opened, he explored her. Tasted her.

Melanie didn't hold back. With her petite little hands wrapped around his shoulders, he felt her nails as they dug into his skin through the material of his shirt when her tongue met his. Slowly they entered and retreated, a sensual dance with their mouths made in perfect synchronization.

Melanie's scent, her taste, her feel, drew him under a spell that only she had the anecdote for. Only she could cure with her words, her promises.

Her love.

Love. That word didn't make Alex freeze now. He knew it with every fiber of his being. He loved this woman. He wasn't sure how it happened or why or even when. But he knew it for the truth that it was and there was no way he would let it go. Let her go.

FOREVER GRATEFUL

Slow and steady wins the race, Lambert.

He pulled out of their kiss. Her breathing mirrored his own, wild and erratic. Her eyes were dazed as she tried to regain focus. And her lips–her beautiful, perfect lips–were a little swollen and damp and still lured him in. He reached his thumb up and rubbed the moisture off, looked straight into those teal orbs as the words tumbled out.

"Marry me."

Aimee Martin

Chapter 12

"A sound heart is the life of the flesh: but envy the rottenness of the bones." Proverbs 14:30

She stood in the shadows of the building and watched them. They didn't know that she had snuck out the back door as soon as they were out the front. So they had no idea that she stood there and spied on them. Her anger and jealousy raged at the sight of them.

Him with his arms around her. Her with her tiny little, boyish body as she clung to him like some damsel in distress.

Ha! Damsel in distress, my butt. I saw the warning look in her eyes. She's tougher than he thinks and will definitely need to be watched out for.

But she'd dealt with troublesome girlfriends before,

scared them off with what her former psychiatrist used to call a black heart. Good thing she'd gotten out of that mental ward before they decided to make her seventy-two hour hold a more permanent one. Tried to brainwash her into thinking something was wrong with her.

She knew better than to believe that psychoanalysis crap. There was nothing wrong with her. She just wasn't afraid to be more aggressive in order to make sure things always went her way. The shrink told her it was that aggression that had gotten her on the sixth floor at Brown's Psychiatric Hospital in the first place.

All because that last 'girlfriend' had been too clingy and she'd had to take drastic measures to get to the man. This one wouldn't be any different, she could tell, and her resentment made her hands itch with the need to slap the woman. But she wasn't afraid to bring that hostility back out if it meant she would get what she wanted.

Denise always got what she wanted.

And she wanted Alex.

.　　.　　.　　.　　.

July 3, 2014

Ted Wilson walked down the hallway at Dalton Management. He felt at home and out of place at the same time. He hadn't stepped foot inside these halls since he'd resigned two years ago. He wouldn't be here now if it weren't for Melanie. Normally he would call a client with any information he found. But this, this had made him too unsettled.

Maybe because Mel was so close to him. Probably too close. He should have given the name off to someone else at his firm for the simple reason of being too emotionally involved. But this was his Mel, his surrogate daughter, and he needed to take care of it himself.

He arrived at her door, made sure to keep his head down so he hadn't had to interact with anyone who knew him from before. He knocked three times and stood back to wait. A minute later Melanie stood in the open doorframe and smiled widely at him.

"Ted! I wasn't expecting you," she exclaimed and then in a quieter voice, "What are you doing here? You said you'd never set foot back in this building."

She stood aside and waved him in. He went to one of the black leather chairs in front of her desk and sat, waited for her to close the door and get settled in the chair beside him before he explained why he was there.

"I never planned on coming back in here. Never had a reason to until now."

"What's going on? You're being cryptic."

"Listen, kid. I ran that name that you asked me to.

Denise Sanders."

"And?" she prodded.

"Keep in mind that I didn't dig too deep; it's only been five days. But what I've already found has me worried." He sighed and pulled out a folder from the brown leather briefcase he'd sat on the floor next to his chair. He opened it, ran through some of the basics.

"Denise Haley Sanders. Twenty-four year old Caucasian female. Driver's license says one-hundred and twenty-five pounds, five foot nine. Red hair, brown eyes."

"Ted," Mel interrupted him. "I know what she looks like. Why don't you cut to the chase? I was right, wasn't I? Something's wrong with that woman." When Ted hesitated again, she pushed him a little more. "I'm a big girl. I can handle it."

"Alright. She's bad news, kid. I'm talking criminal record and psychiatric hospital bad news. Her rap sheet's got multiple harassment charges, a few Breaking and Entering's, two restraining orders issued against her. And…"

"And? What is it, Ted?"

"Aggravated assault with a deadly weapon."

Ted watched a myriad of emotions flit across Mel's face. Shock, disbelief, anger, terror. Her throat worked up and down as she swallowed repeatedly.

He reached across her desk and grabbed her bottle of water, handed it to her. She took it. Her hands shook as she held it tightly between both palms like a lifeline. After she took a small sip from the bottle, she looked into his eyes and asked the question he was afraid she was going to.

"Who did she assault?" Her voice wavered.

"From what I could gather, it was in relation to an old boyfriend. He also happened to be one of the people who'd filed for the R.O. Apparently she wasn't too happy when he broke things off. When he started seeing someone else, she went after the new girlfriend with a tire iron." Ted took a breath and then, "Mel, this Denise almost killed her. The report said the girlfriend was in the hospital for a month, half of that time spent in a coma. Word is she's still in a wheelchair.

"I don't know what you've done to get her attention. But you need to be on the lookout. Hire a bodyguard, extra security, something. If you feel the slightest twinge of fear, of someone following you or messing with you, you call me. Immediately. You got it?"

"Yeah. I got it. But I don't think it's me she'd be after. She tried to set her hooks in Alex and he's back in Texas. I'm sure I'll be fine."

"Did you hear what I said? She didn't go after the old boyfriend. She went for the other woman."

"I know, but____"

"But nothing," he cut her off. "You just be careful. Promise me?"

"Okay. I promise," she whispered and couldn't quite hide the way her lips trembled.

He knew Mel would hate it if he hovered, so Ted stood and Mel did the same, slowly. She followed him to the door and gave him a hug, thanked him for the information. He slung his right arm around her shoulders and held her close.

"Anything, anytime, you call, kid."

She nodded against his chest and he kissed the top of her head and let her go. As he walked back down the suffocating hall, he prayed she'd never know what that Sanders woman was capable of.

Chapter 13

"And ye shall seek me, and find me, when ye shall search for me with all your heart."
Jeremiah 29:13

August 1, 2014

"Mel? Did I lose you?" The voice on the other end of the line was muffled but still loud enough that it caught her attention.

"No, Manny, I'm here. Sorry. I just got sidetracked reading this contract. Your contract."

Not a total lie. Manny Garcia's new sponsor contract for a well-known shoe company sat in front of Melanie, open to page four. She just wasn't actually reading it. Specific requirements the professional third baseman from Saint Louis had scribbled down in blue ink stared back at her. The words blended together like watercolors that'd been washed away.

Instead of finalizing the details of this contract, she replayed one of her last conversations with Alex before he'd left California a little over a month ago. Again.

"I don't think there's anything in here that the board will have an issue with," Mel told the ball player and struggled to keep her mind on task. "So I'll finish with the corrections and fax it back to you for signatures. Then we'll get it over to their office and you'll be ready for commercials and photo shoots in no time."

"That's great! Thanks, Mel. It's nice to have a manager who's on my side all the way."

"No problem. I'll be in touch."

She put the phone back in its cradle and laid her head back against her chair. She turned to face the window; the evening sun shone into the room and warmed her face. Mel blew out a deep breath and wondered (for the umpteenth time) if she had handled the situation with Alex wrong.

But, really? What was she supposed to have done? He'd asked her to marry him! Granted, laughing might have been a tad harsh but she'd thought he was kidding.

Until she'd seen the honesty, as well as a little hurt, in his eyes. That hurt was enough to make her sober quickly and backpedal to try to ease the sting her laughing had caused.

FOREVER GRATEFUL

"Alex... you can't be serious. We've only known each other for a few months."

"I am serious, Melanie. I've never been more so. I don't care if it's been two months, two years or only two days. For me, it's you. I don't need any more time to know that."

His words, steady and unwavering, caused a lump in Mel's throat with their sincerity. She wanted to believe it. So much. But this was all still new to her–the relationship, the feelings, the vulnerability at putting herself out there–and she needed more time.

"Alex, I..." she started then stopped, looked down at their feet.

He reached out and placed his hands on either side of her face, lifted her eyes to his and ran his thumbs along her jawline in a smooth caress. With a small grin on his lips, he said, "I know. You're not ready." At her nod he went on. "But you will be."

That conversation had whirled around in her mind for the last thirty-four days and every time she got to the point where he'd said "you will be," doubt and hope fought for the center emotion in her chest. She wanted the hope. She held onto it as tightly as her heart would let her.

But that stupid doubt crept back in. It whispered in her ear like a devil on her shoulder that their feelings weren't real or that he could end up being violent or that he couldn't actually be trusted.

And then the little white angel would show up on her other shoulder. It reminded her of the good in Alex. The protective instincts that ran deep and encompassed Mel in its arms. In his arms. Of the honesty she heard in his voice every time they talked. And of the affection she felt inside but was too scared to admit to for fear that Alex would stop pressing her, in spite of his promise not to, and simply let her go.

"I won't stop asking you, Melanie," Alex said on the dreary Sunday afternoon. Clouds framed the sky like an opaque gray shadow as he prepared to leave. "I'm going to keep at it until I wear you down. Eventually you'll see how real I am and how great we are together and you'll say yes."

He leaned in and brushed his lips across hers once, twice, and landed hard a third time before he pulled away and walked over to Ted, who waited in his car to take Alex to the airport. Mel stood in front of her condo's lobby door, one hand gently laid across her tingling lips, and gave a weak wave to Alex as he rode off.

Despite her fears to the contrary, Mel knew he'd meant what he had said. Alex wouldn't stop asking her to marry him. She just hoped that she was ready to say yes before it was too late.

Am I actually considering this? she thought.

The answer was yes, she was, because for the first time in her life she had something that felt like it was meant to be.

FOREVER GRATEFUL

And in order to take what he was offering, she had to get past what had happened to her. To let that dark cloud go so that she could bask in the sunshine that came with Alex.

She hadn't told him about it yet, but Mel had done some research into this whole God thing. She'd looked up testimonies and theories on Google and Wikipedia. She'd even dug her Gramma's old bible out of one of the boxes full of mementos from the house she spent so much time in growing up; before her Gramma died.

Mel hadn't started reading the book, yet. But it sat on her coffee table in her living room, black leather dusted off as it waited to be opened. Called to be opened. Every night she stared at the gold glossy inscription, chewed her bottom lip, and tried to see an answer in those nine letters–*Holy Bible*– so that she wouldn't have to actually turn the pages. And every night those letters stared back at her, dared her to take a chance at what lay beneath the black cover.

She couldn't explain it, but somehow Mel knew that she would never be able to move forward with Alex if she didn't at least try to understand where his faith came from. And if she was even more honest with herself, she wanted to understand that faith on a personal level, too. To see if there was peace for her there.

Maybe that faith would be the key to finally moving on for good.

The beep of a text brought Mel's eyes down to her cell

sitting in her lap. She couldn't suppress the smile when she saw Alex's name lit up with the bright blue backlight.

They talked every day, usually several times a day. And every message or call broke a little bit more off of her guard. When she talked to him, Alex made her feel free from all the stress–past and present–like a bird that floated in the sky by the force of the wind. He made *her* want to fly.

Hey darlin'
You busy? I miss you.

Darlin'. Out of all the endearments Alex called her, that one was Mel's favorite. Maybe because it made him seem like such a southern gentleman or because no one had ever used that name for her. Ever. She didn't know which and she didn't care. As long as he kept saying it.

Hey, yourself.
Not too busy. Just got off
the phone with a client.

She hit send quickly and then typed out another before he could respond.

I miss you, too.

Mel tried to picture Alex as he would look when he read the second message. He'd still be at work at Jaxson's since it was only three in the afternoon there. Was he guzzling water in a sweat soaked t-shirt as he leaned against that huge barn? Or maybe inside the barn, taking advantage of the cool air from inside. Would he smile in that mega-watt way when he saw those four words? Or more shyly in case someone was nearby, watching him.

She caught herself as she did this more and more lately. Daydreamt about what he was doing or what he was wearing and if he thought about her as much as she did him. She wanted to see him again.

> What's it gonna take to
> get you back to Texas
> to see me?

Mel frowned at the text with a laugh. Did he have some sort of signal into her mind or something? She shook her head at Alex's uncanny ability to say what she was feeling and replied.

> Your sister's baby shower.
> I promised I'd be there
> for it in January.

The twinge of regret that she wouldn't see him sooner than that struck Mel in the belly like a lead ball. She missed his deep laugh and his sense of humor. She missed his beautiful honey eyes and sexy, curving smile. She missed the comfort she got when she was with him.

Two and half months might as well be a lifetime. Could they hold onto what they had for that long with only calls and texts?

> Then I guess I just
> have to come back to L.A.

Instead of texting him, she punched in his number and called.

"No response to that?" he said by way of a greeting, making Mel laugh.

"I guess not. Or maybe my fingers were tired of typing. But the most logical reason for calling is that I wanted to hear *you*."

She sensed the smile in his voice when he replied.

"I think you miss me more than you're letting on, Miss Moore."

"And I think you're a sweet talker, Mr. Lambert."

"You love it." He laughed and never denied her playful accusation.

"Did you mean it?" she asked quietly.

"Yeah, I did honey. I need to see you. Make sure you're still real and that I didn't dream you up in some heat induced stupor from working at the ranch."

"I was worried for the first couple of weeks after you left that… I was afraid you might decide this was too much to deal with."

"I'm not going anywhere. Some things are worth the wait and you, sweet Melanie, are worth much more."

"Sweet talker," she mumbled again, which made him snicker.

"I need to get back out in the pasture. Jax needs help moving the rest of the late-season calves closer to the branding pen. Can I call you tonight?"

Mel really wanted to spend more time on the phone with him. Now, tonight, every day.

But she knew she needed to bite the bullet and open her Gramma's book, too. Every time Alex spoke those softhearted words to her, she felt even more compelled to get some kind of answer so they could move forward.

So as much as she longed to talk to him until the wee hours of the morning, she had to turn him down.

"Actually, there's some stuff I need to take care of at home tonight. I'm not sure how long I'll be at it. Can I take a rain-check until tomorrow?"

"Sure." He hesitated. "Is everything okay? I didn't say anything wrong, did I?"

"No, Alex. You've said everything right. I'll call you tomorrow. Bye."

"Bye, darlin'."

She heard the click on the other end of the line and it was like a judge had beaten his gavel to his desk. A final verdict. Mel pushed up from her chair and moved into action. She quickly gathered her purse and briefcase, contracts and office memos that she hadn't gotten to yet and made her way to the garage, grateful that she had let Becky go home early since it was a Friday. She didn't want to have to field any more probing questions about Mel's mysterious visitor a month ago.

Forty minutes after she left the office at one o'clock, she walked into her condo. She changed into a pair of jeans, a faded red and black SDSU t-shirt and a pair of flip-flops. She took Kass down for a quick walk around the building, picked up the waste after, and headed back upstairs.

Now that she had decided to go through with her plan, she was anxious to get started.

Mel locked the front door after she and Kassie were inside, gave the dog some food and water and sat down on her couch with her own water glass. She picked up the black book carefully, handled it like a fragile one-hundred-year-old letter, and laid it on her lap.

She ran her fingers across the gold script, took a deep breath and opened her Gramma's bible.

.   .   .   .   .

Later that night Alex sat at one of the dozen tables inside The Bar with his brother, Aaron, and Jax. The men sat close to one of the pool tables while they took a break from their game of Cutthroat (a game of pool played with three people instead of just two).

Alex peeled the label off of his untouched beer and tore the soaked paper into small pieces. He missed Melanie and tried to figure out how he'd be able to head out to see her.

Aaron and Jax sat reclined on their barstools. Aaron in

his jeans, royal blue polo shirt and tennis shoes looked every bit the runner, especially with one of those watches that kept track of everything from your heart rate to when the sun came up. He was the complete opposite of Jax, who was in his customary Stetson, jeans and boots. But they were best friends and Alex was grateful they'd so willingly brought him into the fold since he came back.

He regretted that he and Aaron had grown apart over the years he'd spent in the Navy. But now that he was back at home in Lake Shores, he looked forward to rebuilding that relationship. As well as building a stronger friendship with his new brother-in-law.

The two had been talking about their wives and marriage and kids. Alex wanted to join in but what could he contribute? He didn't have any of those things. But he wanted them.

"Hey." His brother's voice brought his head up. "What's going on with you? You've been sulking around here for the last few weeks, ever since you got back from that little California trip. Missing those beach babes that bad?"

Jax laughed into his own bottle across the table, no doubt because he knew exactly what had Alex looking so lonely. Brin probably told the man everything and Alex knew that his sister and Melanie talked on a regular basis. Had she told Brin about their weekend?

"Yeah, Alex. What's got you so beat up?" Jax chimed in

with a smirk and earned a scowl from Alex.

"Nothing. I just got some personal stuff on my mind. And no, it's not beach babes." The last he directed to his brother.

"Just one babe, right?" Jax again put his smart-aleck two cents in and pushed his hat up on his forehead. His eyes gleamed with mischief under the glow of the yellow bar lights that hung overhead.

"Is this about that Mel chick?" Aaron asked before Alex could answer. "I thought you two just had dinner while you were on the West Coast."

Alex fidgeted in his seat. He felt bad that he hadn't opened up to his brother about his feelings for Melanie. But really, they were guys. Guys didn't do sappy conversations and tell each other their hopes and dreams on love like a bunch of pig-tailed schoolgirls.

"Don't call her that, Aaron. She's not just some 'chick.' Her name is Melanie," Alex cautioned his brother.

"Alright, alright. So it is about her, then?"

Alex only nodded his head and worked on turning that label into twice as many miniature pieces. He could feel the stares from the guys and fought off the urge to just up and leave.

Then again, maybe he needed to suck it up and use them as a sounding board. Get some advice from the old married men. He smiled at his thoughts, looked up at the two and sighed. Resignation made him start talking.

"Melanie is... she's different from any other woman I've ever dated. There's something about her that just calls to me. I feel, I *know*, that God put her in my path for a reason. But she hasn't had an easy go of it with life so it's been hard for us."

"What happened?" Aaron asked, all kidding aside.

Alex could tell the big brother inquisition was getting ready to come out when Aaron–and Jax–both leaned in closer to him.

"That's not my story to tell. I'll just say that she doesn't exactly have the strongest belief in faith." *Or any*, Alex thought to himself. "But I know that can change. I'm trying to help her see it, see life and faith and God for all that they're worth."

He went on to tell them about the dates they'd had in L.A. How he'd gotten her to see the beauty that God created, and was helping her to open her heart and mind to what more could be offered to her. He left out the parts about Denise; there was no point in bringing up someone who had no bearing on what he wanted with Melanie.

Aaron and Jax sat quietly and listened. Neither said anything until he'd finished and Jax was the first one to speak.

"So what's the problem? It sounds like you were making some headway with her."

"I think I might have scared her." He paused, debated, before he sputtered out the rest. "I asked her to marry me."

Alex placed his hands in his lap and ducked his head to avoid the stunned frowns he knew were coming. He wasn't prepared for his older brother's outburst.

"You did what?!" Aaron said. His voice rose with each word and the other patrons looked their way. Aaron gave a little wave to everyone in apology and more quietly said, "What do you mean you asked her to marry you? You've only known this woman for a few months. Are you crazy? Or just stupid?"

Alex bristled at the childish tone his brother used on him. He wasn't crazy and he wasn't stupid. His hands clenched beneath the table with the need to deck Aaron. Lord knows it wouldn't be the first time.

But they were adults now, not a couple of hormonal teenagers, and Alex knew if he threw punches it wouldn't solve anything.

So he went for the metaphorical slap in the face.

"How long had you known Jess before you knew she was the one, huh?" At Aaron's silence, he turned the question to Jax, who had remained quiet during his brother's rant. "And what about you with Brin?"

Acquiescence showed on both of their faces as they sat back in their chairs.

"Touché," Aaron said at the same time that Jax replied

with, "You're right."

"I'm sorry, Alex," Aaron continued and stared toward the back corner at nothing in particular. He smiled and got a soft look in his eyes as he turned back to Alex. "I knew the moment I laid eyes on Jess that I wanted to marry her. We were both running on the old dirt track around the football field. It was evening, dark coming up quick. I had stopped to tie my shoe and she ran right into the back of me, knocked us both on our butts. She had a big smudge of dirt on her cheek and I thought she was the most beautiful woman I'd ever seen. And when she told me, none too kindly, to get off the track next time I had to tie my shoes, I knew she was it for me.

"I guess sometimes I forget that you're a grown man and not that scrawny kid who used to follow me around. Hell, you've seen the world, faced off with drug cartels out in the ocean on your deployments. Who am I to say that what you feel for her isn't real?"

"Yeah. I remember when I saw your sister in the church for the rehearsal. That light from the stained glass touched her face and it hit me in the gut like a raging bull. She looked like an angel basking in the sun. I knew right then it was her."

"See, that's what I was talking about," Alex told them and scooted to the edge of his chair in his excitement to have them understand. "When we met at yours and Brin's wedding in April, Jax, talking to Melanie was so easy. Hearing her laugh, seeing her smile, she drew me in like this... siren and her song. Bad example, I know," he conceded before they had a chance to mock him when he compared Melanie to a siren.

"But you get what I'm talking about. And ever since then, all I think about, all I feel, is her. It's Melanie because she *matters*. But now I don't know what to do, where to go or how to move forward."

Aaron twirled the bottle that sat in front of him, a thoughtful expression on his face while he looked at the table in silence. After a minute, he looked up and suggested, "You need to tell her."

"I did. I asked her the day before I left if she would marry me. She said it was too soon, that she wasn't ready."

"No, moron. You need to tell her that you love her."

A breath whooshed out of Alex's lungs like a deflated balloon.

Love. Of course I love her. But I never told her. How could she think I was serious if I didn't tell her?

For some reason, though, asking her to marry him seemed a lot easier than telling her that he loved her. He could handle her saying no because he knew it wouldn't always be a 'no'.

But if she didn't love him?

"What if she doesn't feel the same way?" he asked

quietly.

"You tell her anyway. And you keep telling her over and over until she knows you're speaking the truth. And when she finally believes you, you say it again." This from Jax.

"Okay. Yeah, you're right. Both of you. I need to see her."

Jax smiled as he took a drink from his beer and stood. He grabbed his pool cue that'd been leaning against the back of his barstool.

"I think we can work out a long weekend for the ranch. I could use a little extra time with my wife, anyway."

Alex and Aaron both groaned at the suggestive grin on Jax's face and Aaron warned him, "Seriously, dude. I know Brin's your wife but she's also our sister. Keep it to yourself."

"Yeah!" Alex agreed. He felt lighter in his heart now that he had some sound advice from the two guys. He grabbed his own cue and stood, too. "Now let's get back to some Cutthroat."

.   .   .   .   .

Mel sat with her hands frozen, the bible opened to the first page. She stared at an envelope with her name written across the front in shaky, bold, capital letters. She'd stared at that envelope for the last ten minutes and wondered how in the heck it had gotten there. Who had put it there, and why?

She knew she wouldn't get any answers by just looking at it so Mel picked up the white envelope that was crinkled around the edges from being stuffed in a book and then a box.

Her hands trembled when she flipped it over and slid her index finger under the seal. The sound of the envelope as it ripped echoed in her silent home.

Inside she found sheets of paper that had been tri-folded to fit in the packet. She pulled them out slowly and laid them on her lap, still folded. The pages were yellowed like stained teeth; time had taken its toll on the paper.

Mel's breath caught in her throat when she opened the papers and immediately recognized her Gramma's beautiful script. The date in the top right corner was just one and a half months before she had died, when Mel had only been eighteen.

A water drop landed on the black ink and Mel gently wiped it away and grabbed a tissue from the coffee table. She dabbed her eyes before more tears could fall. Her lips trembled with grief and longing as she read the words that tried to blur before her.

November 14, 2007

My Dear, Sweet Melanie

If you're reading this then know that I am up in Heaven, smiling down at you and dancing because my prayers have finally been answered.

FOREVER GRATEFUL

From the time you were just a little girl, I wanted to hold you and love you and give you a foundation for life that was based on the Lord. But it wasn't my place. I was just the grandmother. So I did what I could with the time I had with you, planted seeds that I hoped would one day sprout into full-grown faith. My guess is that now you're finally ready to see what's on the other side and I hope you listen carefully.

Christianity is not about a religion. It is about a relationship with our Creator. It is feeling love even when we are too broken to love ourselves. It is knowing that someone is looking out for us even when we slip and fall and feel alone. It is believing, with your whole heart, that no matter what sin you have committed, you can be redeemed. You have only to ask.

Your mother, my daughter (bless her beautiful and free-spirited heart) never could grasp this when I tried to explain it to her during her childhood. She found it suffocating because she couldn't open her mind up enough to believe that everything around her was put here by Him. And I understood when you followed in your parents' footsteps. I saw how you longed to be a part of their life and I don't blame you for it. But now you're a grown woman and I hope you can see the truth for what it is. And it most certainly is not us coming from some speck.

Faith is the unshakeable belief in something. You have to build on it, like trust, and nurture it the way you would a budding rose. You have to feel it, even in darkness, like a blind man feels his way through life. And you have to cherish it for what it is... a connection, *a devotion, a pure entity. It is not perfect nor is it meant to be. Imperfections are what make us human and what can endear us to God even more, so long as we always <u>strive</u> to be what He wants for us, which is a perfect life.*

Everything that has happened in your life has happened because it was meant to. The good times were to remind you of happiness. The bad times to remind you of humility. The sad ones to give you a chance to hurt and come back restored. He has never put more on your shoulders than you could handle, even if it felt the opposite at times.

You are a strong, beautiful woman with a big heart. One that is full of love to give. Accept Him and He will always be there. Anytime you feel doubt or fear at this new and exciting journey, I want you to remember these words...

God has kept you here for a reason. You have survived because He has a plan for you. You have made it to this point in your life because you are blessed. Release and let go of all past hurts. Recognize them for the illusions that they are. The will of God will never take you where the grace of God cannot protect you.

Open your heart, sweet granddaughter, and be happy.
All my love, always,
Gramma
P.S. Since you have my bible open, read Ephesians 2. It's one of my favorites.

Melanie's breath shuddered and caught in her throat as she imagined her Gramma's voice, her soothing and melodic tone saying these words aloud that she wrote years ago. She reread the letter twice more before she set it down on the couch beside her and laid a hand on the pages as if she could feel her Gramma's presence in them.

Mel turned back to the open bible, gave a small giggle at the way her Gramma had put that last dig in there in her typical tongue-in-cheek way. She flipped through the thin pages and smiled at the notes written in the borders of each one. The underlining of sentences and circling of words that Gramma must have regarded as important. She finally made it to the section called Ephesians, almost at the very back, and found the right chapter.

Some of it was difficult to translate–thees and thous and words with -est and -eth at the ends–but she managed to get through the entire chapter. Then she read it again. And again. On the fourth time, verse eight stood out above all the others. It called to Mel like it was written for her and her alone.

"For by grace are ye saved through faith; and that not of yourselves: it is the gift of God."

Mel read the line again. Something took hold inside of her and wouldn't let go. It was a feeling of understanding, of courage. It was a feeling of peace. Like a heavy rain washing away the dirt from a street, the verse swept into her and washed away all of her doubt on God and why He had let that rape happen to her.

"I did survive," she murmured to herself.

It wasn't about God *letting* that happen. It was about

- 259 -

how she had the courage, from Him, to stand up afterwards and not be defeated. And how could anyone go through something like she did and come through on the other side feeling more determined without divine intervention? They couldn't. At least not without a heavy burden carried on their shoulders along the way. Why did it take her so long to see it?

Because you blamed Him instead of thanking Him for getting you back, Mel.

The answer to all the questions she'd had about why that horrible incident had happened to her was so clear now. Her Gramma's last words and the verse she read worked together in her mind, made her see that it was never about the bad, but the good that came of it. It was about learning to be a person who was grateful instead of spiteful. It was about trusting and gaining faith.

Tears flowed from her eyes while the emotions swirled in her heart. Gratitude, amazement, clarity. Faith. She believed, wholeheartedly.

Mesmerized by the resolution just that one chapter gave her, Mel flipped through the pages, anxious to learn more, get more answers. She immersed herself in her Gramma's bible, read the notes the older woman had made to help her understand the scriptures better.

Several hours later, when the sun had set and the room was cast in a soft glow from the large white, porcelain lamp on the end table, Mel was ready to call it a night. To rest her head and heart from the overload of information.

But one last verse caught her eye and when she read it, she got the answer to a question she hadn't even known was there. A question that'd waited patiently inside her mind for its turn to be discovered.

"Let love be without dissimulation. Abhor that which is evil; cleave to that which is good."

The *Romans* verse was underlined and circled, with her Gramma's notes in the border saying to *Always Love*. Don't hide love, cling to it. But she'd been doing the exact opposite for five years. She'd hid from any chance at love–even the strange and casual love from her parents–and in the process let that evil keep hold of her heart.

Sure, she knew now that it was God's will and her determination that helped her to survive. But she'd been letting evil and those wicked men keep her from one of the most vital feelings in life. Love.

She wanted to feel love again. She wanted to be wrapped up in its warm embrace, cradled to its bosom like a nurturing mother.

She wanted Alex's love.

But I already turned him down? What if I'm too late?

Mel wouldn't let her doubts keep her from fighting. She quickly placed the letter back inside its envelope and then into the pages of the bible. She grabbed her cell phone and pulled up websites, made reservations, while she ran down the hall to her bedroom.

Once she got the two confirmation emails, she got her red carry-on suitcase from under her bed and packed clothes for three days inside. She walked into her bathroom, threw all her toiletries into a smaller red bag and laid it inside the case, too. As she zipped the luggage, she called her assistant.

"Becky?" she said when the girl answered on the other end. "I hope I'm not calling too late."

"Of course not, Miss Moore. It's only eight-thirty." *Right... she's probably out partying with her friends on a Friday night.* "Did you need something?"

"Well, yes. I kind of need a little favor. A big favor, actually." Mel stopped and took a breath, afraid that Becky would say no and she would be stuck. She had to make this work, no matter what the cost. "And I know it's short notice so I'll make it worth your while."

"I'm sure it's not that big of a deal, Miss Moore. What's the favor?"

"Could you come and stay at my house for the weekend and watch my dog? I have to go out of town."

Chapter 14

"And this I pray, that your love may abound yet more and more in knowledge and in all judgment." Phillipians 1:9

August 2, 2014

I can't believe I let Jax talk me into coming out here at six in the morning. On a freaking Saturday.

When Alex and the guys were leaving The Bar last night, Jax had asked him to come over early this morning because a dozen calves needed to be loaded up and taken to Houston for the quarterly livestock auction. He should have said no. He could have.

But Jax had given him a job when he came back and Alex felt like he owed the man. Besides, as soon as the cattle were loaded onto the trailer, he'd be headed back to his parents to go back to sleep.

Where the heck is everybody? Alex thought in annoyance while he leaned against the stock trailer, alone.

The sun barely peeked over the horizon, shy in its ascent into the dark midnight sky, and it reminded Alex of a baby playing a game of peek-a-boo. He took a swig of his coffee, let the dark-roasted aroma fill his nostrils as it helped chase away the sleepy yawning he couldn't seem to stop on his own. He looked up to watch the last stars flicker out, their flame taken over by the deep orange and purple glow of the awakening sun.

He brought his head back down to stare into his coffee then jerked when something grabbed the gleam of the rising sun and caught out of the corner of his eye. He stood up straight from the trailer and watched the shiny, silver sedan as it pulled into the driveway between Jax and Brin's house on the left and the barn, where he was, on the right.

The windows were tinted, the rims sparkled and the car was spotless. Or it was before the dust from the drive settled on the car like fresh snow in the middle of a northern winter. He hadn't seen any movement inside the vehicle.

Since Brin and Jax hadn't made their way outside yet– *And the rest of the hands are still MIA*–he walked over to see if he could help whoever the mystery person was.

When he was a few steps from the car, the driver door opened and a blonde head appeared from inside as it slowly rose above the doorframe. She faced away from him, looked toward the house, but he would know that golden wheat shine anywhere. Alex stopped dead in his tracks and waited, his breath stuck in his lungs and his heart hammered out a beat any marching band would've been proud of.

Slowly, Melanie turned her head around, searched, until her eyes landed on Alex who stood not more than five feet from her, next to the passenger side of the car. The expression in her eyes as she looked over her shoulder at him was filled with excitement and apprehension.

He opened his mouth to ask her what she was doing here but the words wouldn't come out. So he waited.

Melanie closed the door to the car and walked around the hood, stopped directly in front him. She looked up into his eyes and nervous energy poured off of her. She licked her lips. Alex wanted to kiss her right then but again, he waited.

"Hi," she finally said, her words a whisper that blended in with the early morning breeze.

He didn't say anything. He was still too shocked. Melanie started to fidget. Her feet stepped back and forth like she was standing on hot coals. Her hands twisted around the cell phone she held. She looked down at the ground and took a deep breath, her chest rose and fell heavily. When she looked back up, he watched her determination come through. She stood still and straight and lifted her chin high.

"Something's happened, Alex."

That put him on alert.

"What's wrong? Are you hurt? Did someone mess with you?" He reached out to run his free hand up and down her arms, looked over her body to check for any sign that she had been harmed.

"No." She shook her head back and forth and stilled his roaming hand with a palm on his forearm. "It's quite the opposite, in fact. Someone helped me."

"You came over fifteen hundred miles to tell me that someone helped you? I don't understand."

"I'm not sure I do either."

"Tell me what happened, honey," he spoke, his tone soft but firm as he gave her no room to be uncooperative.

"I will. I'm going to. But first I need to say… you need to know that… Crap! This was so much easier in my head." She closed her eyes again and ran a hand over her make-up free face. She looked down at the phone still in her hands, fiddled with it for a second, then looked back at his face. A slow beat started to play from her cell.

Music? She's playing music?

"Melanie, what are you____"

"Just… just listen, Alex."

He nodded and listened to the song play. He recognized the voices of Lady Antebellum, thanks to his sister and her constantly putting one of their CDs on repeat. Snippets of the first verse caught his ear, made him perk up in hopeful understanding.

Walking in the wrong direction. Building walls around my heart. Time to let it go.

Alex gazed deep into Melanie's eyes, got lost in the aquamarine depths while he searched for the words she tried to relay with this song. Then the chorus began and he could feel his breathing pick up faster than before as her message came out loud and clear in the broken pieces that registered in his brain.

I'm ready to feel now... No longer afraid...
Time to move on... Without the fear...
I'm ready to love again.

He reached down and set his coffee mug on the ground, took the phone from Melanie on his way back up and kept his eyes locked on hers. He turned the volume down to a barely there echo–because no way did he want to stop listening to what she was saying through the lyrics–and reached over her shoulder, laid the phone on the roof of her car. With his hands now free, Alex reached up and cupped her face. His fingers tangled in her hair, thumbs ran along her jaw and he tilted her chin up to keep their connection.

"Are you really sure you mean it?" he questioned quietly, afraid that if his words were voiced too loudly they would carry this moment away from them.

She nodded in his hold. He blew out a quick breath as a smile started to creep on his lips. Just as he brought his mouth down to hers, Melanie stopped him, her palm light on his chest.

"I'm not there, yet, Alex. But..." She licked her lips again. "But I'm ready to try. For you. For us."

Aaron's words from the night before came back in that moment. *"Tell her,"* he'd said. Melanie might not be there. But he was.

"I love you, Melanie."

He watched her eyes for any hint of fear or the need to run and saw none. Her mouth formed a silent "O" but no sound came out. Her shoulders sagged–*in relief, maybe?*–and her eyes fluttered closed for only a second before they were open again. She regarded him with careful hope. Just as she started to say something, he spoke up first. He wanted to make sure she understood what his intentions were.

"I heard what you said. That you're not there yet, but you're ready to try. And that's fine. It's perfect. I just wanted you to know that when you are ready, I'm here. And that I love you." He swallowed thickly as he fought to make her see the truth in his words. "What happened back in L.A., what I asked, it wasn't some slip of the tongue. I meant it Melanie. I want to marry you."

"Why?"

He fought off a weak smile at her whispered question that showed how self-conscious and vulnerable she still was.

"Because you're it for me."

FOREVER GRATEFUL

Tears glistened in her eyes, made the blue-green color look like a tropical ocean. And when she smiled, two escaped from the corners of her lids, ran down her cheeks in a happy escape. Alex leaned forward and kissed them away. The salty moisture made him want so much more. He pulled back slightly and rested his forehead against hers and asked the question that had hounded him since he saw her step out of the car.

"Can I kiss you now, honey? I need to. I'm dying here."

When she gave a feminine sniffle and nodded her head yes, Alex didn't waste another moment. He dove in and took her lips with a yearning that was so deep, so elemental, he groaned with the contact.

Her soft lips fit against his perfectly, molded to his like a second skin. The tears that fell from her eyes as he kissed her seeped in between their mouths and smoothed the way for him to turn his head and deepen the kiss. He kept his left hand on her jaw but brought his right arm down, wrapped it around her back, grabbed her waist and held her tightly to him.

Melanie inched her hands up from his chest to twine around his neck. When he gently coaxed her to open her lips for him, she grabbed onto his hair and held on for dear life. But she never stopped kissing him.

And when her tongue tentatively touched his, shy but resolved, he held her tighter and danced his tongue with hers.

Their mouths moved in flawless harmony with each other. When Alex tilted his head left to kiss her deeper, Melanie moved hers right to accommodate. When Alex kissed her harder, she gave her lips to him willingly. And when he backed off a little, she took control and kissed him forcefully, never willing to break the passionate contact.

Both of Alex's hands roamed over her back now, fit her into the protective cocoon of his body. He wanted to block out the rest of the world while he kept Melanie in this bubble where it was only them. Their embrace. This kiss.

But he knew when his limits were being reached. He wanted to kiss her, to romance her. Not scare her away because he moved too fast.

He slowed the kiss, brought it down a level and placed small caresses across the seam of her lips. He kissed her cheeks, her nose, her forehead. One last lingering touch on her lips and he leaned back, just a few inches to see her face. He smiled at the dreamy way her head lolled to one side. When she opened her eyes they were glazed over with desire but cleared quickly at the loss of contact. Alex ran his thumb along her lower lip, damp from their kiss.

"How did you know where to find me?" he asked as he removed his hand from her mouth and tucked her hair behind her ear.

"That's what you want to ask right now? You kiss me like it's the last thing you're going to do on this earth and the only thing you can think to say is 'How did I find you?'"

"Sorry. I'm trying to get my mind off of that kiss before I forget how to be a gentleman," he teased. "And for the record, I do plan on making sure that the last thing I do is kiss you."

Melanie shook her head at him but her sweet smile belied the annoyance she tried to pull off.

"I called Brin last night when I got to the airport. Around nine, I think. Well, eleven here. I told her I had to see you and asked where would be the best place to find you. She asked what time I'd be in Lake Shores and when I told her, she said to just come here." Melanie shrugged, like her explanation was both easy and obvious at the same time.

"Wait. When did she tell you this?" Alex asked as suspicions ran through his mind.

"Here it would have been around eleven, maybe eleven-thirty. Why?"

That little... he got a call at eleven last night and I'd bet my best pair of boots that it was Brin, setting this up, Alex thought to himself as he replayed last night and the out-of-leftfield question from his brother-in-law.

He thought it was strange that Jax had waited until the last minute to ask for Alex's help loading the cattle. But last night he hadn't paid too much attention because he'd been too focused on finding the time to go see Melanie.

"No reason. Let's get out of here. I've got something I

want to show you."

Alex threw his right arm around Melanie's shoulders and guided her back to the car. After she sat down in the passenger seat, he leaned in and kissed her quickly on the lips, straightened and closed the door. As he walked around the back of the car, he looked into the living room window of the house to his left.

There, in the glow of a lamp, stood Brin and Jax. His sister was in front of her husband and held a steaming mug in both of her hands. Jax's forearms rested on her shoulders. They both smiled and gave him a wave when he shook his head at them. A laugh bubbled out at their perfect meddling.

Alex slid into the driver's seat, started the car and reached for Melanie's hand, linked their fingers together.

"So where are you taking me?" Melanie asked him and smiled when he kissed each of the knuckles on her left hand. He rested their joined hands on his thigh.

"To my favorite place."

.   .   .   .   .

I can't believe I actually did it. Hopped on a plane and flew to Texas with no plans except to tell Alex that I was ready.

Mel smiled at her thoughts as the scenery rolled by out the window of her rental car. That Alex was driving. It was early in the morning, only six-thirty, and dawn was slowly turning the sky from that deep navy of night to a dark orange and violet, the colors mixing together in the sky like they were on an artist's pallet. The gently rolling hills came to life as the day awakened, greens dotted with yellow wildflowers flowing in a breeze. Tall oak trees began to cast shadows around their branches.

"I thought there were only fourteen hundred miles between us," Mel said as she stared out the window to her right.

Alex coughed and laughed at her out of the blue question before he asked, "What? Where did that come from?"

"Back at the ranch, when I told you that someone helped me. You said, "you came over fifteen hundred miles…" I thought it was fourteen." She looked over to Alex.

"Fourteen hundred to Houston. By the time you drive here, to Lake Shores, it's just over fifteen." He was trying not to laugh at her, Mel could see it in the way he rolled his lips inward.

Before she had a chance to tell him that she knew that– it'd just been a long night and her brain wasn't quite working–the car started to go up an incline and Mel looked forward to find that they were driving over a bridge. A really steep bridge. As they crested the top and began their descent, Mel's breath caught in her throat at the sight before her.

The ocean, as far as the eye could see, stretched out for miles in front of and on either side of them.

She grew up in California; seeing the ocean was just a regular day for her. But with the rising sun only lighting part of the water and the white-capped waves crashing into the shore, it felt like something new.

A small part of her brain whispered that it was because she was seeing the water and beach as a different person, a faithful person. And she believed it.

This. This is what Alex had been trying to get her to see when he'd been in L.A. The beauty that her heart and mind weren't ready to accept then, but are now.

Alex's fingers tightened around hers and she looked over to see him glancing at her with a smile on his lips. He drove straight after coming off of the bridge, right onto the sand, and hung a left. He parked by the dunes and turned off the engine.

"You know I live by the beach, right? I've lived there my whole life." Mel couldn't resist teasing him.

"Yeah. But that's your place. I wanted my woman to see mine."

His woman?

Any other man would have gotten an earful at calling her 'their woman.' But not Alex. She'd be anything he wanted her to be.

"Come on. Walk with me to the water."

FOREVER GRATEFUL

They both got out of the car and met at the trunk, took off their shoes and placed them on top of the car. Mel was still wearing her old jeans and Alex had on a pair, too, so they both rolled them up to their calves. Then he took her hand and led her to the beach's edge where the warm water gently lapped at their toes.

They stayed in that spot for a few minutes, watching the sun come up over the horizon, and saw several fish jump out of the water, their scales glowing silver in the sun's rays. Alex turned and started walking down the beach with her hand still enclosed in his. The place was quiet and still, except for the few people who had braved the early morning hours to fish in the surf.

"When I was a kid, we used to come here all the time," Alex said, breaking the silence. "The whole Lambert family. Me, my parents, Aaron, Brin. We'd all meet up with aunts and uncles, cousins. It'd look like a circus with all of the cars and barbeque pits and volleyball nets. Kids running around yelling and adults making fools out of themselves playing chicken in the ocean. But we had such a blast." He sounded sad as he reminisced about that time.

"As we got older we weren't able to come as often. There were always sports' tournaments, church obligations, school functions. Life just got too busy, you know? By the time I was a teenager, we rarely ever saw the whole family together, just a few people here and there. It made me miss those times we'd spent out here. The times when everything was simple.

"I'd come out by myself on the weekends when I was a junior and senior in high school, sit in the sand and just watch the waves. Sometimes I'd bring a fishing pole and throw a line out. But mostly I would just think. Wish for those days when family had come first."

They stopped walking and Mel watched Alex as he watched those same waves he used to stare after as a young man. There was a furrowing in his brow as he remembered his past and Mel wondered why his mind was so troubled about it when it sounded like his childhood was wonderful.

Compared to hers, anyway.

Just as she was ready to ask him why he'd brought her out here if the memories only made him sad, he turned to her. He wrapped his arms around her waist and Mel felt him link his fingers together behind her back, caging her in his embrace.

She walked her hands up his forearms–taking a moment to enjoy the sinewy muscle that jumped under her fingertips– and placed her hands on his shoulders. His hard chest pressed against hers, made her feel soft and feminine. His strong legs stood on either side of hers and kept her locked inside of his hold.

But she didn't feel suffocated or panicked like she normally would because memories from that night crept into her mind. She felt protected and safe because she knew that Alex would never hurt her.

She looked up to his face and found him staring at her. His beautiful eyes roamed over every inch of her face and she swore she could feel it as if he were caressing her with his fingers. His hair blew with the breeze coming off of the water and a thick lock landed on his forehead. His jaw–that looked like chiseled stone–was covered in with light brown stubble. She brought her left hand up to push that wayward curl back and ran her hand down along his cheek, enjoying the tickle that stubble caused on her palm.

"I brought you here because..." he stopped and swallowed hard, his Adam's apple bobbing with the movement. Mel had to fight the urge to lean forward and kiss that part of his throat. She wanted to give him a chance to finish what he was about to say.

"The reason I decided to get out of the Navy, not make a career out of it, was because I was ready to get back to that simple life. The one where family is what matters. Not a job or money or status. Family. I brought you here because I want that. With you. Marr____" Mel placed her hand over Alex's mouth, stopped him from finishing what he was about to say. Again.

"Not yet, Alex. I don't want to have to tell you no again but I will if you ask me that. Just wait for me to get there and be patient, please," she begged as she removed her hand.

"I've waited my whole life for you, Melanie. I don't mind waiting a little longer."

She smiled, for the sweet sincerity of his words as well as in relief at his agreement. And she knew he meant it, too. He would wait as long as it took for her to come to grips with the concept of a future for them.

So Mel decided now was as good a time as any to tell him what brought on the sudden trip to Lake Shores. And hopefully they could start moving closer to that future.

She turned to watch the water, imitating how Alex had been as he'd watched the waves when he'd told her of his family coming here so often when he was younger. Mel thought that if looking out at the ocean made opening yourself up easier, then she would take any bit of help she could.

So she kept her gaze on the water that was a dark silvery-grey as she started to talk.

"Do you remember when I talked to you about my Gramma and how she was a Christian?" she began and then continued without waiting for a response. "After I asked you to tell me about God, I started thinking about her. And I remembered always seeing her with her bible close by. Sometimes she had it open on her lap; other times it was just somewhere within reach. I'd forgotten how much I associated seeing that black leather-bound book with all things Gramma.

FOREVER GRATEFUL

"When she died almost seven years ago, I was eighteen. I was out on Christmas break from my freshman year of college. I'd come home to spend the holidays with my parents. But they neglected to tell me that they were going to be in D.C. for some protest about people cutting down pine and fir trees to use as Christmas trees in their homes."

Mel gave a short laugh at the absurdity of what her parents had done. It was Christmas. A time to be with family and enjoy one another and all they'd thought about was they're next 'statement'.

"So it was just me and Gramma at her place and honestly, I was happy about that. She lived in this little cottage style home that she and my Grandpa bought right after they got married. He died before I was born so I never knew him but I could pick out his picture from twenty yards away because Gramma had them everywhere in the house. It only had two bedrooms and one bathroom but the living room and dining room were huge and it had this great country kitchen. She was always in there cooking.

"We made chocolate chip cookies, laced popcorn on string and wrapped it around her little five foot artificial tree, wrapped presents. She put on my old Alvin and the Chipmunks Christmas cd and laughed while I sang *Christmas Song* in my most nasally voice. She told me as long as she had her granddaughter with her, she'd have the best present in the world. It was probably the greatest

Aimee Martin

holiday I'd ever had.

"When I woke up on the twenty-third, I went to make some coffee and grab the newspaper from her front porch. She was usually awake before me but we'd stayed up late the night before so I didn't think too much about her still being in bed. By the time I finished my second cup of coffee and I still hadn't heard a peep out of her, I decided I'd check on her.

"I'll never forget what she looked like. Like she was sleeping and dreaming with this little smile on her lips. The only thing that made me realize different was how pale she was, almost gray. I walked to her bed and felt for a pulse but didn't find one. I knew she was gone. I called the police and told them what had happened. They came out with the coroner who said that she'd passed away peacefully in her sleep and told me to call my parents. I did and do you know what my mother said?"

Now Mel looked over at Alex who was watching her intently, empathy evident on his handsome face as he gently shook his head no.

"She said, "There's nothing we can do for Gramma now. She's part of the universe again so you need to let her rest. We'll be home in time for New Year's." That's it. No crying, no anger, no coming home to help. I was furious and I think that's when I started having doubts about their beliefs. Luckily Gramma already had most of her funeral arrangements made but I had to put the ball in motion because she had listed me as next of kin. I guess she knew my Mom wouldn't put much effort into a funeral. We buried her next to my Grandpa on the twenty-sixth. I boxed up everything that I knew she wouldn't want to be sold or given away and put it all in a storage building. Then I contacted a real estate agent, had them put the place on the market and went back to school on the thirtieth, before my parents came back."

Mel turned back to that silver-gray water as she went on.

"The point of that story is that I wanted you to understand how much I loved her, my Gramma. I appreciated her and admired her and it nearly broke me when she died. When you started to tell me about God, I felt this pull from her. I swear it's like she was calling to me, telling me to go to that storage building and get her things.

"So I did. I went and got one box, just one, and went home to open it. Laying on the top, wrapped up in white tissue paper, was her bible. It took me two weeks of staring at it on my coffee table but I finally opened it."

She stopped when she heard Alex's sharp inhale and his hand tightened around her fingers. She squeezed back to let him know that she was okay but kept her gaze forward.

"There was a letter inside. It was addressed to me and when I opened it, it was… it was from her. She wrote it about six weeks before she died. There was quite a bit in there but in a nutshell, she was explaining what Christianity and faith meant. And she listed a chapter she wanted me to read. Ephesians 2. I read it about three or four times before I finally saw it. The verse that made it all click into place.

"It said that by grace you are saved through faith and that it's the gift of God. And I got it. I just…" she paused and turned to face Alex one more time. "I just got it. I survived that rape and it was a gift. I realized that I needed to stop thinking about the bad of that night and focus on all the good that has come since.

"It felt so amazing to have that clarity that I started reading more. For hours, Alex. Right before I was ready to call it a night, another one popped out at me. *Let love be without dissimulation; abhor that which is evil*–"

"*Cleave to that which is good,*" Alex finished.

"How did you know that?"

"It's from *Romans*, my favorite book in the bible."

Alex grabbed Mel's free hand and wrapped his arms around her. He rested their joined hands on the small of her back, keeping her immobile in his embrace. He leaned forward and ran his nose along the tip of hers and Mel's eyes fell closed at the tender stroke. She felt his lips brush a soft kiss where his nose had just been and opened her eyes to see him staring at her.

"So you think I'm good, huh?" he asked with a smirk.

Mel slowly shook her head. She leaned her chest against

the hard planes of Alex's and brought her mouth within an inch of his, whispering against his lips, "No. I think you're perfect. For me."

And as Mel laid her mouth on Alex's, leisurely tasting him, she felt the truth in her heart even if she was too scared to say it, yet.

She felt love.

. . . . .

Alex pulled Melanie closer into his chest as they watched the water darken in front of them, the pale blue from the day turning into a deep cobalt, while the sun set behind them.

He sat on the sand with his legs propped up and Melanie rested in the V of his body, his knees bracketed on either side of her. His arms were wrapped around her middle and she lazily ran her fingertips over the skin of his forearms, making him shiver inside at her soft touch.

They were still at the beach, had been there all day. After Melanie had told him about the letter from her Gramma, they went back to the car and sat on the trunk while the morning grew warm and beach patrons started showing up. Very little was said for the better part of an hour. Alex had mulled over what Melanie had admitted, tried to find a way to help her see that what she had just been through–her awakening faith with the help of her grandmother's letter–was all she needed to put her trust in him and their future. To move forward.

It was there, in the scriptures.

Melanie, while not unhappy by any means, had seemed more contemplative to Alex. He'd caught sight of her several times with a frown on her face, like she was thinking too hard or struggling with a decision. But then she would look over and notice him staring and quickly wipe that frown away, replacing it with a smile. He knew she was just trying to work it all out in her mind so he never brought it up.

He was happy just to be with her.

They'd grabbed their shoes as the morning turned into early afternoon and had walked two miles down the beach to an old shack of a restaurant called Blacktip's, the name burned into a massive wooden shark that stood guard over the entryway. The small building was constructed of hardy plank and covered in a faded yellow paint, with screen windows that had seen better days and doors that were loose and squeaky on their hinges. There was a concrete porch all the way around for people to sit out and enjoy the ocean while they ate, white and green plastic tables and chairs the only furniture so that wet bathing suits didn't do any damage to anything more expensive.

He and Melanie had walked inside to the counter and each ordered fish tacos with sides of cole slaw and fries, then taken their baskets out to the porch to eat. It was almost eleven-thirty by the time they sat down, the sand underneath the table and chairs scraping against their shoes like sandpaper.

They talked while they ate, some about the food and a little about the different people on the beach. A handful of teenaged boys tried to show off in front of Melanie by fighting over a soccer ball with their feet ten yards away. But instead only made her laugh when three of them got tangled together and face-planted in the sand.

A couple of little girls that couldn't have been more than six or seven ran from the beach up to the restaurant, beating their trailing parents inside to order their own lunch. Alex noted the way Melanie wistfully stared after the tow-headed girls and wondered if her biological clock was ticking.

And then he'd remembered imagining her pregnant with his baby just two months ago and said a silent prayer that that time would come for them.

The afternoon wore on, more people came and went from Blacktip's, and still the two sat in their plastic chairs at their plastic table. Whether they were laughing together or just sitting silently, the entire day was just comfortable. And easy.

When the dinner crowd had started to trickle in and a local band–The Red Water Highways–had started to tune up for their Saturday night show, Melanie and Alex had finally left the diner and headed back to the car.

He'd asked her if she was ready to leave but Melanie had been adamant that she wanted to be here when the sun went down. "From dawn to dusk on the beach with you" is what she'd said she wanted.

So here they were, watching as dusk came and went and the night began to fill with stars again, their twinkles like miniature lights millions of miles away playing a game of flashlight tag.

Was it really just this morning that I watched the stars disappear for the day? Alex thought.

So much had happened today. It made seeing Melanie get out of that car, completely surprising him, seem like a lifetime ago instead of just twelve hours.

"Melanie?" he spoke softly, leaning in to whisper in her ear and grinned at the way she shivered when his breath touched her skin.

"Yeah?"

"I love you."

"I know."

And that was enough, that she knew how he felt and wasn't running scared from it. It was a step in the right direction. Alex was going to take Jaxson's advice and keep on telling her until she was ready to fully accept it and return his feelings.

Melanie turned her upper body in Alex's arms and

watched his face, a smile on her face.

"What?" he asked, wondering why she had moved.

"You don't even realize you do that, do you?"

"Realize I do what?"

"Hum. You were humming." She placed her right hand on his cheek, running her palm over his day old beard. "What was that song?"

Alex had to think for a second because she was right; most of the time he didn't know he was humming. But when he finally realized what song it was, he laughed and leaned his cheek farther into her hand, thinking that no truer words had ever been spoken. Or sung.

"It's a song from Green River Ordinance called *Dancing Shoes*."

"Do you know the words?"

"I know the ones that matter… My loving arms are for you."

Whether it was the words or Alex humming them that caused it, he wasn't sure. But no sooner were the lyrics out of his mouth than Melanie turned completely around and sat up on her knees. Her arms wrapped around his neck, her hands latched onto the hair at the nape of his neck.

Alex brought his hands to her waist and marveled at how small she felt, how perfect. With her face barely a hairsbreadth away from him, he could see her eyes shimmer in the moonlight, could see them thin as her smile grew wider.

And then she brought her mouth to his and he lost all train of thought.

Her lips were soft and full. The breathy moan that escaped her parted mouth egged him on and he brought her body flush with his, cupped the back of her head to hold her still. Her hands worked their way down and around his back, sliding under his shirt, and the feel of her cool fingers tickling his spine was almost his undoing.

He shuddered in desire and they both fell back to the sand.

Alex turned his body, never taking his lips from hers, until he was resting on his left elbow and his right hand slowly worked down the column of her throat. He smiled at the sound of disapproval she made when he moved his mouth over to follow the same path, teasing her erratic pulse with the tip of his tongue and moving over to nibble on the lobe of her ear.

He slowly worked his lips across her neck, placed a wet kiss in the hollow of her throat, and made his way back up to her waiting lips.

But he stopped when he saw the look in her eyes; one of longing but also of fear.

Dammit, Alex! Get control.

"I'm sorry, darlin'. It seems I have a hard time restraining myself around you. Please, please don't be afraid of me."

"I'm not afraid of you, Alex. I'm afraid of me. What if I can't ever… you know…"

"I promise you, Melanie. We will not make love until we are married. I don't want you to have any doubts as to why I'm here. It's not for your body or your money or your name. I'm here for you. I always will be."

"You sound awfully sure of yourself, Mr. Lambert."

Alex sighed in relief at her teasing, glad that he hadn't frightened her off with his inability to control his wanderings.

"No more than I'm sure of you. Of us. You'll see it, too, when you're ready."

"I'm not so sure about that." She turned her face away, looking out at the miles of sand.

"Why?" He brought her face back with his hand on her cheek, frowning when he felt the wetness left there from tears. "Why don't you think you'll see?"

"I haven't told you my whole story, Alex. And I'm afraid that when I do you might not feel the same way."

"You listen to me, Melanie. Nothing, and I mean *nothing*, is going to change the way I feel about you."

"We'll see," she whispered, the words floating away with the sea breeze blowing over them.

Aimee Martin

Chapter 15

"Wrath is cruel, and anger is outrageous; but
who is able to stand before jealousy?"
Proverbs 27:4

August 25, 2014

Mel sat at her desk and fought the urge to wad the letter
into a ball and throw it into the trashcan at her feet. There
was no reason for the envy flowing through her. She'd made
her decision those years before and she needed to accept it.
Getting mad at her best friend wouldn't change the past.

But no matter how much she told herself that the anger
and jealousy she felt was unjustifiable, Mel just couldn't
quite bring herself to believe it. She closed her eyes and took
a deep breath, tried to relax her emotions and still her
resentful thoughts.

Aimee Martin

She read the letter again.

August 21, 2014

Dear family and friends,

We would like to introduce you to our baby boy, Brandon. No, he isn't here yet! He is expected to arrive on February 13, 2015, just in time for Valentine's Day. We are so excited and he is so beautiful that we couldn't wait to share him with you.

We also wanted to prepare you for a little something extra.

Brandon will be born with an additional 21st chromosome. You probably know someone with this condition. It's called Down Syndrome. But did you know that there is so much more that can be done today to give our baby a bright, wonderful future? Our baby will be born healthy. A fetal echocardiogram has ruled out any heart defects! We rejoice that God has fearfully and wonderfully knit him within the womb, and we praise Him for the awesome gift that Brandon is.

We hope you will love him as much as we do. But we do understand that not everyone will share our views. We ask two things; please do not ask us to consider termination or adoption. He is our son and our joy over his impending birth holds no bounds. We are alright. We had a brief moment of concern but we placed our worries at the foot of the cross. All that remains is love.

Secondly, we ask you to share our blessing. Get to know our baby. When you do, we know you will love him.

God bless you all,

Brin, Jaxson and Brandon

Shaking her head at the joy and optimism bouncing off of the letter, she asked herself yet again what was wrong with her.

Brin is going to have a baby with a genetic disorder. And she is going to love that baby unconditionally. What's so wrong with me that I couldn't love mine?

But Mel knew the answer to that before the thought had even finished writing itself out in her mind. That baby had been conceived because of rape. And Mel had felt lost, scared, alone with no one to turn to for help or advice.

So she had done the only thing that had made sense at the time. The only thing that she thought would help her to put that ugly time behind her.

She had aborted the baby. Her baby.

She didn't know then that her baby was a gift from God, regardless of the circumstances. She'd committed one of the greatest sins.

How could He ever forgive her when she couldn't even forgive herself?

Aimee Martin

And that–Mel's failure to forgive and believe that God can forgive, too–was the crux of her reticence of moving forward with Alex.

Alex deserved a whole woman, an unblemished woman. She wanted that for him, wanted nothing but happiness for him. And despite Mel's feelings of hope for a future and the love she felt growing every day, she didn't think she could ever be that woman for Alex.

Not when her sin would be hanging over her head and her heart for the rest of her days.

Mel put her head on her desk and cried, tears soaked the letter underneath her face. Her shoulders shook with her sobs and her stomach cramped with the emotional pain that was released with her whimpers.

She cried for what had been taken from her; her innocence.

She cried for what she had so recklessly abandoned; her baby.

She cried for what she was about to lose; Alex.

Because Mel knew that she was going to have to give him up.

Chapter 16

*"Bear ye one another's burderns, and so
fulfill the law of Christ." Galatians 6:2*

September 6, 2014

"Hey Dad," Alex said to his father, Mitch, when he
walked into the kitchen for a cup of coffee.

The man was sitting at the table with his own mug and
the newspaper laid out before him.

"Morning, son," he replied without looking up from the
funny pages.

Alex took his steaming cup of joe and sat down across
from his father, stared out the window to his left. The sun
was rising slowly on this Saturday morning, kind of like
Alex, and he could still see the dew that coated the lawn like
glittering diamonds. He brought his mug to his lips and blew

on the liquid before he took a sip, hoping the Columbian roast would work quickly to get his brain moving, something that seemed to take more effort over the last few days.

"You got something on your mind, Alex? You're staring at the yard like it holds the answers to the world's biggest problems." His Dad's voice brought Alex's gaze over.

"No. I mean yeah, something's on my mind. It's nothing." He looked down into his coffee and sighed before he looked back up to meet his father's gaze. One that clearly said "BS."

"It's Melanie."

"Ah. I had a feeling it was about a woman. You want to talk about it? I mean, I don't know her very well. At all, really. But I've found that most women are the same when it comes to confusing men."

Alex chuckled at his Dad and the man's predilection of placing all females in a mystifying category like mythical creatures.

"That's just it, Dad. Melanie isn't like most women. She's different. Special."

"Then what's the problem?"

"It's just… When she came down here about a month ago I thought we had hit a milestone. That we were going to start moving forward in our relationship. I told her I loved her, that I wanted to marry her. And I meant it. She hasn't said it back, yet, but I know she feels the same way. I know it.

"But something's changed in the last couple of weeks. I'm not sure what it is but I can feel her pushing me away. It's like she's trying to, I don't know, isolate herself or something. And I can't figure out why or how to pull her back. I'm afraid I'm losing her." This last he whispered. His fear choked his throat so much that the words were hard to get out.

Silence stretched between them while Alex thought of Melanie and his Dad quietly took in everything Alex had said. Several moments passed before the older man finally spoke up.

"You really do love her, don't you?" At Alex's affirmative nod, Mitch continued. "Then you need to go to her. You fight for her, with whatever it takes. Make her see that you belong together."

"But Aaron and Jax said that I should just be patient and keep telling her I love her. And that eventually, when she's ready, she'll realize that she loves me, too."

"And you believe a couple of wet-behind-the-ears newlywed men? Over me? Boy, I've got more experience with stubborn women in my pinky finger than those two have in their entire bodies. Combined!"

"Yeah, I guess you're right." Alex laughed. "Still, they managed to catch them a couple of great women so they must be doing something right."

His Dad leaned back in his chair, took his coffee with him and held the mug right in front of his mouth before gloating, "Who do you think taught them all they know?" He smirked and took a sip of his drink before he set it back on the table. The smile disappeared as seriousness came back.

"I know I'm not Jax's father and that I didn't really teach him anything. His old man did a fine job raising that boy and I've been honored to call him son-in-law. But I did raise Aaron. And you. And I didn't teach y'all to just sit back, twiddling your thumbs, waiting for life to fall into place. You want something, you go after it."

Alex distractedly nodded his head at his Dad's words. The man was right. Alex had never been one to sit by and wait for anything in his life. Why should it be any different with Melanie?

It shouldn't. I should be going after her harder than I've gone for anything in my life.

"You're right, Dad. Absolutely right."

"Of course I am. The question is… what are you going to do about it?"

Alex stood from the table and pushed his chair in, his hands rested on the back of the slatted wood as he stared his father straight in the eyes, and conviction made his voice stronger.

"I'm going to find a way to go after my woman."

An hour later Alex stood outside the front door to his

sister's house and waited for someone to answer it.
Impatiently, he pushed to doorbell two more times, thinking
that maybe they hadn't heard it the first three times. Then he
knocked on the big oak door.

While his hand was still raised, the door swung open to
reveal an angry looking Jaxson.

"Calm down, Alex," Jax said, relaxing only a little when
he saw his brother-in-law on the other side of the threshold.
"What are you doing here? It's eight-thirty in the morning.
On a Saturday. It's the only day I get to sleep in and you're
taking that away from me."

Alex pushed by him, ignoring the fact that Jax was still
in his boxers with a pearl snap shirt thrown on, unbuttoned,
and walked into the entryway without an invitation.

"I know and I'm sorry. But I had to come over." He
looked around the corner of the hall expecting to see his
sister coming from the direction of their bedroom. "Where's
Brin?" Alex asked.

"She and Tina went to Houston today to do some
shopping for the nursery."

Well that explains my Mom's absence this morning, Alex
thought.

"They probably won't be back til late tonight so if you're
looking to talk to her, you might want to come by
tomorrow."

"No, I actually needed to talk to you." Alex stared at Jax

and stood up straighter. He took a deep breath, fortified his resolve. "I came by to tell you that I quit."

Silence.

No "What do you mean you quit?" or "What's this all about?" or even a simple "Fine." Jaxson just stood there with his arms crossed over his chest, staring at Alex like he had a third eye. His height and the deadly stare might have been intimidating if Alex didn't know what a softie Jax really was. But after three minutes, and still nothing, he did begin to fidget a little.

"Is this about Mel?" Jax finally asked, his head cocked to the side as he studied Alex.

"Yeah. Listen, I appreciate the job and all the help you've given me since I've been home. It means more than I could ever tell you. And I'm really sorry if this is putting you in a bind. But I have to go to her. I feel like something is happening with us, with what we've been building, and I need to go get her, to make her mine."

"Alex, I____"

"Please don't try to talk me out of this. I know what you and Aaron told me. And I've listened to it for the last month. But circumstances have changed. What would you do in my shoes? Would you let Brinley walk away?"

"No." Jax smiled lovingly at the mention of his wife. "I would have gone after her with guns blazing. But I wasn't going try and talk you out of going."

"You weren't?"

"No. I was just gonna tell you that you'll always have a job here. If you want it. So go, take all the time you need. And when you get things sorted out with Mel, if you find yourself back here in Lake Shores, The Burnt Aggie will be waiting."

"Thank you, Jax. For everything."

Alex leaned in and gave his brother-in-law a half hug and Jax did the same, both of them slapping the other hard on the back before pulling away.

"Now get outta here and go get your girl."

.   .   .   .   .

"Slow down, Kass. Easy girl," Mel said to her dog, the words wheezing out of her mouth as she tried to keep up with the pup.

After spending the day cooped up inside, fighting down the urge to pick up the phone and call Alex, Mel had decided that she needed a little fresh air. If she would have known how much energy had been bottled up inside her dog by being indoors all day, she probably would have reconsidered the jog.

The evening heat had waned with the setting sun and a slight northern breeze helped to cool her skin that was flushed red with the exercise.

Aimee Martin

The sidewalks were fairly empty, most people getting ready for a night out on the town, so Mel and Kass were able to make their way back to the condo without suffering through too much crowding.

They rounded the corner of Wilshire and Hope Street, turned left, and Mel saw the revolving glass doors of her building. She pulled Kassie to a walk and raised her hands above her head with the leash in her left. She took deep breaths, tried to slow her heart rate. She waved to Paul, the doorman, as she and the dog passed through the doors and headed straight for the elevator.

I've met my quota for exercise today. I'll take the lazy way up if I want to.

Alone in the elevator, Mel bent over and stretched her hamstrings some, moved her hips from side to side. Kassie apparently thought it was time to play when she started nipping Mel's ponytail, causing her to lose her balance and fall back on her butt.

"Kassie!" she scolded the dog but couldn't hold in the laughter as her sweet pup bounded into her lap for kisses. She was still laughing when the ding sounded and the elevator doors slid open.

Mel tried to get around Kass to keep the doors from closing but her dog wouldn't move fast enough. Frustration started to creep in when she said, "Kass, no," and only got tackled again. She landed hard and tried to silence her muttered "oomph" right as a hand darted out to hold the door open.

And then the voice, gliding through the narrow opening, filled her ears with its deep timbre and caused her skin to break out in goose-bumps.

"Looks like you need a hand."

The elevator door finally started to recede, revealed a set of long legs encased in faded denim, muscular thighs straining against the fabric that was beginning to tear from years of wear. Next came a tanned and corded forearm partially covered with a white long-sleeve. Then the chest, concealed in what Mel now knew was a white henley t-shirt, with a hint of enticing tanned throat visible at the neck.

And finally–*Finally!*–came the face.

A chiseled jaw supported a set of full lips that were curved into a half smile, begging to be kissed. The straight nose and pronounced cheekbones added a softening to the raw masculinity. And the most beautiful set of honey-colored eyes gazed down at her with a mix of amusement, yearning and love.

"Alex," she breathed, his name like a plea on her lips.

He squatted down in front of her on the elevator floor and placed his hands around her elbows. Callused palms sent electric tingles racing up her arms and made her shiver. He slowly guided her up so that she was standing again. Keeping his knees bent slightly so that his eyes were level with hers, he brought his mouth close to hers.

"Hi, baby." And he laid his lips across hers.

Mel threw her arms around his neck, got lost in him, before she heard a loud yelp. She and Alex both jerked back and Mel realized that she had accidentally jerked on Kass' leash.

"Oops, I'm sorry girl." Mel bent down to rub her dog's head who whined a little in return, moving her eyes to Alex like she was waiting for an introduction. Mel stood straight again and asked Alex, "You didn't get to meet her before, did you?"

"No. You said you'd put her in your bathroom so that she wouldn't bother me. But I love dogs." He squatted down so that he could pet her dog.

"Oh, Alex, be careful! Kass…" she stopped, her head tilting as she watched her dog lick Alex in the face and roll over onto her back for a belly rub.

He laughed and obliged, scraping her belly and calling her a "good girl" before looking back up to Mel.

"What were you saying?"

"Nothing. Kassie, well, she's usually a little standoffish with people she doesn't know. Sometimes protective, mainly over me. It's one of the reasons I got her. But you… she just… how did you do that?"

"I told you I love dogs," he rubbed Kass one more time and stood back up. "And they love me, too."

So do I, Mel thought but didn't have the courage to say.
"What are you doing here, Alex?"

"Why don't we get out of this elevator, into your place
and I'll tell you all about it?"

Without asking he took Kassie's leash from Mel's hand
and walked down the hall, stopped in front of Mel's door
where there was a navy carry-on duffel bag sitting on the
floor.

She watched him, dumbfounded, until the elevator doors
began to close again. She quickly ran out to avoid getting
stuck and heard Alex laughing as she pulled her key from the
hidden pocket inside her running shorts.

Walking over to him, she shot him a scowl while she
unlocked the door and strode inside with Alex–still
chuckling–and Kassie at her heels.

Tossing her key on the entry table, Mel headed into the
kitchen and grabbed two bottles of water from the fridge.
She walked over and sat in one corner of the couch while
Alex unhooked Kassie's leash. He tossed it on the coffee
table and sat down on the couch in the opposite corner, took
the bottle Mel held out to him.

For several minutes they simply stared at each other, the
only sound the gentle lapping from the dog bowl as Kass
drank deeply. When the dog laid down on the tile and let out
a long sigh as she placed her head across her front paws, the
silent spell broke and Alex finally spoke.

"I quit my job at the ranch."

"Wait, what?" Mel asked, her brow furrowed in confusion. "I thought you liked working there?"

"I did. I do. Jax wouldn't let me actually quit so I guess I'm on a sabbatical."

"But, why?"

"Because you need me."

"I never said that____" she started to argue but Alex cut her off.

"I didn't say you did. Sometimes it's just a feeling, something that you just know. And whether you want to admit it or not, I know it's true. You need me, Melanie." He placed his water on the table and scooted over on the couch, took her hand in his which was cold from the bottle. "And I needed you, too."

"I'm here, Alex. You have me."

He gazed at her with a sad smile on his lips, his eyes squinting a little as they moved back and forth between hers.

"Do I? Really? 'Cause it feels like you've been pulling away from me for the last two weeks."

She started to shake her head no, to deny what he was saying, but she stopped because it was true. Ever since she got that letter from Brin she *had* been pulling away.

"Why? I want to know why, Melanie."

"I don't know."

"Don't do that. Don't lie to me, or yourself."

"Alex, I… it's not some simple answer," she sighed, not liking the feeling in the pit of her stomach. One that made the bottom drop out from anxiety and worry that he wasn't going to let this go. That she was going to have to come clean with him. "You wouldn't understand."

"Try me."

She watched his face, determination made his jaw firm and his lips set in a straight line. His eyes never wavered from hers, like he was looking directly into her soul, and the love he said he felt for her shone through. Mel was terrified of losing that love once she bared it all to him.

The thought of never having him gaze at her with that affection again made her lips tremble and tears threatened to fall.

Mel stood up from the couch quickly. The water bottle she'd placed in her lap fell to the floor and rolled underneath the table. She ignored it. If she was going to do this–actually tell him about the pregnancy–then she couldn't sit still while she did.

She couldn't bear to watch his face fill with revulsion, which she was sure would happen.

She walked over to the windows looking down on Wilshire and paced back and forth. Lights flickering on outside cast long shadows inside. They followed her every move like the shame she'd carried for years. She had one hand up near her mouth and was biting her thumb nail compulsively while her left hand was wrapped around her waist, trying to hold in the nausea.

Just get it over with, Mel. Tell him, let him storm out. And when he does, you can start putting the pieces of your broken heart back together.

Resolving herself to the inevitable, Mel stopped pacing and faced the windows. She squeezed her eyes tightly closed and pinched the bridge of her nose, tried to ward off the tension headache that was threatening.

When she opened her eyes and wrapped both arms around her middle like a shield, she stared, unseeing, at a neon sign directly across the street.

And began to talk.

. . . . .

"You know that old saying, 'If I knew then what I know now,' that you always hear older people talking about?" She peeked over her left shoulder at Alex and when he silently nodded she turned back to the window and continued. "I never really got that. Never understood how someone could say that they would make different choices in their life based on knowledge they've gotten over the years. At least, I didn't until a month ago."

Alex watched Melanie carefully. She spoke softly, so soft that he wanted to stand up and close the distance between them so that he could hear her better. But he sensed that she needed space right now so he stayed put.

"I haven't been completely honest with you, Alex." He sat up straighter in his spot on the couch, the hair on the nape of his neck stood on end as he prepared for the worst but prayed for the best.

"That rape..." *Please don't tell me she made something like that up,* Alex thought when Melanie paused. "That wasn't the worst thing that's ever happened to me. I mean, it was terrible and I had nightmares for months. I was scared to go anywhere, afraid that people would see "Rape Victim" blazing across my chest like a scarlet letter. Or treat me differently when all I wanted was to be normal again. Whatever that is," she whispered her last sentence.

"About five weeks after that night, I noticed that I was getting sick a lot. And I was tired all the time no matter how much I slept at night. I might have been a virgin but I wasn't naïve and I knew what was happening, what *had* happened. So on my way home from class one day I stopped by the drug store on the corner of my street and bought three home pregnancy tests. When I got home I laid them all out on the bathroom counter and just... stared. I remember sitting on the bathtub and looking at them, thinking to myself, "Those can't be real. I'm not actually getting ready to see if I'm pregnant. From being raped." And every time I had one of those thoughts the nausea would hit and I'd be perched over the toilet.

"By the time I finally got the courage to just get it over with it was dark outside. There was a tiny nightlight plugged into the wall and it'd cast this ominous glow across the vanity mirror that barely gave enough light for me to see what I was doing. But I couldn't turn the overhead on; it felt like a spotlight and I just wanted to hide.

"I grabbed all three tests and took them in the same sitting. Once I'd put the caps on them and laid them on the floor next to the toilet, I brushed my teeth, changed into a big nightshirt and crawled into bed. I cried myself to sleep, terrified about what waited for me in the bathroom despite the fact that I already knew. Women's intuition, I guess."

Dear God, Alex thought to himself. *Why? Why her? Wasn't the rape enough?*

But he knew that questioning God wasn't the answer. For whatever reason, He had felt that Melanie could handle it.

He held his breath until it felt like his lungs were going to explode. Then he slowly released it and waited for Melanie to keep going.

But she stood still as she quietly faced the windows. Her shoulders shook slightly and Alex knew she was crying. He ached to comfort her and was just beginning to stand and take her in his arms when she turned toward him with a hand out.

"Sit. Please. I can't say this if your arms are around me."

She angrily wiped away the tears from her cheeks and turned back to the window, standing a little straighter like she was forcing herself to not cry anymore.

"When I dragged myself into the bathroom the next morning, I just stood over them, looking down at those three sticks like they were snakes ready to strike. They were all positive, of course. I sank down to the floor and cried, for hours. And then I went back to bed. I didn't know what else to do."

"What about your parents? Didn't you call your Mom, ask for her help?" Alex asked, anger over their lack of concern for their daughter made him speak his mind.

"Dear God, no. They knew about the rape. The emergency room doctor from the hospital I went to a couple days afterwards called them and they came down. They put on a big show while we were there, coming across to all the staff as loving parents. But as soon as we left they started talking about different young men that ran in the same hippie circle as them. It's like they thought that since I wasn't innocent anymore I'd be willing to get into that whole "free love" thing. When I adamantly turned them down, they ran off to Oklahoma and we never talked about that night again."

"That's not right, Melanie. They shouldn't have done that to you, treated you like that."

"I know. But you can't change who your parents are,

right? It was just easier to let them go than to fight."

She sounded so dejected, disappointed even though she'd supposedly made peace with the way her parents were. And Alex couldn't stand to sit there while she stood, ten feet away, feeling lost and alone.

He stood from the couch slowly and she turned to watch him. But this time she didn't tell him to stay where he was. He took that as a good sign and carefully walked over to her, wrapped his arms around her waist, covering hers that were still crossed around her belly. He linked their fingers together and laid his chin on her shoulder, wanting to make sure that Melanie knew he was here for her. She stayed facing away from him and he heard her sniffle once before continuing.

"A few days later, when the shock had worn off, I made a decision. I was getting ready to graduate. I was alone. I was pregnant because of a *rape*. None of it felt right, like it was meant to be that way. So I made the appointment for three weeks later."

"What appointment, honey?" Alex asked but, dear Lord, he already knew. And his heart was breaking for what she had been through.

"I had an abortion."

Now she turned to face him, keeping her arms around herself. He could see her eyes brimming with tears in the dark, glossy teal pools, ready to spill over at any minute. Her lower lip trembled and she took it between her teeth to make it stop.

But it was the expression on her face that did him in.

It wasn't that she looked like she was sad or hurting. She looked ashamed, sickened, and Alex couldn't understand why. Was she ashamed over herself? Her parents? Sickened by the path she took? He got that what she went through was a life-changing event but she'd handled it the only way she thought she could.

Melanie wasn't a Christian then. Her grandmother had already passed away, her parents were nonexistent. She didn't believe that God brought the bad as well as the good into our lives, so how could she have known that the baby was a gift?

He couldn't hold it against her. He was far from perfect. But he could do whatever it took to make her see that she was still redeemable. He was ready to tell her, too, when she started in first.

"You should be running, Alex. Far away from me as fast as you can."

He slowly shook his head at her, confusion made his brow furrow so hard he could feel the wrinkles in his forehead.

"Why would you think that? Why on earth would you say that I should be running away from you?"

"Because I'm tainted, Alex. Damaged. And you deserve

to be with a woman who isn't as messed up as me. Someone unblemished and redeemable."

"I deserve to be with you," he whispered into the dark room. Her shoulders started shaking again with the sobs she tried to hold in. He tightened his arms around her waist and went on. "You're not tainted, Melanie. You're a survivor. An unbelievable, strong, beautiful survivor. What you went through would make most people give up, lose hope. But you fought on. You survived."

"But I killed that baby! Alex, I'm going to Hell. And I can't condemn you, too because of my mistakes."

"Melanie. Our God is a loving and forgiving God. Do you regret what happened? Do you regret what you did?"

"Yes," she said emphatically, her eyes sliding closed. "I don't regret the rape. Not anymore. Because it opened my eyes to what can and does really exist in the world and, ultimately, made me tougher. But I'll never forgive myself for not having the foresight to know that the baby was a gift. For carelessly getting rid of it. And if I can't forgive myself, then how can I expect God to forgive me?"

She opened her eyes and tears rolled down her cheeks like tiny streams of heartache.

"He will. If you are truly sorry, and you truly accept Him, then He will forgive you. You only have to ask. You can, honey. I know you can."

"But you____" she began and he cut her off.

FOREVER GRATEFUL

"I'm going to be with you every step of the way."

Alex brought his hands up to her face and cradled her cheeks, his thumbs gently brushing away the wetness. He searched her gaze, hoping to find any sign of acceptance. It was there, a tiny sliver of hope fighting to shine through the doubt.

But that sliver was all he needed.

Because he knew that no matter what she thought, neither of them were going to be condemned. He was going to see to it that she accepted forgiveness. From herself and from God.

When her shoulders sagged and she blew out a small breath, he knew he had just won the battle. They had a lot of war left but he meant what he said. He wasn't going anywhere.

"I love you, Melanie."

She smiled at him through her tears.

But even with that sweet grin, he could tell that she was trying to figure out a way to send him off again. To wrangle herself away from a situation that she thought was going to end up causing him pain. And she couldn't have been more wrong, because the only pain he would ever feel was if she left him.

"You might as well stop trying to fight me on this. You're never going to win."

And then, in her eyes, he spotted the first sign of

resignation in the way those sea green depths softened and gazed adoringly back at him. He felt it in the way she finally removed her arms from her waist and walked them up his biceps until they wrapped around his neck and linked together tightly.

He saw her begin to cave to what he knew was inevitable. Their future.

"I already have."

Chapter 17

"Let him kiss me with the kisses of his mouth: for thy love is better than wine." Song of Solomon 1:2

October 17, 2014

Mel grabbed her glass of wine from her kitchen counter and checked the time from the clock on the microwave. It was only seven at night in L.A. but it was already nine in Lake Shores. She decided it wasn't too late, sat down on her couch and picked up her phone.

After she took a sip of her wine, she set the glass down and dialed, the ringing loud in her ear as she waited.

"Hello?" Brinley answered on the other end.

"Hey there, gorgeous. How's pregnant life?"

"Mel! Hey, how are you?"

"I'm good. Great, actually. How are you feeling?"

"Same here. Tired. But I guess that's to be expected right? I'm starting to show now, too. I don't know who likes to rub my belly more... Me or Jax." Brin laughed.

"Ah, so he likes the little extra cushion, huh?"

"I'm going to pretend you didn't just say that. But yes, he loves laying his hands on my stomach and waiting to feel Brandon kick. It's sweet. And sexy."

Mel felt her throat close up as a multitude of emotions swelled inside her. A sadness of never being able to experience what Brin was describing was front and center, though. She cleared her voice before she spoke, not wanting her friend to ask any questions.

"I bet it is," she managed and then, "How about everything else? How've you been handling everything today?"

"You remembered," Brin said and sniffled on the other end. "Ugh. These damn hormones. I'm crying about everything." Mel stayed silent, gave Brin a chance to calm herself down. "I'm handling it okay. Each year gets a little easier, you know? Most days I'm fine. But every now and then lately I'll hear one of Annie's songs on the radio and end up crying in my car. I really was fine until I got pregnant, though, so I'm going to keep blaming these hormones," she said with a touch of anger in her voice.

Mel laughed at the way Brin's words were all over the

place. She could just imagine the trouble Jax must be having trying to keep his wife happy all the time.

"Enough about me. I don't want to cry anymore," Brin decided. "What's been going on with you? Any new clients?"

"No, same ones. They keep me busy though because four of them are all working on sponsorship deals and my boss has me handling them alone."

"Uh-huh. And how are things with Alex?"

Mel hesitated. How much should she tell her friend? Does she want to know all the details or just the cliff's notes version? After a moment, she decided on the short but sweet.

"They're really great, Brinley. Alex is... well, he's fantastic. He's helped me see the light in so many ways. Ways I never imagined there being a light to see but with him it just gets brighter and brighter every day."

"Yeah, Alex is something special. Of course, I'm partial since he's my brother."

"Well I guess I might be a little partial, too then since we're dating."

"You sound so happy, Melanie."

Mel thought about that for a minute. And she realized she was smiling, her cheeks aching from grinning so big. Her heart was thumping loudly in her chest just thinking about Alex. And the flutters she often got when he was around danced in her belly as if he were there with her.

"I am, Brin. He makes me happy."

There was a beat of silence before Brinley asked a question.

"Do you love him?"

.   .   .   .   .

September 7, 2014

Alex and Mel were driving down the Pacific Coast Highway. It was just past dusk, the night turning the ocean to their left a deep, midnight blue. The breaking waves were highlighted in the rising moonlight and their white caps shined like an undulating beacon.

They had just enjoyed a dinner at Uncle Pat's, a place Brin had told Alex he had to try while he was out here because he hadn't gotten around to it the last time back in June. And since Mel had never been there either, they'd decided to give it a try.

The fried fish had been exceptional, the French fries crisp and salty. And the easy-going atmosphere had left the two feeling happy and young and carefree.

Alex's phone was plugged into the radio and he had someone named Pat Green playing, softly crooning about a Dixie lullaby. Mel had never heard of the singer before but Alex loved him. Said he was true Texas country music and she was enjoying the lilting melody.

FOREVER GRATEFUL

They had the windows rolled down in her little Audi and the wind was whipping her hair around her face, golden strings tangling in her eyelashes and mouth. But Mel didn't mind. The briny air wafting inside the car from the ocean and the peaceful music filling her ears were like a balm to her tired soul.

Yesterday, when she had finally confessed everything to Alex, she had been scared but prepared for him to leave. To run away from her and never look back.

But he'd stayed with her, never wavering in his support and love. What meant more was that he'd never questioned her actions. He'd said that all of her mistakes could be forgiven now that she accepted God. Mel was still a little unsure of the likelihood of that but she felt lighter in her soul knowing that Alex believed it and believed in her. It boosted her self-esteem, gave her a new optimism on life, and made her want to try. For him.

"I wonder what that is," Alex said, his quiet statement bringing Mel's head around to look at him.

"What?"

He pointed off to their left, up ahead on the beach. She could see tons of different colored lights–bright oranges and yellows, whites and fluorescent blues, even deep reds–taking up a large section on the beach in the distance. But they were still too far away to see what was going on.

"I don't know what it is," she answered.

Two miles down the road, they were finally able to get a glimpse of what lie on the sand next to a large pier jutting out into the water. Mel watched the huge circle move around and around in the sky like a flying wheel and heard the screaming laughter of children being flung around in an oversized swing.

"It's a carnival!" Mel exclaimed, her voice raising an octave as she watched in awe at the action that was just out of reach.

"You like carnivals?" Alex asked, glancing over to her with a smile.

"Of course. I mean, who doesn't? But it's been a long time since I've been to one. Years."

"Hmm." That was all Alex said before her turned the car onto the next exit ramp and headed west toward the colorful lights.

"What are you doing?"

"I'm taking my woman to a carnival."

Mel's opened her mouth to say, something, but then closed it again when no words came out. Surprise and elation made her bounce up and down in her seat like, well, like a kid going to a carnival.

Alex pulled the car into a row with dozens of others and parked between a beat up old, red Chevy truck and a gray minivan. He turned off the ignition and quickly got out to head over to the passenger side of the car. Excitement had

FOREVER GRATEFUL

Mel jumping out of the car before he had a chance to open the door for her. They met at the hood and he reached over and grabbed Mel's hand, ran his thumb along the backs of her knuckles as he pulled her forward to the fair laid out before them.

He bought them tickets at a booth just outside an entrance gate and they both got black stamps on the back of their hands that were in the shape of a clown. When they walked through the gates and into the funfair, sounds and smells assaulted Mel.

Popcorn and hot dogs smelled salty. Funnel cakes and cotton candy smelled so sicky-sweet that Mel thought she could get a toothache just from looking at them. Loud dings sounded off to their right where a teenage boy was smiling at a girl next to him and swinging a hammer, trying to raise a bell as high as it would go on a pole. Kids ran around in circles, laughing loudly as they raced away from their parents with streams of yellow tickets flowing from their fingers. Spooky music played loudly from a haunted house that was set up to their left. A man with a bushy, black, handlebar mustache and wearing tight red spandex pants and a red vest stood on a podium, boasting about being able to guess anyone's weight.

It was all so much to take in that Mel just stopped, frozen in one place as she slowly spun in a circle to see everything that surrounded them. Memories from childhood came barreling into her mind and she grinned, laughing as she remembered being a little girl and begging her Gramma to let her ride every single ride.

When she stopped turning, her eyes landed on Alex. He was standing three feet away, watching her with his arms crossed over his chest and a smirk peeking out on his beautiful lips. Seeing him standing there, with his jean-covered hip cocked out and amusement pouring off of him, Mel felt her heart swell with adoration.

She ran the few steps to him and he opened his arms, wrapped them tightly around her when she threw herself into his embrace. She locked her hands around his shoulders and he buried his face in her hair, lifted her several inches off the ground as he stood tall with Mel in his arms.

"Thank you for this," she whispered in his ear, not sure whether he would even hear over the giddy commotion around them.

But he brushed the hair off of her neck and placed a tender kiss there, right over her beating pulse, and said, "Anything for you, darlin'."

When he set her back on the ground, he kept his left arm around her back, his hand resting possessively on her hip. His right arm swung out in a half circle, indicating everything in front of them and he asked, "What do you want to do first?"

Mel looked around and her eyes settled right in front of

them, at the large Ferris wheel circling the sky. She glanced back up at Alex and tilted her head toward the ride with her eyebrows raised, the question evident. He looked to where her head was pointing and back at her with a smile and nodded his head.

They took off running to the ride, laughing like a couple of teenagers in love.

It's because you are in love, Mel's mind said to herself but she chose to ignore it for now. To not stress over feelings and instead just enjoy the moment.

The ride was just coming to a stop when they reached it and they waited in line while old passengers got off and new ones got on at every stop. When it was finally their turn to board the last available seat, Alex gave the man running the ride their tickets and led Mel into the bucket with a hand on her back. The attendant started to strap them in when Alex held his hand up.

"I've got it. Thanks."

The man shrugged his shoulders and walked off to throw their tickets in the trash. Alex pulled Mel closer to him so that they were hip to hip. Instead of using separate straps, he extended the length of one and strapped them in together. That one little action made Mel's heart pick up, and not because of the anticipation from the ride. Being close enough to smell him—woodsy and clean and something solely Alex— had her stomach doing flip-flops with wanting to touch him, to taste him.

She looked up at him and saw that same desire in his eyes, smoldering in its intensity. And once upon a time that would have terrified her.

But Mel knew that Alex was always in control. And she trusted him implicitly. She knew that she was safe with him.

He raised his hand to signal to the guy manning the ride that they were ready, never taking his eyes off of hers. The bucket jerked forward then back before it slowly started to creep up, heading toward the dark sky. The wheel picked up speed as they rode higher and higher and Mel's breathing started racing right along with it.

She leaned toward Alex, placing her hand lightly on his chest, and felt the muscles twitch under her palm. Alex wound his arm around her back and pulled her even closer to him, his fingers digging into the skin at her waist.

Her gaze traveled down from his eyes and landed on his mouth, the urge to kiss him causing her to lick her lips involuntarily. She looked back up and saw Alex breathing heavily through his open mouth as he watched her.

He lowered his face, brought his mouth to within an inch of hers, and whispered, "Fly away with me, baby."

The words feathered across her lips right as he connected them, sealing his lips over hers with a ferocity that had Mel shivering.

And the only thing she could think of as he moved his

mouth slowly across hers was, *I love you.*

.   .   .   .   .

Heaven, Alex thought as soon as his lips touched Melanie's. *Pure Heaven.*

He wasn't sure he would have been experiencing a kiss like this–a kiss that melted into him and he felt all the way down to his toes–if he hadn't made the quick decision to bring Melanie here. He didn't even know why he had decided to turn in.

Maybe it was the wistful look on her face as she stared at the bright lights. Or the longing he'd heard in her voice for a time when everything was happy and easy instead of full of responsibilities.

Whatever the reason, he'd found himself exiting the highway and heading here.

And he was relieved he did. Because regardless of the fact that he probably sounded like a woman right now– thinking about feeling a kiss down to his toes–it was the most amazing thing he'd ever experienced. And he'd give just about anything to have this feeling, this kiss, this woman with him for the rest of his life.

Her lips were soft and a little wet from when she'd licked them (a move that had almost made him groan aloud with the craving to taste her right then). Her body was warm pressed up against him. Her fingers strong as they clutched the fabric of the blue polo shirt he was wearing.

And her scent. That trace of something light and floral that was so uniquely Melanie hung in his nose and made Alex squeeze her tighter, desperate to have that scent wrap around his whole body.

When the movement of their bodies shifted and he could feel them descending instead of ascending, Alex slowly pulled away from the sweet temptation that was Melanie's lips. Her eyes were closed, her mouth slightly open, her cheeks flushed.

She was beautiful.

He reached up and ran his thumb along her lower lip; her eyes fluttered open and stared at him. And then she placed a kiss on the tip of his thumb and laid her head down on his shoulder.

At that moment, with Melanie resting on him, his arm wrapped around her and the carnival lights glowing brightly before their eyes, he knew what true contentment meant. His heart was full of love. His soul felt more at peace than it had ever been. His entire being felt whole.

He never wanted it to end.

But too soon, after several rotations of the wheel, the ride began to slow. One by one, the passengers were switched out of the buckets, the Ferris wheel starting and stopping with each change. They were at the very top of the wheel, their bucket swaying gently back and forth while they waited for the switch taking place over two hundred and fifty feet directly below them. Melanie sighed against his shoulder and Alex leaned over and kissed the top of her head.

"You okay, honey?"

"Oh, Alex. I'm more than okay. It's perfect." She turned her head up to look at him. "You're perfect." He started to shake his head at her, to deny what she claimed, but Melanie kept right on at it. "I keep waiting for the other shoe to drop. To wake up one day and realize the last three months have been some kind of fairytale. And every day, you do something else that amazes me even more. I'm afraid you might be too good to be true."

"Ow!" He exclaimed, reaching down to rub a spot across his ribs. "Woman, did you just pinch me?"

"Just making sure you're real," she said with a grin that quickly turned into laughter.

"Don't you know that *you're* the one who's supposed to be pinched to see if you're dreaming or not?"

"Sure I know that; but pinching hurts. I didn't want to get hurt."

"I'll never hurt you, sweet Melanie. You know that, right?"

All laughter gone now, she swallowed hard and nodded her head yes then turned to look back out across the carnival lights. The sounds from the games below were more muffled up here but music could be heard clearly from a dance floor that was set up on the outskirts of the carnival, close to the pier. Alex decided that's where he would take her next.

Fifteen minutes later, they were finally off of the Ferris wheel and Alex held Melanie's hand, pulled her in the direction of the dance floor he'd seen. They walked over to a drink stand and he ordered them each a lemonade. The two sat down at one of the picnic tables surrounding the floor and drank quietly, waiting for the song to finish playing.

When the chords of the next song began, Alex set down his drink and pulled Melanie up from the table. He walked backwards onto the floor and pulled her into his arms. He took her right hand in his left and placed his other hand on the small of her back. She wrapped her other arm around his neck and he guided her around the floor, humming to the tune from Ed Sheeran. The overhead lights went out right as the chorus began and he and Melanie both looked to the sky, admiring the thousands of stars that were twinkling like fireflies.

He started to spin her in circles as he sang each passing line of the song.

Take me into your loving arms. Spin. *Kiss me under the light of a thousand stars.* Spin. *Place your head on my beating heart.* Spin. *I'm thinking out loud.* Spin. *Maybe we found love right where we are.* And then he dipped her low, expecting to see her laughing eyes gazing back at him.

But she wasn't laughing. Her eyes were round and glossy, like she was holding back tears. Her lips were trembling. Her breathing was fast.

"I love you, Alex."

And just like that, his heart stopped.

Slowly he brought her body back up until she was chest to chest with him. He searched her face for any sign of remorse or regret that she had let those three words–those three beautiful, amazing, perfect words–slip out. He saw nothing but sincerity as the corners of her mouth started to tip up.

Consumed by the joy swelling inside him, Alex closed his eyes and released the breath that had been stuck in his chest. He brought his hands up to her face, cradled her cheeks like fine china, and laid his forehead down to rest on hers.

"Say it again," he whispered against her lips.

"I love you." She wrapped her tiny hands around his wrists, squeezing them lightly. "I love you, Alex."

No sooner had the words slipped out of her tempting lips did he crush his mouth on hers. The relief and excitement at hearing her finally, finally tell him she loved him had him kissing her with more intensity than he'd planned. Alex forced himself to lighten his kiss, teasing the seam of her lips with his tongue. And when she opened for him, lightly stroking him in return, a growled sigh escaped him. In appreciation. In pleasure.

In love.

He tore his mouth from hers and peppered her face with kisses. Small strokes across her cheeks. Light pecks to her eyelids. Feathery caresses to her forehead and chin. All the while murmuring, "I love you, I love you so much," over and over again.

As the song drew to a close and the dance floor lights came back on, Alex pulled back to look into Melanie's eyes. The tears she had been holding onto ran in small streams down her cheeks but there was nothing but pure bliss in her gaze. He couldn't hold back the laugh that bubbled out as his heart swelled.

He reached down and wrapped his arms around her waist and lifted her off the ground. She threw her arms around his neck and buried her face in the crook there when he started spinning her in a circle, giggling through her tears.

Shouts of "woo-hoo" and "yeah" and "awe" rang out around them with loud applauding. Alex stopped spinning and Melanie lifted her head from his shoulder.

They looked all around them at the people who had ceased their dancing and were smiling and clapping at them. Alex only smiled wide in return but Melanie tried to hide her face back in his neck.

He wouldn't let her. He set her on her feet and grabbed her hand, gave a small salute to their little crowd.

And then, just because he couldn't hold in what he was feeling, he yelled, "She loves me!"

The roars and claps got even louder, making Melanie and Alex both wince a little. But she was laughing now, too. Alex swept in for another kiss to her lips, gave the group one last wave and pulled her from the floor, back through the gates and out to her car.

When they got there, Alex backed Melanie up to the passenger side of the car. She leaned her back against the door and he caged her in, placed his hands on the roof on either side of her head. His heart beat wildly, his stomach rolled in nervousness. But his heart, his heart filled to bursting with love as he leaned in close to her mouth.

"Marry me, Melanie," he whispered against her lips.

She froze, the smile falling from her face. Her eyes that had been shining so bright took on a sad note and he knew what she was going to say before the words even came out.

"No. Not yet, Alex. I'm just not there yet. But please don't give up on me."

"I'd never give you up, baby. Even if you have turned me down three times."

"Technically it's only been two." She smirked at him. "I stopped you from fully asking the last time, remember?"

"Yeah, I remember," he sighed. "Doesn't make it bruise my ego any less, though."

Melanie tilted her head to the side and got a sympathetic

look on her face. She raised her right hand and laid it across his cheek.

"Don't stop asking me, Alex. I promise, one day, I'll say yes."

"Just not today?"

"No. Not today."

He turned his head and laid a gentle kiss in the palm of her hand then closed her fingers around it and held her fist to his chest, right over his beating heart.

"Say it," he whispered.

She grinned as she leaned on her tiptoes, brought her mouth to his as she whispered back the words that she knew he wanted, needed to hear.

"I love you, Alex Lambert."

"I love you more, Melanie. Always."

.　　.　　.　　.　　.

October 18, 2014

Mel sat at her kitchen table with her laptop open and a contract sitting in front of her. She was highlighting the signature lines, the neon yellow sticking out in stark contrast to the white paper. As she flipped page after page filled with black ink, she thought about how different her life would have been if she'd ended up on the other side of these contracts. If she hadn't been so scared of the stage.

Just thinking about being up in front of hundreds of people gave her a case of the cold sweats.

She was glad that her work kept her out of the limelight. And that she was able to do it in the privacy of her own home. Like now. Where she could work and sit in her pajamas all day and take multiple breaks to daydream about Alex if she wanted to.

Just thinking about him now had her warming all over, touching her fingers to her lips as she remembered the way he'd kissed her when she'd told him she loved him. She could feel heat as it seeped through her palm when she recalled the tender kiss he'd placed there. She touched her cheek and could imagine clearly that it was his hands cradling her face with reverent care.

So this is love... she thought.

Not what she'd had with Justin. Or rather, what she had *believed* they'd had. That was some kind of mirrors-and-magic show, an illusion. But this, with Alex, was real. And she loved it.

She remembered coming home after their impromptu visit to the carnival. The had snuggled on the couch under a cotton quilt–both fully clothed–and watched as the sun came up, the glow slowly lighting the buildings across the street. She'd run her fingers up and down his forearms (probably her favorite place on him) and he had softly run his fingers through her hair.

And just before the last shadows disappeared across the street, she had again whispered "I love you" to Alex and fallen into a deep sleep.

Later that morning, she'd awoken to the smell of coffee, bacon and eggs. They sat side by side on barstools and ate at her kitchen counter. They laughed over the way the teenage boy had tried to impress his girlfriend the night before. And the embarrassment that had been obvious on his face when he' only gotten the bell to go halfway up the pole. They exchanged timid smiles as they both talked about dancing with the lights out and only the stars illuminating the air around them.

And then Alex had abruptly stood up and taken Mel into his arms, singing and dancing with her in the middle of her living room to no music other than what came out of his mouth. She had giggled at the suddenness of it but danced right along with him, smiled at him as he stared into her eyes and serenaded her.

She closed her eyes and could still hear his voice and feel his hand on her lower back as he pulled her close and smell the coffee on his breath as he brought his mouth down to hers.

Her phone ringing beside her brought her back to the present and out of the carnival (and subsequent) memories. She smiled widely when she saw Alex's name as the incoming call. She answered before the first ring finished.

"Hey, babe."

"Hey, darlin'. Whatcha doing?"

"Nothing really. Just going over some contracts for work. What about you?"

"Headed home. I've been at Aaron's. Me and Jax were over there watching the Longhorns play. It was a good game, too. They beat Oklahoma in the Red River Rivalry. I love college football."

After his ode to football, a hush fell over the line for a few seconds.

"I miss you," Mel said.

"I miss you, too," Alex responded, all traces of football talk gone. "That's actually why I was calling you. I needed to ask you something."

"Okay."

"I want you to come spend Thanksgiving with me. With my family."

Mel was quiet on the other end, taking in what it meant to spend a major holiday with her boyfriend's family. It didn't matter if his sister was her best friend. This was a big step. Huge.

At her continued silence, he asked, "Melanie? You still there, honey?"

"Yeah, I'm here. Are you sure? I mean…" *What? What am I trying to ask him?* "I'm just saying that if you want to wait until things are more serious or we've been together longer for me to really get to know your family, it's fine."

"I'm going to marry you, Melanie. It doesn't get any more serious than that. And my family already knows."

"You told them?" Mel could keep the surprise out of her voice.

"Of course I did. Listen, my family is very close. And you're going to a part of that. It would really mean a lot to me if you came down for Thanksgiving."

Well hell... it's hard to deny him anything when he gets all sweet and sappy on me. Besides, I want to.

Mel's last thought caught her a little off guard but she wasn't ashamed to admit that it was true. She did want to go to Lake Shores. She did want to spend the holiday with Alex's family. She wanted to have a traditional turkey dinner with love and laughter and tryptophan comas.

"Okay," she told him quietly.

"Okay? You'll come?"

"Yes. I'll come."

Alex sighed on the phone, the sound heavy like the fate of the free world had been held in the hands of that one answer, her answer. And now he could breathe again knowing that she was coming, was going to be with him and his family.

She only hoped she didn't do anything to screw it up.

Chapter 18

"Let us come before his presence with thanksgiving, and make a joyful noise unto him with psalms." Psalms 95:2

November 26, 2014

Mel watched the clouds float by outside of the airplane window and tried to pick out shapes in the white fluff, like she used to do when she was a kid. She caught herself doing this kind of thing–reminiscing about less stressful times, innocent times from childhood–more and more lately. She wondered for a while what had brought the change about.

But if she was honest with herself, she knew exactly when it had happened.

It was in September, when Alex was with her in California.

It was when he had done something so incredibly sweet and thoughtful-took her to that carnival-that she couldn't help but to admit her feelings for him.

It was when she had finally told him that she loved him.

Ever since that moment, she felt like she could float on those fluffy white clouds outside the window. "Floating on cloud nine" as the saying went. And she got it, now. She got what that old adage was trying to portray; the feeling of being high on life.

It was amazing to her how much more fulfilled her life felt ever since she accepted that there was a God, as well as her love for Alex. How much more at peace she felt. She didn't know how she would ever be able to thank Alex for showing her all that life had to offer. But she was never going to stop trying.

The pilot came over the speakers and told the passengers that the plane was getting ready to make its descent. As she buckled her seatbelt and again looked out the window to her right, she saw the runway come into view. Rows and rows of cars lined up outside the airport, people waiting to pick up and drop off their loved ones. And she imagined Alex down there, waiting for her.

She smiled in anticipation of seeing him again. Finally.

The plane dropped and Mel's stomach did a dip with it. The wheels screeched on the blacktop as the plane landed and slowed, coming to a crawl at the end of the runway. The pilot slowly maneuvered them to their gate and the flight attendants walked down the aisle, telling everyone they could start collecting their belongings while the systems were shut down.

Normally Mel would sit patiently and let the other passengers go ahead of her. But not today. She was too anxious and excited.

She grabbed her red carry-on from the over-head compartment and stood with the handle in one hand and her purse slung across her opposite shoulder. As soon as the attendants gave the signal, she moved into the aisle and followed the string of people out of the plane and into the gangway. When she finally came out on the other side, into the busy airport, she stopped and looked around, searched for the tall man with sandy brown hair and honey eyes.

Her gaze moved back and forth from one side of the waiting area at Gate E to the other. On her third pass around, she finally spotted him, leaning against the wall of windows to her left that overlooked the runway she had just come in from.

He had his right ankle hooked over his left and his arms were crossed in front of his chest, making his biceps bulge underneath the dark gray t-shirt he was wearing. Dark blue jeans covered his long legs and a pair of black military boots looked almost menacing on his feet.

But his face, his face was etched with happiness and

love. His eyes shone brilliantly like amber jewels. And his lips were set in a perfect half grin, waiting for her. She didn't make him wait any longer.

Dropping the handle of her suitcase and laying her purse down on top of it, Mel ran to him. He stood straight from the window with open arms and caught her right as she jumped into him. Alex lifted her off the ground, spun them in a circle while she laughed in his ear and kissed his neck over and over.

When he set her back on her feet, he braced her face with his hands and brought his mouth down to hers.

"Say it," he whispered against her parted lips.

"I love you."

She felt him smile right before he molded their mouths together, connected them in the way she had longed for. Just the faintest touch of his lips, barely brushing across her own.

But it was all she needed to feel the bottom drop out of her belly, again, and her heart race at simply being with him.

"Come on," he said as he pulled back and wrapped his left arm around her shoulders, anchoring her to him. "Let's go home."

Mel ignored the jolt those three words brought to her. The thrill at hearing Alex say "home" and including her in it. She was just happy to be with him again. She didn't need to overthink anything else.

They walked to where she had dropped her things and

she picked up her purse while he grabbed the handle of her
suitcase. With his hand caressing her shoulder, she reached
around and grabbed onto the belt loop of his jeans, holding
him tightly to her around his waist. Together they walked out
into the sunshine, the light blinding after being inside the
darker airport. He guided her to a black four door Chevrolet
pickup truck with new license plates.

"Is this yours?"

"Yep. I just got it last week. Do you like it?" he asked as
he put her suitcase in the back seat and opened the front
passenger door for her.

"It's beautiful." She climbed into the cab and slid across
the seat, running her palm across the smooth black leather.
She looked up to find him staring at her with a confused and
almost agitated look on his face. "What?"

"It's a truck."

"Yeah. So?"

"Trucks aren't *beautiful*. Manly, tough, hardcore… yes.
Beautiful… no."

Mel rolled her lips together to keep from laughing at his
defensive tone and struggled to keep her shoulders from
shaking.

Boys and their toys.

"You're right. I'm sorry." She took a deep breath and
promised herself she wouldn't laugh at what was obviously a
touchy subject. "It's not beautiful. It's very masculine. And

rough around the edges. Can you just imagine how diehard of a truck it would really look like covered in mud?"

He paused in closing the door and looked at her sideways, a scowl taking over his handsome face.

"Now you're just mocking me. And cruelly, too, I might add."

She couldn't help it any longer and started to laugh.

"I'm sor–" he shut the door on her apology.

Mel fidgeted in her seat as she watched him walk around the hood and climb into the driver's side, wondering if she might have gone too far.

But just as she was about to apologize more sincerely, he leaned across the seat and wrapped his hand around the back of her neck. He jerked her to him, kissed her quickly on the lips and pulled back to look into her eyes. She spotted the laugh lines around the corners of his eyes that contradicted his bogus anger.

"I love you."

"I love you, too."

"Even if you are mean."

He sat straight in his seat and started the engine, checked the rearview mirror before pulling out into the traffic exiting the airport pick-up lanes.

Mel watched the scenery fly by as Alex drove them from Houston to Lake Shores. High rises and clustered suburbs gave way to open fields and houses no closer than a half a mile. Cattle and horses dotted both sides of the highway, some laying in the sun and dozing off while others grazed in shadowed areas surrounded by large oak and cedar trees.

Alex reached across and took her hand, brought it to his mouth to kiss her knuckles. He rested their joined hands on his thigh and hummed to the radio that was playing some sort of slow, country tune.

Mel watched his face, the golden skin across his cheekbones highlighted whenever the sun peeked out from behind the clouds in the sky. His lips were curved up at the corners and clearly indicated how at ease he was.

Her gaze roamed down and took in his muscled arms. The bicep in his left flexed as he maneuvered the steering wheel to pass a car. The bronzed skin on his right forearm stretched taut, the sinewy muscle showcased just how fit he was. And the calluses on his palm that held her hand sent those wonderful tingles up her arm. She cherished those calluses. They told her how much he worked with his hands and how capable he was of protecting her. He was a blue collar man, so different from anyone in her life.

She loved it. She loved him.

Soon they were pulling into the small town that Alex called home. A single stretch of road, simply called Main Street, guided them toward the southern edge of town. Older men sat in rocking chairs in front of stores, some falling asleep in the warm, fall weather while others waved at the passersby and talked animatedly to each other.

Older cars lined the street on both sides. People walked up and down the sidewalk dressed in well-worn jeans and boots, faded shirts. It seemed as if everyone who lived here was comfortable with the simple life. Like no one needed what most of society deemed the "necessities of life" and instead focused on the relationships around them. Mel wondered what it would feel like to live in a place like this. And if she could ever feel at home here.

At the end of the street, Alex turned right. Mel looked over him, confused.

"I thought I was staying at Brin and Jaxson's?" she asked, knowing that the road to their place was in the opposite direction.

"You are. But I wanted to show you something first." He glanced over at her and gave her a reassuring smile. "It'll only take a few minutes."

He took another right at the end of the second road and turned into a worn driveway, parked the truck in front of a house.

The outside was painted a pale yellow that looked like a canary with faded feathers. There was a short, white picket fence lining the front yard and it wrapped around to the sides of the house where it was replaced with a six foot high wooden fence, also painted white, to add more privacy.

FOREVER GRATEFUL

White clapboard shutters bordered the windows and a concrete porch lined the entire front of the house, complete with two white rocking chairs and a small, wooden, slatted table standing in between the two.

"Why are we here?" Mel asked, never taking her eyes off the charming place before her.

When Alex didn't immediately answer, she turned her head and found his anxious gaze watching her. He had turned in the seat so that he was facing her and his fingers drummed nervously on his thigh.

"I bought it."

He shrugged and swallowed hard, his Adam's apple sliding up and down his throat slowly.

"A truck *and* a house? Planting some roots, huh?"

He only nodded his head, that anxious look still marring his normally cheerful face.

"Why don't you look happy about it? This is a big deal, Alex. You bought a house. You should be excited and celebrating and proud."

"I am. It's just…" he trailed off.

"It's just what, Alex?"

"Call me optimistic but I was hoping that, one day, when you're ready, you might want to live here. With me. As my wife." He cleared his throat. "I bought it… for *us*."

.   .   .   .   .

Alex watched Melanie's face as his words sank in.

First there was surprise. Maybe that he had bought the house in general. Possibly that he'd bought it with her in mind. Or it could be because he had brought up the subject of marriage. Even if he hadn't actually asked her yet. Again.

Then there was a little bit of fear. That one only lasted for a few seconds but he saw it. Fear of the unknown? Or fear because this was all pushing too far, too soon? Maybe she was afraid because, despite telling Alex she loved him, Melanie had no intention of ever marrying him. And that thought scared Alex, too.

But finally he saw what he had been looking for. He saw excitement. And happiness. Her beautiful face took on a light that was full of wonder and love and trust. Trust in him or their future, he wasn't sure which. But he didn't care. That trust, no matter where it was directed, was enough to have him feeling hopeful, optimistic about his decision to buy this house.

He sighed heavily in relief.

"Do you want to go inside?"

"Absolutely."

They both got out of his truck and he met her at the hood, grabbed her hand and led her up the worn walkway to the front porch. Cracks in the concrete stood out in the surface, the heat and humidity of Lake Shores causing damage to the slab.

"I'm planning on having this replaced." He pointed to the ground as he guided her over one particularly large crack. "I just closed on this place last week so I haven't had a chance to really do anything yet."

"It's fine, Alex. I'm sure everything is perfect."

"Well..." he trailed off, figuring he'd let her see for herself just how much needed to be done.

They stepped onto the front porch and Alex released Melanie's hand to get the keys from his front pocket. He looked sideways at her when the keys jingled free and saw that she stared at the rockers with a wistful expression on her face.

"I love these. My Gramma used to have some just like them only they were stained a dark brown."

"We can stain them if you want to."

"No." She smiled over at him. "I like them just the way they are. White. Like a blank canvas."

"Or a fresh start," he countered and her grin grew.

Alex unlocked the door and stepped aside to let Melanie walk in first. He followed closely behind her when she stepped over the threshold and reached to the right to hit the light switch. Her breath caught as the front room was bathed in light.

"Yeah, I know. It's pretty barren right now. But I thought that... I was hoping that maybe you'd want to decorate it together."

"Oh, Alex. It's beautiful." She turned and looked over her shoulder at him, a teasing smile on her lips. "Can I call the house beautiful? Or is that inappropriate, too?"

"Ha. Ha. Aren't you just the little comedian?"

She winked at him and turned back around to walk further into the house. The living room, dining area and kitchen were all connected in one large space. The living area was on the left with a large fireplace made from white stone. The only piece of furniture was a dark yellow and white striped couch complete with dark yellow throw pillows.

The dining room sat in the middle with a square oak table and four high-backed chairs. Directly behind the table was a set of French doors that led out into the backyard.

The kitchen was to the right. It was bathed in sunlight from the two windows nestled in the corner above the stainless steel sink. The whitewashed cabinets with brushed nickel hardware matched the gray granite countertops. The stainless double oven was set back in the far wall.

The maple wood flooring underneath their feet was stained a deep honey and ran from one side of the house to the other.

"It's a split floor plan so there are two bedrooms and a bathroom over there." He pointed to a hallway to their immediate left. "And the master bedroom and bathroom are over here," he said, angling his head to their right. "The backyard has this great garden area, too. There's nothing planted in there right now, obviously. But the people I bought the place from said they had vegetables and fruits planted there every spring. I figured we could plant something together. Sometime. So, where would you like to go next?"

"I want to see the bedroom."

Alex swallowed thickly and prayed that his restraint would hold. He'd promised Melanie he wouldn't make love to her until they were married. But going into what he hoped would one day be their bedroom, in marriage, was definitely going to put him toward the ends of his limits.

"Okay," he said, his voice hoarse with emotion.

He reached down and took her dainty hand in his and pulled her to the hallway on the right. She followed behind him quietly and Alex could feel her eyes on his back, making his skin prickle with anticipation. Was she having as much of a struggle right now as he was? Or was he just being an out-of-control man?

Get it together, Alex!

He took a deep breath when they reached the door at the end of the hallway. Again he opened it and let Melanie walk in first. He stepped up behind her and placed his hands on her hips when she stopped just inside of the room, looking at the almost empty space in front of them.

He hadn't been lying when he'd told her the place was

barren.

There were only two pieces of furniture in the room. A whitewashed chest of drawers, that matched the kitchen cabinets, was on the wall that backed up to the rest of the house, on their left. And directly across from it, on the opposite wall, was a bed of that same faded white wood. The sleigh style headboard and footboard framed a king sized mattress and was covered in white sheets and a thick, pale yellow cotton quilt. Dark yellow accent pillows lay against the two sleeping pillows. Alex realized that it kind of looked like a yellow cloud.

"If you don't like it we can change____"

"I don't want to change a thing, Alex. This..." she turned in his arms and wrapped her hands around his neck. "This is exactly what I picture when I think of an old farm house. A country house. It reminds me of Gramma's. And I always felt so at home there." She turned to look back at the room, their room. "I feel that here, too."

"You don't know how happy it makes me to hear you say that," Alex whispered into the quiet room and leaned his forehead against hers.

He rubbed the tip of his nose up and down hers before leaning in to give her a soft kiss on the lips. He forced himself to pull back and not let the kiss get carried away. Especially with the temptation of a bed so close at hand.

I will not break my promise to her. I will not break my

promise to her. Lord, give me the strength to not break my
promise to Melanie.

Despite Melanie's muffled sound of protest when Alex
leaned away from her mouth, he grabbed her by the hand and
pulled her from the room. They made their way back into the
kitchen and he pushed her up next to the counter tops.
Melanie placed her hands on top of his shoulders and Alex
grabbed her around her waist, easily lifted her off the
ground, and set her down on the gray granite.

And just because they were now at eye level, he leaned
in and kissed her again.

I'm a glutton for punishment, he thought as he traced her
lower lip with his tongue.

She shuddered against him and he wrapped his arms
around her, held her tight against his chest. Melanie
responded to him eagerly, her knees anchored on his hips
and her hands grasped the shirt covering his stomach. She
kissed him back fervently and her tongue tangled with his
like it was the last thing she'd ever get to do. Or maybe like
kissing him was the one thing she had been craving since
they last saw each other. God knows it's all he'd wanted.

This. Her lips, her body. Her heart.

"Stop," he murmured against her mouth. "We have to
stop, honey. My discipline only goes so far."

Melanie immediately complied and leaned back, taking
her hands from his shirt and wrapping her fingers around the

edge of the counter. He watched her knuckles blanch white with the effort to keep her hands to herself and he chuckled, relieved the he wasn't alone in battling the difficult vow they had made to each other.

Removing himself from temptation, he walked backwards across the kitchen and leaned against the stove on the opposite side of the space. He even crossed his arms over his chest, dug his fingers into the skin under his arms, to keep from reaching for her again. As nonchalant as he tried to appear to be, Melanie saw right through it and started laughing at his pose. Maybe even hers, too. So he laughed with her.

"Maybe we shouldn't be alone together anymore," she said in between fits of giggling.

"If you'd learn to keep your hands to yourself, woman, we wouldn't be having this problem."

"Me? You're the one who caged me in just a second ago."

As soon as the words left her mouth, the smile fell from her lips. And Alex knew, without a doubt, that she was thinking of the last time she had been caged in. Temptation be damned, he walked across the floor and took her gently by the shoulders.

"I would never hurt you, Melanie. You know that, right?" She only nodded her head so he went on. "You are the most important thing to me, baby. I will always protect you. From everything. And if you ever feel that you need protecting from *me*, then I'll take care of that, too. Okay?"

She raised her hand and laid her palm upon his cheek, softly running her fingers along the stubble there.

"I won't need protecting from you, Alex. Never you. I know you'd never harm me."

"Are you still afraid of those men?"

She shook her head from side to side, adamantly saying no. It made Alex wonder why she wouldn't feel any fear when thinking of those monsters.

"Do you want to tell me why?"

"No, not yet. I will one day, I promise. But not today, okay?"

"Okay, honey. Not today."

She sighed, her chest rising and falling with her relief as she nodded her head at his agreement. He leaned in and placed his lips on her forehead, just rested them against her soft skin.

"How about we get you to my sister's? We're gonna have a big day tomorrow. It's already coming up on evening and I know you must be tired after your flight."

"Yeah. That sounds good. Thank you."

Alex helped Melanie down from the counter and they made their way back through the house and outside. He looked up at the sky as they walked to the truck. The setting sun was turning the sky into a painter's pallet of deep pink and orange. It looked like someone had cut open tangerines and grapefruits and laid them out amongst a dark blue table. Crickets were starting to chirp, waking up from their day-long rest and ready to hunt for the night. A couple of big gray doves flew overhead, cooing as they made their way back to their nest.

He was so caught up in what was going on around them that he hadn't realized Melanie had stopped walking until he felt the pull on his hand. Turning to look at her, Alex saw that she, too, was watching the sky to their west. The last rays of the day highlighted the hair that was loose around her shoulders. A slight wind blew making the strands flow like a spider's silk, golden silk. She was so beautiful she took his breath away.

"Thank you, Alex," she said, still looking at the sky.

"For what?"

Now she turned to look at him and he walked the two feet to her, wrapped their linked hands around to rest on her lower back.

"For inviting me here. It's so peaceful. Every time I'm here I feel like the world just stops. Like everything around us pauses to let us have this one moment in time. This one, perfect moment. So thank you."

"I feel the same way. But you make it perfect. It's you. None of this–the house, the sky, the town, this *moment*–none of it would matter without you here in it. It's you, baby."

FOREVER GRATEFUL

"I love you."

Dear God, Alex would never get tired of hearing her say that.

"Not nearly as much as I love you." He kissed her on the tip of her nose and pulled her toward the truck. Again. "Come on. Let's get you to Brin's."

. . . . .

November 27, 2014

Mel sat at Brin's table in the breakfast nook of her kitchen, opened jars of pickles, olives and cranberry sauce and laid them all out on a crystal relish tray for Thanksgiving dinner. It was one o'clock and everyone was supposed to be here at two.

Brin ran around the kitchen-in a "waddling penguin" type way since her belly was growing so large-and tried to finish the side dishes that were baking in the oven and rolling out the dough to make dinner rolls with.

"Hey Brinley, why don't you slow down? You've got an hour before your family shows up. I don't want you falling and going into premature labor because you're running around like a chicken with its head cut off just to get stuff finished."

But Brin had told her, while she took out the dressing

and put in the sweet potato casserole, to expect everyone at any time.

"My family has a tendency to show up unannounced whenever they feel like it. So I want to be ready."

Mel laughed so hard she had tears in her eyes. When Brin asked what was so funny, Mel told her it was because Alex had a habit of doing that, so she was well acquainted with that fact.

"But didn't *you* show up *here* without warning, too?" Brin had asked mockingly.

"Touché."

And just then the doorbell rang. Brinley froze with the rolling pin suspended in the air. She threw an "I told you so look at Mel" before laying the pin down and going to answer the door. Loud male voices could be heard from around the corner as they yelled "Happy Thanksgiving" and began asking where the food was.

Mel turned in her chair and watched the three Lambert men come around the corner with Brinley, her mom, Tina, and her sister-in-law, Jessica trailing behind. Her dad, Mitch and older brother, Aaron walked right into the kitchen like they owned the place, looking for scraps on the counter. The women were close at their heels, slapping their hands away and trying to shoo them out of the kitchen.

But Mel wasn't paying any attention to them. Not really. Her eyes were glued to the man who stood just inside the doorway with his hands in the back pockets of his jeans and his right hip cocked out. His white button down shirt was starched and ironed with the sleeves rolled up, revealing his tanned forearms. His hair was finger combed back and a single lock fell forward making Mel's hands itch to brush it back.

"Hey," he said quietly.

She stood from the table and Alex's eyes roamed down the length of her while she made her way over to him. He ran his thumb along the hem of her sleeveless, sheer beige blouse. The tip of that finger rested underneath the cream camisole she wore underneath, tickled her belly. His gaze moved to her skinny-jean encased legs and down to her brown riding boots. He looked back up into her eyes and leaned in closer to her face.

"Hey, yourself."

"You look beautiful."

"You're looking mighty handsome, too, there babe," she whispered against his mouth, anticipating his kiss.

And right before his lips touched hers, they noticed that all the talking and arguing from the kitchen had stopped. Mel and Alex both turned their heads in that direction to see the other five people staring at them. The women all with sappy expressions on their faces and the men with knowing smirks across theirs.

"Don't you guys have anything better to do than

eavesdrop on us?" Alex asked and threw his arm around Mel's shoulders while she ducked her head into the crook of his neck and hid her flushed face.

"Not at all," Aaron replied, crossing his arms across his chest like he was taking a stand. "Please, by all means, don't let us interrupt what you two were doing." Jess elbowed him in the ribs, making him jerk and grab the now tender spot. "Ow. What'd you do that for?"

"Leave them alone," she scolded him and then turned to Brinley. "Where's Jaxson?"

"Oh, he went to put some hay out for the horses so he wouldn't have to worry about it after dinner. He should be back any minute."

No sooner had the words left Brin's mouth did Jax walk in from the back door, bringing with him the smell of oats and cut alfalfa. He smiled at everyone as he placed his cowboy hat on a peg just inside the door.

"Happy Thanksgiving, everyone!" He walked over to Brinley and placed a hand on her belly, his large palm covering most of the baby bump. "How's my baby?" he said quietly while staring into Brin's eyes and then leaned down so that he spoke to her belly. "Both of them?"

Brin placed her hand over Jax's and said, "We're good."

Mel watched the exchange—just like everyone else—with a small smile. She looked up at Alex to find him staring down at her, a smile of his own gracing his full lips. He squeezed her shoulder in a way that clearly said "That'll be us one day." And for once, the thought of that, of being pregnant with Alex's child, didn't scare her.

Instead she felt hope.

"Okay, guys. Out of the kitchen, all of you. Dad, Aaron, Alex? Why don't you go in and turn on the TV? I'm sure there's a football game playing on one of the channels. Jax, babe? Go shower and change for dinner. We'll eat in thirty minutes."

The men all departed to their designated places, deciding not to argue with the hormonal pregnant woman. Mel, Jess and Tina all got to work helping Brin finish in the kitchen.

Half an hour later, all ten of them were sitting down at the large dining room table. Jaxson asked Mitch to say their blessing for them and the older man complied. He gave thanks to God for the food they were about to eat, asked blessings on the hands that prepared it and gave a tearful thanks for bringing his whole family—new and old—together to spend the holiday as one. Everyone echoed his *Amen* and began reaching for the food.

The fair spread out before them made Mel's mouth water.

A turkey roasted to a golden brown, dressing, sweet potatoes, homemade noodles, mashed potatoes and rolls all on large serving platters barely left enough room for their place settings. Two bottles of white wine made their way around the table, skipping over Brinley, and a pitcher of sweet tea sat in the corner of the table for refills. As the platters were passed around next, everyone began talking and laughing, sharing stories from Thanksgivings past.

So this is what it's like to have a family Thanksgiving? Mel thought to herself and watched the familial camaraderie with a mix of regret at missing it her whole life and joy at being included now.

Alex squeezed her hand underneath the table and she smiled at him.

"You okay?"

"I'm great. This is great. Thank you."

"You're wel–" His words were cut off by a loud crash outside.

Everyone jumped up from the table at once.

"What the heck was that?" Alex uttered, taking the lead in the line of people making their way to the front door since he was closest. Mel brought up the rear, a feeling in the pit of her stomach making her nervous to see what had happened.

When they were all on the front porch, Mel heard the gasps coming from the women and the curses coming from the men. She wheeled her way to the front of the group and froze in shock and horror at what she saw.

Alex's truck–his new, beautiful (she didn't care what Alex said, it was beautiful) truck–sat in the gravel driveway with a brick smashed through the front windshield. And

FOREVER GRATEFUL

white shoe polish across the side, the words blazing in the sun like some awful beacon. A warning.

He's Mine! Back off!

Aimee Martin

Chapter 19

"Remember not the sins of my youth, nor my transgressions: according to thy mercy remember thou me for thy goodness' sake, O Lord." Psalms 25:7

Right as Alex closed the front door of Jaxson's and Brin's house after showing the sheriff and his deputy out, the men descended on him like piranhas on a wounded fish.

"What the hell is going on, son?" Mitch demanded first.

Alex looked over at Melanie who was sitting on the couch with her legs tucked up underneath her. Her face was pale and her eyes were still a little wild and scared. He waited for her to look up at him and when she did, he raised his eyebrows in question. She gave a nod of her head, giving him permission to tell his family what this was all about.

"Y'all are gonna want to sit down."

He waved his hand to the rest of the empty furniture and the men all went and sat by their wives. Alex walked over and stood directly behind Melanie, placed his hands on her shoulders. Whether to give her strength or himself, he didn't know. But he let the feel of her slender frame under his palms fuel him and told his family what their suspicions were.

"You need to keep in mind that what I'm about to tell you isn't necessarily the facts. It's what Melanie and I suspect, but we have no real proof. Only our intuition." He looked down at Melanie when she reached up a hand and held onto his right one, gave him a reassuring squeeze. "It started the first time I went out to California, back in June. Melanie and I met at this place called The Taproom."

Alex went on to explain the entire situation with Denise. How she had tried to pick him up, how Melanie had swooped in and put her in her place. Melanie added that she remembered seeing how enraged Denise had looked when they'd left the bar but she didn't think any more about it. She definitely didn't think the "Stalker-Woman," as they were now calling her, would take things this far.

Next Alex told them about how he had taken Melanie to the country bar and Denise had shown up there, too. About how Melanie had started grilling the woman for personal information.

Which reminds me... Alex thought and placed his hand

under Melanie's chin, lifted her face to him.

"Why did you do that? You never told me what you were up to."

Melanie bit her lip and looked a little embarrassed. She took a deep breath and closed her eyes.

"You remember Ted?"

"The driver? Sure, he was great. What's this got to do with him?"

"He's not just a driver. Actually, he's not a driver at all. He just did that as a favor to me." She opened her eyes and looked at him as she went on. "He used to work security for Dalton. When he left a couple of years ago, he opened up his own private investigating firm."

Alex's shoulders tensed up and his heart started racing at what he knew was coming. But he couldn't stop himself from asking, "What did you do, Melanie?"

"Well… um… I gave him all that information about Denise and asked him to do a check on her. I had this bad feeling Alex. And I'd learned to never ignore those feelings again. Not like I did *that* night."

She spoke this last quietly and Alex knew why. No on here knew about what had happened to her five years ago. But he did, and he understood her need to go with her gut instinct. His shoulders slumped back down as he realized what Melanie must have felt to take the measures that she had.

"I'm sorry, honey. I never should have put you in that position."

"Oh, Alex. It wasn't your fault. How could you have known that Denise was going to turn in Crazy-Stalker-Woman?" He smiled at her dig on the other woman. "Besides, I should be the one who's sorry. If I would've just let her have you that night, none of this would have happened."

He felt his eyes bug out of his head and his mouth dropped open in shock. He was about to yell at her for even thinking that when she started laughing. Not just laughing. Hooting and hollering so loud that she bent over at the waist and held her stomach. His mom and sister joined in followed by his sister-in-law and the other guys.

"I'm sorry, babe. I'm kidding. Really, it's not funny. This is a very serious situation. I just thought we could all use a laugh. I'm sorry," she said again.

He scowled at his family, who were all still chuckling.

"Oh you guys are just hilarious. I'm glad you think this is a laughing matter. Maybe if I just go look Denise up right now I could put an end to all this jealous harassment."

"No!" Melanie shouted above the din of snickers still coming from his family. She stood and walked around the back of the couch, wrapped her arms around Alex's waist. "I'm sorry. But she doesn't get you now."

"She doesn't?" Mel shook her head no at his question.

"And why is that?"

"Because I love you. And the only way she'd get you now is if she could pry you from my cold, dead fingers. And even then, I don't think I would let you go."

"I love you, more, baby. And I'm not going anywhere."

His brother cleared his throat from across the room, reminded Alex that they had an audience.

"Sorry," he said to everyone else and guided Melanie back to the couch, took the empty cushion next to her. "Okay. So what did Ted the P.I. have to say about the Stalker-Woman?"

"She's crazy." Alex laughed this time and Melanie interrupted him. "I mean it, Alex. She's nuts. She was on one of those psychiatric holds once, that Ted found, and she has a long list of criminal history."

"What kind of history?"

"Breaking and Entering, restraining orders, you name it. But the worst..." she stopped and licked her lips.

Alex could see the pulse in her throat pumping faster and knew that whatever she was about to say was getting her worked up and had her scared.

"What's the worst, honey?"

"Aggravated assault with a deadly weapon."

The room was silent. Alex felt his breathing speed up as he tried to grasp what Melanie was saying. The urge to lock her in a room, to protect her at all costs until this woman was far away from them, was so high that it took all his restraint to not go caveman on her and drag her off over his shoulder.

She had her hands clasped together in her lap and wrung them together nervously. She chewed on her bottom lip and wouldn't make eye contact with anyone.

He reached over and grabbed her hand, making her flinch. But then she linked her fingers with his and he ran his thumb along the inside of her wrist in soothing strokes.

Alex knew she wasn't going to want to expand on this anymore but he needed to hear the rest. And he thought that maybe it would help her, too, so that she would realize how serious the situation was.

"Who did she assault, honey?"

Nothing. She stayed silent, still chewing her lip. He could feel the tremors in her hand and knew that whoever had been hurt, whatever had happened, had scared her.

"Melanie?" She raised her gaze to his and there it was. The fear in her beautiful blue-green eyes that he wanted to get rid of forever. "Who got hurt?"

"From what Ted could find, Denise had been with this guy. When she started to get possessive, the guy called it quits. But she kept at him, kept harassing him. Even after he'd started seeing someone else. Then she started harassing his new girlfriend, too. Tried to warn her away from the guy."

Oh, no. This isn't going how I thought it would. I

thought it was gonna be the guy who ... his thoughts were cut off as Melanie continued.

"Denise went after the new girlfriend with a tire iron. Ted said he read the reports and that it was brutal. She almost killed her. They filed charges on her but she was able to get off because of some insanity deal. The judge had her checked into a psychiatric hospital for a hold and for anger management classes and basically let her off with a slap on the wrist."

"Melanie, sweetie, are you and Alex in danger?" Alex's mom, Tina, spoke up from across the room, worry etched on her face.

Melanie looked the woman straight in the eye and said, "I don't know. I didn't think so but Ted warned me to be careful. Judging by what happened today, I think I might have been wrong."

"We'll figure it out, okay?" Alex told Melanie. "You're going to call Ted and fill him in on everything that took place today. And when you go home, you're going to have him find someone to watch over you, twenty-four-seven, until we get this straightened out."

He wrapped his arm around her shoulders and she laid her head against his chest, clutched the fabric of his shirt tightly in her hand.

"I won't let anything happen to you, baby. I promise."

She nodded against his chest. He stroked the back of her

hair and looked across the room at his entire family. All three men looked like they were ready to go to the ends of the earth to help him protect Melanie. And all three women were ready to offer comfort and support. He gave a slight nod of his head to all them, that one movement clearly showing his appreciation.

"Can you all give us a minute?" he asked the small crowd.

"Sure thing, Alex." This from Brinley as she tugged on Jax's hand. He helped his pregnant sister from the couch, guided her back to the kitchen.

Aaron and Jessica followed behind them and Jess laid a reassuring hand on Alex's shoulder as she passed.

His parents were the last ones to leave. His mom had tears in her eyes but never let them fall. His dad stopped right in front of them and said, "Melanie. We consider you a part of this family, now. And we take care of what's ours. That means you."

Mel looked up from Alex's chest and gave his dad a small smile.

"Thank you, Mr. Lambert. That means a lot me."

His dad patted him once on the back and went to the kitchen with the rest of his family. When they were all gone, Alex wasted no time moving Melanie close to him. He lifted her and set her across his lap, wrapped his arms around her back and laid his forehead against hers.

"Okay, truth time. How are you really feeling right now?"

"I'm scared, Alex. What if she tries something when I'm back in California? You won't be there. But even if you were, could you really keep me safe?"

"Don't you do that!" She looked shocked by his little outburst. "Don't you expect me to cower like a rat the way that Justin kid did. I'm not him. And I will protect you. Do you hear me?"

She nodded her head yes with wide eyes. He took a deep breath and cradled her cheek in his right hand, rubbing circles on her lower back with his other.

"I'm sorry. I didn't mean to yell. I just... I love you so much and I'm scared, too, okay? But no matter what, you will be safe."

"Do you know what scares me more than anything?" Her voice was barely above a whisper, the words just loud enough for him to hear and not carry into the kitchen around the corner. "What scares me most is what this whole situation is going to do to me. I mean, if something were to, God forbid, happen to you or me, how is my faith going to withstand it? I'm just a baby at this and I'm worried that my faith in God might not survive."

That's what she's most afraid of? I can help her with that tomorrow.

"Melanie, I want you talk to someone." She started to

shake her head no, no doubt thinking he meant some sort of shrink. "Not that kind of someone. I want you to talk to my minister from church. I think he could really help you to see that once you let the Lord into your heart, there are so many ways to go up from there. Will you do that for me? Will you talk to him?"

Alex could see the indecision in her eyes. Her old nonbelieving-self competing with her new, faithful character. He stared into her eyes, his own bouncing back and forth between her aquamarine gaze.

"Please."

"Alright." She sighed. "I'll talk to your minister."

.　　.　　.　　.　　.

November 28, 2014

Mel held onto Alex's hand like it was a lifeline as they walked to Blacktip's, the restaurant the two had been to back in August.

When Alex had called her this morning and said he'd be picking her up at eleven to go meet his minister, Reverend Pierce, she'd assumed they would be going to a church. Which, understandably, had made her even more nervous since she hadn't been in one since she was a little girl staying with her Gramma.

FOREVER GRATEFUL

So when he'd picked her up a half hour ago and headed to the beach, up and over that steep bridge she remembered so well, she'd asked him where they were going.

"I told Reverend Pierce you might not be comfortable at the church since you're, you know, new to this. To confiding in a clergy and praying and *believing*. So he suggested we meet someplace where you would feel more at ease. And I thought of Blacktip's because we had such a fun and relaxing time there a few months ago. Is that okay?"

He had glanced over at her, worry etched on his face that he might have made the wrong choice.

"It's fine," she'd told him. "Honestly, I think I'd be nervous no matter where we were."

"You're going to be okay, baby. I promise."

"Will you be there with me?"

"No." He sounded a little defeated when he'd answered. "This is something that you have to do on your own. But I'll just be down the beach. At our spot. So if you start to feel overwhelmed or panicked or anything at all, you call me and I'll come get you. Okay?"

"Okay."

Alex had pulled onto the sand at their spot and Mel stared at the water, just like last time, and the way the surface glittered silver in the sunlight. There weren't as many people out this time of year. It wasn't cold, but the wind blowing in from the gulf had a chill to it.

They'd walked to the restaurant in silence. Alex gave Mel the time to prepare and was supportive by just holding her hand.

He guided her up the few steps to the concrete deck and she saw that the minister was already there, sitting in one of those green plastic chairs and waiting for them. She stopped walking, just for a second, and Alex turned to look at her. Mel looked from the minister to Alex and saw empathy in his eyes. He knew how hard this was for her.

Alex was the only person in the entire world she'd ever shared her past with.

He gave her a small smile and nodded his head slightly, encouraging her. She took a deep breath, set her shoulders back, held her chin high and walked the last few steps to the man waiting.

Reverend Pierce was older, she would guess in his fifties, with dark brown hair that was peppered through with gray. Laugh lines crowded the outside corners of his eyes and made him seem like a happy and easy going man. He stood and smiled at Mel when they stopped at the table, held out his right hand. She took it, still holding onto Alex's with her other hand.

"You must be Melanie. I'm Anthony Pierce, but you can call me Tony."

"Nice to meet you. Please, call me Mel. Everyone else does.

"Not everyone," Alex chimed in, looking down at her with love.

"You're not everyone," she whispered.

When she looked back at Tony, he was watching them with a look of interest. Interest in what she wasn't sure. Could be those few words she and Alex had said to each other. Or maybe the look that had passed between them.

Either way, she got the feeling that there was going to be a lot more soul-baring today than she'd originally thought.

That's what you're here for, Mel. To get it all out and find peace fully.

"Okay," Alex began, breaking into her thoughts. "I'm going to leave you two alone. Tony, it was good to see you." He shook the minister's hand, who returned his words with a nod. Then Alex turned to Mel and said, "I'll be right down the beach." He leaned in and kissed her on her cheek, whispered in her ear, "You'll be fine, honey. Just be open and honest and listen to what he has to say."

Mel nodded against his lips but didn't trust her voice to be able to speak without begging him to stay with her, to walk her through what she was supposed to say and do. Alex stepped away and started to walk backwards towards the steps. Their arms outstretched and held onto each other until the very last second. When the contact broke from their fingers, he turned and strode down the steps and back along the beach the way they'd come.

Aimee Martin

Mel turned to face the older man and again he smiled at her, holding his hand out to indicate the free chair across the table from him.

"Why don't we sit, Mel?" She did and he followed suit, folding his hands together on the table top. "So, where would you like to start?"

"Has Alex told you anything? You know... about my past?"

"No, Mel, he hasn't. He said this was your story to tell. That you needed to be the one reveal it to me and I agree with him."

He watched her closely and she glanced down at the plastic separating them like it was a green hole that she knew would only be filled with her words.

"It's not a pretty story. There aren't any hearts and flowers." She looked back at him, at his kind eyes. "It's a rather sordid tale, to be honest."

"I'm not here to judge you, Mel. Only God can do that. I'm here to listen. To help you understand that no matter how *sordid* you think your past is, it's never too disgraceful to give to the Lord. To let Him help and heal you. I'm here to let you talk to someone who'll be impartial and, hopefully, give you some words of wisdom."

"Okay."

"Okay."

He leaned back in his chair and placed his crossed hands

over his belly, the picture of calm reassurance.

"September was five years ago from the night it all started. Actually, I guess it started when I was growing up with hippies for parents and raised agnostic. But that one night in September in Oh-Nine changed it all for me."

She took a deep breath and began to examine the table again, rubbed her index finger along a groove in the plastic, hoping that if she didn't look at the man across from her then getting the words out would be easier.

"I was a senior in college and dating this guy named Justin. We'd gone out to dinner to celebrate our engagement of sorts. It happened when we were leaving the pub and we ran into these three men. Monsters, really."

And Mel went on to tell the minister, a complete stranger, the entire story of what had occurred that night. Of her pain and fear and even the shame that she felt afterwards, when those beasts were gone and she was all alone in that alley. She told him about being sick at seeing all that blood staining the concrete underneath her and how broken she'd felt, physically and emotionally.

She told him about how she'd been a virgin. And that even though she didn't believe in God, not back then, she'd still been saving that part of herself that she'd considered sacred. And when those men took that from her all she could imagine, the only reality she could grasp on to, was that there had to be no God. Why else would that have happened to her? In her mind, at that time, she could only question what kind of heavenly being would let something so horrific and damaging take place in the life of a young woman who never hurt anyone or anything.

"Let me ask you a question, Mel," Tony began when she took a breath from admitting her old perception on faith. "Have you ever thought that maybe it wasn't God organizing that night, but Satan?"

"I'm not sure I understand."

"There have been times in biblical history, and our mainstream history, where God has let Satan try his hardest to get someone to leave their faith behind. You see, if a person denounces God, then they become a soul destined to Hell unless they wholeheartedly repent. There's a book in the bible called Job that tells the story of a man with undying faith."

"Yeah, I think I've heard Brin talk about that before."

Tony nodded his head at her response.

"It's a very popular book. And for good reason. Anyway, Satan thought he could get Job to leave God behind if only enough bad things happened in his life. But God didn't believe that. So he gave Satan free reign to try to ruin Job's life, the only stipulation being that Job could not be killed.

"So Satan went after Job with everything he had. From boils covering his entire body to losing his land and station in life. His wife left him and his children died. And do you know what Job did in regards to God?"

"I would assume he cursed Him. The man had every right to."

"But that's just it." Tony leaned onto the table, his excitement at discussing this age-old story evident. "He didn't curse God. He cursed his birth but always stopped short of accusing God. See, Job knew that his faith would be his saving grace. He knew that the only way out of the living hell he was enduring was to keep his faith in God because God was the only one who could save him. So he prayed and praised and never lost sight of the Lord."

"So he died sick and poor and alone?"

"Not at all." Tony smiled at Mel. "When it became obvious that Job would never lose his faith, God appeared to him and said *"Gird up thy loins like a man."* And He blessed Job for what he'd gone through while never losing faith. Job married again and had more children. He was given double of his original riches. And his health was restored until he died an *old* man.

"My point here, Mel, is that regardless of *who* puts you through hard times, you can't give in and lose your faith. If it's because of Satan, then God will bless you for staying true to Him. And if it's God testing you, then He will also bless you for making it to the other side and never doubting His will for your life."

Mel looked into Tony's eyes for a few seconds before

turning to gaze out at the crashing waves as she thought about what the man had said.

When she'd read the letter from her grandmother, she'd already come to the conclusion that for whatever reason that night had happened, she had survived because she was *meant* to. She had survived because of Him, not in spite of Him. Knowing that made everything Tony was saying easy to agree with.

The harder pill to swallow–and what she feared would never be forgivable–was what had ensued after that night. The pregnancy. The abortion.

And it was those two things that she really needed some clarity on, needed to know if and when and how she could ever be forgiven for one of the greatest sins. Mel squinted her eyes against the glare from the sun on the water's surface fifty yards out. Then she took a deep breath and started talking again.

"I get what you're saying about all of that."

"Good."

"But that's not where my insecurities about faith lie. There's more to the story." She looked back at the minister. "To my story."

Tony nodded encouragingly at her, willed her to continue.

"A little over a month after that night, I found out I was pregnant." Mel paused and watched Tony's face for any sign of realization about what was going to come next. Seeing none, she went on. "I was so scared. First, I was furious, and then sad, depressed. When I finally got to the acceptance phase, I knew what I had to do. Or at least, what I *thought* I had to do" She paused again, determined to meet his eyes when she finally spoke again.

"I had an abortion. Tomorrow will be the five year mark."

Mel waited for him to criticize her or spew judgments at her or maybe just get up and leave. He did none of those things. Instead he just sat there with sympathetic eyes, waiting for her to keep talking.

"Alex has been helping me to see that there *is* a God, and so has a letter I found from my grandmother. And I do believe. Absolutely, unequivocally believe. But how can God ever forgive me for killing that baby? How can He accept me as a member of His eternal family when I did something so selfish and malicious?"

Tony continued to watch her with a look of sadness in his kind, brown eyes. Mel didn't understand; he should be yelling at her right now and showing disgust over what she'd done. And to top that off, he was actually smiling at her.

What does he have to be happy about?

She kept on her little rant while he sat silent across from her.

"So even though I believe that I survived that rape for a

reason, and with God's help, I'm not sure I'll ever be able to believe that God could receive me when I aborted a baby. It's got to be the most unforgivable sin, right?"

Instead of answering her question, Tony leaned forward and took Mel's hands in his. They were warm and soft, comforting. And then he asked a question of his own.

"What's her name?"

"What's whose name?"

"Your baby. What's her name?"

Mel was so shocked at his response that she sat frozen; her mouth gaped open and her eyes grew wide as she stared at him. The only thing she felt, other than shock, was horror. How could he ask her what she'd named a baby that she'd killed? She closed her mouth and shook her head from side to side, confusion and disbelief making her mute.

Mel opened her mouth to speak and then closed it again, unsure of what she actually wanted to say. Her heart was racing; she could feel it pounding on the inside of her chest like a jackhammer. Her breathing was speeding up and she was afraid she might hyperventilate.

Then she blurted out the only words that repeated themselves in her brain.

"What do you mean 'What's her name'? She... he... *it* doesn't have a name." Her voice rose in anger and she couldn't do anything to stop it. "There's no name! I killed it!"

She tried to remove her hands from within his grasp but

he held them steady.

"Before I formed thee in the belly I knew thee, and before thou camest forth out of the womb I sanctified thee..." Tony finally said.

Mel's brow furrowed in confusion and she asked, "What?"

"Jeremiah 1:5. It's a word from God and He's saying that He knows the babies before they have been established in their mother's womb."

"Wait..." Mel began but any further words got caught as she tried to understand what Tony was telling her. She cleared her throat and tried again. "Are you saying that God... that He knew my baby?"

"Yes. Just like He knew you. To God, the only difference between *your* existence and your *baby's* is recognition."

Mel shook her head again at what he was saying, something she seemed to be doing a lot of since she sat down with this minister.

"I don't understand what you mean. How is recognition the only difference between that baby and me?"

"When God made man, the first thing He did was give that man a name. Adam. He then had Adam name all of the animals of the land and the fish in the sea and the birds in the sky so that man could *recognize* what those creatures were. And then He made woman and had Adam give *her* a name.

Eve."

"Okay. I think I understand all that. But that was all at the beginning so of course God had to have names then. Isn't everything and every person that's come about since then named because of man and not God? Didn't he back off after that and let Adam and Eve basically take over from there?"

"In a sense, yes. But God was always there with them, in here." He took his right hand from Mel's and placed it over his heart. "And it's not just God that has always known us. We have known Him, too. About twenty-five hundred years after Adam was created there lived a man named Moses. God came to Moses in the form of a burning bush and told him to set His people free from slavery in Egypt. Moses asked the voice 'Who shall I say sent me?' and God said *"I am that I am." Exodus 3:14*. It means that just as He knows us by our names and souls, so, too, we know Him by His name.

"Recognition. It's what allows us all to have relationships. Be it with our Heavenly Father or each other. God knows your baby has a soul; she's with Him in heaven. But you need to do what all mothers since the beginning of time have done in regards to their children. Mothers bring their baby to her bosom and claim the baby as her own and give the baby a name."

Tony released Mel's hands just as quickly as he took them several minutes ago and stood from the table.

FOREVER GRATEFUL

Mel to looked up at him, baffled, as everything he had said replayed in her mind.

"This is an intimate moment."

"What is?" Her voice was a squeaky whisper.

"Naming your baby. I'm going to go grab a cup of coffee and give you a minute to think of baby names for her."

"There is no baby!" Mel's voice finally came out loud and clear as she yelled at him. "I killed it!"

He walked to her side and laid his hand on her shoulder, looked down at her pale face when he spoke.

"No human being on the face of the earth has the power to destroy a soul. She is as alive today as you and I. And she needs a name."

Then he patted her shoulder twice before walking behind her to enter into the restaurant, leaving Mel to stare into the empty space across from her as his words slowly began to click into place, like the gears of a lock lining up.

In somewhat of a daze, Mel stood from the table and walked to the bottom step of the deck, sat down on the weathered wood, wrapped her arms around her legs and resting her chin on her bent knees. Tears slowly ran from the corners of her eyes and the wind blowing in off of the coast made the wetness sting against her cheeks. The minister's last words rang in her ears over and over again until she felt like she could see them written in the sand at her feet, as well as hear them.

Aimee Martin

She's alive. Her soul isn't destroyed.

Mel's breath hitched in her throat as she finally comprehended what Tony was telling her. Her baby wasn't dead. Her baby is alive and healthy and happy in heaven, eternally. The tears came steadily as she whispered words–words that floated away on that breeze before anyone else could hear them–that were meant only for her daughter. And somehow she knew, from the bottom of her heart, that her baby was a little girl.

"Sarah. Your name is Sarah. Oh, God," she cried quietly. "I'm so sorry, my sweet baby. I'm sorry that I didn't give you a chance to live. I'm so sorry that I took your life for granted and didn't understand what a blessing you were. I know you would have changed my life had I only given you a chance.

"No, you *are* a blessing. Even though you aren't here, in my arms, I know that you *have* changed my life. I always thought that what had happened and getting pregnant was for the worst. But I was so wrong, baby. You've changed my life for the better. My sweet Sarah, it wasn't Alex or Gramma's letter that changed me. It's this. Right now. Knowing that you are thriving in the arms of our Lord regardless of what my sins were has made me realize that He was with me all along, waiting for me to come to Him. And to you. Oh, Sarah. I'm so sorry."

Her tears got too thick in her throat and she couldn't talk

anymore. She buried her face in her hands on her knees and cried. She cried what she had lost, yes, but more for what she had found. Knowledge and recognition, just like Tony had said, that her baby girl's soul lived on.

Tiny fingers wrapped themselves around the hair by the side of Mel's face, tucking it behind her ear. And then Mel felt small lips lay across her wet cheek. She jumped and turned to find where the sensations were coming from. Her breath halted and she froze.

A little girl of about four years old with bright blonde hair and aquamarine eyes sat down next to her on the step, smiling as she reached over and placed her tiny hand in Mel's and gripped her fingers. Her skin was so pale it was translucent, and her smile was happy with relief.

"I forgive you, Momma," the girl breathed. "Thank you for naming me. It means Princess," she said with an impish twinkle in her beautiful eyes. "Sarah, your princess. Bet you didn't even know that." Her voice was so small, just like her body. "I will always be your Princess. It's all going to be okay now. You're going to be okay, Momma."

The little girl laid her head on Mel's lap and that's when Mel felt it. There was a warming in her chest, like a comforting hand wrapping itself around her heart. She felt little tendrils of heat spread from her chest and work their way down throughout the rest of her body, wrapping her in a warm cocoon from the inside out.

And she felt a peace, a tranquility unlike anything she had ever known, settle deep inside her soul.

"Do you feel it?"

"It?" Mel asked and gently placed her hand down on the silky curls lying across her thigh.

"The Holy Spirit."

Mel's hand froze in its downward stroking.

Is that what this warming is?

"Yes, Momma," her daughter answered, reading her thoughts. Sarah raised her head and laid her little hand across Mel's chest, right over her beating heart. "He's here. And always will be if you ask Him to. Just like me."

Mel's lips quivered, making her words sound like vibrations as she answered, "Yes, sweetheart. I feel it. And I don't ever want to lose it." She looked from her daughter's eyes that were so like hers and turned her gaze to the sky, to the white clouds floating overhead like a symbol of hope calling to her.

"I ask you, God, to please come into my heart. I ask that you forgive me for my sins. Have mercy on me and my stupid, childish mistakes. Please come into my soul and give me a chance to make my wrongs right in your eyes." Mel looked back down at her little girl and then, "Give me a chance to redeem myself so that I may one day live eternally with You and Sarah. Please, Lord, protect my baby until I can be with her again. Amen."

FOREVER GRATEFUL

Sarah smiled and nodded her head in acceptance, her face lighting up like the morning sun, making her entire body glow in happiness.

Therefore if any man be in Christ he is a new creature: old things are passed away; behold, all things become new. You are forgiven, dear child. Go in peace and show your love for the Lord to one and all.

The words weren't spoken aloud but Mel heard them all the same. In her head and her heart. She felt them in her soul.

"We'll always be with you, Momma. Forever."

Just as her last word was spoken, Mel heard the door to the restaurant swing open and bang closed. And right before her eyes, Sarah's form began to shimmer like a mirage, her smile still in place. Mel watched as another hand grasped Sarah's and guided her down the beach. That was all she saw–just a hand–but it was enough that Mel knew her daughter was safe in the hands of Jesus.

Mel was so overcome with that feeling of peace and relief that she couldn't even feel sad that her daughter was gone. She reached up and laid her own hand across her heart and knew that Sarah was there, just like her little girl had said she'd be. Tears flowed freely from her eyes but this time, they were tears of joy.

Tony sat down on the step next to her, right where Sarah had just been, and handed her a cup of coffee. Mel shook her head like she was coming out of a trance and took the mug, cradled it in her palms as her waterworks continued. Tony reached around and laid his hand across Mel's back, rubbing up and down in a soothing motion.

"Are you alright?"

Mel could only nod her head while she looked at the minister, tears streaming.

"Did you name your baby?"

"I did," she began and laughed, excitement at her new beginning making her happier than she'd ever felt. "Her name is Sarah. She told me her name means Princess. I talked to her. She forgave me."

Tony cocked his head to the side, his brow furrowed and his lips turned down at the corners, confusion evident in his expression. Something had clearly happened here. Sarah did indeed mean Princess and he seriously doubted that Mel knew Hebrew.

"She was here, Tony. And she forgave me. I know it; I feel it. In here." She laid her right hand back across her heart again.

Tony slowly nodded his head in understanding, a smile forming on his mouth as he asked, "And what about God?"

"I felt Him with me the whole time. And I heard Him. Well, not really heard, but His words were there. I asked Him into my heart and for forgiveness. And He gave it, freely.

"It was so amazing."

FOREVER GRATEFUL

More tears and laughs, Mel was still stunned at how willingly God had been to forgive her. She would never take that for granted.

"I asked Jesus to take of my daughter and I know He will. He loves me. They all do. And I know I'll see my baby again one day. I can live with that, happily. I belong to God who created the world. Nothing will ever separate me from Him."

"You've done well, Mel. You've been saved," Tony said but Mel's gaze was torn from the man's kind eyes, drawn instead to the form walking down the beach toward them.

"Excuse me," she muttered as she stood and raced across the sand.

Alex scooped her up in his arms when she reached him and spun her in a circle. She laughed and cried into his shoulder and felt his own smile against the skin of her neck. He slowly stopped spinning and gently set her down on the ground. Taking her face in his hands, he ran his thumbs underneath her eyes, wiped the tears away, and placed a tender kiss on her lips.

"You okay?"

"Oh, Alex. I'm better than okay. I'm saved."

He smiled, his eyes twinkling and glistening with tears of his own.

"I'm so proud of you, baby. I love you."

"I love you, Alex. Always."

Aimee Martin

Chapter 20

"Ask, and it shall be given you; seek, and ye shall find; knock, and it shall be opened unto you." Matthew 7:7

December 25, 2014

Mel walked down Pacific Avenue at Venice Beach and marveled at how much had changed on the Boardwalk since the last time she was here. Granted, she hadn't been down since a year after her Gramma died. It had just been too painful, brought too many memories that broke her heart.

But now her heart was whole again and she was able to face those memories head on with nothing but fondness and happiness.

Being with Alex, admitting her love for him those few months ago, had released some sort of dark chasm that had hung over her. And ever since, Alex's love had begun filling that crater with goodness and light and promise.

And then there was the confession, the revelation. Accepting that her Sarah was real and alive and well in Heaven with God brought home a peace that she had only dreamt about but never hoped to have.

The name, Sarah, just popped into her head and yet, because her daughter told her the meaning of her name, this miracle was shared. Even the minister knew what she'd seen was real. He'd asked her if she knew Hebrew. Mel laughed at the memory. The spirit of a little child told her the meaning of the name she'd chosen for her and gave her a confirmation that would last a lifetime. Nothing would ever take that beautiful experience from her.

In times to come, when her faith would try to weaken, she could look back to that heavenly visit and regain her peace. And knowing that the Lord had forgiven her, even after she struggled and fought so hard against it, made her feel like there was nothing but purity waiting for her and Alex and their future.

And Sarah, her beautiful Princess? Mel knew she'd see her again.

Alex.

He had been so determined but so patient, waiting for her to get to the same place he was. Owning the love that was flowing between them. And now, with that honest love pouring freely from her, Mel saw the world in a different way.

Like now, on the Boardwalk.

When she'd come here in December on the one year anniversary of her Gramma's death, back in two-thousand and eight, tears had clogged her vision and an ache had taken over her chest. Anxiety had made her sweat and shake and feel like she was going to throw up so bad that she swore she would never come back. Not if those feelings were all she had to look forward to.

But now, six years after that first experience, there was no ache or anxiety. No sweating or shaking or nausea. Granted, it was actually two days after the anniversary but she figured her grandmother would understand since this whole inner-peace thing was so new to her. She still had tears in her eyes but they were sweet and full of promise. For the first time since Gramma's passing, Mel felt close to her again.

And it was all thanks to Alex for showing her the beauty of trust and love through him and God. Mel couldn't help but feel that her grandmother would be proud. She prayed it was true.

When she reached the pier she walked over and sat on one of the many benches lining the walk. The faded green wood was hard on her back as she leaned against it. But she embraced the slight discomfort as she watched the people walking by, because it meant she was *feeling* again.

The sun was beginning to set and it warmed the left side of her face, casted orange glows on everyone.

Well, everyone except for the tall man with dark, mocha skin wearing a black suit and sunglasses who hung in the shadows thirty yards away. Mel knew Ted had hired the man to keep an eye on her, at least until the situation with Denise was taken care of. The first couple weeks were hard; she kept wanting to call Ted and tell him to have the man back off. But now she barely noticed him. And she had to admit, knowing he was there gave her a sense of comfort. As long as he kept his distance (which he always did).

Mel ignored his presence and focused on the other people who walked down the Boardwalk. Even though it was Christmas night, people were still out and about. Maybe walking off their big dinners or just grabbing a bit of fresh air after cleaning up from presents. It soothed Mel to know that she wasn't alone in her need to be out in the open on this day.

A family of five–mom, dad, two teenage boys and a little girl no more than six–passed in front of Mel. The little girl wore a bright red, velvet dress and squealed as her older brothers held each of her hands, swinging her up off the ground. The parents walked a few steps behind them, holding hands and smiling at their children.

A man around her age rode by on a unicycle, quickly

heading down Speedway. He was wearing biker shorts and had a bright yellow Mohawk. The three bowling pins he was juggling did nothing to take away from his clothes. Or lack thereof.

Performers, Mel thought with a smile.

As she brought her head back around her gaze caught on a man walking out of a shop one block up and a little to the right from where she sat. She watched him walk past the corner of Washington Boulevard and Dell Avenue. He was older, maybe in his fifties, with a head full of silver hair. His shoulders looked strong; his posture was straight almost to the point of being rigid. But what made her stare was the naval working uniform he had on. The many shades of overlapping blue had an obvious effect on the man's demeanor. His face was stern but content. His attitude was reserved but untroubled. Everything about him portrayed discipline and dedication.

He reminded her so much of Alex.

Even though Alex had retired from the Navy, Mel could picture him at that age, revealing all of those same qualities the older man was portraying that were ingrained on a person when they joined the military. Or so she'd heard.

Mel continued to watch the man walk down Washington, headed in her direction, and she began to wonder about him. She played with different scenarios in her mind of where he was going and what he would be doing.

Maybe he was off to meet his wife and go to dinner or a movie. Or he could be looking for a gift for his grandchildren since he appeared to be the right age.

Of course, it was possible that he was alone and was just out killing time before he went home to an empty house.

Once upon a time, that last thought probably would have been first and foremost in her mind because she'd been so cynical about 'happy ever afters' and the people who claimed to have them. But now, now she knew better. She knew that those happy ever afters existed in real life and not just fairy tales.

She was living one herself.

The thought of her own fairy tale, her life with Alex, brought a smile to her lips. She closed her eyes and let the sun continue to warm her cheek while she imagined all that the future would hold for them.

When a shadow fell across her face and blocked the glow to her left, she opened her eyes to see what was in the way of the fading sun. Her breath caught in her throat and she gasped.

"Alex. Why are you… how did you…" she stuttered. Taking a deep breath to clear her thoughts, she tried again. "What are you doing here? I thought you were going to spend Christmas with your family and come out on the thirtieth?"

His relaxed stance while he grinned down at her with his

hands in the front pockets of his jeans was at complete odds with her racing heart. His broad shoulders stood out in his dark blue t-shirt and Mel itched to stand up and throw her arms around them. To feel the strength she knew was there, hidden under the navy cotton. But she was frozen to the bench, stunned as to why and how he was here.

"I spent this morning there," he began, his deep voice settling the pounding in her chest. "And while I watched my parents open their presents from each other, smiling at one another with love, I realized that I didn't want to wait for New Year's Eve. I couldn't wait."

He removed his hands from his pockets and walked around Mel's legs to sit on her right side. She followed his movements with her eyes until he was right next to her on the bench, sparing only a quick glance down when he reached over and took her hand in both of his, before looking back up into his eyes.

"That love and devotion they shared this morning, that they share every day, is what I wanted this Christmas. I didn't need any presents under a tree. I needed you."

All of the people around them blurred in her periphery, tunnel vision took over as Mel stared at Alex and saw what was in his gaze. Love and devotion, just like he'd said.

But also truth.

He absolutely meant what he was saying and Mel felt herself fall just a little bit more in love with him right then.

That he was willing to leave his family–on a holiday that she knew meant a lot to him–and come here made Mel realize just how committed he was to this relationship. To her.

"Oh, Alex. I needed you, too." Tears pooled in her eyes but she blinked them away. "I didn't know just how much until right at this moment. This, you being here, is the best present I could have ever asked for. Thank you."

Alex pulled on her hand, making her lean in toward him until her chest was laid up against his and she felt his strong heartbeat in tune with hers. He brought his lips down, giving her a small peck that held more affection than any heated kiss could, and whispered, "Merry Christmas, love."

.　　.　　.　　.　　.

December 29, 2014

It had been four days since Alex made the spur-of-the-moment decision to fly to California on Christmas. He and Melanie's original plans were for him to have flown in tomorrow. But just like he'd told her that night at Venice Beach, he couldn't stay away.

Luckily he had spoken with her that morning when he'd called to wish her a Merry Christmas. So when he showed up at her condo–letting himself in with the key she'd given him at Thanksgiving–and saw that she wasn't home, he knew exactly where to find her.

When Alex had first spotted her on that bench with the evening sun aglow around her, she had taken his breath away. Her beauty, her innocence. And her determination to make a better life for herself than what her past had tried to dictate. He thanked God right then and there for bringing them together and prayed that his love for her would always be as strong as he felt then in his heart.

After walking up to her and surprising her–*Man, I wish I could have captured the look on her face when she saw me*–they walked along the Boardwalk until the sun had fallen fully beneath the horizon. The stars had begun to twinkle right as the seagulls flying overhead had squawked their final calls for the day and flew off to sleep for the night. They'd made their way to her car parked in a lot several blocks from up from Pacific and drove back to her house.

If he could have had his way, they would've been back in Lake Shores, at their new house, cuddled up in front of a fire. But since there weren't any fireplaces in her building, they settled for a cluster of ten candles of varying sizes on the coffee table. The smell of gardenia floated through the air around them and Alex hadn't known if it was from the candles or the woman he held tightly in his arms. He didn't care, either.

Alex had reclined on the couch and Melanie had sat in front of him, in between his legs. She'd idly stroked the tips of her fingers up and down his left forearm that was wrapped around her shoulders and clasped the fingers of his right hand that rested on her belly. In that moment, Alex knew what true happiness was.

He had the woman of his dreams in his arms. He had her love. And they had a future just waiting for them to reach out and grab.

He couldn't wait to get started.

When midnight rolled around, Alex had suggested they get some sleep. He had walked Melanie to her bedroom and gave her a kiss goodnight. It might have lasted a little longer than he'd anticipated but he'd managed to pull away before things got out of hand. With a final touch of his lips to her forehead, he'd closed her in her room and walked across the hallway to the spare bedroom. Stripping down to his boxer briefs, Alex had climbed into bed and dreamt of the day that he would finally be able to sleep in the same bed as Melanie.

In the days since his arrival, Alex and Melanie had done everything from shopping (yes, she did finally drag him to Rodeo Drive) to going to the movie theater to strolling down the Hollywood Walk of Fame. They ate out at lunch and usually stayed home to cook dinner together, preferring that time alone without prying eyes.

Because it never failed that Alex would reach over and kiss her in the middle of their meal. Or grab her and start dancing to the tune of running water while they were washing the dishes.

Today, because he had requested a change of pace from all the excitement the last few days, and because the weather was unseasonably warm at seventy-seven degrees, they had decided to spend the afternoon at the beach. Instead of going to one of the more heavily populated areas, they drove down to Malibu where Brin's house was so they could take up space right off her back deck, giving them more privacy.

After unlocking the front door with the key his sister had given her, Melanie led him through the house to the back doors, off of the deck and onto the warm sand. Alex set the tote bag she'd packed that morning down and laid out the two beach towels. Melanie quickly sat down on one to keep it from blowing away, giggling as Alex fought with his own towel that blew around his ankles before he got it flat and managed to sit before it floated off in the breeze.

Then she reached into her bag, grabbed a pair of sunglasses and put them on. She pulled out an iPod, queued up a song by Ella Fitzgerald, and laid it next to her head on the towel. Alex watched her movements, how graceful they were, and marveled at how composed she was even when she wasn't trying to be.

But when she laid back on her elbows, all thought of grace and composure fled from his brain. What was left was a natural urge to climb over onto her towel and kiss her deeply. To show the few other beach patrons walking around that this beautiful woman next to him was his and his alone. And he fought down the deepest urge to carry her off to the nearest courthouse so that a judge could marry them.

That was the feeling that was the most surprising to him. Especially seeing as how, even though he'd asked, she hadn't even said yes yet.

But she will. I know it.

Alex rolled over to his side and propped his head up on his elbow so he could take in every inch of Melanie. Her head was tipped back so the sun could wash over her face. Her hair fell down to touch the towel beneath her and it looked like a golden curtain. She wore a black bikini that was covered on top by a white tank, allowing Alex just small glimpses of what lay hidden beneath. Covering her bottoms and legs was a sheer pink material with big marigolds imprinted on it. He thought it was some type of bathing suit cover-up skirt.

Whatever it was, the split that ran up the length of her left leg showcased a tan and toned calf and thigh. His hand itched to remove the material from her right leg so he could see if it was as beautiful and enticing as her left.

To keep his free hand busy, he picked up a handful of sand and let the tiny grains sift through his fingers while he let his eyes continue to caress her.

Finally sensing his gaze, Melanie turned her head and smiled when she saw him watching her. Turning back to the sun overhead, she said, "What are you doing?"

"Nothing. Looking at you."

"I figured that. So I guess the right question would be *why* are you looking at me?"

"Because I can." Alex put some cheekiness into those three words, made it seem like that was all the reason he needed.

She laughed at his answer and the sound was a sweet melody that rang from his ears down to his toes. For the first few months that he and Melanie dated, those laughs were few and far between.

But ever since her trip to Lake Shores for Thanksgiving– ever since her eye-opening confession about her baby to Tony–he noticed that she laughed more and more.

And the fact that he was the one to elicit those laughs made his chest swell with pride.

"I love hearing that."

"Hearing what?"

"Your laugh."

Melanie turned her head to look at him again, pulling her sunglasses down her nose as she did. He thought his statement might bring out some kind of sweet response from her. But he could tell by the little smirk on her face that that wasn't going to happen.

"You must not get out much if that's all it takes to make you happy."

"Don't be a goober. Lots of things make me happy. You, everything about you, just happen to be at the top of the list."

"Did you just call me a 'goober'?'"

Now it was his turn to laugh at the way her expression morphed from playfulness to one of disbelief. Like the sound of that childlike word was so foreign to her that she didn't know how to respond.

"Yes. Goober. Kind of like dork, only less well-known."

"Hmm. I'm not sure how I feel about that."

"Yes, you do. You feel like it's a term of endearment and you love it. Even if you won't admit it."

"Maybe," she said. But a smile teased the corners of her lips and Alex knew he was right. "I think I still like some of your other ones better, though."

Now Alex did roll over onto his hands and knees and slowly crawled toward her. Like a panther stalking his prey. He positioned himself right up next to her chest, forced her to lie back on her towel. He placed his hands on either side of her head, leaned down and spoke in a soft voice.

"You mean honey?" He kissed her left cheek. "Or baby?" A peck to her right cheek. "Maybe darlin'?" He brought his face back just enough to stare into her eyes, getting lost in those blue-green depths. "Or love?"

By the way her breath caught on that last one he figured it was the sweet nothing that meant the most to her.

"Because you are. My love."

FOREVER GRATEFUL

And he laid his lips across hers. What he meant to be just a small touch, a little taste of her lips, exploded into something bigger. He should have known better. Every time he kissed his Melanie a fire exploded inside him and he couldn't ever seem to get enough.

He leaned an elbow to the ground and wrapped that hand around the back of her head, brought her closer to him. He brought his right hand to her face, skimmed his fingers down her jaw until they landed on the side of her neck. He felt her pulse pounding beneath his palm and his picked up the same rhythm when she delicately touched her tongue to his, slowly delved deeper.

He gave back what she was offering ten-fold. Showed her with his mouth exactly what she was doing to him, stimulating in him. A possessive need and yearning to have her, to love her in more ways than one.

But you promised her you wouldn't make love to her until you were married.

His thoughts were like a bucket of ice cold water on his desire and quickly put out the flames that she ignited in him with the smallest gesture.

Alex forced his mouth away from Melanie's, ignoring the protesting moan she gave, and rested his forehead against hers. Their panting breaths mingled with one another and he closed his eyes to try to get back his control.

"I'm sorry, baby. I didn't mean for that to happen."

Alex felt her cool hand reach up and lay across his cheek, waiting there until he opened his eyes and looked down at her. She smiled, a look of tenderness crossing over her face at his remorse.

"Please, don't be. I'm not. Every time you kiss me, hold me, touch me…" she paused and swallowed thickly. "You help to make those bad memories go away, overcoming them like you would an enemy and keeping them in the past where they're supposed to be. What you give to me, Alex, by kissing me and touching me, is a gift. One I'm not sure I'll ever be able to repay. But I'm sure as hell going to try."

"You make me sound like some kind of saint. When I'm anything but, Melanie. I've had my share of past enemies; just like you."

"Name one," she whispered, her soft voice floating on the sea breeze.

"Promiscuity."

"What do you mean?"

"When I was younger, I wasn't exactly the most well behaved Christian boy. I dated lots of girls, slept with some of them. Along with a few that I wasn't dating. And that's not something I'm proud of. Most parents refused to let their daughters go out with me after word got around. That's not exactly the picture of perfect obedience."

"How old were you?"

"How old was I?" His brow furrowed in confusion as he

repeated her question. She nodded her head and he blew out a quick breath before answering, "In high school. Seventeen, eighteen. That's one of the reasons I joined the Navy. I could see that I was headed someplace dark and knew that I needed to get out. Joining the military was the only thing I could think of that would help to bring me back to the man I wanted to be. That and remembering my relationship with God."

"Alex, one of the things you've taught me these past few months is that no one, ever, is beyond redemption. No one is beyond forgiveness. You were just a kid; you didn't know any better."

"I should have," he interrupted and Melanie placed her fingers over his mouth to shush him.

"I remember the teenage boys with raging hormones when I was younger. Honestly, it's a wonder any of you make it to adulthood." Alex laughed beneath her touch and she went on. "My point, Alex, is that just because you made a mistake, doesn't mean that you're a bad person. It doesn't mean that God doesn't love you. As long as you… what's that word? The one where you ask for forgiveness?"

He reached up and wrapped his hand around her wrist, kissed the center of her palm, before bringing her hand down, away from his mouth to rest on his chest.

"Repent."

"Yes, that's it. As long as you repented, then you'll be

forgiven. Right?"

"Yeah." He smiled at her innocence, the purity of her faith that was so new and yet still strong. "How did you get to be so smart on theology?"

"I had a good teacher."

He leaned in and pressed his lips to hers, soft and sweet, then rolled back over onto his own towel. He kept her hand in his, rested them in the sand between them.

They stayed like that, quiet and reflective, for several long minutes. The waves crashed into the shore like white noise, blocking out all of his misgivings from just moments ago. The sun hid behind a big, white cloud but its rays peeked through, long and thin lines of pale yellow reached out to touch them.

Alex heard Melanie sigh in what he assumed was contentment and he couldn't help but feel the same way. Like they were in their own little bubble, protected from the outside world and kept safe with only their love and happiness surrounding them.

It made what he was about to bring up all the more hard. But he knew that before they could fully move on with their life, he needed to know the last details of what had happened to Melanie that night.

And he hoped that her newfound faith would help to give her the strength to go over the final moments.

"Hey, baby?"

"Hmm?"

"You mentioned something a few minutes ago and I've been meaning to ask you about it."

"What's that?"

"You said that my kiss, my touch, helps to take away all of those bad memories from that night." He paused and bit his lip, wondered if maybe this wasn't such a good idea after all.

"What about it, Alex?"

Well, that solves that worry.

"Whatever happened to those men? I mean, you never talked about anything beyond what they did and then the pregnancy after. I was just curious as to whether or not they were ever arrested."

She was silent for so long that Alex was afraid he might have lost her. He sat up and turned his body so that he was facing her and what he saw made him stop breathing for a second.

He'd expected tears, maybe fear evident in her expression. He did not expect to see the look of acceptance. Or the small smile playing on her mouth.

"You don't have to tell me, baby. I couldn't ever find the right time to ask. I guess there isn't ever really a good time to bring something like this up," he reassured her. "But honestly, if it's too much, just say so and we can leave it at that."

Melanie released his hand so that she could sit up and face him, mirroring his position. She removed her sunglasses and looked into his eyes and, yes, there were tears there but she blinked them away.

Then she turned to look out at the ocean to her right as she spoke.

"They were never arrested, Alex. I didn't even go to the police. After their warning I was just too scared."

"But Melanie____" he started to protest but she cut him off.

"No, Alex, don't. Just listen. Okay?"

"Alright."

"I guess you could say that what they got was far worse than jail," she began and then stopped, like the words were stuck in her throat.

"I don't understand, honey."

She took a deep breath, her chest rose and fell underneath that white tank top and black bikini. When she turned to look back at him, the tears were gone. In their place was a look of pure courage and it made him proud to know that she was willing to do whatever it took to move past that hurt. Including baring details that he was sure she'd rather leave in some dark corner of her mind.

But when a minute had passed and she still hadn't said anything, he prompted her.

"Why do you say they got something worse, Melanie?"

FOREVER GRATEFUL

"Because they're dead, Alex. All of them."

· · · · ·

September 12, 2009

She'd finally quit throwing up.

After the heaving stopped, the realization of what had just happened began to sink in. Mel knew she had to get out of that dark alley. She had to get home.

She jerked when a pair of hands reached for her arms and she let out a shriek. She looked up into a pair of brown eyes staring down at her with a mix of shock and disgust.

Funny. She used to think those eyes were beautiful. Full of promise for a future that they had just decided on sharing.

Now, she looked at Justin and saw only a shriveling piece of man. A coward who would do nothing for her as the years went by except hold her back. There was no way in hell she was going to let that happen.

Jerking her arms away from his too-soft hands, she practically screeched at him, "Get away from me!"

"Mel. Come on, it's me. Justin. Let me help you."

"You mean like you helped me when those three men were attacking me?" She managed to stand, albeit on shaky legs, and squared her shoulders at the worm in front of her. "You can't help me. You won't. Not if it's going to put your life in any kind of danger."

She turned and slowly made her way to the entrance of the alley. She placed a hand on the rundown red brick wall to her left for support, hoped to find a cab close by to take her home.

"We need to get you to the hospital or something. Come on, Mel. Cut me some slack, here."

Anger had her whirling around on Justin. She wobbled as her balance was tested but managed to stay upright.

"Cut *you* some slack?" she asked, incredulous. "Three men just *raped* me and you want me to cut you some slack?!"

He at least had the decency to look ashamed. Good. He should feel that way.

"You're no better than those men. You hid in that corner–" she threw her arm in the direction of the place where Justin had spent the last hour, "–and did nothing but shrink away. Right when I needed you most. You're not worth it. You'll never be worth the effort I've put into this relationship. I don't ever want to see you again. Please. Just leave me alone."

Her voice quivered on those last few words but Melanie managed to hold the tears in. Turning back toward the alley opening, she made her way to the sidewalk and looked both ways. Half a block down on her right was a car, its *TAXI* sign on top lit up like a bright, yellow banana shining in the dark night.

The thirty steps it took to make it to the cab seemed to take forever on Mel's tired and battered body. But she finally–*Finally!*–made it to the door and slipped into the backseat.

The driver glanced at her through the rearview mirror then did a double take, looking much longer the second time.

"Are you okay, Miss?"

"I'm fine. To the University, please. Hamilton Dormitory."

"Are you sure you don't need to go to the hospital?" Mel closed her eyes and shook her head, not wanting the man to see the shame on her face. "Okay," he said and drove off toward her dorms.

She didn't even think about looking behind her to see if Justin was still there.

When the cabbie dropped her off and she tried to pay him his fare, he waved the money away. Told her that this ride was on the house. She accepted his generosity and trudged up the stairs to the building's front door. Taking a right at the first hallway, she walked all the way down to her room at the end and let herself in.

Luckily, her roommate, Allyson, was gone for the night. Out to some party her boyfriend's fraternity was throwing. Mel closed the door once she was inside and locked the deadbolt, leaned against the cold wood for a minute as tears threatened.

No! You're stronger than this, Mel!

Using her pep talk for momentum, Mel pushed off the door and went into the bathroom that she and Allyson shared with two other girls. Stripping down to nothing, Mel threw her clothes into the trashcan next to the toilet, not even bothering to see if they were salvageable.

Anything that could remind her of tonight had to go.

She turned the shower on and stepped under the steamy spray, turned the heat up as high as she could stand it. She hoped that maybe the scalding water would remove the touch of those men's hands and mouths. But no matter how hard she scrubbed, she could still feel them, like a ghost's fingers running along her body.

Mel gave up after scrubbing her body three times and her hair twice. She shut the shower off and wrapped up in one of their big, pink, fluffy bath sheets. Wrapping another one around her wet hair, Mel brushed her teeth and walked out into their room, over to her bed that set next to the window.

She curled up under the white cotton quilt (bath towels and all), laid her head on the pillow and finally let the tears that had been trying to fall for the last two hours take control. They rained down her cheeks like Niagara Falls, relentless in their effort to soak her face and pillow. She didn't know how long she cried for but it was long enough for her to fall asleep before the tears stopped.

September 13, 2009

Mel woke when the bright morning sun filtered in through the cracks in the blinds to her left. Her head ached like a sledge hammer was beating on it. Her eyes felt gritty and swollen. Her throat was dry and it hurt to try and swallow.

She pushed herself up in bed and moaned with the effort. Her entire body hurt; everything from her face to her toes were sore and if she hadn't known better she'd have thought she'd been in some kind of wreck. What hurt the most–her most feminine areas–brought back memories from the night before and she realized that it had actually happened. That she hadn't just experienced a horrible nightmare.

Hoping that if she just ignored the discomfort then the memories would go away, she clenched her jaw tightly and forced herself out of bed.

Mel made a point of not looking into the mirror while she went to the restroom or brushed her teeth. After splashing some cool water on her face and gulping down an entire bottle of water from Allyson's mini-fridge, she went back to bed. Mel curled up with a pillow between her legs as well as one hugged tightly to her chest. Something about the soft cushion helped to alleviate some of the pain.

She reached over to her nightstand and grabbed the remote, turned on the television. One of the local news programs was on, some reporter going on and on about the water department's problems keeping track of the online payments of customers.

Mel was getting ready to change the channel when the reporter cut back to the anchor, an older man in his forties with salt and pepper hair who'd been on this station for as long as she could remember. But it wasn't him, per se, that made her stop from changing the channel.

No, it was the footage they were showing of a fiery car crash. And the pictures of the victims of the crash that they displayed in the upper right corner of the screen. Three faces that she knew she'd never forget for the rest of her life.

It was the faces of the men who had raped her the night before.

Chapter 21

"The Lord will also be a refuge for the oppressed, a refuge in times of trouble."
Psalms 9:9

Mel stared at the television in a kind of daze. Anger mixed with relief which mixed with confusion. They fought for the front running place in her mind.

Why couldn't this have happened two nights ago?

The bitter thought caused her body to tremble. She'd never been an eye-for-an-eye type of person before. But apparently when a horrible enough injustice was done to someone, even the most caring person could become spiteful.

Or so it seemed if her current feelings were anything to go by.

Shaking herself out of her frozen stupor, Mel reached

for the remote that had fallen from her hand when she saw those faces and turned up the volume. The anchorman's voice echoed in her silent room.

"... *but according to the police, no other cars were involved in the accident that took place around Two a.m. The reports we've received from eye witnesses state that the car was swerving all over the highway at a high speed when it seems that the driver lost control of the car. The black sedan then rammed straight into the concrete median. Paramedics arrived at the scene seven minutes later but they were too late. A leak in the gas tank caught on fire due to the sparks put off from an electrical short circuit, igniting the car into a ball of flames. Onlookers said the heat could be felt from fifty yards away and that the stench coming from the vehicle was 'unlike anything they'd ever smelled'. The San Diego Fire Department battled the flames for less than ten minutes before they had the fire under control. Unfortunately, the three passengers of the automobile had perished before the firemen were able to pull them from the car. The police were able to identify the bodies from dental records and have notified the families. No word yet on whether alcohol or drugs were involved. Stay tuned for more information on this story as it unfolds, tonight at Six.*"

As the anchor went on to another story, Mel turned off the TV and watched the black screen like the footage was still playing.

FOREVER GRATEFUL

She could see the fire from the hood of the car rising up like fingers to reach for the sky. She could see the mangled metal that had once been in the form of an automobile. And if she closed her eyes and thought real hard, she'd swear that she could almost smell that scent the witnesses had said was so sickening.

When she opened her eyes she felt the tears running down her cheeks and let them go unheeded. She needed to cry. She needed to feel something other than the relief that those monsters were gone from this world forever, never able to hurt another woman.

But she couldn't.

Relief was all that was there.

And despite what they had done to her the night before, she fought down a laugh that tried to bubble up from her throat. Mel placed a hand over her mouth to stifle the laughter, thinking she must be going crazy.

Oh, God... I'm nuts!

And then the laughs came out regardless of her efforts to stop them. Hysterical laughter that caused her to bend at her waist and fall face down onto her pillow. Her shoulders shook and her belly cramped.

But when the twinge of pain in her lower body made her jerk, the laughter again turned to sobs. Now her shoulders shook for an entirely different reason.

And the only question that kept going through her mind

was, "Why couldn't they have died *before* they raped her?"

·   ·   ·   ·   ·

December 29, 2014

While Mel had recounted the story of that night, she'd turned back toward the water, let the waves rolling in toward her calm her nerves. It kept her voice steady. A smile formed as a thought hit her.

"Have you ever noticed that it seems we always have these kinds of conversations near the water?"

Alex was quiet beside her, not answering her question or saying anything at all to what she'd just revealed. She glanced back at him.

"What kinds of conversations?" he countered quietly.

"Heavy ones. The kind that are full of troubling feelings and struggles. Every one we've had has either been by the water or on the water, like when we went whale watching. It just struck me as coincidental, that's all." Mel searched his eyes for any kind of understanding or sign that he agreed and saw none. "Why aren't you saying anything, Alex?"

"I'm thinking. Give me a minute."

Mel bit her lower lip and turned back to the ocean, preparing for a break-up. How could he not want to end things with her? She'd just admitted to basically being happy when she'd seen that those men had died. She was a bad person. Horrible.

"What's going on in that beautiful little head of yours?"

She only shook her head in response, emotion clogged her throat and made it impossible to talk. Mel sensed Alex scoot closer to her before she felt his hand on her chin. With his thumb and forefinger he turned her face back to him. His honey eyes stared into hers, darted back and forth with concern.

"What is it, honey?"

"I'm just waiting for you to break up with me."

Confusion made his forehead furrow, a deep crease forming in between in his eyebrows.

"And why would I do that?"

"Because I'm a terrible person. Because I was happy that those men were dead. And it's not right."

"It may not be right. But I'd say that it's perfectly normal, Melanie. What you went though, what they did to you, was bound to cause some resentment in you. I can't think of a single woman that wouldn't feel the same thing if they'd been in your shoes."

His empathy made her cry. The understanding in his tone made her feel unworthy of someone so good.

"I think that what makes it the hardest is that deep down I had planned on going to the police. Even though they'd warned me not to. I just… I needed a little time. And I guess when I saw that crash on TV, saw that they'd been killed, I felt a little cheated. Like my chance to make them pay for what they'd done had been taken from me."

"I think a more apt explanation is that God intervened."

Now it was Mel's turn to frown in confusion. She slowly shook her head as she said, "I'm not sure I understand. What do you mean that God intervened?"

"I mean that He protects His people. And He's willing to do so at any cost."

"But I wasn't a believer then. Why would God do that for me?"

"He knows everything, Melanie. You might not have been a believer then but He knew that one day you would be. And He exacted out the punishment to those men as He saw fit."

Mel still wasn't getting what Alex was saying. But before she could ask him what he meant, he went on to explain on his own.

"*Dearly beloved, avenge not yourselves, but rather give place unto wrath; for it is written, Vengeance is mine; I will repay, saith the Lord.*"

"What is that?"

"It's from *Romans*. I've told you it's my favorite book in the bible. There's a lot to learn from those sixteen chapters. You should read it sometime."

"But what does it mean?"

"It means that you aren't supposed to take revenge out yourself. But that you should give wrath the space to take form, God's wrath. And it says that vengeance belongs to God and God alone. His wrath, His punishments, are far greater and more just than any here on earth. So while you could have gone to the police, and those men more than likely would have gone to jail, God saw fit to make them pay with a greater sentence. Their lives.

"I don't want you to think that this happens in all cases of someone who's been wronged here on earth. It's quite the contrary, actually, and why too many people who claim to be Christians get upset when God doesn't act in retaliation on their behalf. But once in a while, retribution that clearly comes from God becomes apparent.

"He knew what that night had done to you. He knew that a baby would be conceived. He knew everything that would happen after. So He chose to step in, Melanie. And honestly, I think that's when He started to work on your heart and your faith. You just needed some guidance to know that that's what was happening in your life. You needed someone to help you see that God has been with you through everything."

"I needed you, Alex."

"Not nearly as much as I've needed you, baby."

He stroked his fingers along her cheekbone, the touch barely there and yet she still felt a pulse of electricity shoot through her from the gentle caress. When his hand moved farther down, past the column of her throat to land on her chest, she felt her heart pick up speed right underneath his palm. She laid her hand over his, grabbed hold of his fingers and squeezed tightly.

"Or maybe," she said, "we needed each other."

He smiled in response.

As he leaned in and brushed his lips across Mel's, she knew that she would never stop needing Alex. His touch, his kiss, his love. The humor that he was ready to let loose with one word, always making her laugh. The protective instinct that she knew ran deep inside him, constantly evident in the way he kept his arms around her, shielded her from anything he thought might be a threat. Whether the sun or the rain or a pair of viscous eyes that belonged to a redhead, he was there to keep her safe.

Everything that made him who he was became as vital to her as the air she breathed.

In that moment, with his mouth closed around her own– teasing her with little flicks of his tongue against hers–and his arms wrapped around her body and his hands holding onto her ribs tightly, Mel knew that Alex was it for her.

And she prayed that when the time came, she'd have the strength to face her fears. To throw caution to the wind and be with him in every way possible; from emotionally to mentally to physically.

FOREVER GRATEFUL

"Ask me again, Alex," she whispered as she buried her face into his neck and sucked in a lungful of air, breathless from his kiss.

"Ask you what?"

"You know." Mel left the sentence hanging, expecting Alex to say those two words that she wanted to hear, now, before she lost her nerve.

She watched him swallow hard. His Adam's apple bobbed up and down, and she leaned over to place a tender kiss on that small bulge of his throat. His breath hitched when her lips met their mark. She leaned back to look into his eyes and anticipation swirled in her belly as she waited.

"Baby steps," he finally answered.

What? Those are not the two words I wanted him to say.

"No, Alex. That's not what I–" he placed his fingers over her mouth.

"I know what you want me to say, Melanie. But I think you've had it right all along. We need baby steps if we're going to have any shot at this lasting. And I want it to last. So… baby steps."

Mel couldn't hide the disappointment in her eyes when they closed, blocking out his face. Or in her body as her shoulders sagged. But the uncertainties that tried to creep in made her want to run and hide.

Did I make him wait too long? Does he have too many doubts about us now? Has he changed his mind and is just trying to find a way to let me down easy? Or... dear God, did I read him wrong this whole time and he doesn't really feel what he said?

A strong finger ran along the crease in her forehead, attempted to smooth out the wrinkles.

"Stop that," his deep voice commanded.

"Stop what?"

"Stop over thinking this. Nothing has changed between us. Nothing is going to change with our future. We just need a little more time, okay? I'm not going anywhere, honey."

"Okay." She blew out a breath and opened her eyes.

He stared down at her with different emotions playing on his face. Good-natured humor, happiness, understanding. And there was most definitely love.

A heavy sigh escaped her lips and he smiled, probably thinking the sound to be exasperated. He'd be right.

"You know that old saying, 'Patience is a virtue'?" Alex nodded his head at her so she went on. "I don't think I like that virtue very much anymore."

He threw his head back and laughed, a big belly laugh that made his whole body shake. And since she was still wrapped up in his arms, she shook right along with him. When he looked back down at her, he just shook his head with a smile still gracing his full mouth.

"My God, I love you so much, Melanie." He bent his head, his lips just an inch from hers and whispered against her mouth, "Tell me."

"I love you more, Alex."

.   .   .   .   .

December 31, 2014

Alex glanced at the clock on the microwave in Melanie's kitchen, noted that it was eight-thirty, and smiled to himself, ready for the day ahead. He figured she'd be waking up any time now, the smell of coffee and bacon strong as it hung in the air like a thick cloud.

Sunlight filtered in through the window at the end of the kitchen, bathing the area in a bright morning glow. Melanie's dog, Kass, lay curled up next to his feet. Her nose sniffed the air and her big, black puppy-dog eyes begged for a drop of food.

He had his phone out on the counter, the music app playing an album by Brad Paisley. He hummed along to the music while he scooped up a pancake from the frying pan and laid it on one of the two white plates on the bar, quickly turned and poured more batter into the pan.

While that one was cooking, he poured some orange juice into two glasses and set them both next to the plates. A bowl of strawberries and blueberries sat mixed together in between the place settings along with an empty coffee mug.

He tipped his own mug up, drained the last of the rich brew, set it next to his plate.

When the batter began to sizzle and pop behind him, Alex turned and flipped the pancake just as a new song came on his phone. He smiled and sang the lyrics while he patted the pancake down with the spatula.

And then he heard the giggle.

Turning just his head, he looked over his shoulder and saw Melanie standing in the hallway entrance, just on the other side of the living room. She leaned against the doorjamb in a long white t-shirt that came down almost to her knees and her hair was in a messy bun on the top of her head.

She was the most beautiful woman he'd ever laid eyes on.

"Are you laughing at me?" he asked, turned around to lean his jean-clad butt against the counter and crossed his arms over his bare chest. He grinned to himself when her eyes followed the movement and stared at his upper body for a full minute before she cleared her throat and looked back up.

"Not *at* you. *With* you, babe."

"But I'm not laughing."

"True." She took a deep breath, her chest rose and fell heavily. "But if you could see what I see, then you would be."

Before she realized what his plan was, Alex was across the fifteen feet separating them. He took her into his arms as she squealed in surprise and pulled her tight against him with his left hand on the small of her back. His right hand took hold of her left.

"Maybe instead I'll just make you part of the show."

And he twirled her around the living room, into the kitchen, right past Kassie and back toward the hallway. All through the condo, Alex led Melanie around in a quick step dance and sang the song at the top of his lungs.

When he got to the second verse, she gasped as he sang, "You see a priceless French painting; I see drunk naked girls." As she stopped dancing with him and her mouth hung open, he asked, "What?"

He shrugged his shoulders and got her body moving again, whispered for her to listen as the chorus came on. Then she laughed when the words sunk in.

"Just a guy, huh?" He nodded his head and smirked at her. She wound both her hands around his neck, held on to the hair at the nape of his neck. She leaned in and kissed him quickly. "Well I kinda like you being a guy."

"You do?"

"Uh-huh." She held up her thumb and forefinger, a centimeter of space between the two. "Just a little."

"Well then let's see what we can do to make that more than just a little."

- 433 -

But right as his mouth got next to hers, the smoke alarm started blaring from the kitchen. Alex and Melanie both jerked away from each other and looked that way, noticed the small amount of smoke that rose toward the ceiling from the stove.

"Shit!" Alex raced back to remove the pan with the burning pancake from the burner. He placed it in the sink and started fanning the smoke with a dish towel. And this time he knew for a fact that Melanie was laughing at him. "This is your fault, you know."

"Mine? I didn't do anything."

"Oh yes, you did. Giggling at me earlier, looking all cute in your morning hotness. You sidetracked me and now I've burned the pancake. So–" he tossed the towel on the counter as the last of the smoke disappeared and the alarm finally quit beeping, "–you get to share yours with me."

"Fine. But you can get the coffee."

"Deal."

After pouring the mugs and setting them on the kitchen bar, he walked around the counter to take his seat next to Melanie, placed a kiss on the side of her head as he passed her. She cut the pancake in half, gave him the larger of the two, and scooped up some berries on top, covered the entire thing with whipped cream (the kind from the can).

He took the can from her and did the same, gave a squirt of the white foamy topping to the tip of his finger.

FOREVER GRATEFUL

Melanie was too engrossed in her bacon and didn't see his hand coming until it was too late. He wiped the cream on the tip of her nose, laughed loudly when she turned to stare at him with a stunned look on her face.

"Payback, baby. I'm very serious when it comes to cooking."

She had a cheeky gleam in her eye as she wiped the cream off with a dainty finger, looked at the little glob before sticking her finger into her mouth and gently sucked it off. And Alex had the strange suspicion he might have started something here that he wouldn't be able to finish.

Before he knew what was happening, Melanie had the can and was shaking it and squirting the whipped cream all over him. They were both laughing as streams of white flowed through the air, some making contact with his chest while others landed on the floor. Alex managed to wrestle the can away from Melanie, gave her a good squirt on her neck. She squealed and jerked away, tried to run. He reached out quickly to catch her and they both slipped on a pile of whipped cream on the tile floor.

He just managed to turn them so that he landed on the ground first, taking the brunt of the fall, and she landed on top of him. The air whooshed out of his lungs but he was too happy to notice any pain.

They stared into each other's eyes as their laughter died down, small pants coming from both of their mouths. She smelled like sweet cream and bacon and woman.

The little glob of whipped cream on the side of her neck called to him like a long lost love. Slowly, he leaned his head up and brought his mouth to the sweetness, licked it up like a lollipop.

Melanie shuddered in his arms.

"Alex?"

"Hmm?" he hummed as he brought his lips to the other side of her neck, placed an open mouth kiss to her beating pulse. He waited there, with his mouth against her sweet skin, expecting her to say something about slowing down. Which he had every intention of doing, but sometimes a little prolonged anticipation just made everything better.

"You're getting my shirt covered in whipped cream."

He hastily brought his face back, speechless that she was worried about the cream and not him. Not directly, anyway.

"What?"

"I said, you're getting whipped cream on me. And this happens to be one of my favorite nightshirts."

Disbelief turned into slyness. Alex squeezed her tighter to him and moved his chest in a back and forth motion, smearing the cream all over her shirt.

"How's that? Is that better?" he asked, his voice rising through the sounds of her high pitched laughter.

"No!" she yelled and laughed harder as he found a ticklish spot right behind her ribs and attacked there in earnest. Her head was raised, her eyes closed as she fought for control. "Okay, yes, it's fine. Please, stop tickling me. I can't take it!"

Taking mercy on her, Alex stilled his hands but kept his palms splayed over her sides. Her laughter started to subside, her body slowly came to a rest. She brought her head back down and opened her eyes. In those blue-green depths he saw everything that he was sure was evident in his own.

They'd been over it a hundred times; they didn't need to go over it again.

So he settled for placing a short, tender kiss to her lips, murmured, "I love you" against their softness.

She responded with the same and then he sat up with her on his lap. Wrapping his hands around her rear end to steady her, Alex stood in one fluid motion with Melanie in his arms. He fought off the urge to carry her to bed and placed her back on her stool at the bar. With a shared smile, they dug in to finish their breakfasts.

Without any more whipped cream.

That night, for their New Year's Eve celebration, they had decided to forgo attending one of the massive parties Los Angeles was known for. Instead, Alex had made reservations at an Italian restaurant, a five star place known for their homemade pasta and imported wines. At least according to Brin.

At Six-Forty-Five, Alex waited in the living room on the

couch for Melanie to finish getting ready. His right knee bounced up and down and nerves threatened his control. His palms felt sweaty so he swiped them across his leg, hoped that the black slacks wouldn't show the wetness. His charcoal grey, long-sleeved, button-up shirt felt tight around his neck so he unbuttoned the top button, figured no one would care since he wasn't wearing a tie anyway.

He was just about to get up and start pacing when a feminine throat cleared from several feet away. Alex looked up from his lap and stiffened. He knew his mouth was hanging open and figured there'd be drool pooling in a minute. His eyes bulged out of his head. His heart sped up at the sight that stood before him.

He slowly rose from the couch and made his way over to Melanie.

A black dress with spaghetti straps and a deep V neckline graced her beautiful body. There was an overlay of lace that shimmered in the evening sun as she fidgeted in place with a silver clutch in one hand and wool shawl in the other. He raked his eyes down her long legs and groaned appreciatively at the four inch silver stilettos that covered her feet, tiny strips of leather crisscrossing all the way up to just above her ankle.

His gaze moved up her body, smiling as she did a turn and showed him her bare back. She faced him when he stood directly in front of her. Her aquamarine eyes were almost grey tonight with her smoky eye shadow. Her lips glistened a deep red, begging to be kissed. And her blonde locks fell in long waves, curled and flowing across her shoulders and down her back.

"You... you look stunning, baby. Absolutely breathtaking."

He leaned in and kissed her cheek, not wanting to chance coming into contact with her lips and having his plans shot for the night.

She placed her purse under her arm and reached up, smoothed her hand over his now-open collar and hummed softly as she grinned coyly at him.

"You're looking pretty handsome yourself." She ran her fingers through the hair on the side of his head, tucking some of the longer strands behind his ear. He clenched his fists at his sides to keep from grabbing her. "Are you ready to go?"

"Yeah." He cleared his throat. "Yes, let's go. Our reservations are in fifteen minutes."

Alex helped Melanie wrap the shawl around her shoulders. She placed her hand in the crook of his elbow and he led her to the door. He turned before walking through, held a hand out to Kassie in a "stay" motion, and locked the door behind them. Then they made their way down the elevator and out into the evening air.

Her feet stopped when they walked right up to the black Towncar and Ted stepped out of the driver's side door. She looked up at him in surprise.

"Did you do this?" He smiled and winked at her in response. "Well, you're just pulling out all the stops tonight, aren't you?"

Ted leaned over, kissed her left cheek as he opened the back door for them and said, "Happy New Year's Eve, kid. You look beautiful."

She smiled at him, whispering a "Thank you" as she stepped inside and took a seat.

"Everything ready?" Alex asked Ted as he shook the man's hand. Ted nodded in the affirmative and the two men shared a knowing look before Alex climbed into the car next to Melanie.

They held hands on the drive to the restaurant, the stillness of the night outside permeating into the quiet of the car. The nerves that Alex had battled just a few minutes ago disappeared. In their place was an assurance unlike any he'd felt. And a calm that everything in his life was just as it should be.

When Ted pulled up to Ma Sarti's on Broadway, Alex hopped out before the older man had a chance to come around. He reached his hand in and helped Melanie out. Giving a nod to Ted, he turned and guided her into the white and glass paneled French doors.

Italian classical music played softly in the background as soon as they crossed the threshold. The large room was dimly lit with crystal chandeliers strategically placed every twenty feet, their illumination set low.

A maître d' greeted them, complete in a black tux with stark white shirt and tie. The man had black hair slicked back and stood straight with an air of confidence and dignity, his deep voice oozed sophistication.

"Good evening, Mr. Lambert. Miss Moore. Please follow me; your table is right this way."

Melanie looked over her shoulder at Alex as he gently grabbed her elbow and directed her to follow the man. Her eyebrows rose, reached for her hairline, but the smile on her face lit up her expression, showed him that she was pleasantly surprised.

There were very few other patrons in the restaurant to interfere with his need for perfection tonight. But it wouldn't have mattered if there were a hundred. Thanks to his sister, Alex had planned this night a few weeks ago and already had a small room reserved in the back for just the two of them. He prayed everything went as planned as he thought of the amount of money he'd put into this one date.

No amount of money is worth her happiness, though.

When the maître d' opened the dark wooden door, he and Melanie stepped into a room no larger than twenty feet by twenty-five feet. Another one of those chandeliers hung from the ceiling. The music playing in here was Italian also, but some type of opera singer blended her voice with the accompaniment. Her soprano pitch added a sweet melody that made him think of a lover's song and he smiled.

In the center of the room was a round table with a bleach white tablecloth. There were two full china place settings laid out, complete with crystal glasses and every piece of silverware known to man. There was a sideboard on the right wall with three warmers covered with silver, domed lids. A young woman with hair as black as the maître d' stood next to it and waited to serve the dishes that Alex had made the decision to order earlier in the day.

"Enjoy your meal, Mr. Lambert. Miss Moore." The older man bowed slightly and exited the room. The door closed behind him with a soft click.

Alex pulled out Melanie's chair at the table, waited for her to be seated before he took his own chair across from her. He stuck a finger up in the air and the waitress came straight to the table with a bottle of wine in hand. She held it up in front of him and he quickly glanced at the label, gave a nod of his head for her to pour.

When he looked across at Melanie, she was grinning at him. "Have you become a connoisseur since the last time we had wine at a restaurant?"

"No. The wine was already ordered with dinner. I was just checking for a price tag. Apparently they don't put those on the bottles here."

Melanie laughed and the rich sound had him chuckling

with at her.

"Exactly how long have you been planning this night?"
He shrugged his shoulders, playing dumb to her question.
"Okay," she huffed. "Keep your secrets. I can keep some,
too."

Before he could reply, the waitress set a glass of the
white wine–chardonnay this time–in front of Melanie. She
took a sip and sighed in approval. Alex followed suit and
then they sat back while the waitress followed the wine with
salads, serving them both right there at the table.

Romaine lettuce, toasted almonds and slices of raspberry
were coated with a balsamic vinaigrette and a dusting of
fresh ground pepper. For a salad, even Alex had to admit that
it was good. He and Melanie ate their first course in silence,
enjoyed the food and occasional sip of wine.

When they'd both finished, the waitress came and took
their plates away, set a bowl with fresh baked bread and
garlic butter in between them. Steam rose from the bread and
Alex stared through it at Melanie. Their eyes met and held,
sensual tension built and ran high as he did nothing to hide
how much he wanted her.

She bowed her head first, picked up her wine glass with
a dainty hand and brought it to her lips. She licked the
remnants of the golden liquid off her lower lip and Alex
squirmed in his chair, biting back a groan at the desire to
taste her.

"You sure do like to go all out, don't you?" Mel's soft voice broke into the quiet.

"For you? Absolutely. And don't ask me 'why you' again."

"I wasn't going to. I'm done asking that, doubting the good that's come into my life. Now I'm ready to just accept it. Accept you."

Her words slayed him, his resolve and patience. Alex didn't want to wait for the last course. He didn't want to wait for the dessert of cheesecake with a fudge chocolate sauce to be delivered. He didn't want to wait to feed her bites of the rich cake, kissing away sauce until their plate was clean.

He didn't want to wait for anything anymore. Now was the time

Swallowing hard, he set his napkin on the table and stood. Melanie's eyes followed him as he walked around the small table and came to a stop directly in front of her. He stayed in that spot for a few minutes, his hands in his pockets as he stared at her. There was a question in her gaze, but he didn't answer her unspoken query.

He slowly lowered himself down, onto one knee.

·　　　·　　　·　　　·　　　·

Oh, dear God. This is it! Mel thought as Alex knelt before her.

FOREVER GRATEFUL

She'd waited for this to happen, wanted this to happen. But after Alex's little speech about them needing more time the other day, Mel had put the hope of it out of her mind, knowing that this would come soon enough.

Apparently, three days was all the time Alex had needed.

She looked down at his handsome face and fought back the tears that threatened to fill her eyes. She wanted to see him clearly.

Alex took her left hand in both of his, rubbed his palms over her clammy fingers. A small smile graced his lips before he took a deep breath and spoke.

"Melanie. I had this entire night planned out. Dinner and dessert. A big speech. Fireworks later on. But just like what happened when you walked into my life, I realized that sometimes the best laid plans go astray. I didn't plan on working at my brother-in-law's ranch. I didn't plan on buying a house in Lake Shores. I didn't plan on falling in love so soon after I got out of the Navy. I didn't plan on you.

"But I thank God that He knows what needs to happen in our lives at just the right moment. Because *we* needed to happen, darlin'. *We* needed to find each other when we did so that we could end up right here. In this perfect moment. Together.

"We've both had a past that tried to break us and instead helped to define who we are today. A past that might have toughened us up more than normal but has ultimately opened our hearts to chance. It's helped to turn us into the kind of people who appreciate the goodness and the light in life. You and I... we both deserve to find our own goodness. And for me, that's you.

"Your spirit and strength amaze me. Your beauty and grace leave me breathless at times. And your love, that you've given to me so freely, has filled my soul with a happiness that I know most people only dream about."

Mel wanted to stop Alex right there and tell him that he was her dream. That it was *his* love and devotion to her that allowed her to return his feelings. But she held her tongue. Her lips trembled and the tears that she'd tried to hold at bay now fell in small rivulets down her cheeks.

"Now is the time for us, Melanie. Now is the time for our future. And I can't envision living it without you by my side. I love you. I want to spend the rest of my life showing you just how much, being the man that you know will always be here for you, with you. I want to always be the one to put a smile on your face, to hold you when you cry. I want to laugh with you while we squirt whipped cream all over each other. I want to walk hand in hand down the beach every weekend."

He pulled a ring out of his pants pocket, looked down at it as he twirled the white gold in his fingers. Mel watched the light glint off of the large, round center diamond. And as he spun it, rainbows of colors shined onto the floor from the much smaller–but just as beautiful–diamonds that wound around the band. It was the most beautiful ring she'd ever seen and her breath hitched at how perfect it was. At how perfect Alex was.

For her.

"I want to watch every sunrise with you in my arms." He brought his eyes up from the ring and looked at her with a longing that said he'd do anything to have that happen sooner rather than later. "And I want to go to bed loving you every night. Forever.

"Will you marry me, Melanie?"

Mel scooted from her chair and sat on her knees right in front of Alex. She didn't spare the ring another glance, looked only into his eyes as she placed her hands on his cheeks.

"Alex. The woman I am today, right at this very moment, is here because of you. You're the one who brought me back to life. You showed me how to live again. The woman you fell in love with is only here because *you* helped to bring me here. It's you, Alex. It's always been you."

She brought her mouth to his, almost knocked him back as she threw her arms around his neck and her body against his. She felt tears fall on her lips and didn't know if they were from her or him. It didn't matter. The salty taste only added a sweetness to the taste of Alex, the taste of their future.

Abruptly he pulled back, his hands on her waist as he held her away.

"Is that a yes?"

She didn't answer him. Instead Mel just held out her hand, waiting. She watched through a watery daze as Alex slid the ring onto that most important finger of her left hand, right past the last knuckle to settle in a perfect fit. Mel wiggled her finger up and down and laughed as the prism of colors danced across hers and Alex's skin.

Alex brought her hand up to his lips, kissed the place where her ring now rested. He turned her hand over and placed an open mouth kiss right in the center of her palm and brought her hand to his chest, covered it with his own.

"You've made me the happiest man on earth."

"Not yet, I haven't. But soon. Very, very soon."

"We have all the time in the world, baby."

Mel brought her face right up to Alex's again, molded herself to his powerful form and relished the feel of his arms going around her to keep her in place.

"We have a lifetime, Alex."

Chapter 22

"There is no fear in love; but perfect love casteth out fear: because fear hath torment. He that feareth is not made perfect in love." I John 4:18

Mel tried to concentrate on the dinner that was laid out before them. But after Alex's proposal, all she really wanted to do was go back to her place, lie on the couch and have one of those good, old-fashioned make out sessions with Alex. The kind that teenage kids are known for sneaking in when their parents aren't watching. Because that's what Alex made her feel like. A teenager, madly in love with not a care in the world.

Focus, Mel! Stay in the moment and just enjoy the night.

She glanced up from her pasta to find Alex staring at her. He wasn't touching his food, either which made her not feel so guilty about not being able to actually taste the food. And judging by the look in his eyes–smoldering and impatient–he was thinking the same thing she was.

"What are you thinking about?" she asked him.

"How much I want kiss you." She grinned as he spoke her mirrored thoughts. "And how I'd love nothing more than to take you to Vegas so we can get married by one of those Elvis impersonators. And check in to the nicest suite we can find. And make love to you. As my wife."

Mel's breath caught in her throat at the vivid picture Alex had inadvertently placed in her mind. Images of him, gazing down into her eyes as he made love to her, brought a warmth to her chest and belly. Feelings that she used to be sure she'd never feel in regards to being with a man ambushed her and she squirmed in her seat, fought down the urge to tell him to do just that.

If someone would've told her six months ago that she'd be ready to get married, to give herself to a man wholly, she'd have called them crazy.

But now, all she wanted was to skip the wedding and get right to their honeymoon.

"I'm thinking that, too."

"But I won't do that," he admitted. "You deserve the best and I'm going to give it to you. So–" he leaned forward, placing his elbows on the table, "–have you given any thought to what kind of wedding you want to have?"

"Alex, you just asked me. Twenty minutes ago. I think I might need a little more time than that to plan."

"Of course you do. But surely you have an idea. Don't all little girls dream about their wedding?"

"Yes," she confessed. "But I gave up those dreams five years ago. Until recently, until you, I didn't think I'd ever have a need to imagine those dreams again."

Alex smiled at her, a look of empathy on his face as he reached out and took her hand in his, twirled the ring on her finger.

"I'm sorry. I didn't think about that."

"You don't need to apologize, babe. Honestly, all those things I thought I wanted in a wedding and a marriage are different now. I used to dream about being a princess with a huge tulle gown and sparkling tiara. Hundreds of people there to witness the ceremony. You know, the big "to-do" that little girls think is important."

"And now?"

"Now I don't need the world to witness some extravagant wedding. I just need you. Something small and intimate."

"Ugh," he groaned. "Don't say things like that."

"What?" she asked, unsure as to what had made him upset.

"*Intimate*. It puts thoughts in my mind that I'm trying very hard to not focus on right now."

Mel giggled and squeezed his hand as she admitted, "Me, too."

"How soon can you plan a wedding?"

She thought about it for a minute, about what she wanted for their day. She smiled as an image played out in her mind and she knew that it was exactly what she wanted.

"I have an idea." Alex nodded his head at her to continue. "I'm thinking about a backyard wedding. At your new house in Lake Shores."

"*Our* house," he corrected.

"Right. Our house. It'd be perfect. Your family, a few of our close friends. We can have it right at sunset and spend our first night as husband and wife in our home." She bit her lip as she waited for a response. "Does that sound okay with you?"

"It sounds perfect, just like you said. All I need is you by my side, saying 'I do'. The rest is just details."

"Okay, then. I'd say let's do it as quickly as possible."

"How quick?"

With all of the details already laying out in her head, she knew it wouldn't take long.

"How about six months," she asked him.

"Are you sure you can get it done that fast?"

"Positive. Besides, I don't want to wait any longer than absolutely necessary to call you my husband."

Alex pulled on her hand to get her to lean across the

table toward him. He met her halfway and brought his lips to hers in a sweet kiss, the tiniest of touches from his tongue that made her lower lip tremble.

"I like the way you think," he murmured against her mouth. "I love you."

"I love you, too. Now." She sat back down in her chair and picked up her fork. "You said something about fireworks."

An hour later, Alex and Mel left the restaurant with a to-go bag in hand. Neither had wanted to stay for dessert and since it'd already been ordered, the waitress boxed it up for them so they could take it home.

Ted waited at the curb for them and when he saw the glint of the diamond on her finger, he reached out and took Mel in his arms. She returned the hug, her arms around his neck as he held her close. This man had been more like a father to her the past few years than her own and she was thankful for the part he played in her life.

"Were you in on this little secret?" she whispered.

He chuckled as he set her away from him and lifted her hand to inspect her ring.

"Yes, I was. Nice job," he said to Alex and then to her, "You're not mad are you?"

"Of course I'm not mad. I'm assuming this means Alex got your stamp of approval."

Ted turned and held his hand out to Alex, shook it and

clasped him on the back as he said, "Yeah, he does."

"Thank you, sir. That means a lot coming from you. I know how highly Melanie thinks of you."

"Just don't hurt her," Ted warned and Mel rolled her eyes.

"Never."

"Okay, okay. Enough with all this macho stuff. Alex promised me fireworks and it's now almost eleven, so we'd better get going to wherever you two had planned before it gets too late."

With that Mel opened the car door herself and got in. Alex slid in beside her as Ted got in the front. Reaching across the short distance separating them, Alex grabbed Mel around her waist, lifted her off the seat and onto his lap.

"Hey," Ted spoke from the front. "You two keep in mind there's not a partition in this car."

"Sorry, Ted," Mel told him as she stared into Alex's eyes. "But I'm gonna kiss my fiancé so you'd better keep your eyes on the road and not the rearview mirror."

She heard his deep laugh from the front seat as she wound her arms around Alex's neck and brought her mouth to the side of his throat. She kissed him there, lightly, right on his beating pulse and Alex's arms tightened around her. Slowly, Mel moved her lips around to his Adam's apple, placed her mouth there as it bobbed under her touch. She moved up and rested her lips against his chin for the briefest of seconds before she couldn't take the torment anymore. She was trying to tease him but only succeeded in torturing herself, instead.

Mel brought her face up and laid her lips on his, her body sinking into his at the sweet feeling. One of Alex's hands came up from her waist and he laid his palm against her cheek, the roughness causing her to shiver. His thumb traced a path along her jaw as his fingers toyed in the hair at her neck. His hot touch was soft and gentle, coaxing her to open up for him.

And she did. She took what he offered, tasted him and gave him herself in return. There was no hesitation because she trusted him to not go any farther than they had promised. She trusted him with her body. With her mind.

She trusted him with her heart and that was the most important. That, and the fact that he entrusted her with his. And she'd cherish it for the rest of her life.

Starting tonight.

.　　.　　.　　.　　.

You have to stop this Alex, before it gets out of hand.

He knew the truth of his thoughts before they'd even finished forming in his brain.

But Melanie smelled so good, felt so good sitting in his lap, that he didn't want to let her go just yet.

And he couldn't get enough of her mouth. Of her taste and the way she gave herself over to his kiss. Everything about her was pure Heaven on Earth and it all started right there, with her lips.

But he knew when he'd reached his limit. And with Melanie getting restless on his lap, that limit approached quicker than normal.

Gently, Alex leaned away and broke their contact. He fought down a grin of satisfaction when he saw the disappointed look on Melanie's face. And just because he was apparently a glutton for punishment, he leaned back in and kissed her on the side of her neck, right below her ear. She shivered in response and Alex caught a whiff of her perfume as it floated into his nose from the spot where his mouth rested against her soft skin. He breathed it in–breathed her in–for a second more before he forced himself back one last time.

"Why'd you stop?" she asked, breathless, and this time Alex couldn't help the proud smirk that crossed his face.

"Someone's gotta be the voice of reason."

"You're right. I'm sorry. I guess I don't really know when things get to be too much."

"It's okay, baby. I was kind of teasing you about the voice of reason thing. But what you said is right. I've reached the edge of my control and we need to stop before we do something irresponsible and break our word to each other."

FOREVER GRATEFUL

"Okay," she whispered and closed her eyes as Alex ran his fingers down her cheekbone and across her lips, wiped off the wetness that was glistening there, even though he really wanted to kiss it away. "But you're going to have to let me go."

"I'll never let you go."

"And I don't ever want you to. So how about we settle for you letting me get back in my seat?"

Alex helped her to scoot off his lap and back onto the seat, brought her hand to his lips and kissed her knuckles. She opened her hand on the side of his face and he leaned into the touch, loving the feel of her skin against his and the look of love on her face. He linked his fingers through hers, kissed them one last time before he laid them down to rest in his lap.

Thirty minutes after leaving Ma Sarti's, Ted pulled up at a pier in Marina del Rey that was teeming with hundreds of people. Melanie looked outside at the crowd, frustration obvious in the way her shoulders slumped, and Alex smiled because he knew that she was hoping for a more quiet setting.

His smile turned into a chuckle as she frowned when, instead of pulling into the parking lot at the pier, Ted turned down an old, paved road covered with sand blown in from the shore. Confusion played a big part on her expression right now and Alex couldn't help but find it funny.

Aimee Martin

The older man kept on driving, followed the dune to their right as he headed south, farther away from the pier and the lights and the people.

About a half a mile down, Ted brought the car to a stop, turned in his seat and looked back at them.

"Here you go."

"What are we doing here?" Melanie asked, her gaze going back and forth between Alex and Ted.

Instead of answering, Alex opened the door and got out of the car, held his hand out for Melanie. She took it, a little hesitant, and followed him around to the other side of the car. He stuck his head in the front window, said to Ted, "We'll see you around one."

And then, after tapping the roof of the car a couple of times, Alex pulled Melanie by the hand, over the dunes and onto the sand as Ted drive off.

He heard her deep inhale behind him when she took in the site laid out before them. A black and blue wool blanket was spread out on the sand, held down on the four corners by a radio, a small red and white ice chest and two old lanterns (the kind that still use kerosene).

The lamps put off a deep yellow glow and illuminated the plaid fabric like a miniature pool on top of the sand. The radio was tuned in to a local oldies station, Bob Marley's legendary voice singing about Redemption. Alex walked over to the blanket, still pulling Melanie behind him, and kicked off his shoes before he stepped onto the cover.

When he turned back to Melanie, she was looking down at the scene before her like it was a foreign land. Her mouth was open, her brow wrinkled.

"You're awfully cute when you're surprised."

She finally snapped her head up and looked at him, her mouth closing, opening and closing again, at a loss for words. And still standing in the sand in her silver high heels.

He squatted down onto his haunches, gently took her left foot in his hands and rested it on his thigh. He undid the tiny buckle–albeit a little clumsily–and tossed the shoe next to his. Slowly, he ran his fingers up the inside of her foot, past her ankle all the way to the top of her calf, gently massaging as he went. When he leaned down and laid his lips along the inside of her ankle, she grasped onto his shoulders and he could feel her whole body tremble. Then he set that foot down and repeated the process with her right foot, her hands holding on to him the entire time.

Now barefoot, Alex pulled Melanie down, right onto his lap, and swallowed her surprised squeal with a kiss. Just a quick caress of his mouth against hers before she pulled back to look him in the eyes.

"What have you done, Alex?"

"I told you earlier I had this whole night planned out. Dinner, dessert and fireworks."

"Yes but… but I thought that…" she stopped.

Aimee Martin

"You thought what, baby?"

"I thought that since you'd already asked me to marry you that maybe the plans were going to change."

"Not a chance. I worked hard on this night and I plan on seeing it through to the end. If that's alright with you."

"Okay," she said quietly, smiled in acceptance. "Then why don't you show me what you've got in that ice chest over there."

"With pleasure."

Melanie scooted off of Alex's lap. He leaned over and grabbed the chest, moved it to the center of the blanket in between them. Alex opened it and brought out a small bottle of champagne and two glasses. He set them down and reached back in for the bowl of strawberries, placed one in the bottom of each glass. Then he popped the cork on the champagne and poured half a glass for each of them.

Handing a glass to Melanie, Alex lifted his in the air and waited for her to clink her glass with his. The small sound echoed around them as he said, "To us."

She smiled and countered, "To our future."

They both took a sip of the bubbling drink right as the first lights lit up the sky, followed by a pop loud enough to shake the sand beneath them. Melanie looked up in awe, a quiet "Oh," came from her mouth. Alex set his glass on the top of the ice chest, took Melanie's out of her hands and set it next to his.

FOREVER GRATEFUL

Then he laid down on his side, held his upper body up with an elbow, his head in his palm, and pulled her down into the crook of his shoulder. She snuggled in with her back to his front as the fireworks kept on, and he brought his right arm around to hold her across her middle.

While she watched the sky, Alex looked down at Melanie's profile. Her face lit with the colors that sparked in the sky. Red and orange made her fair skin look flushed. Blue and green blended with her eyes, made them more vibrant than normal. Yellow and white shimmered along her dress; the black lace looked silver in the brightness.

And every now and then one of the booms from the little explosions in the sky would be loud enough to make her flinch, and Alex would tighten his hold on her.

After thirty minutes of watching the blazing show overhead, the fireworks picked up speed, three and four blasting at a time to be immediately followed by several more. The sky was bright, the colors mixed together like a painter's canvas, until finally the last of the fireworks burst overhead. The smoke could be seen drifting away through the air and the scent of sulfur hung heavy, a cloud of gray and white blowing in the sea breeze.

"I've always loved to watch fireworks," Melanie whispered into the night.

"Me too."

"Thank you." Melanie turned in Alex's arms, her back

now lying flat on the sand as she stared up at him. "For everything. Tonight was the most magical night of my life. It was perfect."

"You're welcome." Alex splayed his hand across Melanie's belly, his palm rasped against the fabric of her dress as he brought his lips down and kissed her forehead. "Thank you for saying yes."

"Happy New Year, Alex."

"Happy New Year, love."

.   .   .   .   .

January 2, 2015

After the fairytale that was New Year's Eve, Alex had decided that he should stay at Brin's house so that they could give each other a chance to "cool off". Mel had agreed with him, even if a little reluctantly.

Yesterday he had come over to her place just in time for breakfast. The two had spent the day together and walked around the city. Holding hands as they strolled down Melrose Avenue looking into vintage store windows had never felt so good and so incomplete at the same time to Mel. She wanted his hands on her face, her back, holding her in place while he kissed her.

But at the same time she didn't want to tempt herself to a

point where she might not be able to say no. And she didn't want to put Alex in that position, either. Not when they'd come so far and were so close to the day when things would change between them.

Change for the better, Mel thought as she finished blow drying her hair.

Since they'd stayed up so late on New Year's Eve, last night they'd called it an early night. They'd had a light dinner back at The Seafood Café and Alex had dropped Mel off at her condo, again heading back to Malibu (after a very thorough and heated kiss goodnight at her door).

Tonight, Mel had asked if Alex would take her someplace she'd never dreamt of going but that she knew he would definitely enjoy.

A gun range.

"Are you sure you want to go shoot a gun, darlin'?" he'd asked when she'd made her request.

She couldn't tell him that something about knowing how to shoot would make her feel safer until this whole issue with Denise was resolved. She didn't want him to feel inadequate or even responsible for the antics of the other woman.

But it wasn't just that. In all honesty, she *had* always wanted to learn how to shoot. Ted had planned on teaching her but he'd been so busy getting his new agency off the ground the last couple years that he hadn't had time. So she figured she'd ask her hunky, Navy-trained fiancé.

"Yes! It's fun, isn't it?"

"Well... yeah. I just never thought it'd interest you, that's all. But if you really want to learn, I'd love nothing more than to teach you. I have to warn you though... something about shooting a gun gets your blood flowing so I don't want you trying to jump my bones when we're finished, okay?"

"What?! I would never___"

"Uh-uh, no excuses to weasel your way out. Just promise me."

"Okay," she conceded, *"I promise."*

After a quick text to Ted for the range information, Mel had made the call to reserve a lane–whatever that was–for her and Alex at the L.A. Indoor Sporting Range. She was due to pick him up at two so they could ride over together. He'd offered to drive, said that he was starting to get the hang of the heavily populated city and its many streets. But Mel had been unyielding in her decision that she be the one to drive today. Something about watching Alex drive, commanding the car with ease while his forearms flexed with each sure movement, was getting to be too hard on her. It tested the limits of her restraint and she needed a break.

She walked Kass down to the corner and back, let her pup take care of business before locking her up for the day. She took a last look at herself in the floor length mirror in her bedroom and was satisfied with her appearance.

Dark blue skinny jeans, camel colored, long-sleeved

tunic with pockets and flat, brown leather booties. Her hair was in a ponytail so she wouldn't have to worry about it getting in the way and her makeup was minimal, just a little mascara and some clear lip gloss.

She grabbed her purse and keys from the entry table, walked out the door, locked it behind her and headed down to her car in the garage. Sending a quick text to Alex at precisely one-thirty, she let him know that she was on her way and pulled out into the sunshine, smiled at the bright blue, clear skies overhead and thought that life couldn't get much better than this.

Thirty minutes after texting Alex, Mel pulled up in front of Brin's house, got out of the car and headed up the walkway. She shivered when she was about fifteen away.

Strange, Mel thought. *It's not even cold out.*

When she got to the door, she froze right as she reached to grab the knob. The door was ajar. Only by a few inches so it was possible that Alex just left the door open, knowing that Mel was going to be there soon.

No, no he'd never do that. Something's not right.

Mel reached around in her purse, searched for something, anything, that she could use for protection. All she came up with were the keys still clutched in her left hand. Figuring it'd have to do, she wrapped her fist around the longest one, set her purse down on the front porch, grabbed her cell out of the side pocket, and slowly walked inside.

As quietly as she could, Mel tiptoed down the entry hall, thanked God that she'd chosen a pair of shoes that didn't click on the tile. She made it to the corner where the kitchen began and glanced right, saw nothing out of the ordinary. Continuing on her way, she walked into the open living room, noted that not a thing seemed to be out of place.

Maybe I'm imagining all this, her mind battled with itself. *No, something's wrong. I can feel it.*

Staying on track, Mel turned left at the hallway off the living room, headed to the bedrooms. The first one she got to was an office of sorts. The desk was organized as was the large bookcase behind it. Two chairs sat in front and a leather rolling chair sat behind it, all untouched.

Mel backed out and headed right, toward the master bedroom. Her heart beat wildly in her chest and the palpitations caused an ache. Her breathing was speeding up, too, and she forced herself to slow down as she crossed over the threshold. She stopped and swallowed a screech when she saw a pair of boot-covered feet on the floor, the rest of the body hidden from the bed.

Wait a minute. I know those boots. Those are…

When it sank in that those were Alex's shoes, Mel rushed over, found him lying face down on the floor. She looked around, searching for anyone else in the house, then turned back to him and fell to her knees by his head. She grabbed his shoulders, shook him gently. There was blood on the back of his head, not a large amount but enough to have Mel worried. Not knowing what'd happened, and not wanting to risk hurting him, she stopped shaking him and placed a hand in the center of his back, rubbed to try to rouse him.

"Alex," she whispered. Nothing. "Alex, wake up. It's me, babe. It's Melanie. Come on, open your eyes for me."

"That's not going to work so you might as well just shut up."

Mel stiffened at the voice that came from behind her. Fear and anger now filled her entire being until she thought she'd burst from it. She closed her eyes, took a deep breath and turned around, thankful that most of her body was hidden from view by the bed.

"Denise."

Aimee Martin

Chapter 23

"Be not overcome of evil, but overcome evil with good." Romans 12:21

The Crazy-Stalker-Woman tilted her head to the side, the move calculating, like something a scientist would do when studying his experiment. There was evil in her eyes and a snarl on her lips.

She wasn't as well kept as she had been the other times Mel had seen her. In fact, Denise looked downright haggard. Her hair was a mess of tangles and hung over half of her face; her makeup looked like it'd been on for days, black smudges under her eyes. Her black skirt and top were wrinkled and there was a run in her pantyhose up her right leg.

But the most threatening thing about her was the small gun she held in her right hand.

"You don't sound surprised to see me."

"Should I be?" Mel slowly set her phone on the ground. "What did you do to him?"

Keep them talking, keep them occupied.

Ted's words–instructions that he'd been adamant she memorize when she'd first started at Dalton, young and impressionable–bounced around in Mel's head. Forced her to stay focused.

Mel kept her eyes on Denise as she slowly tapped out three numbers on her phone, turned the earpiece volume down. She glanced behind the crazy woman, expected to see her "bodyguard" bust through the door at any minute. But he never came.

She and Alex were on their own. For now.

"I asked what you did to him?" Mel repeated her question when she was sure someone had picked up on the other line.

"I didn't shoot him if that's what you're asking. I don't want Alex to die." Denise took a step forward, the gun shook in her hand. "Just you."

"And you think that if you kill me then Alex will come running to you for comfort?"

"Yes. I'll make sure he does. You're too naïve to understand how far a woman's wiles can get us in life. It's a pity you'll never have the chance to figure it out, either."

Denise took another step toward her and Mel pushed the

phone closer to the bed so that it was almost hidden completely from view.

"If you didn't shoot him then why is he bleeding?"

"Well I couldn't very well have him awake when I killed you. So I hit him with this–" she held up the butt of the gun and Mel saw dark red there, "–to knock him out for a while. He'll be fine, just fighting a little headache when he wakes up."

"You knocked him out with your gun?" Mel wanted to make sure that the person on the phone was getting all the information. "That doesn't seem like the right course of action to get him to be with you, Denise. In fact, I'm almost positive that's a sure fire way to get him to run the other way."

"Then I guess I'll have to take measures to make sure that doesn't happen. Like getting you out of the picture. Besides, it's not like he actually wanted you anyway. Think about it. Why would Alex want you when he could have this?" She ran her free hand up and down her body like Vanna White.

There was a small part of Mel's brain that thought maybe, just maybe, Alex wasn't really unconscious at her knees. Maybe he was acting, scared of the woman in front of her. That little devil on her shoulder tried to whisper that he was just like Justin, that all men were. But Mel pushed it back; she knew that Alex was good and strong and protecting. And he'd help her if he could.

"Now," Crazy-Stalker-Woman said with narrowed eyes, "why don't you make this easy and come on out from behind there?"

Mel didn't want to. She wanted to stay right by Alex so that when he woke up, he'd know that she was there. That she'd be with him.

But she didn't want to take a chance on Denise doing anything more to harm him. He was already bleeding, who knew for how long, and Mel would do anything this crazy woman asked if it meant this scenario would come to an end quicker.

Palming the phone in front of her, Mel snuck it into the front pocket of her shirt and rose from the floor.

"Slowly," Denise commanded. "Hands up."

Mel obeyed, placed her hands in the air as she stood. She ignored the fear in her gut and focused on the anger that poured through her. Anger that this woman had hurt Alex. That she'd disrupted their lives right as they were getting started. That she had the audacity to come after a man–*Mel's man*–who clearly didn't want anything to do with her.

Denise raised the gun until it was pointed at Mel's chest, moved it in a "come here" motion, and Mel slowly walked away from Alex, toward the other woman. Keeping the gun up, Denise grabbed Mel's ponytail with her free hand, yanked to get her to move out of the bedroom. Sharp pains erupted on her scalp and reminded Mel of the last time someone had pulled her hair like that. She forced her mind to stay in the present, to not go into that dark place where the memories from the rape lingered.

Once in the living room, Denise shoved Mel onto the couch. She plopped down on the center cushion, bounced up and down from the force. The two women stared at each other, animosity between them so thick it was tangible.

"What now? Are you going to shoot me?"

"Yes."

That one word brought the fear back to Mel. She didn't want to die. She didn't want to have overcome everything in her past only to have her future taken away. She wanted to lead the life God had set out before her.

God, Mel realized. *Oh, dear Lord, please help us. Be with us right now. Show me the way out of this.*

"So long, Melanie," Denise spat out Mel's name like it left a sour taste in her mouth.

And then several things happened all at once. Mel watched the scene play out before her, everything in slow motion, every detail with absolute clarity.

"You don't get to call her Melanie," came a deep voice from right behind Denise. A voice that had Mel gasping in sweet relief. "I'm the only one that gets to call her that," Alex said, a low growl taking over his normally calm tone.

Before he could make a move to grab the gun out of

Denise's hand, the back door flew open. Mel turned to see Ted storm in, a gun of his own raised and pointed directly at Crazy-Stalker-Woman. Denise could see that she was running out of options; it was evident in her wide eyes and the way her body shook.

She started to turn the gun on Ted who stopped her, saying, "Don't even think about it, lady. You need to put that away and you might make it out of here alive."

"I don't think so old____" Denise's words were cut off when the front door slammed open with such force it left a hole in the wall.

"Hands in the air! Now!" yelled a muscled police officer in a dark blue uniform. One more just like him filed in behind, followed by a man and woman in working suits. Detectives.

Mel felt the air whoosh out of her lungs and she closed her eyes, finally feeling like they were going to be okay.

"No. If you want this gun, you're gonna have to come and take it from me."

Denise's refusal had Mel's eyes popping open again.

What in the world is wrong with this woman? Doesn't she see she has no way out of this? Mel thought in confusion.

Then she remembered that they were dealing with an unstable person.

The officer who busted through the door inched his way toward Denise, who now had five guns pointed in her direction. Alex remained right next to her and despite the fact that he'd been lying unconscious not ten minutes ago, looked ready to pounce.

The officer was an arm's length away and one hand reached out to grab the gun. Denise spun away, took aim right at Mel. She closed her eyes, waited for the shot that would surely end her life. When the loud pop echoed throughout the room Mel screamed, instinct made her wrap her arms around her head and bend over. She thought she heard another scream after hers but the blood pounded in her ears and everything sounded like a distant echo.

Mel expected to feel the agonizing burn that she'd heard gunshots evoked. She waited a beat, then another. And another. Still, she felt no pain. One at a time, Mel opened her eyes.

There was the source of the yelling. Alex had Denise on the ground, her arms wrapped around her back while he held her wrists together in a tight, vise-like grip. She squirmed and screamed for him to let her go, yelled obscenities at Mel, kicked out her legs in any attempt to break free like a rabid dog.

Alex leaned over and whispered something in Denise's ear. Mel was too far away to hear what it was but whatever the words were had Denise stilling, her entire body rigid as a look of pure defeat crossed her face.

One of the officer's came up next to Alex, took Denise's

hands and snapped a set of handcuffs on her. He and the other officer hauled her out of the house. Crazy-Stalker-Woman never made another peep.

She's gone. Thank you, God!

Ted walked across the room, laid a comforting hand on Mel's shoulder and headed for the two detectives. The three huddled in the kitchen in quiet conversation.

Alone in the living room, Mel slipped from the couch and crawled over to Alex where he sat on his knees, hands clasped together in his lap. Mel reached out, took his hands in hers and waited for him to look up at her. When he did, it broke her heart to see the anguish there. And pain.

"Alex, we need to get you to the hospital." He shook his head at her, pulled on her hands and brought them to his chest. "Yes. You're bleeding. You probably need stitches. You might have a concussion."

"No. I'm… Melanie, I…" He hung his head and swallowed, tried to get his words together. "I'm so sorry, baby. So damn sorry."

"Alex, you don't have anything to be sorry for. Why would you say that?"

At this he looked back up at her like she was the crazy one.

"Because I didn't protect you. I'm responsible for that woman–" he flung his arm toward the front door, "–being here. For putting you in danger. Melanie, baby, if anything would've happened to you I don't know..." he choked. "I don't know what I would have done. How I would've ever forgiven myself."

"No, babe, no. You didn't have any control over what she did. She isn't well, Alex. She's sick and you can't blame yourself for her actions. It's over. And besides–" Mel reached up and placed her hands on his face, held his cheeks, "–I'm fine. She didn't hurt me."

Alex laid his palms over Mel's, linked their fingers together and squeezed tight, almost to the point of pain. But Mel knew he needed that connection, needed to know that she was, indeed, alright.

And then his eyes pooled with tears, big droplets caught in the corners but he didn't let them fall. Mel's did, though. Just seeing how emotional Alex was, how much of a weight this was putting on his shoulders, had her crying. For him, for her. For what they'd been through.

But most important was the relief and happiness she felt and the tears that came with *those* feelings. Tears for the future that was now clear and ready to be lived.

Tears of hope and faith and love.

"Alex, I____" she began but he interrupted.

"I know how scared you must have been, Melanie. With the way that woman cornered you like those... men. I just don't want anything to take you back to that time. I don't want you thinking that I can't, or won't, protect you. Because

I will. I promise you, baby, I'll always be here for you, always protect you and take care of you."

"I know that, Alex," she said. "I know you will. And I promise I'm alright. I didn't go to that dark place in my mind. I think I started to but... but do you know what's different this time around? Why I was able to push all that aside?" He shook his head at her. "It's because I knew, without a shadow of doubt, that you would protect me. You, Alex, with your strength and conviction and heart, would have protected me. If you could have. And since you couldn't, I felt like I owed the same to you. This time was my turn to be the strong one."

"But you shouldn't have to be."

"Tell you what... I promise to let you be the strong one next time, okay?" He finally laughed and a smile cracked through the frown that had taken over his face. "I love you."

Alex leaned his forehead against hers and Mel closed her eyes, breathed in the scent of him and thanked God that they were alive.

"I love you. So much."

A throat cleared, coming from the kitchen. Mel and Alex both looked over to see Ted standing there with a detective to his right. He held out a hand to help Mel up, did the same for Alex and when he wobbled on his feet, Ted helped him into one of the barstools.

"Miss Moore, Mr. Lambert. I'm Detective Arnie White," the older man began. He looked to be in his fifties, like Ted, with a still fit body, broad shoulders. Dark, wavy brown hair covered his head and his matching beard was sprinkled through with gray. But his eyes spoke of years of experience and a kindness that Mel appreciated right now. "Ted here has been filling us in on the situation. I'm real sorry you two got put in this position. I think we've probably got everything we need to file a report down at the station. That is, if you want to press charges."

"Yes," Mel said at the same time that Alex declared, "Absolutely."

"Okay then. Walker, you got anything you want to add?" he said to his partner.

She was younger, maybe early thirties, and petite. Blonde hair and brown eyes, the woman could easily pass for a kindergarten teacher. But when she stepped forward and shook Mel's hand, Mel could feel the strength those small hands held and figured this lady detective probably packed a mean punch.

"No, Arnie, I don't think so. Sir," she said to Alex, "that was some restraint you showed there. I'm not sure I would've been able to stop at holding that woman's hands back if she'd had a gun on my husband. You must be one of the good ones." And then to Mel, "Be sure you hold on to this one."

Mel laid her hand across Alex's back and leaned into his side, smiled into his eyes as she responded, "I plan to."

"If you two could just come down to the station so we

can get your statements, then we'll get everything taken care of." Detective White craned his neck, looked at the back of Alex's head and the gash there. "Maybe after you've gotten that taken care of at the hospital."

"Sure thing, Detective," Alex said.

"I'll bring them down as soon as he's stitched up, Arnie." This from Ted.

The detectives left, the sounds of the front door closing and the click of the lock reverberated throughout the now quiet house. Ted walked back into the kitchen after showing the detectives out and looked at Mel and Alex, studied them with a stern look on his face. Mel waited to be reprimanded for not taking better precautions.

The lecture never came.

"What happened to that bodyguard," she finally asked when Ted never said anything.

Ted's shoulders slumped, almost in guilt. He hung his head and took a deep breath. When he looked back up Mel could see the remorse there, the self-blame.

"I called him off for the day. We hadn't seen or heard from that woman in so long that I figured maybe she'd given up, moved on. I knew you'd be with Alex today. I thought... I thought you'd be safe. I got careless and I'm sorry. This is my fault. It never should have happened. I never should have called off the dogs until she was stopped."

"Ted," Alex broken in. "I'm gonna tell you the same

thing Melanie just said to me. This wasn't your fault. She was crazy and you had no control over what she did. It happened, it's over. Now it's time for us to move on."

Alex looked at Mel, wrapped his arm around her waist, kept her close.

"All of us."

. . . . .

Alex stared into Melanie's eyes–her beautiful aquamarine eyes that'd almost been taken from him–and thanked God that the day turned out the way it had. He meant it when he'd told that he didn't know what he'd have done had anything happened to her. He'd have been lost, that's for sure. Lost and alone.

He felt so stupid for letting that woman get the jump on him, not being more on guard. But everything had been so peaceful lately, so perfect. Alex guessed that he, like Ted, got careless. Too caught up in his happiness that he hadn't been as vigilant as he should have been.

They could all play the blame game for hours and never agree on whose shoulders the responsibility fell. And it didn't matter anymore, either. Like Mel said, it was over.

"I have a question." Melanie's soft voice broke into the quiet. Alex and Ted both looked at her, waited while she chewed on her lower lip, confusion on her face. "I heard a gunshot. But when I opened my eyes, everybody was still alive and well." She looked at Alex. "Well, mostly. Anyway, what happened?"

Alex looked at Ted and gave a short nod, asking the other man to explain.

"Well," Ted began, "right before Alex tackled Denise to the ground, he grabbed her hand and pushed it up, pointed that gun in the air and away from you. She must have pulled the trigger right as he did."

"So what happened to the bullet? What did she shoot?"

Instead on answering, Ted pointed his hand up toward the ceiling. Melanie's eyes followed his aim and her gasp at what she saw had Alex squeezing her tighter into him.

There, right over where he had wrestled Denise to the ground, was a hole in the ceiling. Chips of texture and paint were missing from around the hole that was less than an inch in diameter. Alex knew that Melanie was looking at that hole, imagining what it would've looked like if that was a person rather than sheetrock.

He pulled on her waist, made her sit on his leg, and kissed the side of her neck, whispering, "It's over, remember? Don't think about it. Don't even look at it, okay?" She nodded and her skin slid against his lips.

"We have to get that fixed, Alex, or Brin will never let us use her place again."

Alex couldn't help it; he laughed out loud at Melanie's

worry and Ted joined him. He thought for sure she'd be freaking out at what kind of damage that bullet would cause to a person. Not about the hole in his sister's ceiling.

His arms tightened around Melanie while his chuckles subsided and he sucked in a breath when a sharp pain shot through the back of his skull. Melanie noticed it and stepped out of his arms but he pulled her right back in between his legs and kept her there.

He was never letting her go again.

"Alright you two, let's get over to the hospital so we can get Alex stitched up. Then we can take care of business at the station and put this mess behind us."

"Sounds good to me," Alex agreed.

He stood and Melanie wrapped her arm around his waist, giving him support. They followed Ted out of the house, got in the man's Towncar and headed to the hospital.

January 4, 2015

It'd been two days since the incident. After the emergency room doctor had run a CAT scan to make sure he didn't have a concussion, the doc had put eight staples in Alex's head to close up the gash left from the butt of Denise's gun. He and Melanie had then spent three hours at the police station going over every detail from their first encounter with the woman til the day she broke into Brin's house.

And that was when Alex had admitted that she hadn't actually broken in. She wasn't invited by any means. But he'd been getting ready when Melanie was due to arrive so he'd unlocked the front door, figuring Melanie could just walk in when she got there. He had no idea that Denise would be the one to discover the unlocked door and take it upon herself to enter without permission.

And that was a mistake he'd regret for a long time because it'd almost cost he and Melanie their lives.

Detective White had assured them that Denise wouldn't be able to harm them for a long time. Even though they were sure that her lawyer would plead insanity, White knew that the D.A. would demand a long stint in a mental hospital followed by jail time because of her criminal history. Alex and Melanie hadn't cared what happened to her. As long as she was out of their lives for good.

After they had left the station, Alex and Melanie picked up some Chinese take-out and headed back to her place. They'd eaten in relative silence, both thinking about the day. When Alex tried to leave, to go back to Brin's, Melanie had begged him to stay. He didn't know if it was because she didn't want to be alone or didn't want *him* to be alone. And honestly, he hadn't cared.

Because he needed to be close to her, too.

He'd awoken in the middle of the night in the guest bedroom to the sound of crying coming from across the hall.

FOREVER GRATEFUL

When he'd walked into Melanie's room, she was sitting upright in bed with her arms wrapped around her bent knees. She'd been rocking back and forth and weeping.

He went and sat on the bed next to her, took her into his arms. She'd buried her face in his neck and cried even harder while he rubbed circles on her back. And then she'd looked up into his eyes, taken a deep breath and said, "I don't to wait six months, Alex. I don't want to wait any longer that absolutely necessary. I want to marry you, be your wife and never miss out on a single thing with you."

"That's fine with me, darlin'. Whatever you want, whenever you want it, I'll be right there by your side."

"Okay. Then I want to get married as soon as possible. This month."

Alex tried to hide his shock and failed miserably. Melanie laughed at him, wrapped her arms around his neck and kissed him, right on the corner of his mouth.

"Don't look so scared. You're going to make me think you're having second thoughts."

"It's not that. It's just… can you do that? Get ready for a wedding in just weeks?"

"Yeah. With your help I can."

"Of course I'll help you, baby. As much as a man's able to, anyway."

Melanie took a deep breath and looked like the weight of the world had been lifted from her shoulders. Alex reached up and wiped away the remaining tears on her cheeks, kissed the few drops that still hung on her eyes.

"Will you stay with me, Alex? Please? I don't want to be alone tonight."

Alex warred with himself on the decision for all of sixty seconds. When he saw her desperate look, her face still shaken with fear, he knew he'd give Melanie whatever she needed. And if that meant battling his hormones to help his love get a good night's sleep, then so be it.

Melanie had crawled under the sheet and he'd laid on top of it, pulled her back into his chest. She laid her head on his shoulder and he wrapped his left arm around her waist, held her close. She was asleep in minutes, her heavy breathing like a lullaby to him.

He followed her into unconsciousness.

Yesterday they'd spent the day at Brin's, cleaning up the mess left over from the run-in with Denise. He'd gotten in touch with a contractor who would be out there patching the ceiling up today.

In the meantime, Alex and Melanie made phone calls to let their families know what'd happened. Melanie didn't want to call her parents; but she did at Alex's insistence. And after a very short conversation, she hung up with a look of resignation.

"How'd they take it?" Alex asked.

"About how I expected. They asked if I wanted them to

come home. I said no, that I was okay."

"And? What about us? Did you tell them about the wedding?"

They sat in Melanie's living room on opposite ends of the couch. At his question Melanie scooted over and planted herself right in Alex's lap, laid her head on his chest. She ran her fingertips across his throat and waited a beat before she answered.

"They said they were very happy for me. For us. And that they look forward to the day they'll get to meet you. But–" Mel paused, wrapped her arm around his belly, "–they couldn't possibly makes plans to get to Texas in three weeks," she mimicked what he guessed was her mother.

Alex bent his head and kissed her temple, a light brush of his lips across her smooth skin.

"I'm sorry, baby. I know how much you wanted them to come."

"Actually, I don't really mind, Alex. I'm going to have you. Your family and Ted. And I've been in touch with my college roommate, Allyson. She's going to be there, too. That's all I need. Does that make me a bad person? That I don't mind that my parents aren't going to see me get married?" She looked up into his eyes.

"No. You could never be a bad person. What it means is that you've grown. You don't care about the details. You care about the end picture."

"I care about you."

"And that's all that matters." He wrapped his palm around her chin and brought her face up, kissed her lips and forced his brain to stay focused, to not get distracted by her lithe body sitting on top of his. "I love you, Melanie."

"I love you." She returned his kiss with enthusiasm, her arms tightened around his neck. But when her lower body started to wiggle impatiently Alex set her back, held her at bay with his hands on her waist. "Sorry," she said quietly, blushing and bowing her head as a giggle escaped her tempting lips.

"Three weeks, love. That's it. Until then maybe we need to think about cutting the snuggling out. At least a little."

"Deal," she agreed and slid off his lap. Now sitting on the cushion next to his, Alex grabbed her left hand and laid it in his lap, traced circles around her palm and twisted the engagement ring he'd given her. "What about your family? What did they say when you talked to them?"

"They were worried about what'd happened. Mom and Brin wanted to come out, make sure you were okay."

"Me?"

"Yes," he laughed. "You. I guess they figure since I'm a man I don't need any coddling. Anyway, I told them you were fine. That we were taking care of each other. Aaron and Jax wanted to come out to fix the house but I told them we'd already taken care of it. I think my Dad is the only one who handled it well. He said he'd make sure they all got their concerns under control before I got back."

"When are you leaving?" Mel asked and Alex heard the sadness there.

"The sooner the better I think. Keep in mind, woman, you've put a lot on me. I have to get the house ready for a wedding at the end of the month."

"I have every faith in you and your abilities."

"Uh-huh. When do you think you'll head my way? And what do you think your boss is gonna say?" That's what worried Alex more than anything.

Melanie had a job here in California. He didn't expect her to move to Texas, to give it all up for him. At least not right now. But he worried that she'd be putting her career in jeopardy by taking time off so soon.

"You let me worry about my boss. I have a *lot* of time built up to take off. I'll handle it."

Alex was suspicious at the way she'd answered him but he trusted her enough to know she'd do what she said.

"What about the wedding? Did they say anything about that happening so soon?"

"Are you kidding? My Mom and sister have known this was coming. They've been chomping at the bit to get the green light from you to start planning. Mom said if you'd give her a call and let her know what she can do on her end, she'll get started right away. I don't know who's more excited about our wedding... me and you or Mom and Brinley."

"I say let them be excited about the wedding," Mel whispered as she leaned in and kissed Alex on the side of his neck.

He knew he was squeezing her hand to keep from grabbing her and forced his fingers to release their hold on her.

Big mistake.

She walked her fingers up his chest until they wrapped around his cheek, pulled his face to her. And she said against his lips, "We can be excited for the wedding night."

As Alex kissed Melanie back, and his hand held the back of her head to keep her still, he decided he completely agreed with her.

Chapter 24

"Wherefore they are no more twain, but one flesh. What therefore God hath joined together, let no man put asunder." Matthew 19:6

January 22, 2015

Mel looked around the house and smiled, thinking to herself, *We did it. We actually got it done!*

The last two and a half weeks had her feeling like a busy-body, her nose in every detail that was being planned and put into place. She'd tried to give Tina and Brin free reign to take care of nailing down the decorations here in Lake Shores while she took care of wrapping things up in Los Angeles.

But try as she might, Mel constantly called and checked

up on the orders being made and the planning that was being done without her presence. To ease her guilt, Mel reasoned that it *was* her wedding. If they got upset with her hounding them, Tina and Brin never showed it.

And now the time was almost upon them. In two days Mel would become Mrs. Alex Lambert.

She couldn't wait.

Since she'd gotten to Texas three days ago, Mel had been staying at the house–hers and Alex's house–and he'd been staying with his parents. During the days they had gone to a home furnishings store in Brazoria that Jax had told them about and picked out new furniture for their house. In the evenings they'd usually go to dinner with his family, the women all caught up in the upcoming wedding and the men engrossed in anything *but* the wedding.

At night Mel and Alex would spend time cuddled up together on the couch in their living room in front of the fireplace. The wood would crackle and pop like Rice Crispies, smoke would billow up in gray, translucent clouds to float through the damper. The scent of burning oak would fill the room and surround them just like their blanket. It was perfect.

And then Alex would leave, driving the three minutes across town to stay at his parents so they weren't testing their limits, something that Alex reminded her daily were running thin.

FOREVER GRATEFUL

Right now, Alex was on his way back from Houston. Ted, as well as her friend Allyson, both flew in today and he'd volunteered to pick them up so she could finish getting the house ready.

The furniture had all been delivered and Alex, Aaron and Jax had spent hours rearranging it to Mel's liking. Alex had hung all the pictures, mirrors and clocks throughout the house that Mel had picked out. So while he was gone, she finished laying out area rugs (Kass had already claimed the big rectangle one in the living room as her own), towels and putting clean sheets on the beds.

Taking one last look at the dining room table adorned with a big crystal vase, wildflowers overflowing from it, and the taupe place settings in front of the four chairs, Mel smiled in approval and went to take a shower.

Thirty minutes later, with her hair blown dry and lying straight around her shoulders, a little lips gloss on her lips, Mel was just finishing getting dressed when she heard the front door open. She quickly buttoned her skinny blue jeans, threw on her sapphire blue sweater and rushed out the bedroom as the front door closed.

"Baby," Alex called out. "We're here." Mel rounded the corner and watched as Alex set the second of two suitcases on the entry hall brown marble floor. "Melanie, where are…" he trailed off as he turned and caught sight of Melanie standing in the hall doorway.

He slowly stalked over to her and Mel noticed the look in his eyes. The one that said he wanted to eat her up, over and over. When Alex reached her he brought a hand up, trailed a finger down the side of her face and wrapped his hand around her neck.

"You look beautiful."

And he kissed her, parted her lips with his own and slipped the tip of his tongue inside to tangle with hers, not caring that there were two other people in the room with them. In fact, he didn't even seem to remember until there was a loud cough behind them.

Alex jerked his head back, turned and saw Allyson smiling sweetly at them while Ted scowled. Shrugging his shoulders, he mumbled an, "I'm sorry," without looking the least bit so. Looking back down at Mel, he gave her a quick peck to her forehead and patted her on the butt. "Go say hi to your guests. Before I steal you away to the bedroom."

Mel grinned at him, fought down the urge to tell him okay, and walked over to where the other two waited.

She rushed to Allyson first and they both squealed like little girls getting splashed with water from rambunctious boys. She hadn't seen Allyson in three years. Mel had forgotten how small she was.

Being just over five feet would hinder most women, keep them from being thought of as grown and capable. But not Ally.

FOREVER GRATEFUL

Her family was from Montana, owned a hunting ranch somewhere in the southwest region. She'd come to California to get a degree in public relations and hoped to land a job as a publicist after. That's how they'd met at UCSD; Mel and Ally had several classes together since their majors were so similar.

Ally was two years older than Mel, twenty-seven, like Alex. Her long, chestnut brown hair hung halfway down her back and her matching eyes were large and round and stood out as a focal point in her heart-shaped face. She was beautiful.

And a spitfire when someone got on her bad side.

Mel remembered a guy in their Media Relations Management class that'd tried to hit on Ally. After she repeatedly turned the guy down, and he kept right on asking her out, Ally had finally threatened to share the videos she had of him snoring in the library to the entire school, thereby preventing him from getting another date. Ever. The guy left her alone after that.

"Allyson," Mel said, leaning back to look at her old friend at arm's length. "You haven't changed a bit. How are you?"

"I'm good. Things have been busy at the ranch since we just finished up black bear season two months ago. We're trying to tag our animals, see what our count is now that season is over."

Allyson had to go home to Montana after graduation to help her Dad and brother out at the ranch. She'd had an older brother that passed away unexpectedly and her Dad asked her to come back. Mel thought it was a shame. All that school, all that money, and Ally never got to put it to use, even for a little while.

"Daddy wasn't too happy that I was cutting out in the middle of our work. But Momma told him to get over it. Friends' weddings are more important. And I gotta say, Mel," Ally whispered, leaning in close to Mel's ear, "you got yourself a hot one over there. And a military man to boot." She nodded her head in Alex's direction where he stood in the kitchen, pulling out sandwich fixings and bottled waters.

"Yeah," Mel agreed. "I do."

"Alright, kid. Get on over here and give me a hug before you get all wrapped up in college tales with Ally or kissing with Alex."

Ted held his arms out, waited on Mel. She walked into them happily, wrapped her arms around his waist.

"Thanks for being here, Ted."

"Are you kidding? I wouldn't miss this for the world."

"That's good. Because I have something I need to ask you," Mel began.

Alex walked in to stand by her and placed a comforting hand on her lower back. She reached around with one hand and held onto him while keeping her other on Ted's arm.

FOREVER GRATEFUL

Mel swallowed thickly, looked into the older man's eyes and asked, "Ted, will you... would you... do you think you could walk me down the aisle?"

Ted took a quick breath and his eyes got wide. He opened and closed his mouth several times. And then a smile graced his face and his eyes crinkled at the corners.

"I'd be honored to, Mel. Truly honored."

．　　　．　　　．　　　．　　　．

Alex breathed a sigh of relief when Ted agreed to walk Melanie down the aisle. Not that he actually thought the man would say no. But he knew how much it meant to Melanie and he was happy that she'd have someone she loved and respected to offer her over to him.

As he stood there watching Melanie talk and laugh with two of her best friends, he thought of what was to come for their future. Of the talks and laughs they would share. Of the family they'd one day have, God willing.

The sun filtered in through the open blinds on the window next to the door, highlighting her golden hair and making her skin glow. She took his breath away. He couldn't wait for the next two days to be over with.

He couldn't wait for Melanie to finally be his. In every way.

"Alright you three," he broke in to their laughter, "We

need to eat lunch and get y'all settled in." Ally was staying here with Melanie and Ted would be staying at the Bed and Breakfast on Main Street. "The rehearsal is due to start at four-thirty. We've got less than four hours before everyone else starts to show up here."

Grabbing Allyson's suitcases from the floor, Ted and Alex took them to the spare bedroom while the women went into the kitchen.

The time for wedding practice would be upon them soon.

At just after four, Alex's family descended on their little yellow house like a pack of wolves. Boisterous laughs came from the living room where the men had gathered and took shots at Alex, thanks to a picture of him on the mantle.

He remembered the day the photo was taken. He'd been in L.A. with Melanie, back in September, and she'd asked him to blow her a kiss. Little did Alex know that she'd waited with her phone to take a snapshot of him in the moment. Melanie now had the picture–in black and white and enclosed in an antique white, wooden frame–proudly displayed front and center above the fireplace.

He didn't mind, though. If the photo made his woman happy, then the men could laugh all they wanted to.

The women were all talking, five feminine voices going at once from the kitchen where platters of vegetables and fruits were being laid out. Alex swore there were at least three different conversations going on in there and wondered, briefly, how they could keep track of all that was being said. Then he decided he didn't really care that much and went to grab a beer.

Outside in the backyard, on the new cedar deck he and his brother had built, Alex found the ice chest, grabbed a light beer from inside and twisted the cap off. He fiddled with the lid in one hand, took a swig of his beer and looked out at the garden at the back of the yard.

He and Melanie hadn't had a chance to plant anything in there yet so his Mom had brought over big pots full of flowers from her place. "To add some color for the wedding," she'd said.

Right in front of the garden plot was a white arbor that stood almost seven feet high and half as wide. He knew that Melanie had florists coming the next day to fill the lattice work that closed in the back of the arbor with fresh flowers. He could already picture standing in front of that contraption, facing Melanie before their family and friends and vowing to love her forever.

He was ready now. Ready to start their lives together. Ready for their wedding night.

Alex took another swig from his beer, feeling too warm of a sudden in his gray button down dress shirt and black slacks.

A hand clasped him on the shoulder and Alex turned to

see his brother, Aaron, standing to his right as he looked out at the arbor, too.

"You ready, little brother?"

"Yeah." Alex smiled, no doubt looking like a lovestruck idiot. Which, of course, he was. "To be honest, I'm ready for the wedding part to be over. Hell, I'm even ready for the honeymoon to be over. I just want to get back and start our lives, you know?"

Aaron nodded his head but didn't say anything. Alex looked over at him and noticed the small frown on his brow.

"You okay?"

"Huh?" Aaron asked then shook his head and looked back at Alex. "Yeah, I'm fine. Just thinking. Remembering."

"Remembering your wedding?"

"No. I was like you. I didn't care about the ceremony other than saying those words that would tie me and Jess together."

"Then what're you thinking about? You've got a look on your face."

"A look?"

"Yeah. A look. One that clearly says something's wrong."

Aaron reached behind them, grabbed his own beer from the ice chest, opened it and stared out into the backyard again. He was silent for a minute. Alex waited while his brother got his thoughts together.

FOREVER GRATEFUL

"I was remembering what is was like when Jess and I first got back from our honeymoon. How everything was so new and perfect and just... right. Easy."

"And it's not now?"

Aaron turned to look at Alex and shrugged. "Sometimes. But Jess... she's been pushing to get pregnant. Said something about her biological clock ticking away and that she didn't want to wait until she was halfway through her thirties to get started." Aaron and Jess were the same age; both of them turned thirty-three this past fall. "I don't know. I think since Brin and Jax are getting ready to have a baby it's put that desire front and center."

"And that's a bad thing?" Alex asked, not understanding what the issue was.

"For me, yeah. I'm just not ready. Half the time I don't feel responsible enough to take care of just the two of us. How am I supposed to be a father when I feel like that?"

Aaron looked into Alex's eyes, seeking an answer. But Alex was the little brother. He didn't know what to say. He didn't even know what Aaron was feeling; he wanted to have children with Melanie as soon as possible.

"I don't know what to say, Aaron. Have you tried praying about it?"

"No." Aaron's shoulders slumped and he turned back to the yard. "I guess I should."

"That's where I'd start," Alex admitted.

"Start on what?" came a small voice from behind them. Alex and his brother turned to see Allyson standing there, grabbing a bottle of water from the chest. He looked to Aaron, confused, when he felt his brother stiffen. Alex figured it might just be because the two hadn't met yet, and made introductions.

"Ally, this is my brother, Aaron Lambert. Aaron, Allyson Marx. She was Melanie's roommate in college."

"Nice to meet you, Aaron." Ally held her hand out but Aaron just looked at it like it was a snake waiting to bite. She dropped her hand and tilted her head, studying Alex's older brother. "You know, you catch more flies with honey than vinegar. Maybe if you tried being a little more engaging then that scowl of yours wouldn't push people away. Excuse me."

Alex watched her walk away, back into the house, before he turned to his brother.

"Dude, what the heck was that? Did you have to be such a jerk?" Aaron stared at the door Ally had just walked through. "Aaron." Alex snapped his fingers in front of Aaron's face, brought his gaze back over. "What was that all about?"

"I don't know. Something about her just set me off. Made me uncomfortable."

"Well try not to be so nasty next time."

"Yeah, okay. Sorry," Aaron said. Clapping him around the shoulders again, his brother pulled him toward the house.

"Come on, enough about my problems. You've got a great girl in there waiting for you. Let's get this rehearsal going."

Alex didn't miss the way Aaron was quick to change the subject and made a mental note to talk to him more about his issue later. Right now, he had a fiancé to find.

By six o'clock that evening, Alex, Melanie and their bridal party–Aaron and Jax as groomsmen and Allyson and Brinley as bridesmaids–had run through the wedding ceremony no less than five times. He confessed to Melanie when they were alone at the arbor that he didn't understand the need for that many run-throughs. All he had to do was repeat after the minister. But Melanie insisted that there was more to it than that. And that if he didn't pay attention then she'd make him pay for it later.

She didn't find the humor when he'd offered to let her punish him the night of the wedding. In the bedroom.

As the night wore on, the temperature started to drop down into the low fifties. Alex lit a couple of industrial heaters his parents had given them as an early wedding present to take the chill away. There were folding tables and chairs set up in between the heaters and everyone filled their plates with fried chicken (thanks to Tina and Brinley), mashed potatoes and fried okra and headed to the tables to eat. Alex and Melanie had already finished eating and stood in the corner of the yard, looked over the ten people in attendance tonight.

His parents, Aaron and Jess, Brin and Jax, Ted and Allyson as well as Tony and his wife Lisa. It was exactly what Melanie had told Alex she wanted. Holding her hand, with her head on his shoulder as they watched their intimate crowd mingle, laugh and talk, he couldn't have agreed more.

"I guess we need to get this night wrapped up, don't we?" Melanie said and looked up into his eyes.

"Yeah. There's a lot that has to be done tomorrow for the ceremony the day after. We all need to get some rest."

"Okay," she sighed and leaned up to kiss his neck, right next to his Adam's apple.

"Don't start that now," Alex mumbled and pulled Melanie closer to the tables. "Alright everyone." Alex waited for the talking to die down and all eyes to fall on him. "Melanie and I want to thank you all for your help these last few weeks. We know it hasn't been easy to get everything ready and there's no way we could have done it without you. It means the world to us.

"I want to say a special thank you to Brinley. If it wasn't for you, I never would've met the love of my life. No matter what happens, you've given me the best gift I could've ever asked for. Ow," he exclaimed, looking down and seeing Melanie's cocked eyebrow. Chuckling, he said, "Well, second best. Right behind Melanie saying yes." And then back to their laughing guests, "We know with your support that our love, our life, will be blessed. Anything you want to add darlin'?"

"Yes. Not so long ago I didn't believe in God."

Melanie waited until the surprised gasps stopped and Alex tried not to look shocked that she'd brought that up.

"I didn't believe in 'happily ever afters' or divine intervention. Until I met Alex. He's shown me what it's like to have faith beyond measure. To be strong enough to move past a life of doubt."

She looked up into his eyes and Alex's breath halted, his eyes tearing up at the emotion he saw.

"He's shown me what it's like to love unconditionally. I only hope and pray I'll be able to give back to him what he's given me as our future unfolds."

Alex bent his head, captured her mouth as soon as the last word rolled off her tongue. It was just a sweet sipping of lips, a small taste of what was he was feeling. Of what was to come.

"You've given me more, baby. Just by being mine."

"That's enough!" came a male voice followed by another saying, "Get a room already!"

And then the feminine voices scolded the men, saying, "Be quiet!" and "It's sweet. Leave them alone."

Alex ignored the catcalls from around them. He placed kiss after kiss upon Melanie's face—each cheek, forehead, nose—then he rested his forehead against hers and whispered against her lips, "Two days."

Aimee Martin

.   .   .   .   .

January 24, 2014

Mel woke up before her alarm clock. One at a time her eyes popped open. She lay in bed on her side, faced the window to her right. Early morning sunlight filtered in from the sheer white curtains, dust motes hung in the air like confetti. Through the window Mel could see into the backyard, could see the arbor that was covered in yellow roses and sunflowers with lots of white filler flowers–bouvardia, delphinium and jasmine–that gave contrast to the overflowing golden petals.

She breathed deep, like she could already smell the sweet aroma from the blossoms.

Rolling over onto her back, Mel stretched her arms over her head, and sat up, ready to get started for the day. She went to the bathroom, brushed her hair and teeth, and headed for the kitchen to get a pot of coffee going. Just as she poured a mug full of the rich brew and added a little cream, Ally walked in from the spare bedroom.

"Good morning, sunshine!" Mel said and grabbed another mug from the cabinet.

"Morning to you. Oh, bless you," Ally said when Mel handed her a cup of coffee. "So, are you ready? Today's the day you become a married woman. Last chance to run; I'll get the car started if you've changed your mind."

Mel laughed at her friend's teasing. "No more running. I've ran for long enough. I'm ready to marry Alex."

"I think you spent your life running so you could get to him quicker."

"Awe, that's sweet."

"Yeah, just call me Miss Mushy. Okay." She paused, took a sip of her coffee. "Where are we headed first? The beauty shop?"

"We're staying here. I didn't want to go to the salon; I wanted to keep it causal. Brin's got her old hair dresser, Patti, coming to do my hair and a woman named Tiny to do my nails. They should be here by ten to get started."

"Well then you'd better get in the shower. It's already nine and I *know* you've got plenty of shaving to do."

"Ugh, Ally!"

"What? It's true."

"I know." Mel sighed. "Okay, drink your coffee. I'll go hop in the shower. You can use the spare bathroom if you want or wait for me to get done and use the master. It's got a bench." She headed down the hall to the master bathroom.

"I'll wait. Now go, get those legs nice and smooth for Alex," Ally called after her.

Mel could still hear her friend laughing as she turned on the water and stepped into the glass shower.

Twenty minutes later–because yes, Mel did have a lot of

shaving to do–she stepped out of the stall and wrapped a towel around her body, another one over her hair. She walked into the bedroom, headed to the walk-in closet in the corner. She pulled out her wedding day underthings, laid them all out on the bed and admired them for a minute before removing the towel from her body and wrapping an ankle length silk robe around herself. The rest would wait until her hair and makeup were finished.

Just as she tied the sash, Ally strolled in, Brin and Tina trailing behind her. Brin waddled over to her first, wrapped her arms around Mel in an awkward hug with her belly in the way. Quickly shooed away, Tina took her daughter's place but she didn't hug Mel, kept her at arm's length instead. A smile graced her face and a few tears dripped down her cheeks.

"I'm so happy for you and Alex. And I'm honored to be able to call you a daughter. Thank you for making my baby so happy."

"Thank you for raising such a wonderful man, Tina. He's the one who's made me happy. More than I ever thought I deserved."

"You deserve each other, sweetie."

"Yeah," Mel agreed. "I believe we do."

"Okay, ladies. Time to get this show on the road." An older woman–around the same age as Tina–with short blonde-gray hair walked into the bedroom, carting a pink carry-on suitcase with a picture of scissors on the front. She walked right up to Mel, studied her for a beat. Then, "I'm Patti. Let's make your hair beautiful, shall we?"

And then there was a flurry of activity. A chair was brought in from the dining room and Mel was practically pushed into it. Another woman, this one in her forties, walked in with a folding table and a tackle box full of nail supplies. While Pattie started blow drying Mel's hair, the other woman–Tiny–started filing her nails.

Ally, fresh from her own shower, brought Mel a glass of champagne. She accepted it gladly and took a small sip, let the bubbling liquid slide down her throat to settle in her stomach. The warmth helped to calm the nerves fluttering in her belly like butterflies.

Brin had found a radio somewhere, put on a cd full of old eighties music. Mel laughed as Brin wiggled her belly and sang Whitney Houston's *I Wanna Dance With Somebody* at the top of her lungs.

Ally joined in, grabbing a hairbrush from Patti's kit and using it like a microphone as she sang the chorus with Brin.

Tina chuckled from a chair in the corner, rolling her own glass of champagne between her fingers.

Mel looked at each of the three women and felt a sense of harmony. Added to what she felt with Alex–the love and connection–Mel finally felt like she belonged in this world, in this family.

"Where's Jessica?" Mel asked as she realized that the other woman who was to be her sister-in-law wasn't here.

"Oh, she said she had some errands to run. She's going to come with the guys later." This from Tina who sounded almost tolerant, like she was upset that Jess hadn't come.

"Okay," Mel said. She wondered if Jess felt left out for not being *in* the wedding. Then decided no, they didn't know each other well enough so there was no reason for that to be the cause of her absence. Deciding not to dwell on it further, Mel turned to Tiny and picked out a polish for her toes. "That one. The dark red."

And so it went for the rest of the morning until all four women walked around, two cans of hairspray combined on their hair, and Mel was ready to get dressed.

Ally helped Mel put her dress on over her white silk and lace corset and matching panties. The dress Mel had loved from the moment she saw it at the bridal boutique back in California came next. And now that it was on, she fell even more in love with it.

White lace lay over the entire length of white satin. Cap sleeves hung just off the tops of her shoulders and the scalloped neckline rested comfortably just below her collar bones. Fitted through the bust and waist, the dress flared out at the knees and when Mel spun in a small circle, the material swung around her lower legs like a miniature carousel.

FOREVER GRATEFUL

Ally made her stand still so she could do up the row of buttons that ran the length of the back of the gown, from the middle of her back–where the top of the dress rested–all the way down to the small train trailing behind.

Ally finished the last button and Brin strode over, holding Mel's veil. She stood still, faced the windows looking into the backyard, while Brin fit the veil in place and secured it with bobby pins. Mel fingered the white tulle that hung past her elbows, running a fingertip along the floral embroidery, until Brin tapped her on the shoulder, let Mel know she was finished.

Mel stepped into her shoes. A pair of three inch white heels that were covered in lace just like her dress. The peep toe allowed just a hint of the deep red on her toes to be seen. Mel smiled to herself as she thought of the words engraved on the soles of the shoes that no one knew were there. *I* on the right sole and *Do* on the left.

Finished dressing, Mel walked over to a floor length mirror behind the closed closet door and took in her appearance. From her hair that was curled in big ringlets, half pulled up and the rest left to hang around her shoulders, all the way down to her red toenails, Mel finally let it sink in that she was a bride.

And giggled in sweet anticipation, knowing that the next time she saw Alex it would be to walk to him to become his wife.

Aimee Martin

"You look beautiful, Mel," Tina said from her spot on the foot of the bed. The older woman's hands were clasped together over her mouth but Mel could see the smile she wore in the way her eyes crinkled at the corners. "Alex is going to have a heart attack when he sees you."

"I sure hope not, Momma. At least not until after the wedding night."

"Brinley!" Tina scolded her daughter and Mel and Ally laughed at the indignant look on her face.

"What?" Brin shrugged her shoulders, playing off the scold. "It's true." She turned and winked at Mel with a grin on her face.

Mel looked at the clock hanging on the wall above the dresser, saw that it was almost four o'clock. Turning to the other women she said, "Ok, ladies. Let's get this show on the road. I'm ready to go get married."

Brin and Ally both grabbed their bouquets, yellow sunflowers mixed with white and blue wildflowers that Mel had put together herself. Held up against their navy blue bridesmaids dresses, the flowers popped brightly like the sun against a night sky. Mel reached for her own bouquet on the dresser, smelled the big yellow roses with a few white bouvardia (like those outside on the arbor), and let their sweet aroma fill her senses as she headed for the door.

A navy partition screen had been put up along the back of the house and blocked the view from the French doors.

Ted waited next to it looking handsome in a black tux with navy cummerbund and bowtie. He smiled at Mel as she walked up next to him, held his elbow out for her to hold onto.

"You ready, kid?"

"Definitely."

Ally and Brin walked out the doors, down the red carpet aisle that had been laid out on the yard, and took their place to the left of the arbor. As the strains of *Air* by George F. Handel began, Mel took a deep breath and let Ted guide her around the screen corner. When she saw Alex standing at the other end of the carpet her heart jumped into her throat and her mouth popped open in surprise.

Alex stood, in all his masculine glory, wearing his dress blues. Hands clasped together in front of him, his back was ramrod straight, shoulders wide and proud. Mel noticed the slight slump when he saw her but he quickly recovered and held his chin high as he smiled down the aisle at her. She grinned back and walked to him.

Their twenty or so family and friends faded into the background, like elevator music, as Mel focused all her attention on the man who waited for her thirty feet away. She kept her eyes on his honey-colored gaze, their gleam like a guiding light calling her to him.

When Mel and Ted reached the end of the aisle–and Alex–he stepped forward and held out his arm. Ted placed her hand on Alex's forearm and Mel smiled graciously at the man who'd walked her down the aisle before facing the man she was about to marry. She gave Alex's arms a squeeze and heard the medals that hung over his heart jingle like wind chimes as they clanked together when he turned them to face Tony.

"Dearly beloved..." Tony began.

Mel didn't hear anything else until it was time to recite their vows. And even then all she focused on, held close to her heart, were Alex's six little words.

"I promise to always love you," Alex commanded in his deep voice.

And she responded, "I promise to always have faith in you, in us."

When he slid her wedding band on her finger, Mel looked down at the white gold and diamond circle and felt whole, complete in a way she never dreamt was possible. In that moment she knew it was their turn to live in a fairytale world and was ready to embrace their happily ever after.

"You may kiss the bride," Tony said and what his words hadn't been able to do–break into her musing–Alex did in one swift move.

Wrapping one arm around her waist and the other around her neck, Alex pulled Mel tight into his chest and lowered his lips to hers. Ignoring the shouts and claps around them, Mel wrapped her arms around Alex's neck and put everything she felt, every ounce of love and hope and *desire*, into that one kiss. He molded their mouths together, sealed their commitment before God and family with a kiss so searing, so powerful, Mel knew it would be imprinted on her soul forever.

As her fingers clasped onto the hair at the nape of Alex's neck, waiting for him to deepen the kiss, a throat cleared next to them. Slowly Alex lifted his head. His breathing was fast, as fast as hers, and his pupils were dilated as he stared down at her but said to Tony, "Sorry."

And then he smiled, grabbed her hand and turned them to face the small crowd. With a wink in her direction, Alex pulled Mel alongside him, down the aisle and back into their house.

By seven that evening, their wedding reception was in full swing. White twinkle lights hung around the perimeter of the fence, boxing in the yard with their bright glow and fighting for power over the large silver moon that rose high into the sky. Large speakers were set up next to a radio by the back door, waiting to blare the music for the night. Everyone had plates of barbequed chicken and ribs, potato salad and cole slaw but most were already cleaned up and ready for the dancing to begin.

Alex walked over to where Mel stood talking to Mitch, grabbed her around the elbow and spun her to face him. Bending to kiss her on the side of the neck, Alex whispered in her ear, "I think it's time for me to dance with my *wife*."

Mel returned his kiss with one of her own, placed her lips right on his Adam's apple and smiled when she felt him shudder. She wrapped her arm around his waist as he guided them to the center of the yard where tables had been pushed back to allow for a makeshift dancing area. The strains from a song she'd only ever heard Alex hum began and Mel felt her heart swell as she finally got to listen to the lyrics.

As Green River Ordinance sang the words to *Dancing Shoes*, Mel decided her favorite line was, *Just be my woman, and I will be your man.*

When it was time for her to toss her bouquet–an exact replica of the one she'd be keeping–there were four women fighting over the yellow roses while Martina McBride sang *This One's for the Girls*. And when Ally caught it, and tried to hand it off the woman to her left, Mel hollered at her, "You've got to keep it, Ally! Those are the rules."

And then Alex was on his knees at her feet, reaching up underneath her dress to slide off her garter. While Pat Benatar sang about getting hit with a good shot, Mel worked to slow her breathing at the look of hunger in his eyes, of wanting. Neither one of them saw who caught it when Alex shot the thing like a rubber band into the crowd without taking his eyes from hers.

They walked over to a table by the arbor to cut their cake. Traditional white icing was covered in the same yellow, white and navy wildflowers from the bridesmaid bouquets. They both had their small square of cake, ready to feed the other. Mel laid her square on his tongue and whispered to Alex right as his hand got to her mouth, "Don't you do it."

And then he gently placed the square in her mouth.

As she turned back to the table, Mel's face got caught in the palm of Alex's other hand that he'd hidden from her while she'd been distracted. Cake and icing covered the left side of her face and Mel sucked in a breath, annoyance causing her to cut her eyes back at him. Everyone was laughing—including Alex—except for Mel.

But right as she opened her mouth to ream into him for embarrassing her, Alex brought that same cake covered hand up and smeared twice as much of the dessert on his own face. As much as she wanted to stay angry, looking at the white icing and smeared flowers all over his cheek and mouth caused a laugh to bubble up. She couldn't help but to shake her head and smile at him when he'd joined Mel in her cake-face condition.

And then he brought his sticky lips to hers, mingled his icing with hers. She accepted his kiss but gave him a warning.

"You'll pay for that."

"I sure hope so."

As the time closed in on ten o'clock, Alex stood behind

Mel in front of the arbor, his arms wrapped around her waist and her hands rested over his. He leaned in and kissed the side of her neck.

"Have you had a good time tonight, darlin'?"

"Yes," she said, turned in his arms and held onto his face. "It's been amazing. Thank you."

"Thank you for saying yes."

"Alright everybody," a loud voice broke out over the din of laughter and partying. Josh, a friend of Alex's from the Navy stood by the radio with a microphone in his hand. "I believe it's about time for us all to be kicked out of here and leave these two newlyweds alone. But first," he paused and turned to face Mel and Alex. "Alex, you were a great friend while we served together. But I always knew there was something better waiting for you on the other side of the Navy. Now I know what it was. Mel. You two belong together, anyone can see that just by looking at you. And I'm honored to have been here to see you begin the rest of your lives. This song's for you two."

Mel smiled at Alex's friend as he pushed the play button on the CD player. Alex pulled her out to the center of the yard for their last dance. Garth Brooks' booming voice came over the speakers. The words of *When You Come Back to me Again* spoke to Mel and Alex like they were written for them and them alone.

Not a peep could be heard from any of their guests but

the newly wedded couple wouldn't have noticed anyway. Mel only had eyes for Alex and he stared back just as intensely at her. So much passed between their eyes– aquamarine to honey-brown–that it felt like a book of emotions was laid out in the small space separating them. Love, happiness, desire, anticipation. They played a beat of their own to Mel's racing heart.

It wasn't until the last chord played out that Mel and Alex looked around, realized that they were alone. Everyone appeared to have snuck out while they'd been dancing. The air around them seemed to thicken with sensual awareness and Mel licked her dry, nervous lips.

"Everyone left," she whispered into the dark, her voice barely heard above the chirping crickets that called out to the silver moon.

Alex didn't answer, instead just took Mel by the hand and led her through the French doors, down the hallway and into their bedroom. He released her hand to close the door behind them and Mel escaped, walked into the bathroom to remove her dress. She stared at her reflection in the mirror for a minute, steeling her nerves.

You can do this, Mel. He's your husband. He'll never hurt you.

She took a deep breath and threw her shoulders back, held her chin high and turned away from the mirror. When she walked back out Alex had lit a dozen candles and scattered them around the room which now smelled like gardenia and vanilla.

She stood just outside door way with her hands clasped together in front of her belly. She watched Alex, wearing only his blue pants, while he tossed his tie and shirt onto the yellow and white wingback chair in the corner. And then, as if sensing her gaze, he looked over his shoulder at her and the intensity in his eyes had her breath coming in pants.

He turned, slowly made his way to her. Even in the dim light, Mel could see when he swallowed thickly. His eyes roamed over her from head to toes and back up again.

"Are you scared?" Alex asked, his voice low as he brought his hand up to run his fingers along her cheek. Mel couldn't speak, nodded her head instead. "Don't be afraid, baby."

His fingers trailed down her throat, wrapped around the back of her neck and pulled her forward. Mel's hands went to his bare chest to steady herself and she felt his heart pounding hard and fast like hers. She traced the hard planes across his pecs, down to his abs, and rested he fingertips on his waistband. Alex's face came down, lips brushing against the corner of her mouth, tongue teased the seam of her lips, coaxing her to relax and open.

"I just want to love you."

Mel ran her hands back up Alex's hard chest, into his thick hair. She pushed down the anxiety and fright, focused on the feeling of Alex's mouth and strong arms and powerful form engulfing hers. Focused on the love she had for this man in her arms. Opening her mouth, she grazed her teeth along his lips and whispered into his kiss.

"Then love me."

"Always, baby."

Aimee Martin

Chapter 25

"I am my beloved's, and his desire is toward me." Song of Solomon 7:10

January 25, 2015

Alex lay in bed, awake, and looked down at the woman fast asleep in his arms. His wife. It still felt surreal, like a dream he would wake up from at any moment and find that everything over the last six months had been a figment of his imagination.

He bent down and gently brushed his lips across Melanie's temple, just to make sure that she was real. That this was real. Her skin was soft under his lips; her feminine, floral scent clung to his nose, enticing him in its sweetness. And her body was warm snuggled in next to his.

Last night, Alex had been worried about how she would

handle taking that final step as husband and wife. How she would handle him making love to her.

So he'd been gentle, slow, encouraged her to let go of her fears and embrace the sensations he'd given her, one step at a time. She'd been hesitant at first, shy and tense.

And then, like a flower blooming in the spring, its petals opening to let in the warmth of the sun, her body had begun to listen to what it was telling her, what he was telling her. Alex closed his eyes as he thought about last night and how perfect it'd been.

Melanie finished unbuttoning her corset, tossed it to the ground. Alex's breath hitched as he caught his first full glimpse of his wife, at how beautiful she was, her flawless skin. He removed his pants but left his boxer briefs on for now.

Laying Melanie gently down on the bed, Alex crawled up next to her side and rested his palm on her belly, teasing her sensitive skin with small circles. She flinched and giggled, telling him it tickled. He told her to close her eyes, focus on what she was feeling and not what she was thinking. She obeyed, took a deep breath and Alex saw her force her shoulders to relax.

He leaned over, placed his lips right where his hand had been, softly kissed her flat stomach. Her arms jerked on the bed but she kept her open palms flat on the mattress. Alex worked his lips up her torso, skimmed over her chest and stopped at her throat, nipped the hollow there.

He moved to the pounding pulse on the side of her neck, caressed there for a second with his fingertips, followed it with a damp kiss. He cupped her jaw, held her still while he made his way to her mouth and kissed her deeply for long minutes, their tongues mating in the way their bodies naturally told them to.

Alex ran his hand down Melanie's side, skimming over her flared hip until he reached her thigh and the muscle tightened under his touch. He stilled, let her get used to feeling him there. When she relaxed, he worked his way back down her body. Kissed every inch of exposed skin he passed until he reached the place on her body that was made for him and him alone.

Melanie quivered from his touch, anxious at first and then more and more eager as time went on. Until finally, finally, she reached for him and said, "Alex, I need you."

He kissed her, long and deep as he settled himself right where he belonged. "You have me, baby," he whispered against her lips.

Linking their fingers together, he held her hands tight, stared into her eyes and let her see his love–feel his love–as they became one.

Alex sighed as he opened his eyes, tightened his arms around Melanie and forced his thoughts to simmer down. She'd probably be sore and tired this morning. He'd need to take care of her, not ravage her.

He moaned in frustration as a slender, soft calf and foot landed across his legs and he realized that would be easier said than done. He laid his right hand on Melanie's calf, stopped her from rubbing it up and down his leg like a cat winding its tail around someone's ankles. And when she giggled with her face buried in the crook of his shoulder, reached down with his left hand to give her a pinch on her backside.

"Here I thought you were innocently brushing against me while you slept," he said and rolled her onto her back, resting above her with elbows on the bed on either side of her head. "When all along you were intentionally torturing me."

"Not torturing, babe. Teasing."

"Same difference."

"Good morning, husband."

Alex smiled, bent to kiss her lips.

"Good morning, my wife. Did you sleep well? How are you feeling?"

"I slept great. And I feel even better." She stretched her arms over her head. Alex forced his eyes to stay on her face, not where the sheet had fallen away. "What about you?"

"Right next to fantastic. But if you don't pull the sheet back up, I can't be held responsible for my actions."

Instead of pulling it up, Melanie wrapped her arms

around Alex's neck, pulled him closer to her and said quietly, "What if I don't want you to be responsible?"

Alex groaned again, rested his forehead against hers and closed his eyes.

"I'm trying to be careful with you," he admitted.

"I won't break, Alex. And besides… I trust you."

He laid his lips across hers, kissed her tenderly.

"I know you do. And that means the world to me. But just wait, okay? Just for a little while."

"Okay," she huffed. "Then let me up. I have to use the restroom. And I have a present for you. I wanted to give it to you yesterday but there wasn't time. You know… after everyone left."

"Yeah, I know." He grinned at the blush that covered her cheeks, kissed her again. "I have a gift for you, too. I'll get the coffee and meet you back here in five minutes."

He hopped out of bed, grabbed his boxer briefs from the floor and strode from the room before Melanie had a chance to get up, knowing his self-control would break if he saw her with no clothes on. He went to the spare bathroom on the opposite side of the house to take care of his own business, brushed his teeth with one of the extra toothbrushes Melanie had put in there.

Then he went to the kitchen, put on a pot of coffee and got out two mugs while he waited for it to brew. Kassie walked in, nails clicking on the wood floor and tail wagging as he bent to scratch her head. When the coffee finished gurgling he poured it into the mugs. He tossed a Milkbone on the ground for Kass, grabbed his present for Melanie off the counter, placed it under his arm and walked back to the bedroom. And found her sitting in bed, looking down at a large white envelope in her hands.

He paused in the doorway, watched the sunlight highlight her golden hair and the flush on her skin. The pale pink, silk nightgown she'd put on didn't do much to cool his libido. In fact, Alex admitted that it actually intensified it. He knew what lay under that satin fabric and he ached to peel it off her body.

Patience, Alex. Just a few hours. Man up.

Control back in place, he strode forward. Melanie looked up when he reached her and he handed her a mug, walked around the bed to climb in next to her. She took a small sip of her coffee, set it on the nightstand and turned to face him.

"You first," she said.

Without a word Alex handed over her present. It wasn't much, but it meant a lot to him–reminded him of how far they'd come–and he hoped it would do the same for her. She ran her hand over the glossy silver wrapping paper, fingered the navy blue bow tied around it (courtesy of his mother). Just as he was about to take it and open it for her, Melanie slid the bow off and tore into the paper. She tossed the wrapping aside, flipped over the black wooden frame and stared at the black-and-white picture that rested inside.

It was of the two of them, on the boat when they'd gone whale watching. Her hands were wrapped around his back, resting above his waist. His hands cradled her face. They were locked in an embrace and the kiss clearly showcased the love between them, even at that point in their budding relationship.

"Where did you get this?" she whispered, her finger running along the glass, right over where their lips met.

"I'd bought one of those disposable cameras and gave it to Sal the day we went whale watching. I asked him to snap some pictures of us throughout the day. We have about two dozen shots but this one was my favorite. This was where we____"

"Started," she interrupted. "This was our beginning." Her voice was soft, reverent.

"Do you like it?"

"Oh, Alex. It's beautiful. Perfect." She looked up at him and tears swam in her eyes as she smiled. "Thank you. I love it. I love you."

"I love you, too. You're welcome." He leaned over, linked his hand with hers that still rested on the frame's glass, kissed her temple. "Let's go put it on the mantle, front and center."

"Wait." She grabbed his arm when he started to pull

away. "I still have something for you." She picked up that white envelope lying next to her, handed it to him. "Here."

Setting his own coffee down, he eyed the envelope, puzzled as to what could be in there. Without a second thought, he flipped it over and slid a finger under the seal. The paper tore with a loud rip and Alex pulled out a single piece of cream colored stationary. Melanie's name, job title, business email and cell phone stood out in the top right corner, the typed black ink embossed.

But it was the written words taking up space below that that caught his attention. Just four little sentences that had Alex holding his breath, not knowing what to think.

January 12, 2015

Dear Mr. Evans,

Please accept this letter as my formal notification that I am resigning from my position with Dalton Entertainment. I understand that two weeks' notice is standard. However, if at all possible, I would appreciate you releasing me from employment with the company as soon as possible as I will be moving to Texas. Thank you for the opportunities for professional and personal development that you have provided me during the last four and a half years.

Sincerely,

Melanie Moore

FOREVER GRATEFUL

For a full minute, Alex didn't say a word. Just re-read the letter over and over. When Melanie's hand closed over his, Alex realized he'd been gripping the paper so tightly it crinkled in his touch.

"Is this for real?" he finally asked and looked up to watch her eyes for any flicker of doubt. But there was no doubt, only assurance and peace. She nodded her head. "Are you sure this is what you want? You have to know I would *never* ask you to do this, honey. This is your career. It's important to you."

"It *was* important to me. Not anymore. Alex, I took those vows yesterday seriously. I take this marriage, our commitment, seriously. We can't hope to survive if we're spending our time fifteen hundred miles apart. And even if we could, I wouldn't want to. I want to be with you, by your side. And that's right here. In Lake Shores."

"What about your boss? Was he okay with this?"

"Of course not. He basically promised me everything under the sun to try to get me to stay. Even offered to let me work here and only go to California for major events. But I turned him down."

"Why?"

"Because I've realized that the life I led isn't the one I want to lead from here on out. What used to be my dreams are now just… holdups. And they're keeping me from what's most important in my life. You. Us." She chewed on her lower lip, a small crease formed in between her brows. "Are you not happy about this, Alex? I figured you'd be more, I don't know, excited."

"I am. Oh, baby, believe me I'm ecstatic. I just don't want you to make a decision that you'll come to regret later. Or end up resenting me for."

"I won't, ever. I promise you that. You're the love of my life, Alex. And you're more important that any job. My place is with you. Forev–"

Alex cut off whatever she was about to say with his lips, crushing them against hers. Gone was the control telling him to take things slow and easy today. With Melanie's present, her pledge to him and their marriage, she effectively made the caveman in him want to come out and play. To lay claim to this woman. Now.

And Melanie was right there with him.

She scooted down on the bed and pulled Alex forward until he rested on top of her. As her dainty hands wrapped around him, held tightly onto his lower back, he let himself go. Let go of the restraint and limitations and embraced the wild need to be with her.

In that moment, as man and wife with no barriers between them, Alex showed Melanie with his body just how much he loved her gift. How much he loved her.

"Say it," he said against her lips, rocking with her.

"I love you, Alex Lambert."

FOREVER GRATEFUL

He closed his eyes and kissed her harder as they moved slowly together. "I love you more, baby. Always."

.   .   .   .   .

January 26, 2015

Mel stared out the window of the rental car–a silver Toyota Sequoia–as Alex crossed over the Lazaretto Creek Bridge near Savannah, Georgia. They were headed to Tybee Island for their honeymoon.

Honeymoon, Mel thought with a smirk, feeling like she was off in la-la land. Then pinched her underarm and flinched when she felt pain, assuring her it was all truly happening.

When they'd discussed where to go for their first week as newlyweds, Alex had been surprised when she'd mentioned this place. He figured she'd want to go someplace tropical, like most people do.

"I've lived the tropical for my whole life," she'd told him. *"I want someplace quaint. And there's water. A creek and an ocean. It'll just be colder than if we went to Mexico or the Caribbean or someplace like that."*

He'd agreed that the place sounded great and booked them a five-day-four-night stay at a one bedroom house right on the bank of Tybee Creek. One of the reviews of the island said that crossing over the bridge sent you into another dimension, the Tybee dimension. As they drove down Butler Avenue, looking for the Ninth Street exit that would take them to their rental house, Mel could see what the reviewer meant.

Rows of shopping centers lined the side streets they passed, clothing boutiques and bakeries and meat markets, even a small art gallery. They all fought for the top tourist location. Green and white striped canvas canopies hung over the doorways to the shops and the material gently flapped in the breeze.

Men, women and children strolled down the sidewalks, sipped lemonades or coffees and ate little cakes and cookies, no doubt fresh from one of those bakeries.

Big, knotty oaks lined the walks, their thick branches hung over the concrete to shade the pathway for pedestrians. Azalea bushes sat next to green wire trash cans, their bright pink and red blooms just opening up for the season.

They drove past an elementary school where kids played on the playground and rode their bikes around the concrete basketball court.

Off in the distance, on the ocean side of the small island, Mel could see the lighthouse and museum.

They passed a sign indicating the way to Fort Pulaski and Mel made a mental note to see if Alex wanted to go there and take a tour.

FOREVER GRATEFUL

Finally making it to Ninth Street, Alex turned left and headed all the way to the end of the road. They pulled into the drive, Alex shut off the engine and they both stared at the white-washed house in front of them. There was a red tin roof that Mel was sure would be heaven for a rainy night. A cobblestone pathway led to the front door as well as around the side of the house.

Mel stole a quick glance at Alex to see if he was ready and he winked at her, opened his door and got out. Mel hopped out of the car faster and raced up the walk to the door. Just as she was about to turn the knob, Alex's strong arm darted around her, caught her round her belly and hauled her back into his chest. He nuzzled the side of her neck, kissed her there once.

"If you want to play chase, I'll catch you every time."

"Who says I didn't want to be caught?" she said, breathless with the way his lips teased the side of her throat.

Alex's hand tightened on her stomach and her gray cable knit sweater bunched under his flexing fingers. The scruff on his cheek scratched her skin and Mel shivered with how good it felt. In a lightening move, Alex spun her around and walked her backwards until she was up against the front door. He caged her in, placed his hands on either side of her head and leaned down to nip at her chin.

"The game's no fun if only one of us is playing."

"I'll play. Next time. Consider this round a gimme."

"A gimme?" he asked, staring at her through hooded eyes.

"Yeah. As in, 'give me'."

"Oh, I'll give you, darlin'. I'll give you this," he kissed her cheeks. "And this," he kissed her eyelids. "Definitely some of this," his hand came off the door, rested on her hip and squeezed, brought her closer to his body. "But most important, I'll give you this."

The words were barely out his mouth before he kissed her deep, tangled his tongue with hers. That squeezing hand on her hip worked its way to her lower back, slid underneath her sweater, and the feel of his callused palm against her bare skin had her trembling.

Mel hadn't even realized Alex had opened the door until he was walking her into the house, never taking his mouth from hers. She heard the door slam shut as he kicked it with his boot.

"What about the luggage?" she asked, breaking away from his mouth to get the question out.

But he didn't answer, just pulled her back to him with a strong hand on the back of her neck. And then she was floating as Alex picked her up behind her back and knees, carried her down the short hallway to the bedroom. Once there, he set her on her feet, walked her backwards toward the bed.

"I have a compromise. About the game."

"Uh-huh," he murmured. "What's that?"

"How about if we give to each other this go 'round and save the games for another time?"

Alex kept her walking until her knees hit the edge of the bed. She fell onto the pillow-top like it was a cloud. Alex followed her down, kissed her again as he pulled off her sweater.

"Done. Now… no more talking, wife."

They left the suitcases in the car.

January 27, 2015

The bad thing about staying in a rental house instead of a hotel is that you were expected to do your own cooking and cleaning. The good thing about staying in a rental house is that you don't have staff constantly hounding you, hanging around to get you whatever you needed or wanted at a moment's notice. But Alex and Mel didn't care. They'd both rather wait on themselves and be able to come and go without interruptions than to worry about bellhops and wait staff and cleaning crews lurking around.

When they got in around four in the afternoon the day before, they'd been preoccupied for a long while with each other. They finally made it outside to bring their suitcases in and were pleased to find some basic groceries had been provided by the owner of the rental house. After stowing their luggage in the bedroom, Mel had made sandwiches out of black forest ham and Swiss cheese and they'd eaten on the back deck, looking out at the creek twenty yards from the back door.

The water lapped gently in the breeze and a chill reached them from the creek. Alex had grabbed a red wool blanket from the back of the couch inside and wrapped it around them as they sat on a wooden porch swing, watching the dragonflies dart to the water's surface in search of gnats for dinner.

They'd crawled in bed when the moon came out, wrapped in each other's arms and fell asleep, exhausted from the day of traveling.

Today they were going to take a tour of the Tybee Lighthouse. After a light breakfast of toast and fresh fruit, Mel and Alex headed to the car to drive over to the end of the island where the lighthouse stood on a five-acre plot. They pulled up at the entrance gate right as the sun was coming up. It rose up from behind the lighthouse like the New Year's Eve ball, only in reverse, and cast a long shadow in front on the dark green, manicured grass.

Since it was early, Mel and Alex were the only two people there. He parked in a pea-gravel parking lot in front and they both got out of the car, walked up to the doors hand in hand. A short man with silvery-white hair, dark tanned skin that looked leathery from years in the sun and a big, round belly opened the door right as Alex reached his hand up to knock.

"Mornin'!" the short man said. "You two here to take a tour?"

"Yes, sir," Alex answered.

"We usually only give tours in the middle six months of the year, from April to October."

"Oh." Alex turned to look at Mel and she couldn't help her sad smile. She'd really been looking forward to this. "Listen, Mr..."

"Johnson. Marty Johnson."

"Mr. Johnson, sir. Do you think you could maybe make an exception just this once? You see, my *wife*–" he stressed that last word and smiled at Mel as he did, "–and I are on our honeymoon and she was really hoping to get a look at the ocean from the top."

The old man studied Alex and Mel with a frown on his face and Mel thought for sure that he was going to say no. Then his mouth turned up into a smile and his weathered skin wrinkled around his lips and eyes.

"Newlyweds, huh? Yeah I remember when my Eleanor and I were first married back in Forty-nine. I'd have done anything and everything to make her happy, too. And judging by the way this one's smile is lighting up her face–" he pointed to Mel and her smile grew wider, "–I'd say you're in the same boat I was."

"Yes sir. I am. I'll do whatever it takes."

"I don't need anything from you. Just promise me you'll cherish every moment you have together. Both of you. You never know when that one moment will be your last." This last he said with a hint of wistfulness and Mel guessed that his *Eleanor* must have passed away. Swinging the big white door wide open, Marty stood off to the side and swung his arm back, motioning them in. "You two take your time. There're brochures on the table to your right. That winding staircase by the back wall will take you all the way to the top. There's an office over here–" he pointed to the open door along the right wall, "–so if you need something, just come let me know."

He sauntered off into the office and Alex grabbed Mel's hand, pulled her toward the staircase, grabbed a pamphlet on the way. She walked up first and Alex followed. Mel ran her fingers along the brick that had been painted white, the coating chipped and faded, showing the age of the structure and how much it'd been through.

They walked through the watch and service rooms and when they reached the top, Alex went ahead of her, opened a small black, metal door that took them out onto the catwalk of the lighthouse. Mel followed close behind him and sucked in a breath as she came out on top and stood by the black rail.

The ocean spread out for miles in front of them, the

horizon still casting shadows of deep purple as the sun continued to rise. Waves rushed into the shore and even from here–two hundred feet in the air–Mel could hear the whoosh-whoosh-whoosh as the water landed on the sand and rushed back out.

"It says here this place was started back in the Seventeen hundreds and this station was erected in Nineteen-sixteen." Alex's voice brought Mel's gaze to her left where he stood, studying the brochure from downstairs.

Mel plucked the tri-folded piece of paper from him, stuffed it into the pocket of her jeans and took his hand, pulling him around the circle of the balcony.

"Don't read about it, babe. Enjoy it!"

"Okay, okay," he said and walked around the lighthouse.

Mel stayed where she was, watched his progress through nine-foot glass panes surrounding the lantern room.

His powerful shoulders stood out in his dark green windbreaker jacket. His trim waist drew attention every time the wind blew the jacket away from his body. His strong jaw looked hard as he rubbed a hand along it, looking out into the water.

And his lips, looking even fuller from the glass, begged to be kissed.

And then he turned, caught sight of her on the other side of the catwalk. He leaned his face into the glass, blew out a big breath, that made his cheeks puff out. Mel giggled. It reminded her of an old movie she used to love as a kid, *Pete's Dragon.* She had the urge to start singing and dancing her way around the walk, just like the woman from the movie, until she landed in Alex's arms.

She settled for strolling, grazing her hand along the rail as she did. Alex moved away from the glass, leaned back against the railing while he watched her with arms crossed over his chest. When Mel reached him, he pulled her into the V of his body with legs straddling hers and arms around her waist. She rested her head on his chest, listened to the steady beat of his heart mixing with the sound of the waves, and felt happy. There was no other word for it. Just, happy.

"It's beautiful here," Alex said into her hair, lips brushing her scalp. "I think we should make this a regular vacation."

"Me too."

Alex turned his face, rested his cheek against the top of her head and said, "What else do you want to do today?"

Instead of answering, Mel walked her hands up his chest, loving the feel of his muscles twitching under her touch, and wound her arms around his neck. She pulled him down and kissed him, lightly ran her tongue along his lips. He chuckled deep in his throat and the sound brought shivers to Mel's body.

"I do believe you've become insatiable, Mrs. Lambert."

"I do believe you encouraged it, Mr. Lambert."

FOREVER GRATEFUL

Alex wrapped a large hand around her neck, tilted her head way back so that her throat was exposed to his warm lips. He licked a trail from the hollow of her throat to her earlobe, bit it playfully and worked his mouth back to hers. He kissed her deeply and Mel tasted a hint of the French roasted coffee they'd had at breakfast. Mixed with the taste that was pure Alex, it was intoxicating. Mel's hands tightened around his neck, pleaded with him to stop the torment and take her home.

"Guilty as charged, wife," he whispered against her lips. "Let's go home so I can encourage you some more."

"I'm game," Mel said and giggled at the hope that they'd never be through with *these* types of games.

.　　.　　.　　.　　.

January 29, 2015

Any notions Alex had about what marriage would be like flew out the window in the first five days of being married to Melanie. With her, it was like being alongside his wife, his best friend, confidant and lover all rolled into one. It was heaven on earth. It was easy. It was more than he'd ever dreamt possible and knew he'd cherish–just like Marty had asked him to–all the days of his life.

After the morning spent at the lighthouse, he and

Melanie had spent the day in bed, wrapped up in each other, learning one another's bodies in the way a husband and wife should. It'd been close to dawn before they'd finally fallen into an exhausted sleep.

When they woke around ten yesterday morning, they'd decided to have brunch at the Tybee Island Social Club. He'd been hesitant to try one of the locals' favorite drinks–their famous Smoked Bacon Bloody Mary–but he'd done it anyway. And, Alex admitted, found that it was really good. The bacon flavor mixed with the tomato juice made the drink fit in perfect with their breakfast.

From there they'd headed over to Fort Pulaski, taken the forty-five minute tour of the grounds. Some naval men wouldn't care so much about military records that didn't involve the Navy. But Alex found the history surrounding the place–from the National Monument in the form of a canon to the broken down bricks to the grass they walked on where so many men had died–to be inspiring. Standing on that revered ground made Alex proud to have been in the military, served his country.

Melanie had been quiet while he looked out over the lawns, pictured the men falling as mortars and cannonballs tore into them. Imagined the place being used as a housing unit for Confederate prisoners when it'd been taken over by the Union. She'd held his hand, rested her head on his shoulder. And she hadn't complained that their honeymoon had taken a sudden turn down a melancholy road.

Overcome with emotion, Alex hadn't tried to make love to her last night. Just held her in his arms while he thought about the future that was possible for them because of the sacrifices so many men had made. Melanie seemed to be okay with that too since she slept for over eight hours.

Today, on the last day of their honeymoon, Alex was determined to make up for not being very much fun yesterday. They were headed into Savannah for the night.

While Melanie was in the shower, Alex packed up their suitcases, loaded them into the car. She was walking out of the bathroom with a towel wrapped around her body when he came back inside. Her hair was blown dry and curled, make-up already on for the day. He froze in the doorway, considered how bad it would throw their time off if he walked over, took off her towel and laid her down in the bed.

Later, he reminded himself. *You'll have plenty of time for that later.*

"Hey," Melanie said as she walked over to the bed where her clothes for the day were laid out. "Whatcha doing?"

Melanie removed the towel, her back to Alex, and started to put on her underthings. Alex was walking forward when she wrapped that lavender lace around her body without even realizing it. He stopped when he was a foot behind her and Melanie's back stiffened, sensing him there.

She looked over her right shoulder at him, yearning in her eyes. Her lips parted and Alex knew she was waiting for him to kiss her, to take her to bed.

He almost gave in.

Taking a deep breath, swallowing thickly, Alex clenched his hands into fists and stepped back. He smiled at the look of frustration of his wife's face when he did. And promised himself he'd make it up to her later.

"I have a surprise for you."

"A surprise?" She pulled her jeans on, buttoned them up and turned to face him with her shirt the same color as her bra in her hands. "What kind of surprise?" She pulled the shirt on over her head and Alex finally relaxed his hands.

"If I told you, it wouldn't be a surprise."

"Okay. How about a hint then?" She sat down on the bed, pulled on socks and a pair of black low-heeled boots that came to her knees. "Wait a minute," she said, looking around and noticing that their luggage was gone. "Where are our suitcases?"

Alex smiled, shrugged his shoulders.

"Alex. What's going on?"

"They're in the car. We're leaving."

"Already? But we still have one more night. I'm not ready to go back yet." Disappointment was heavy in her tone.

"I'm not either. I don't think I'll ever be ready to share

you with the rest of the world." Alex walked over to where Melanie sat on the bed, pulled her up by the hands, kissed her once on the lips. "We're going into Savannah for our last night."

"Really?"

"Yeah." That's all he said. He might've told her where they were going but he wasn't about to give her any more details than that. "And we needed to leave fifteen minutes ago."

"Alright, alright." Melanie walked into the kitchen, Alex following behind her, and picked up her purse from the counter. Together they walked to the front door, paused and looked back into the little house. "I'm going to miss this place," she said thoughtfully.

"Me, too. We'll come back, baby. I promise." He placed his hand on the small of her back, steered her out of the house and closed the door behind them. "Now let's go."

They both got into the car, buckled up and Alex started the engine, pulled out of the driveway. He drove back down Ninth Street, onto Butler Avenue and headed for Savannah.

Thirty minutes–and two wrong turns–later, they pulled up in front of an old Nineteenth-Century mansion converted into a bed and breakfast, one of the most romantic in the country according to their website. They parked on the side of the street, got out and Alex grabbed a small duffel bag he'd packed earlier while Melanie was in the shower that had all the essentials for one night.

They walked up the path and were greeted at the door by an older woman in her forties with dark brown hair, kind blue eyes and an apron covering her hearty body.

"Afternoon. You must be Mr. and Mrs. Lambert. I'm Mrs. Willis but you can call me Betty. I've got your room all set up for you." She walked into the foyer, Alex and Melanie close behind her. The crystal vases on an entry table held a couple dozen white roses and reflected the sun streaming in through the doorway, put off prisms in every corner. "If you'll follow me I'll take you on up."

They followed the older woman up two flights of stairs to the third story where there was a single bedroom. Walking into the room, Alex saw the bright white comforter covering the king sized bed covered with red rose petals. His first thought was *Cliché* but he quickly got over it when he heard Melanie say under her breath, "Awe. It's beautiful."

The dark stained oak furniture looked to be as old as the house, but built strong and sturdy. A chest of drawers sat on the opposite wall of the bed with a flat screen television on top. A large bay window with window seat sat at the north end of the room, the heavy, red drapes pulled open to let in the winter sun. There was an en suite bathroom to the right and through the open door, Alex glimpsed a large white, porcelain tub with stainless claw feet and a glass walk in shower.

FOREVER GRATEFUL

Melanie walked over to the window, looked out at the city below them, while Alex tipped Betty, thanked her for getting everything together so quickly. She winked at him before she stepped out of the room and closed the door behind her. Alex headed over to Melanie, wrapped his arms around her waist. She laid her head back on his chest, linked her fingers with his.

"It's amazing here Alex. Thank you for doing this."

"You're welcome. But I have a lot more planned. Do you need to freshen up or anything?"

"No." She turned in his arms, kissed his throat. "I'm feeling great."

"Yes you do," he agreed, sliding his hands down to grip her backside and pull her tighter to him. "Let's get out of here before I ruin the whole day by locking the door and keeping you up here for the night."

"That wouldn't be so bad, now would it?"

Alex groaned, kissed her lips and rested his forehead against hers. Cradling her face in his hands, he said, "You're killing me woman. Yes, it would be bad. I have plans." He kissed her once more and pulled away, grabbed her hand and dragged her to the door. "Let's go."

Alex and Melanie spent the rest of the day touring all the historic sights Savannah had to offer. They took a trolley through the historic district, laughing when a Forrest Gump impersonator came and sat next to them, offering them one of his chocolates. They had lunch at a buffet style restaurant that was world-renowned because of its famous owner and chef. They walked along Savannah's Squares, read inscriptions on some of the city's famous monuments. And ended up taking a nap in a small patch of dark green grass underneath a large oak that was covered in moss.

When evening came up, they headed over to another old Georgian mansion that had been redesigned for a restaurant. But instead of eating on the main floor, they headed to the cellar where there was a tavern-style bar. Walking into the dim interior, Alex led Melanie over to a booth in the corner. Like the other booths in the place, this one was covered in black leather with a stainless steel table in front of them. A cluster of white votive candles sat in the center, their small fires flickering on the stainless surface like diamonds.

A long bar took up one wall and two bartenders roamed from person to person, taking orders and making drinks. Dozens of wine and liquor bottles lined the wall behind the bar and ten taps of beer sat in front.

In the left corner sat a white piano, its polished surface glowing blue under the florescent lights. A young man sat at the bench, his fingers flying over the keys as he tapped out a jazz tune.

A young woman in her early twenties with short blond hair, black slacks and a white tuxedo shirt, walked over to their table, set two drink napkins in front of them. Her big smile showed off her white teeth.

"Hi, I'm Susanna and I'll be your waitress tonight. Can I start you off with something to drink?"

Melanie ordered a glass of chardonnay and Alex ordered a pale ale beer from one of their local breweries. They both ordered a dinner of shrimp and grits (one of the local specialties) with side salads.

As they were finishing up their meals and their second drinks, a woman in a red sequined, long-sleeve dress walked up to the platform where the piano was. Her mocha skin lit up under a spotlight that was directed on her. She smiled at the young man at the piano and he nodded his head, began punching out a quick beat on his keys. A few seconds later the woman began singing a fast song, her voice booming and penetrating the stillness of the bar, causing everyone to get up and dance.

Alex stood from the booth, held his hand out for Melanie and guided her to the square, black-and-white checkered dance floor where four other couples took up space. They held hands and spun, twirled around the floor like a twister and laughed as more people joined the crowd and bumped into each other.

When the song finished, the pianist slowed his fingers, the beat changed to one that was gentle and sultry, instantly changing the atmosphere of the room.

Alex pulled Melanie into his arms. She hugged onto his

neck and he held her tight around her lower back. Her head was angled up and Alex rested his face in her neck, breathed in the smell of flowers, Melanie and something else that was becoming much more familiar to him. Desire.

The singer's voice changed from lilting to smoky, the lyrics bounced off her lips like they were reaching out to the couples, pushing them to go and be alone.

Alex kissed Melanie's neck, licked a drop of sweat that rolled down and smiled against her skin when she shivered in his arms. So he did it again. And again. On his fourth pass over her throat, Melanie leaned back, took his face in her hands, crushed her lips against his. He groaned into her mouth. The music and Melanie's body and the heated air around them seeped into his bones and demanded he take Melanie back to their room at the B and B.

Before he could pull her off the dance floor and out of the building, Melanie broke the kiss and looked into his eyes. She swallowed once, licked her lips and Alex tried to go back in, to kiss her again. She placed her fingertips over his mouth, stopped him.

"I love you, Alex."

"I love you too, baby."

He tried to kiss her again and again she stopped him.

"I want you to…. I need…" She stopped, took a breath. "I don't want you to hold back tonight. I want your passion, Alex. All of it."

FOREVER GRATEFUL

Alex knew what she was asking and she was right. He had been holding back from her. Tried to be gentle and easy as they learned one another, as she opened herself up to this new world of love.

But it'd been torture for him, too.

And the fact that she was asking him this, asking him to let go with her, made him both eager to get home and nervous that it'd be too much.

"Are you sure, honey?" He searched her eyes, saw only certainty. She nodded her head and he lost all control. "Come on," he said, his voice gravelly with need as he pulled her to the bar, threw a hundred down on the counter in front of their waitress. "Keep the change," he told her and bee-lined it for the door, headed upstairs and out into the cold night air with Melanie running to keep up with his long strides.

A breeze brought a welcome cooling to his skin. The full silver moon hung overhead, millions of stars surrounding that round ball. Instead of taking one of the taxis lined up and down the side of the road, Alex pulled Melanie along the sidewalk, his heart beating faster with every step. The heels of Melanie's boots click-click-clicked on the cobblestones like a clock ticking away the seconds until they could be alone. Couples strolled hand in hand around them, families sat at bistro tables outside of restaurants, all enjoying the cool night.

But Alex didn't pay them any attention. He had tunnel

vision, focused only on the three-story mansion two blocks away. There was a lamp on in their top floor bedroom and he kept his eyes on the light, let it guide him like a flare.

They made it to the bed and breakfast, walked in the front door and quickly headed up the stairs. Betty stopped them on the second floor landing. Alex came to an abrupt halt so they didn't mow the poor woman over and tried not to let his annoyance at being kept from his room show.

"Good evening. Did you two get to do some exploring today?"

"Yes, ma'am, we did." Melanie giggled softly under her breath as she sensed Alex's antsy demeanor. "I'm sorry we weren't here for the afternoon reception."

"Oh, it's no problem dear. Was there anything you needed before you turn in for the night?"

Alex bent and whispered in Melanie's ear, kept his voice low so that only she heard him say, "I need you. And if you don't quit talking, I'm going to throw you over my shoulder and carry you up that last flight of stairs."

Melanie's eyes grew wide at his threat and Alex let her see the seriousness in his gaze.

"No, Betty. I think we're all set," she said, never taking her eyes off Alex. "We'll see you at breakfast."

The two ran off up the steps before the older woman could get a word out. As soon as they were safely inside their room, Alex locked the door behind them. The click sounded loud in his ears, like a large concrete block sliding into its final resting place.

Melanie stood by the bed, her chest heaving with the same excitement Alex felt. He stalked over to her, picked her up by the waist and tossed her onto the bed. As soon as he came down on top of her, Melanie reached for the hem of his shirt, tried to take it off.

But Alex was having none of that tonight.

He grabbed her by the wrists, pulled them up and over her head, laid them on either side of the feather pillow her head rested on. She looked like an angel with her golden hair spread out around her, her pink lips parted and wet and begging to be kissed. And her eyes, so full of love and longing. For him.

"Alex, please."

"Please what, Melanie? Tell me what you want."

"I want you. Now."

"Then get ready, baby."

Tonight he held nothing back. Alex gave everything he had to Melanie, their bodies frantic to get closer, stronger, tighter around each other, inside each other.

When they collapsed into bed several hours later, their bodies slick with sweat from their feverish love making, Alex held her nestled on his chest.

When his heartbeat slowed and he felt her breathing even out, indicating sleep, Alex said a prayer of thanks to

God for giving him this woman who completed him.

.   .   .   .   .

January 30, 2015

Mel woke to the sound of birds chirping outside their bedroom window. Her eyes focused in that direction and she noticed that they'd forgotten to close the blinds the night before. She blushed at the realization that someone could've seen them.

They could've heard *you too, Mel.*

The thought might have made her embarrassed had it not been for the way she felt this morning. She was a little stiff but sated. Her body was exhausted but her mind was relaxed. She felt well and truly loved.

In every way.

Mel rested her chin on top of Alex's chest and watched him sleep. His mouth was slightly open, little puffs of air brushing her nose. His eyes were relaxed and Mel softly ran her fingers along the laugh lines at the corner of his lids. She wanted to kiss him, wake him up and make love one more time before they went back to their real life. But she glanced at the clock on the nightstand, saw that their plane left in just under three hours and knew they needed to get moving.

She gently unwound herself from Alex's arms and

padded into the bathroom, tended business and brushed her teeth. When she walked back out to grab her toiletries for a shower, she found Alex sitting up in bed. He was leaning with his back against the headboard and the sheet lay around his waist, his hands crossed behind his head, biceps bulging. His powerful chest was exposed to her and Mel traced the contours of muscles with her eyes, wanting so badly to jump right back in bed and nip at those muscles.

He has *made me insatiable,* she mused. And then battled her previous thought with, *He's my husband. I'm allowed to feel this way with him.*

"Good morning, love. What's going on that sweet little mind of yours, honey?"

"Nothing," she lied. And then, because she couldn't *not* tell him the truth, "I'm thinking about what you said the other day… when you called me insatiable."

"Well then come on over here and let's see what we can do about that." Alex threw the sheet back, inviting her to the open space on the bed. But she shook her head no, backed up a few steps until she bumped into the chest of drawers. Alex hopped out of bed, not bothering with clothes, and stalked her like she was his prey, ripe for the taking. He tilted his head to the side when he reached her, a playful smirk on his lips that Mel was dying to kiss away and replace with something else, something sexy.

"Running again, Mrs. Lambert?"

"Never."

And then he got serious.

"I had a thought last night while you were sleeping."

"About?"

"About how much you complete me. Damn," he muttered, laughing. "That sounds so cliché. I'm sorry, I didn't even like that movie. But I can't help that it's true."

"I understand." Mel laughed with him.

"And then I thanked God for bringing us together. For bringing you to me. But most importantly for allowing me the chance to make you happy. And I will, Melanie. I promise to always make you happy. I might not always succeed. But I'll never stop trying. And I promise that no one will ever love you as much as I will."

Mel felt tears pool in her eyes. Tears of love for this man who wasn't afraid to pour his heart out to her in words and songs and dancing at the most awkward times. Tears of happiness that after all these years of being scared and alone she was finally able to let go and be free.

But most of all she knew they were tears of gratitude.

"Alex, I've told you before. I am who I am today, right at this moment, because you never gave up on me. Because God never gave up on me. I don't know where I would have ended up if it hadn't been for you or Him. For the faith you had in me even when I didn't have it in myself. Embracing that faith, believing in it, has helped me to really and truly put my past where it belongs. To forgive and let go of all those bad times so that I can focus on the future. Our future. And because of that I promise to always keep the same faith in you and in us. In God and what He has given us."

"I love you so much, baby."

"I love you, too. For everything you are to me."

"For everything we are to each other, Melanie. We're meant to be a forever story."

"And I'll be forever grateful that it's me and you. Always."

Aimee Martin

Epilogue

"For where two or three are gathered together in my name, there am I in the midst of them." Matthew 18:20

February 12, 2015

Alex held tight to Melanie's hand as they walked down the hallway of the Woman's Hospital in Houston. His sister, Brinley had given birth to hers and Jaxson's baby yesterday and Alex and Melanie were going to meet his nephew. Their nephew.

They'd been back from their honeymoon for two weeks now and settled into marriage smoothly. During the day, Alex would go to work at the ranch and Melanie stayed home to work on their house. Every day he came home to find another project completed. Pictures from their honeymoon being hung around the house, little decorative trinkets that women seemed to like so much placed on tables and dressers and the kitchen counter. She even painted the bathroom a dark yellow because she said it tied into their bedroom better, whatever that meant.

But he loved it. Coming home to his wife and their dog and living the life of a devoted husband felt so domestic, normal. But he knew there was nothing normal about their lives. What they had was special. Alex couldn't wait until they could share that with babies of their own.

But he wouldn't push her. When she was ready, he'd know, and now was not the time.

And that's why he was nervous about coming to the hospital. As excited as he was about seeing the newest member of the family, he was worried that it might have an adverse effect on Melanie. No one else in the family knew what she'd been through. He'd told her if she wanted to tell them it was her decision.

And if she didn't, well, he supported that, too.

But what if something happened and she freaked out seeing the baby? What if she flew into one of those flashbacks and couldn't figure out a way to explain why she'd reacted that way? He prayed that wouldn't happen and asked God to be with them, with her.

Standing outside his sister's room, he paused and squeezed her hand, smiled and asked, "You ready?"

"As I'll ever be." She took a deep breath and blew it out quickly.

"Okay, then," he said, knocked on the door and led her into the room.

.　　　.　　　.　　　.　　　.

Mel paused just inside the hospital room, released Alex's hand so he could go and hug his parents, clasp Jax on the back. Aaron and Jess were there, too, huddled on the couch under the window. Both were staring down at their hands and neither looked up when she and Alex walked in.

Turning back to the rest of the family, Mel smiled at Tina and Mitch, walked over and gave them both a hug. She gave Jax a hug too, congratulated him on becoming a father. His answering smile transformed his face and joy was the only emotion she would use to describe it.

He handed her a cigar with a pink ribbon around it. When Mel cocked an eyebrow at him, the big man just shrugged his shoulders.

"Everybody gets one," Alex said, walking up next to Mel and taking the cigar to put in his shirt pocket next to his own.

Mel realized she couldn't stall anymore, turned and walked to the bed. Brin was sitting up, her hair in a messy bun on top of her head, face clear of make-up. But she was absolutely glowing. Mel leaned down, hugged her around the neck with one arm and kissed her cheek.

"Not fair," Mel said when she leaned back. "How can you have just had a baby and still look this beautiful?"

"I can answer that." This from Jaxson.

"We'd prefer if you didn't," Alex teased.

"Be quiet, both of you. You'll wake the baby," Brin scolded with love. "The secret is motherhood, Mel. It's wonderful. I feel like I could climb Mount Everest. Okay, not really but you get what I mean."

And that right there is what worried Mel. What if she couldn't understand what it meant to be a mother? Yes, she'd forgiven herself for what had happened. And she knew that God had forgiven her as well as her baby. But what she'd never thought about was what if her maternal instinct went out the window all those years ago with what she'd done?

No, she reprimanded herself. *No, that won't happen.*

"Would you like to hold her?" Brin asked and Mel finally looked down to see the little bundle of baby in her friend's arms, a plush pink blanket swaddled tight and a blue, pink and white knit cap on its head.

And then a question struck Mel.

"Wait… I thought you were having a boy? Brandon?"

"We thought so too," Brin said. "Apparently there was a mistake and the lab technician who wrote down all the results from the tests got a few things mixed up. Not that we mind. This little girl already has her Daddy wrapped around her little finger. We just have to go shopping again for clothes. So… you want to hold her?"

Mel couldn't answer; her throat got dry and closed up. She nodded and held out her hands. Brin placed the baby in Mel's arms; the baby made a muffled sound in her sleep then settled in the crook of Mel's elbow. And then she studied the tiny being in her arms.

She saw those beautiful eyes and thought they looked like the sweetest almonds. She saw the baby's tongue poking at its lower lip like it was searching for her mother's breast and thought, *How beautiful and natural.* Mel held the baby's hand in hers, saw the crease in her palm and thought it just made it easier for the baby to grasp onto her Daddy's finger.

In that sweet baby's face, Mel saw the face of God. She saw the work that He created, the love that went into the making of this baby. She looked around the room and saw the love surrounding the baby by her family, could feel that love like it was a second skin.

In that baby's face, Mel felt the hallowed devotion that comes with God's creation.

She brought the little girl to her face, breathed in that sweet baby smell and kissed her forehead. Looking up at Brin, Mel asked, "What's her name?"

"Sarah. Her name is Sarah."

Mel's gaze flew to Alex's. His eyes filled with tears at

the same time that hers did; he knew about Mel naming her daughter Sarah. He smiled at her, placed his hand over his heart and mouthed "I love you" to her.

Mel whispered back, "More."

Then she laughed at the way destiny had played out, at the way God's plans had played out.

From being broken and alone with a daughter in Heaven to being whole and loved with a niece bearing the same name. Somehow she felt, deep inside her heart, that this was a sign from God that hers and Alex's marriage was part of His creation, too. God brought them together. Just like this sweet baby in her arms, their love would have a happy ending.

Because it was just like Alex had said.

Their love was a forever story.

Be on the lookout for the next story in the Lake Shores Series… coming in early 2016

If you enjoyed Forever Grateful, and haven't read the first in the series yet, make sure you check out Forever Home, available at most online retailers.

About the Author

Aimee Martin, an International Best Seller, brings you the next book in her Lake Shores Series, *Forever Grateful*. Her first novel, Forever Home, has sold digital copies in more than a dozen countries including Spain, Japan, France, Australia and many throughout the United Kingdom.

Aimee, from the Texas Hill Country, is a stay at home mother, wife and nurse. She lives with her husband, three children and many animals. When she's not living the life of a wife and mother, she can be found reading and writing. Forever Grateful is her second novel of a four part series of stand-alone novels.

Connect with her via her Facebook page, http://www.facebook.com/AimeeMartinAuthor